RESTLESS HOUSE

RESTLESS HOUSE

EMILE ZOLA

Translated from the French by

PERCY PINKERTON

Introduction by

ANGUS WILSON

LONDON
ELEK BOOKS

Published by
ELEK BOOKS LTD.,
2 All Saints Street,
London N1 9RN

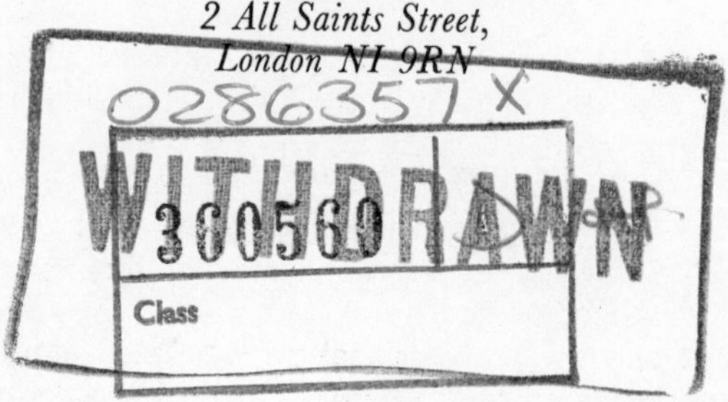

Made and Printed in Great Britain by
A. WHEATON & CO. LTD.
EXETER DEVON

INTRODUCTION

Throughout his career Emile Zola met with outbursts of uncontrolled abuse from the literary critics. Like many idealists who are at the same time ambitious men, he welcomed abuse as much as he disliked criticism. Abuse was after all a measure of his power; criticism too often came from friends or disciples and seemed to him treachery. From his few followers he yearned for praise, from the mass of the people he wished for devotion, but from the established, the successful and the conventional he welcomed abuse. He succeeded in producing all these reactions at their most overwhelming during his defence of Dreyfus; but he tasted the abuse in full measure much earlier in his career. Most of his novels produced violent reactions, but none so violent as *Pot-Bouille, La Terre* and *La Débâcle,* for in these novels he attacked in turn the three chief ideals of the established French Bourgeois society—the Sanctity of Middle Class Marriage, the Honest Virtue of the Peasantry, and the Honour of the Army. The first of these violent storms broke out with the publication of *Pot-Bouille* in 1882.

When we read to-day of the moral indignation that greeted *Ghosts* or *Tess of the D'Urbervilles,* it is difficult to comprehend the strength of contemporary reaction, but with Zola's novels, and in particular with *Pot-Bouille,* this is not so. *Pot-Bouille* remains one of the most extraordinary, the most uncompromising attacks upon that Aunt Sally of nineteenth century novelists, the bourgeoisie. It is not among the four greatest of Zola's novels, the mood perhaps is too monotonous, the objects of satire too mediocre to allow that vast, overpowering energy, by which Zola at his greatest compels his readers into acceptance, to have its full rein. It is, nevertheless, an unique novel; Zola's attack is more complete, more continuous, less hampered by any conventional consideration of good manners than in any of his other novels; he does not perhaps rise to the moments of great tragedy that we find in *L'Assomoir* or *La Terre,* but the macabre and the grotesque, both moods in which he excelled, are sustained throughout in a masterly fashion; and the "black" humour by which he forces his readers to laugh in their moments of greatest unease at which he reveals is found at its best in *Pot-Bouille.* Despite the apparent extravagance of the horror of the story, we are never able to rid ourselves of the conviction that it is a realistic picture; and our belief may well be confirmed by the fierceness of the protest that it drew from his victims. Finally, and this is perhaps Zola's greatest triumph, despite his endless stripping of his characters of every pretension moral and social to which they lay claim, the final impression is one of a deep compassion for these wretched, sterile "respectable" men and women, a compassion as strong as his hatred for the social system which imposes so wasteful a life upon them. In 1882 *Pot-Bouille* made the great bourgeoisie writhe in furious protestation; had it been first published in 1957 it would have evoked the same response.

Much of this unique quality may be explained by the circumstances in which it was written. One of the most remarkable features of Zola's literary career was the constancy with which he kept to his original scheme for his great family chronicle, the *Rougon-Macquart,* of which *Pot-Bouille* forms a part. Originally devised as early as 1869, the series was to cover the whole social structure of France through the loosely knit adventures of a single family, the three branches of which were to represent the new aristocracy of Napoleon III's Second Empire, the bourgeoisie, and the people. The last novel of the series was not published until 1893, and inevitably there were certain growths and changes in the idea as originally conceived, but the main structure planned so long before was remarkably preserved. With the publication of *Nana* in 1880, the lives of the poor of Paris and of those of them who were momentarily raised from squalor by the sale of their physical charms had been chronicled. It was now the turn of the upper middle classes, the men of the professional class, to come under Zola's scalpel and so he designed. This year, however, saw the culmination of Zola's own personal domestic unhappiness. A world literary figure after the publication of *L'Assomoir,* increasingly wealthy, with a devoted and houseproud wife, and a circle of disciples, the outward appearance of the novelist's life was fair seeming. The inner picture was less rosy. Eleven years of sterile marriage had led to increasing pressure upon the affections and tempers of Emile and Alexandrine Zola, a pressure which was not lessened by the need to preserve the public illusion. The nerves of both husband and wife were badly strained; Alexandrine's quick temper too frequently shattered the quiet which Zola's regular discipline of work required, depression had brought constant insomnia to both of them, and in Emile's case occasional bouts of hallucination. The increasingly bad relations between his wife and his beloved, somewhat too ubiquitous mother did not aid matters. The novelist felt increasing need to project this personal misery into literary form—the writer's instinctive means of self-healing. He decided therefore to incorporate into the great series a story of domestic frustration.

Events, however, moved faster than his pen. At the end of 1880, Flaubert, who for all their incompatibility of outlook, was a revered father to Zola, died very suddenly. In the following year, Zola's mother died equally suddenly, in circumstances both mentally and physically distressing. The effect upon Zola was overwhelming, he felt quite unable to undertake any novel so completely personal as the one he had projected. He, therefore, laid aside the scheme—it is typical of his perseverance that it eventually appeared as *La Joie de Vivre* in 1884—and took up once more the novel of the middle classes, *Pot-Bouille*. Much, however, of the black personal mood, savage in his fury against marriage and women, guilty for his own share in his wife's unhappiness—brimmed over into what was intended as an objective, realistic study of bourgeois domestic life.

It had long been Zola's thesis that if the circumstances of the poor drove their women into prostitution, the education of upper middle class girls led directly to adultery. With its combination of prudish censorship upon the physical realities of life and its equally false romantic view of love derived from clandestine novel reading, it could not be a worse prelude to the deadness or the disguised brutality which accompanied the mercenary, arranged marriages for which the daughters of the *bonne bourgeoisie* were destined. The chasm between the maiden's dream and the wife's reality could only be filled, he argued, by an infidelity with the first fair-speaking, romantic looking man that came into the house, especially when the comfortable circumstances of the bourgeois home enforced idleness upon its mistress, which her education had given her no power to occupy. In 1881 he developed this thesis in an article in *Figaro* entitled "Adultery among the bourgeoisie." This article was the prelude to *Pot-Bouille*. The house in which the action of *Pot-Bouille* takes place is a large block of apartments near the Palais Royal, in the centre of Paris and at that time in the centre of the successful middle class world. Into this comfortable, respectable world comes Octave Mouret, a young, attractive adventurer from Provence, a member, in fact, of the Rougon Macquart family. Octave is actuated solely by the desire to make his way in the rich Paris of the Second Empire. He enjoys sex, but without any personal complexes, certainly without any desire for love. The novel tells of his impact upon the bourgeois families in this house. He is the answer, of course, to the meaningless dreams with which these middle class wives pass their days and nights. Gradually the truth about these homes is revealed—women nourishing themselves upon the romance of fifth rate novels, women hysterical with sexual dissatisfaction, women who have come to regard their husbands as automata to be pushed up the social ladder, daughters who hate the mothers who are scheming to find them profitable marriages as sterile as their own. Vabres, Josserands, Campardons, Duveyrier, whatever the slight material and social differences that separate them, differences over which they sweat so much blood of envy and pride, are all living the same lie—a lie of polite social talk, little card parties, small family dances, pretentious musical evenings.

The focus of the novel is inevitably fixed upon the women of the families, for it was the cherished bourgeois illusion that, if men might be allowed the convention of mistresses, "respectable" women were without desire, naturally chaste, that Zola was out to destroy. The novel, he said in his notes, was to deal with three kinds of adultery—adultery through foolish education, adultery through physical distortion, and adultery from sheer stupidity: the wives, mother and daughters of *Pot-Bouille* fall into all three varieties. But Zola had no illusions about the guilt of the men; the eminent architects, lawyers, business men are also lost to any sense of tenderness or love; they fail through coldness, lack of imagination, brutal, inconsiderate lust. By a nice irony we only leave the apartment house to see these respectable husbands mulcted and cheated by vulgar mistresses without any of the attractions of the wives to whom the dead hand of conventional, arranged marriage has made them unable to respond. Nor are the men of the middle classes allowed the superior powers of intellect which they boast over their wives; their "serious" talks on politics—Orléanist, Legitimist, Republican or loyal Imperial—are shown to be as banal as the chatter of their womenfolk about "culture" and dress.

By contrast with the general hypocrisy and outward gentility of the masters and mistresses of the household, Zola gives us, as chorus, the servants. Overworked, "kept in their place," the object of the first economies in any domestic financial crisis, the kitchen underworld had its revenge in the loud-mouthed, salty gossip with which from backstairs and area, it assails the ears of its "betters," gossip which retails in every brutal detail the sordid intrigues that go on in the house, gossip which no mistress dare reprimand because it must be beneath her notice. Perhaps one of the most powerful scenes in the novel is that in which the young bride Berthe's rendezvous with her lover Octave is interrupted before it has begun by the coarse ribaldry of the servants at their early morning tasks in a scene of ample, brutal humour that recalls the bawdy side of Restoration comedy. It is in the world of the servants, too, that Zola lets himself go in the great agony of the maid-of-all-work Adèle, forced to conceal the birth pangs of her unwanted baby.

Adèle is not the only innocent in this black world; many of the characters, notably M. Josserand, are "good," but in the end, one feels, perhaps, that such arbitrary distinctions of "good" and "bad" are beside the point. There is a more complete humanity and compassion that embraces them all. The circumstances, not the men or the women are the villains; for, as I have suggested, this bourgeois world, outwardly prosperous, inwardly sterile is on one level a symbol of Zola's own unhappiness; in his fierce invective he punishes himself, in his compassion he tries to absolve himself. Nevertheless, the middle class readers would perhaps have preferred invective alone; it is less humiliating to receive hatred than pity from those who refuse you every prized pretension. It is not surprising then that *Figaro's* critic declared: "It is time that Paris avenged herself on M. Zola's outrages," and that *Gil Blas'* critic reasserted the great bourgeois creed: "It is still the middle classes who best represent the measure of good, solid French qualities."

I have dealt at length on the moral and social aspects of *Pot-Bouille,* because Zola is pre-eminently a moralist and a social chronicler, but as a work of art or of entertainment, it is a remarkable novel. Rich in irony that merges into broad comedy, superb in melodrama, its most striking quality is the dexterity and ease with which Zola handles so many groups of characters and so many plots, carrying them along by flowing narrative, intertwining and untwining the various strands without confusing the reader. It is this quality—the most important for the translation—which the present version by Percy Pinkerton catches so admirably. If Zola has been comparatively unknown to English speaking readers, it has been because of the poor quality of translation available to the general reader. When the Lutetian Society undertook the translation of

Zola's main works in 1894 and 1895, the echoes of Vizetelly's trial and imprisonment for the translation of *La Terre* in 1888 were still too loud to permit general publication. The series were limited to three hundred copies of each work translated; what was lacking in publicity was, however, made up for in the high standard of translation. Now that Zola's words can be presented to a less prudish public, it is excellent that Pinkerton's work should be made available to the general reader.

ANGUS WILSON.

I

In the Rue Neuve-Saint-Augustin, a block in the traffic stopped the cab which was bringing Octave and his three trunks from the Gare de Lyon. The young man lowered one of the windows, although the cold on that gloomy November evening was already intense. The sudden fall of dusk surprised him in this neighbourhood of narrow streets, swarming with people. The drivers' oaths, as they thrashed their snorting beasts, the perpetual hustling of wayfarers on the pavement, the serried row of shops full of attendants and customers bewildered him; for, if he had imagined Paris to be cleaner than this, he had never expected to find trade so brisk, and it seemed as if offering all its vast resources to any young fellow of energy and daring.

The cabman leant back towards him. "It's the Passage Choiseul you mean, don't you?"

"No, no; the Rue de Choiseul. A new house, I think."

So the cab had only to turn the corner, the house in question, a big, four-storeyed one, being the second one in the street. Its stonework was hardly discoloured, in the middle of the faded plaster facades of the adjoining buildings. Octave, who had got out on to the pavement, measured it and studied it with a mechanical glance, from the silk warehouse on the ground floor to the sunken windows on the fourth floor, which opened on to a narrow terrace. On the first floor, carved female heads supported a cast-iron balcony of intricate design. The framework of the windows, roughly chiselled in soft stone, was elaborate also; and lower down, over the more heavily ornamented doorway, were two Cupids holding a scroll on which was the number, illumined at night-time by a gas-jet from within.

A stout, fair gentleman, who was coming out of the vestibule, stopped short when he saw Octave.

"Hullo! you here?" he cried. "I did not expect you until tomorrow."

"Well, you see," replied the young man, "I left Plassans a day sooner than I at first intended. Is the room not ready?"

"Oh, yes! I took it a fortnight ago, and had it furnished just as you told me to do. Wait a moment, and I'll take you up there."

And, despite Octave's entreaties, he turned back. The cabman had brought in the three trunks. In the hall-porter's room a dignified-looking man, with a long, clean-shaven face like a diplomat, stood gravely reading the *Moniteur*. However, he condescended to concern himself about this luggage that was being deposited at his door, and, coming forward, he asked his tenant, the architect of the third floor, as he called him :

"Is this the person, Monsieur Campardon?"

"Yes, Monsieur Gourd, this is Monsieur Octave Mouret, for whom I took the room on the fourth floor. He will sleep there and take his meals with us. Monsieur Mouret is a friend of my wife's relations, and I beg you to show him every attention."

Octave was examining the entrance with its sham marble panelling and its vaulted ceiling, decorated with rosettes. The paved and cemented courtyard at the back had a grand air of chilly cleanliness; at the stable-door a groom stood polishing a bit with washleather. Surely the sun never shone there.

In the meantime, Monsieur Gourd was taking stock of the luggage. He pushed the trunks with his foot and, awed by their weight, talked of fetching a porter to carry them up the servants' staircase.

Putting his head round the door, he called out to his wife : "Madame Gourd, I'm going out."

The room was like a little parlour, bright with mirrors, rosewood furniture, and a red-flowered carpet.

Through the half-opened door, one caught a glimpse of the bedroom, and of the pink hangings of the bed. Madame Gourd, a very stout person with yellow ribbons in her hair, reclined, with clasped hands, in an arm-chair. She was doing nothing.

"Well, let us go up," said the architect. Seeing the impression made upon the young man by Monsieur Gourd's black velvet cap and sky-blue slippers, he added, as he pushed open the mahogany door of the vestibule :

"You know, at one time he was valet to the Duc de Vaugelade."

"Really!" said Octave, simply.

"Yes, he was; and he married the widow of a little bailiff of Mort-la-Ville. They even own a house there. But they are waiting now until they have got three thousand francs a year before they go and live there. Oh, they're most respectable people!"

About the vestibule and staircase there was a certain gaudy splendour. At the foot of the stairs a gilt figure of a Neapolitan woman supported a jar on her head, from which three gas-jets in ground-glass globes issued. The sham marble panelling, white with pink edges, went right up the stair-way at regular intervals, while the cast-iron balustrade, with mahogany handrail, was in imitation of old silver, with exuberant groups of gold leaves. A red carpet with brass rods covered the staircase. But what most impressed Octave on entering, was the hot-house temperature, a sort of warm breath puffed, as it were, by some mouth into his face.

"Hullo!" said he, "the staircase is heated."

"Of course," replied Campardon; "all self-respecting landlords go to that expense, nowadays. The house is a very fine one—very fine."

He looked about him as though testing the solidity of the walls with his architect's eyes.

"My dear fellow, the house, as you will see, is a thoroughly comfortable one, and only lived in by thoroughly respectable people."

Then, as they slowly went up, he mentioned the names of the various tenants. On each floor there were two sets of apartments, one facing the street, and the other the courtyard, their polished mahogany doors being opposite to each other. He first of all said a word or two about Monsieur Auguste Vabre. He was the landlord's eldest son: that spring he had taken the silk warehouse on the ground floor, and occupied the whole of the *entresol* himself. Then the landlord's other son, Théophile Vabre, and his wife, lived on the first-floor back, and in the floor overlooking the street lived the landlord himself, formerly a Versailles notary, but now lodging with his son-in-law, a counsellor at the Court of Appeal.

"A fellow who is not yet five-and-forty," said Campardon, as he stopped short. "That's not bad, is it?"

Two steps higher up he turned sharp round and added:

"Water and gas on every floor."

Under each high window on the landing, whose panes, with the *à la grecque* border, lit the staircase up with a white light, there was a narrow velvet-covered bench. Here, as the architect pointed out, elderly folk could sit down. Then, as he went past the second floor without mentioning the occupants, Octave asked:

"And who lives there?" pointing to the door of the principal suite.

"Oh, there!" said he. "People one never sees, and never knows. The house could well do without such as they. However, there are blemishes to be found everywhere, I suppose."

He sniffed disdainfully.

"The gentleman writes books, I believe."

But, on reaching the third floor, his complacent smile came back. The apartments facing the courtyard were subdivided. Madame Juzeur lived there, a little woman who had seen much misfortune, and a very distinguished gentleman, who had hired a room, to which he came on business once a week. While explaining matters thus, Campardon opened the door of the opposite flat.

"This is where I live," he said. "Wait a minute; I must get your key. We'll go up to your room first, and afterwards you shall see my wife."

In those two minutes that he was left alone, Octave felt penetrated, as it were, by the grave silence of the staircase. He leaned over the banisters in the tepid air which came up from the hall below; then he raised his head, to hear if any noise came from above. There was a deadly calm, the peace of a middle-class drawing-room, carefully shut in, admitting no whisper from without. Behind those fine doors of lustrous mahogany there seemed to be veritable abysses of respectability.

"You will have excellent neighbours," said Campardon, as he reappeared with the key; "the Josserands on the front floor—quite a family; the father is cashier at the St. Joseph glass-works, with two marriageable daughters. Next to you are the Pichons; he's a clerk. They're not exactly rolling in money, but are thoroughly well-bred. Everything has to be let, hasn't it? Even a house of this sort."

After the third floor the red carpet came to an end, and was replaced by a plain grey drugget. Octave's sense of dignity was slightly wounded thereby. Little by little the staircase had filled him was awe; he felt quite fluttered at the thought of living in such a thoroughly well-appointed house, as the architect had termed it. As he was following the latter along the passage to his room, through a half-opened door he caught sight of a young woman standing beside a cradle. Hearing a sound, she looked up. She was fair, with light, expressionless eyes; and all that he got was this marked look, for the young woman, blushing, suddenly pushed the door to with the bashful manner of someone taken by surprise.

Campardon, turning round, repeated :

"Water and gas on every floor, my dear boy."

Then he pointed out a door opening on to the servants' staircase—their rooms were overhead. Then, stopping at the end of the passage, he said :

"Here we are at last."

The room was large, and square-shaped, the design of the wall-paper being blue flowers on a grey ground. It was simply furnished. Near the alcove there was a washhand-stand, leaving just room for anyone to wash his hands. Octave went straight to the window, through which a greenish light entered. The courtyard loomed below, depressingly clean, with its even pavement, and its cistern with a shining copper tap. Not a soul, not a sound; nothing but rows of windows, devoid of a birdcage or a flower-pot, displaying all the monotony of their white curtains. To hide the great bare wall of the house on the left, which shut in the quadrangle, sham windows had been painted on to it with shutters eternally closed, behind which the walled-in life of the adjoining apartments seemed to be going on.

"This will suit me perfectly," cried Octave, delighted.

"I thought it would," said Campardon. "By Jove, I took as much trouble as if it were for myself, and I carried out all your written instructions. So you like the furniture, do you? It's all that a young fellow wants. You can see about other things later on."

And as Octave shook him by the hand and thanked him, while apologising for having given him so much trouble, he added in a more serious tone :

"Only, my good fellow, there must be no rows here, and, above all things no women. 'Pon my honour! if you were to bring a woman here, there would be a regular revolution."

"Don't be alarmed," muttered the young man, somewhat uneasy.

"No, let me tell you, for it is I who would be compromised. You see what the house is. All middle-class people, and so awfully moral. Between ourselves, I think they rather overdo it. Ah, well! Monsieur Gourd would at once fetch Monsieur Vabre, and we should both be in a nice mess. So, my dear chap, for my own peace of mind's sake, I ask you, do respect the house."

Overcome by so much virtue, Octave declared on oath that this he would do. Then Campardon, looking round him warily and lowering his voice, as if fearful of being overhead, added, with shining eyes :

"Elsewhere, it's nobody's business, eh? Paris is so big; there's plenty of room. I myself am an artist at heart, and personally I don't care a damn about such things."

A porter brought up the luggage. When everything had been put straight, the architect took a fatherly interest in the details of Octave's toilet. Then, rising, he said:

"Now let us go down and see my wife."

On the third floor the maid-servant, a slim, dark, coquettish-looking girl, said that madame was engaged. In order to put his young friend at ease, Campardon showed him over the flat. First of all, there was the big white and gold drawing-room, profusely ornamented with sham mouldings. This was placed between a little green parlour, which had been turned into a study, and the bedroom, into which they could not go, but the architect described its narrow shape and the mauve wall-paper. When he took him into the dining-room, all in imitation wood, with its strange combination of beading and panels, Octave, enchanted, exclaimed:

"It's very handsome!"

There were two great cracks right through the panelling of the ceiling, and in one corner the paint had peeled off and showed the plaster.

"Yes, it's effective," said the architect, slowly, with his eyes rivetted to the ceiling. "You see, these kind of houses are only built for effect. The walls, though, won't stand much knocking about. That's not been up twelve years yet, and it's already cracked. They build the frontage of handsome stone, with all sorts of sculpture about it, give the staircase three coats of varnish, touch up the rooms with gilt and paint; that's what fetches people, and makes them think a lot of it. Oh, it's solid enough yet! it'll last as long as we shall."

He led Octave through the ante-room again, with its ground-glass windows. To the left, overlooking the courtyard, there was another bedroom, where his daughter Angèle slept; all its whiteness, on this November afternoon, made it seem mournful as a tomb. Then, at the end of the passage, there was the kitchen, which he insisted on showing to Octave, saying that he must see everything.

"Do come in," he repeated, as he pushed the door open.

A hideous noise assailed their ears. Despite the cold, the window was wide open. Leaning over the rail, the dark maid-servant and a fat, ill-favoured old cook were looking down into the narrow well of an inner courtyard, which lighted the opposite kitchens on each floor. With backs bent, they were both screaming; while from below arose the sound of gross laughter, mingled with oaths. It was as if a sewer had brimmed over. All the domestics of the house were there, letting off steam. Octave thought of the middle-class majesty of the grand staircase.

As if warned by some instinct, the two women turned round. At the sight of their master with a gentleman they looked surprised. There was a slight hissing noise, the windows were shut, and all became once more silent as the grave.

"What's the matter, Lisa?" asked Campardon.

"If you please, sir," said the maid, in great excitement, "it's that dirty Adèle again. She's thrown a rabbit's guts out of window. You should speak to Monsieur Josserand, sir."

Campardon looked serious, but would not commit himself. He withdrew to the study, saying to Octave:

"You've seen everything now. The rooms are the same on each floor. Mine cost me two thousand five hundred francs; on the third floor, too! Rents are going up every day. Monsieur Vabre must make about twenty-two thousand francs a year out of his house. That will go on increasing, for there is a talk of making a broad thoroughfare from the Place de la Bourse to the new opera-house. And the ground on which this is built he got for a mere nothing, about twelve years ago, when there was that big fire, started by some chemist's servant."

As they entered, Octave noticed, above a drawing-table, and with the light from the window full upon it, a handsomely framed picture of the Holy Virgin, showing at her breast an enormous flaming heart. He could not conceal his surprise, and looked at Campardon, whom he remembered to have been a gay dog at Plassans.

"Oh!" said the latter, blushing somewhat, "I forgot to tell you I have been appointed architect to the diocese—at Evreux, it is. A mere trifle from the money point of view—barely two thousand francs a year. But there's nothing to do—a journey now and again; besides, I've got a surveyor down there. Then, you see, its' rather a good thing if one can put on one's card, 'Architect to the Government.' You can't think what a lot of work that brings me from society people."

As he spoke, he gazed at the Virgin with her fiery heart.

"After all," added he, in a sudden fit of candour, "I don't care two straws about all their claptrap."

But when Octave burst out laughing, the architect felt certain misgivings. Why confide in this young man? He looked at him sideways, assumed a contrite air, and tried to unsay his last remark.

"Well, I don't care, and yet I do somehow. That's about it. Wait a bit, my friend; when you're a little older you'll do like everybody else."

He spoke of his age—forty-two—of the emptiness of existence, and hinted at a melancholy which in no-wise assorted with his robust health. Under his flowing hair and beard, trimmed *à la* Henri IV, there was the flat skull and square jaw of a middle-class man of limited intelligence and animal appetites. When younger, he had been hilarious to the point of boredom.

Octave's eyes fell on a number of the *Gazette de France,* which was lying among some plans. Then Campardon, becoming more and more embarrassed, rang for the maid, to know if madame was at length disengaged. Yes, the doctor was going, and madame would come directly.

"Is Madame Campardon not well?" asked the young man.

"No, she is as usual," said the architect, with a touch of annoyance in his voice.

"Oh, what's the matter with her?"

More confused than ever, he answered evasively: "Women, you know, have always got something the matter with them. She's been like that for thirteen years—ever since her confinement. In other respects she is flourishing. You'll even find that she has grown stouter."

Octave forbore to question further. Just then, Lisa came back, bringing a card, and the architect, apologising, hurried into the drawing-room, begging the young man to talk to his wife meanwhile. As the door quickly opened and shut, in the centre of the spacious white and gold apartment Octave caught sight of the black spot of a cassock.

At the same moment Madame Campardon came in from the ante-room. He did not recognise her. Years ago, when, as a lad, he knew her at Plassans, at the house of her father, M. Domergue, a director of bridges and roads, she was thin and plain, and for all her twenty years, as puny as a girl that has just reached puberty. Now, he found her plump, with clear complexion, and as composed as a nun; soft-eyed, dimpled, and sleek as a fat tabby cat.

Though she had not become pretty, her thirty summers had ripener her, giving her a sweet savour, a pleasant, fresh odour as of autumnal fruit. He noticed, however, that she walked with difficulty, her hips swaying in a long loose gown of mignonette-coloured silk, which gave her a languid air.

"Why, you're quite a man now," she said, gaily, holding out both hands. "How you've grown since our last journey!"

And she surveyed him—tall, brown, comely young fellow that he was, with his carefully trimmed beard and moustache. When he told her his age, twenty-two, she would not believe it—declaring that he looked at least twenty-five. He—whom the very presence of a woman, even of the lowest maidservant, enraptured—laughed a silvery laugh as he delightedly watched her with eyes the colour of old gold and soft as velvet.

"Yes," he repeated, gently, "I've grown, I've grown. Do you remember when your cousin, Gasparine, used to buy me marbles?"

Then he told her news about her own people. Monsieur and Madame Domergue were living quite happily and quietly in their own house; all that they complained of was that they were so much alone, and they bore Campardon a grudge for having thus carried off their little Rose when he had come down to Plassans on business. The young fellow then tried to make his cousin Gasparine the subject of conversation, and so satisfy his curiosity of long standing, respecting a mystery that for him had never been solved—the achitect's sudden passion for Gasparine, a tall handsome girl without a penny, and his hasty marriage with Rose, a thin damsel who had as dowry thirty thousand francs, and the whole scene of tears and recriminations, followed by the flight of the forsaken one to her dressmaker aunt in Paris. But Madame Campardon, though her calm face flushed slightly, appeared not to understand. He could get no details from her.

"And your parents, how are they?" she enquired, in her turn.

"Thank you, they are very well," he replied. "My mother never stirs out of her garden now. You would find the house in the Rue de la Banne just the same as when you left it."

Madame Campardon, who seemingly could not stand for any length of time without fatigue, was sitting in a high easy-chair, her limbs extended beneath her tea-gown, and he, taking a low chair looked up at her with his wonted air of adoration—with his big shoulders, there was something feminine about him, something appealing to women, that touched them and made them instantly take him to their heart. Thus, in ten minutes' time they were both chatting like two old friends.

"Well, here I am, your boarder," said he, stroking his beard with a shapely hand, the nails of which were carefully trimmed. "We're sure to get on famously together, you'll see. It was awfully nice of you to think of the little urchin of Plassans, and to trouble about everything directly I asked you."

"No, no, don't thank me," she protested. "I am far too lazy; I never stir. It was Achille who arranged everything. After all, when your mother told us that you wanted to board with some family, that was quite enough for us to make you welcome. You won't be among strangers now, and it will be company for us."

Then he told her of his own affairs. After getting his bachelor's diploma, to please his family, he had just spent three years in Marseilles, in a large calico print warehouse which had a factory near Plassans. He had a passion for trade, for the trade in women's luxuries, in which there was something of the pleasure of seduction, of slow possession achieved by gilded phrases and flattering looks. And with the laugh of a conqueror, he told her how he had made the five thousand francs, without which he would never have risked coming to Paris, the prudence of a Jew underlying his flighty good-nature.

"Just think; they had a Pompadour calico, an old design—quite marvellous. Nobody jumped at it, it had lain in the warehouse for two years. So, as I was going to travel through the Var and the Basses-Alpes, I suddenly thought of buying up the whole stock and selling it on my own account. It was simply a huge success. There was a regular scramble among the women for the remnants, and to-day every one of them has got on some of my calico. I must say, I talked them over most beautifully! They were, one and all, of my opinion; I could have done what I liked with them."

And he laughed, while Madame Campardon, fascinated and somewhat fluttered at the thought of that Pompadour calico, kept asking him questions. Little bunches of flowers on a light-brown ground—was that the pattern? She had been looking everywhere for something similar, for her summer dressing-gown.

"I've travelled for two years," he went on, "and that's enough. Now there's Paris for me to conquer. I must look out for something at once."

"Why, did'nt Achille tell you?" she exclaimed. "He's got a position for you, and close by, too."

He thanked her, as much astonished as if he were in fairyland, and asked, jokingly, if he would find a wife with a hundred thousand francs a year in his room that evening, when the door was pushed open by a plain, lanky girl of fourteen with straw-coloured hair, who uttered a slight cry of alarm.

"Come in, and don't be shy," said Madame Campardon. "This is Monsieur Octave Mouret, of whom you have heard us speak."

Then, turning to Octave, she said :

"My daughter, Angèle. On our last journey we did not take her with us; she was so delicate. But she's getting stouter now."

Angèle, with the awkwardness of girls at this ungraceful age, took up her stand behind her mother and stared at the smiling young man. Almost immediately Campardon came back, looking excited, and he could not keep from hurriedly telling his wife of the good luck that had befallen him. The Abbé Mauduit, vicar of Saint-Roch, had come about some work—merely repairs, but it might lead to far more important things. Then, vexed at having talked of this before Octave, yet still trembling with excitement, he struck both hands together, and said.

"Well, well, what are we going to do?"

"Why, you were going out," said Octave. "Don't let me disturb you?"

"Achille," murmured Madame Campardon, "that situation, at the Hédouins."

"Why, of course," exclaimed the architect, "I had forgotten that. My dear fellow, it's the job of head assistant at a large haberdasher's. I know somebody there who has put in a word for you. They expect you. As it's not four o'clock yet, would you like me to take you round there?"

Octave hesitated, and, in his mania for being well-dressed, felt nervous about the sit of his necktie. However, when Madame Campardon assured him that he looked very neat, he decided to go. With a languid gesture, she offered her forehead to her husband, who kissed her with effusive tenderness, as he repeated :

"Ta-ta, pussy; good-bye, my pet."

"Remember, we dine at seven," said she, as she accompanied them across the drawing-room to get their hats. Angèle awkwardly followed. Her music-master was waiting for her, and she at once began to strum on the instrument with her skinny fingers. Octave, who loitered in the ante-room repeating his thanks, could hardly hear himself speak. And as he went down the staircase the sound of the piano seemed to pursue him. In that lukewarm silence other pianos, from Madame Juzeur's, the Vabres', and the Duveyriers', made answer, each playing a different air, on every floor; tunes that sounded half-remote, half-religious, as they reached him from behind those chastely solemn walls.

When they got downstairs Campardon turned up the Rue Neuve-Saint-Augustin. He was silent, preoccupied, like a man who is waiting to broach a subject.

"Do you remember Mademoiselle Gasparine?" he asked, at length. "She is forewoman at the Hédouins. You will see her."

Octave thought this a good chance of satisfying his curiosity.

"Oh!" said he, "does she live with you?"

"No, no!" exclaimed the architect hastily, and as if stung at the suggestion.

Then, as Octave seemed surprised at his emphatic denial, he added, in a gentler tone of embarrassment:

"No, my wife and she never meet now. In families, you know——. I've met her myself, and I couldn't very well refuse to shake hands, could I? More especially as the poor girl's badly off. So that now they get news of each other through me. In old quarrels of this sort one must leave it to time to heal the wounds."

Octave determined to question him plainly about his marriage, when the architect suddenly cut matters short by saying:

"Here we are!"

It was a linendraper's shop, facing the narrow, three-cornered Place Gaillon. On a signboard, just above the shop, were the words in faded gilt lettering, "The Ladies' Paradise: Established 1822," while the shop-windows bore the name of the firm, in red: "Deleuze, Hédouin and Co."

"In style it's not quite up to date, but it's a sound, straightforward concern," explained Campardon, rapidly. "Monsieur Hédouin, at one time a clerk, married the daughter of the elder Deleuze, who died two years ago, so that the business is now managed by the young couple—old Deleuze and another partner, I think, both keep out of it. You'll see Madame Hédouin. Ah, she's got a head on her shoulders! Let's go in."

Monsieur Hédouin just then happened to be away at Lille, buying linen, so Madame Hédouin received them. She was standing, with a pen behind her ear, giving orders to two shopmen, who were putting pieces of stuff in order on the shelves. He thought her so tall and attractive-looking, with her regular features and neatly-plaited hair, black dress, turn-down collar, and man's tie. As she gravely smiled at him, Octave, not generally bashful, could hardly stammer out a reply. In a few words everything was settled.

"Well," said she, in her quiet way and her professional grace of manner, "as you're at liberty, perhaps you might like to look over the premises."

Calling a clerk, she entrusted Octave to his care, and then, after politely replying to Campardon that Mademoiselle Gasparine was out, she turned her back and went on with her work, giving orders in the same gentle, firm voice.

"Not there, Alexandre. Put the silks up at the top. Look out! those are not of the same make."

After some hesitation, Campardon said he would call again and fetch him back to dinner. So for two hours the young man explored the warehouse. He found it badly lighted, small, over-laden with stock, which, as there was no room for it in the basement, had to be piled up in corners, leaving only narrow passages between high walls of bales. Several times he met Madame Hédouin tripping busily along the narrowest of the passages without ever catching her dress in anything. She seemed to be the life and soul of the place, the least sign of whose white hands all the assistants obeyed. Octave was rather hurt that she did not take more notice of him. About a quarter to seven, just as he was coming up from the basement for the last time, he was told that Campardon was on the first floor, with Mademoiselle Gasparine. That was the hosiery department, which this young lady superintended. But, at the top of the winding staircase, Octave stopped short behind a pyramid of calico-bales, symmetrically arranged, as he heard the architect talking in the most familiar way to Gasparine.

"I'll swear I haven't," he cried, forgetting himself so far as to raise his voice.

There was a pause.

"How is she now?" asked the young woman.

"Oh, good Lord! she's always the same. One day better; one day worse. She knows that it's all over now, and that she'll never be right again.

Then Gasparine, with pity in her voice, continued:

"It's you, my poor friend, who are to be pitied. However, as you have been able able to manage things otherwise, do tell her how sorry I am to hear that she is still so poorly——"

Without letting her finish the sentence, Campardon caught her by the shoulders and kissed her roughly on the lips in the gas-heated air growing ever more vitiated under the low ceiling. She returned his kiss, murmuring:

"To-morrow morning, then, at six, if you can manage it. I'll stop in bed. Knock three times."

Octave, astounded, but beginning to understand, coughed first and then came forward. Another surprise awaited him, Gasparine, his cousin, had become shrivelled, lean and angular, with projecting jaws and coarse hair. All that she had kept in this cadaverous face of hers were her great, splendid eyes. Her envious brow and sensuous, stubborn mouth distressed him as much as Rose had charmed him by her tardy development into an indolent blonde.

Gasparine, if not effusive, was polite. She remembered Plassans, and she talked to the young man of old times. As Campardon and he took their leave she shook them by the hand. Downstairs Madame Hédouin simply said to Octave :

"Well, then, we shall see you to-morrow."

When he got into the street, deafened by cabs and hustled by passers-by, the young fellow could not help observing that the lady was certainly very handsome, if not particularly affable. The lustrous windows of newly-painted shops, ablaze with gas, flung squares of bright light across the black, muddy pavement, while the older shops, with their dim interiors half lighted by smoking lamps, like distant stars, only made the streets more gloomy by their broad patches of shadow. In the Rue Neuve-Saint-Augustin, just before turning into the Rue de Choiseul, Campardon bowed as he passed one of these shops.

A young lady, slim and elegant, wearing a silk mantle, stood at the door, holding a little boy of three close to her so that he might not get knocked down. She was talking familiarly to an old, bare-headed woman, evidently the shopkeeper. It was too dark for Octave to distinguish her features, but, in the flickering gaslight, she seemed to him to be pretty, and he only caught sight of two bright eyes, fixed for a moment upon him like two flames. The shop formed a background, humid like a cellar, and there came from it a faint odour of saltpetre.

"That is Madame Valérie, wife of Monsieur Théophile Vabre, the landlord's younger son, you know—the people on the first floor," said Campardon, after they had gone a little further. "She's a most charming person—born in that very shop, one of the best paying linen drapers of the neighbourhood, which her parents, Monsieur and Madame Louhette still manage, just to have something to do. They've made some money you can be sure!"

But trade of that sort was past Octave's comprehension, in such dingy holes of old Paris, where, once upon a time, a single piece of stuff displayed in the window was enough. He vowed that nothing on earth would ever make him agree to live in such a den as that.

Thus chatting, they reached the top of the stairs. Dinner was waiting for them. Madame Campardon had put on a grey silk gown, and had dressed her hair most coquettishly, paying great attention to her toilette. Campardon kissed her on the neck, with all the emotion of a dutiful husband.

"Good evening, love; good evening, my pet."

Then they went into the drawing-room. The dinner was delightful. At first Madame Campardon spoke of the Deleuzes and the Hédouins—families well-known and respected throughout the neighbourhood. A cousin of theirs was a stationer in the Rue Gaillon; their uncle kept an umbrella-shop in the Passage Choiseul; while their nephews and nieces were, all of them, in business here and there. Then the conversation turned upon Angèle, sitting bolt upright in her chair and eating listlessly. She was being brought up at home; it was safer, so her mother thought, who, not wishing to speak plainer, winked her eye, by way of a hint that at boarding-schools little misses learnt most awful things. The child was slyly trying to balance her plate on her knife. Lisa, as she was clearing away, just missed breaking it, and exclaimed:

"That was your fault, mademoiselle!"

Angèle struggled to hide her laughter, while her mother only shook her head. When Lisa had left the room to bring in the dessert, Madame Campardon expatiated upon her good qualities—very intelligent, very active, a real Parisienne, never at a loss. They might easily do without Victoire, the cook, who, owing to her great age, was no longer very clean; but, you see, she had been in the service of her master's father, when Campardon was a baby. In short, she was a family ruin that they respected. Then, as the maid came back with some baked apples:

"Conduct irreproachable," continued Madame Campardon, in Octave's ear. "So far, I have found out nothing against her. Only one day off a month, when she goes to look after her old aunt, who lives a good way off."

Octave looked at Lisa. Noticing how nervous, flat-bosomed, and blear-eyed she was, he thought to himself what a high old time she must have at that aunt's. However, he entirely concurred in the views of the mother, who continued to impart to him her ideas as to education; a girl was such a grave responsibility, she ought to be shielded from the very breath of the streets. All this time, whenever Lisa leant across near Angèle's chair to change a plate, the child would pinch her thighs in a kind of mad familiarity, though both were as grave as could be, neither of them moving a muscle.

"Virtue is its own reward," said the architect, sagely, as if to put an end to thoughts that he did not express. "For my part, I don't care a hang what people think; I'm an artist, I am."

After dinner, they stayed in the drawing-room until midnight. It was a sort of orgy to celebrate Octave's arrival. Madame Campardon seemed dreadfully tired; ere long she subsided on the sofa.

"Are you in pain, love?" asked her husband.

"No," she replied, under her breath. "It's always the same thing."

Then, looking at him, she said, softly:

"You saw her at the Hédouins'?"

"Yes; she asked me how you were."

Tears came into Rose's eyes.

"She always well, she is!"

"There, there," said Campardon, as he lightly kissed her hair, forgetting that they were not alone. "You'll make yourself worse again. Don't you know that I love you all the same, my poor darling?"

Octave, who had discretly moved to the window, and pretended to be looking into the street, once more proceeded to scrutinise Madame Campardon's features, for his curiosity was roused, and he wondered what could be the matter with her. But she wore her usual look, half doleful, half good-tempered, as she curled herself up on the sofa, like a woman who submits resignedly to her share of caresses.

At length Octave bade them good-night. Candlestick in hand, he was still on the landing when he heard the rustle of silk dresses as they brushed the stairs. He politely stood back to let them pass. Evidently these were the ladies on the fourth floor, Madame Josserand and her two daughters, coming home from a party. As they went by, the mother, a stout, arrogant-looking dame, stared full in his face; the elder of the daughters stepped aside with a petulant air, while her sister, heedless, looked up at him and smiled in the bright light of the candle. She was charmingly pretty, with tiny features, fair skin, and shining auburn hair, and there was about her a certain intrepid grace, the easy charm of a young bride, as she came back from some ball, in an elaborate gown covered with bows and lace, such as girls never wear. Their trains disappeared at the top of the stairs, and a door closed behind them. Octave was quite amused by the merry twinkle in her eyes.

Slowly he went upstairs in his turn. Only one gas-jet was alight; the staircase, in this heavy, heated air, seemed fast asleep. More than ever did it wear a modest mien, with its chaste portals of handsome mahogany, that enclosed so many respectable hearths. Not a whisper was audible, it was a silence as of well-mannered people holding their breath. But now he heard a slight noise. Leaning over the banister, he saw Monsieur Gourd, in velvet cap and slippers, turning out the last gas burner. Then the whole house was lost in darkness, as if obliterated by the refinement and absolute propriety of its slumbers.

However, Octave found it hard to get to sleep. He tossed about feverishly, his brain filled with all the new faces that he had seen. What on earth made the Campardons so civil to him? Did they think of giving him their daughter later on? Perhaps the husband had taken him in as a boarder just to amuse his wife and cheer her up. Poor woman! what could the extraordinary complaint be from which she was suffering? Then his ideas grew more confused; phantoms passed before him; little Madame Pichon, his neighbour, with her vacuous look; handsome Madame Hédouin, calm and self-possessed, in her black dress; the fiery eyes of Madame Valérie, and the merry smile of Mademoiselle Josserand. How he had grown during just these few hours spent in Paris! This had always been his dream, that ladies would take him by the hand, and help him on in his business. Again and again the faces came back, blending themselves with wearisome iteration. He knew not which to choose, as he strove to let his voice be tender and his gestures seductive. Then, all at once, tired out, exasperated, he gave rein to the brutal impulse within him, to his ferocious disdain of woman-kind, which his air of amorous devotion masked.

"Are they ever going to let me go to sleep?" he exclaimed aloud, throwing himself violently on his back. "I'll take on the first one that wants it. To sleep! to sleep!"

II

WHEN Madame Josserand, preceded by her daughters, left Madame Dambrevile's party in the Rue de Rivoli, fourth floor at the corner of the Rue de I'Oratoire, she slammed the street door in a sudden outburst of wrath that she had been suppressing for the last two hours. Her younger daughter Berthe had again just missed getting a husband.

"Well, what are you standing there for?" she angrily asked the girls, who had stopped under the arcade and were watching the cabs go by. "Walk on, do; for you needn't imagine that we're going to have a cab and spend another two francs!"

And when Hortense, the elder, grumbled :

"H'm! pleasant, walking in all this mud! It will finish my shoes, that's one sure thing!"

"Walk on, I say," rejoined the mother, in a fury. "When your shoes are done for, you'll have to stop in bed, that's all! A lot of good it is, taking you out!"

With bowed heads, Berthe and Hortense turned down the Rue de l'Oratoire. They held up their long skirts as high as they could above their crinolines, huddling up their shoulders, shivering in their opera cloaks. Madame Josserand walked last, wrapped in an old fur mantle that looked like shabby cat-skin. They none of them wore bonnets, but had enveloped their hair in lace wraps, a headgear that made the last street-passengers look round at them in surprise as they tramped along in single file past the houses, with backs bent and eyes fixed on the puddles. The mother grew more exasperated as she thought of many similar home-comings extending over the last three winters, hampered by their smart gowns, in all the black mud of the streets, a butt for the wit of belated loafers. No, she had certainly had enough of it, of this carting about of her daughters to all the four corners of Paris, without ever daring to enjoy the luxury of a cab, for fear of having to curtail the morrow's dinner by a dish!

"So she's a match-maker, is she?" she went on out loud, as she thought of Madame Dambreville, talking to herself by way of solace, not even addressing her daughters, who had gone along the Rue Saint-Honoré. "Fine matches she makes! A lot of pert hussies that come from goodness knows where! Oh, if one weren't obliged to go through it all! That was her last success, I suppose—that bride which she trotted out just to show us that she isn't always a failure! A fine specimen, too, and no mistake! A wretched child, forsooth, that, after making a slight mistake, had to be sent back to a convent for six months to get another coating of whitewash!"

As the girls crossed the Place du Palais Royal a shower came on. This was the last straw. Slipping and splashing about, they stopped and again cast glances at the empty cabs that rolled by.

"On you go!" cried the mother, ruthlessly. "We are too near home now; it is not worth forty sous. And your brother Léon, who wouldn't come away with us for fear of having to pay for the cab! If he can get what he wants at that woman's so much the better! But I can safely say it isn't at all decent. A frump, past fifty, who only invites young people to her house! An old tart that some exalted personage, with the bribe of a head-clerkship, made that idiot Dambreville marry!"

Hortense and Berthe plodded along in the rain, one in front of the other, without appearing to listen. When their mother let herself go like this, oblivious of all the strict rules laid down for their own superfine education, it was tacitly agreed that they were to be deaf. But on reaching the dark, low Rue de l'Echelle, Berthe rebelled.

"There!" she cried. "There goes my heel! I can't stir another step!"

Madame Josserand waxed furious.

"Walk on at once! Do I complain? Do you think it's fit for me to be trapesing about the streets at this time of night, and in such weather, too? It would be different if you had a father like other people. Oh, no; my lord must stay at home and take his ease! It always falls to me to take you about to parties; he'll never be bothered to do so! I assure you that I've had just about enough of it. Your father shall take you out in future, if he likes; you may go to the devil before I drag you about any more to places where I only get put out! A fellow that completely deceived me as to his capabilities, and from whom I have never got the least pleasure! Good Lord! If ever I were to marry again, it wouldn't be a man of *that* sort!"

The girls stopped grumbling. They well knew this eternal chapter in the history of their mother's blighted hopes. With their lace mantillas sticking to their faces, and their ball-shoes soaked through, they hurried along the Rue Sainte-Anne. In the Rue de Choiseul, at the very door of her own house, Madame Josserand had to undergo yet another humiliation, for the Duveyriers' carriage splashed her all over as it drove up.

Fagged and furious, both mother and girls got back some of their grace and deportment when they had to pass Octave on the stairs. But directly their door was shut, they rushed helter-skelter through the dark drawing-room, bumping against the furniture, till they got to the dining-room, where Monsieur Josserand was writing by the feeble light of a little lamp.

"Another failure!" cried Madame Josserand, as she flopped into a chair.

And she roughly tore the lace covering from her head, flung off her fur cloak, and appeared in a gaudy red dress, trimmed with black satin, and cut very low. She looked enormous, though her shoulders were still comely, and resembled the shining flanks of a mare. Her square face, with its big nose and flabby cheeks, expressed all the tragic fury of a queen checking her desire to lapse into the language of Billingsgate.

"Ah!" said Monsieur Josserand, simply, bewildered by this boisterous entrance.

His eyelids blinked uneasily. It was positively overwhelming when his wife displayed that mammoth bosom; it seemed as if he felt its weight crushing the back of his neck. Dressed in a seedy frock-coat that he was wearing out at home, his countenance washed out and dingy with thirty years of office routine, he looked up at her with his large lack-lustre eyes. Pushing back his grey locks behind his ears, he was too disconcerted to speak, and attempted to go on writing.

"But you don't seem to understand!" continued Madame Josserand, in a harsh voice. "I tell you, there goes another marriage that has'nt come off—the fourth!"

"Yes, yes, I know—the fourth," he murmured. "It's annoying, very."

And to avoid his wife's appalling nudity he turned towards his daughters with a kindly smile. They also took off their lace and their cloaks; the elder was in blue, the younger in pink, and their dresses, too daring in cut and over trimmed, had something tempting about them. Hortense had a sallow complexion; her nose spoilt her; it was like her mother's, and gave her an air of stubborn disdain. She was only just twenty-three, but looked twenty-eight. Berthe, however, who was two years younger, had kept all her childish grace, with similar features, only more delicate, and a skin a dazzling whiteness, to be menaced only by the coarse family mask when she had got to fifty or thereabouts.

"What's the good of staring at us?" cried Madame Josserand. "For God's sake put your writing away; it gets on my nerves!"

"But, my dear, I've got these wrappers to do!" said he, gently.

"Oh, yes, I know your wrappers—three francs a thousand! Perhaps, you think that with those three francs you'll be able to marry your daughters!"

By the faint light of the little lamp one, indeed, could see that the table was strewn with large sheets of coarse paper, printed wrappers on which Monsieur Josserand wrote addresses for a well-known publisher who had several periodicals. As with his cashier's salary he could not make ends meet, he spent whole nights at this unprofitable sort of work, doing it on the quiet, afraid that anyone should find out how poor they were.

"Three francs are three francs," he rejoined in his slow, tired voice. "With those three francs you'll be able to add bows to your gown, and get a cake for your guests on Tuesdays."

He regretted the remark directly he had made it, for he felt that with Madame Josserand it had gone straight home, and had touched her pride in its most sensible part. Her shoulders grew purple; she seemed just about to burst forth with some vindictive reply, but, by a majestic effort, she only stammered:

"Good gracious me! Well, I never!" And she looked at her daughters, shrugging those awful shoulders, as if in masterful scorn of her husband, and as much as to say: "There! you hear the idiot, don't you?"

The girls nodded. Seeing himself vanquished, he regretfully laid down his pen and took up a copy of *Le Temps,* which he brought home with him every evening from the office.

"Is Saturnin asleep?" asked Madame Josserand, drily, referring to her younger son.

"Yes, *long* ago; and I told Adèle she could go to bed, too. I suppose you saw Léon at the Dambrevilles'?"

"Of course. Why, he sleeps there!" she rapped out, in a sudden paroxysm of spite that she could not check.

The father, surprised, ingenuously asked:

"Do you think he does?"

Hortense and Berthe became deaf, smiling slightly; they pretended to be examining their shoes, which were in a pitiable state. By way of a diversion, Madame Josserand tried to pick another quarrel with her husband. She begged him to take away his newspaper every morning, and not to leave it lying about all day long, as he had done last night, for instance. That particular copy just happened to contain details of a scandalous trial, which his daughters might easily have read. His utter want of moral principle was evident from such negligence as that.

"So it's bedtime, is it?" yawned Hortense. "I'm hungry."

"What about me?" said Berthe. "I'm simply starving."

"What's that?" cried Madame Josserand. "Hungry? Didn't you get some *brioche* when you were there? What a couple of ninnies! Hungry, forsooth! I took good care to eat something."

But the girls persisted in saying that they were dying of hunger, so their mother at last went with them into the kitchen to see if there was anything left. Their father furtively set to work upon his wrappers again. He was well aware that without those wrappers of his all the petty household luxuries would have disappeared, and thus it was that, in spite of gibes and bickerings, he doggedly kept at this secret drudgery until daybreak, quite pleased, poor man, at the thought that just one more scrap of lace might bring about a wealthy marriage. Though household expenses were being cut down, and funds still proved insufficient to pay for dresses and those Tuesday receptions, he resigned himself to this quill-driving like a martyr, dressed in tatters, while his wife and daughters went tearing about to parties with flowers in their hair.

"Why, it's a perfect pest-house!" cried Madame Josserand, as she entered the kitchen. "I can never get that slut Adèle to leave the window open. She always says that in the morning it makes all the flat as cold as ice."

She went to open the window, when from the narrow servants' yard an icy dampness rose, a stale odour like that of some musty cellar. Berthe's lighted candle threw dancing shadows of huge bare shoulders on the opposite wall.

"And how untidy it all is!" continued Madame Josserand, sniffing about everywhere, in all the dirty places. "She's not scrubbed her table for a fortnight. Those are the dirty plates of two days ago. Upon my word, it's disgusting! And her sink! Just smell her sink, if you please!"

She was gradually working herself up. She upset plates and dishes with her arms all white with rice-powder and bedizened with gold bracelets. She trailed her red skirts through all the filth till they caught in pans shoved under the tables, at the risk of spoiling all her elaborate finery with the greasy garbage. Finally, at the sight of a knife all notched, she exploded.

"To-morrow morning I'll send her flying!"

"What good will that do you?" asked Hortense, quietly. "We can never keep anybody. She's the first girl that has ever stopped three months. Directly they get a little decent, and have learnt how to make a white sauce, off they go."

Madame Josserand bit her lip. As a matter of fact, Adèle, fresh from Brittany, dull of wit and lousy, had been the only one to stop in this wretched abode of middle-class vanity, whose inmates took advantage of her dirt and ignorance to starve her. Scores of times, when they had discovered a comb in the bread, or when, after some nauseous stew they had the colic, they talked of getting rid of her; but then, again, they preferred to put up with her rather than have the bother of finding another cook, for even pilferers refused to take service in such a hole, where the very lumps of sugar were counted.

"I don't see anything at all," muttered Berthe, as she ransacked a cupboard.

The shelves had the mournful barrenness about them and the sham display of households where they buy inferior meat so as to be able to have a show of flowers on the table. There were only some quite clean china plates with gold edges, a crumb-brush with some of the plated silver rubbed off its handle, a cruet-stand, in which the oil and vinegar had dried up; but not a solitary crust, not a scrap of fruit, of pastry, or of cheese. Obviously Adèle's insatiable hunger made her lick the plates clean, and mop up any rare drops of gravy or sauce left by her employers, till she was like to rub the gilt off.

"Why, she must have eaten up all the rabbit!" cried Madame Josserand.

"Yes," said Hortense, "there were the remains of that! No, here it is! I should have been surprised if she had dared to. I shall stick to that. It's cold, but it's better than nothing."

Berthe kept rummaging about, but without success. At last she caught hold of a bottle in which her mother had diluted the contents of an old pot of jam wherewith to manufacture red-currant syrup for her evening parties. Berthe poured out half-a-glass, saying:

"I'll soak some bread in this, as there's nothing else."

But Madame Josserand, with an anxious look, said cuttingly:

"Pray don't be bashful; fill up your tumbler, do, while you are about it. Then, to-morrow, you know, I can give our guests cold water."

Luckily, another of Adèle's misdeeds cut her scoldings short. As she was prying about, on the watch for crimes, she caught sight of a book lying on the table, and then there was a supreme outburst.

"Oh, the slut! She's brought my 'Lamartine' into the kitchen again!"

It was a copy of *Joselyn*. Taking it up, she rubbed it, as if to clean it, and went on saying that, over and over again, she had forbidden her to drag it about with her everywhere to write her accounts on. Meanwhile Berthe and Hortense had divided the little piece of bread between them, and then, taking their supper along with them, they said that they would undress first. They gave a parting glance at the ice-cold oven and went back to the dining-room, the mother holding her "Lamartine" under her exuberantly fleshy arm.

Monsieur Josserand continued writing. He hoped that his wife would be satisfied at crushing him with a look as she went past on her way to bed. But she again sank into a chair facing him, and gazed at him without speaking. This gaze he felt, and it made him so uneasy that his pen sputtered on the flimsy wrapper-paper.

"So it was you who prevented Adèle from making a custard for to-morrow evening," she said, at last.

He looked up in amazement.

"I, my dear?"

"Oh, you'll deny it, just as you always do! Then, why hasn't she made it as I told her to? You know very well that Uncle Bachelard is coming to dinner to-morrow; it's his saint's day, and, unfortunately, on the very day of our party, too! If there's no custard, we must have an ice, which means another five francs thrown away!"

He never attempted to exculpate himself. Afraid to go on with his work he began to toy with his penholder. There was a lull.

"To-morrow morning," continued Madame Josserand, "I shall be obliged if you will call on the Campardons and remind them as politely as you can that we expect them in the evening. The young man, their friend, arrived this afternoon. Ask them to bring him, too. Remember, I wish him to come."

"What young man?"

"A young man; it would take far too long to explain the whole thing to you. I have found out everything about him. I am obliged to try all I can, since you leave your two daughters on my hands like a bundle of rubbish, caring no more about getting them married than about the Grand Turk."

At this thought her anger revived.

"You see, I keep myself in, but, upon my word, it's more than anyone can stand. Don't answer, sir; don't answer, or I shall positively explode!"

He forbore to answer, and she exploded all the same.

"The long and the short of it is, I won't put up with it. I warn you that one of these fine days I shall go off and leave you with your two empty-headed daughters. Do you think I was born to lead such a beggarly life as this? Always splitting farthings into four, denying oneself even a pair of boots, while unable to entertain one's friends in decent fashion! And you're to blame for it all! Don't shake your head, sir; don't exasperate me further! Yes, your fault; I repeat, your fault! You tricked me, sir; basely tricked me. One ought not to marry a woman if one has resolved to let her want for everything. You bragged about your fine future, declaring you were the friend of your employer's sons, those brothers Bernheim, who afterwards made such a fool of you. What! Do you pretend to tell me that they did not make a fool of you? Why, by this time you ought to be their partner! It was you who made their glass business what it is—one of the first in Paris, and what are you? Their cashier, a servant, an underling! Pshaw! You've no pluck, no spirit?—Hold your tongue!"

"I draw eight thousand francs a year," murmured the hireling; "it's a very good berth."

"A good berth, indeed! After more than thirty years' service. They grind you down, and you're delighted. Do you know what I should have done, if it had been me? I should have seen to it that the business filled my pocket twenty times over. That was easy enough; I saw it when I married you, and I have never stopped urging you to do so ever since. But it wanted initiative, intelligence; it meant not going to sleep like a blockhead on the office stool!"

"Come, come," broke in Monsier Josserand, 'are you going to upbraid me for being honest?"

She rose, and, approaching him, brandished her "Lamartine."

"What do you mean by honest? First of all, be honest towards me; others come second, I hope! And I tell you again, sir, it is not honest to take a girl in by pretending to want to become rich some day, and then to lose your wits in looking after someone else's money! It's true, I was most beautifully swindled! I wish to goodness things could happen over again! Ah, if I'd only known what your people were like!"

She paced up and down the room in a rage. He could not check a movement of impatience, despite his great desire for peace.

"You ought to go to bed, Eléonore," said he, "It is past one o'clock, and I can assure you this work must be finished. My relatives have done you no harm, so why discuss them?"

"And why shouldn't I, please? Your family is no more sacred than anybody else's, I presume? Everyone at Clermont knows that your father, after selling his solicitor's practice, let a servant girl ruin him. You might have married off your daughters long ago if he had not picked up with a bitch when over seventy. He swindled me, too, he did!"

Monsieur Josserand turned pale, and replied in a trembling voice, which grew louder as he went on:

"Look here, don't let us begin the old game of abusing our relations. Your father has never yet paid me your dowry of thirty thousand francs, as he promised."

"Eh? What's that? Thirty thousand francs!"

"Just so; don't pretend to be so astonished. And if my father was unfortunate, yours has behaved most shamefully towards us. We never got to know exactly about that will of his; there were all sorts of shuffles so that your sister's husband should get the school in the Rue des Fossés-Saint-Victor—that shabby cad of an usher, who no longer condescends to nod to us now. We were robbed, as plain as could be!"

Madame Josserand grew livid with suppressed rage at this inconceivable outburst on the part of her husband.

"Don't say a word against papa! For forty years he was a credit to his profession. Mention the Bachelard Institute in the Panthéon quarter, and see what they say! And as for my sister and her husband, they are what they are. They swindled me, that I know; but it's not for you to tell me so, and I won't bear it; do you hear me? Do I ever twit you with your sister, who ran off with an officer? Oh! your relations are charming folk, aren't they?"

"Yes, madam, but the officer married her. There's Bachelard, that brother of yours, an unprincipled——"

"Sir! are you going mad? He is rich, he makes as much as he likes in his commission agency, and he has promised to give Berthe a dowry. Have you no respect for anyone?"

"All very fine; give Berthe a dowry! I wouldn't mind betting he doesn't give her a sou, and that we shall have to put up with his revolting habits for nothing. Whenever he comes here I'm quite ashamed of him. A liar, a rake, an adventurer, who takes advantage of the situation; and who, seeing that we grovel before his fortune, for the last fifteen years, gets me to spend two hours every Saturday in his office, to check his accounts! That saves him five francs. We have yet to see the colour of his money!"

Breathless with emotion, for a moment Madame Josserand paused. Then she flung back this final taunt:

"And you, sir, have got a nephew in the police!"

There was another pause. The light from the little lamp grew dimmer; as Monsieur Josserand feverishly gesticulated, the wrappers fluttered about in all directions. As he confronted his spouse, looking her full in the face, she sitting there in her low-necked dress, he resolved to say everything, and trembled for very courage.

"With eight thousand francs one can do a good deal," he went on. "You're always grumbling. But you ought not to have attempted to do things on a scale above our means. It's all your mania for entertaining and for paying visits, for having an 'at home' day with tea and cakes——"

She did not let him finish his speech. "Now we've got it at last! You'd better shut me up in a box at once. Why don't you scold me for not going about stark naked? And your daughters, sir; how are they to get husbands if we see nobody? To think that after sacrificing oneself, one is only to be judged in this despicable way!"

"We must all of us make sacrifices, madam. Léon had to make way for his sisters, leave the house and support himself. As for Saturnin, poor boy, he can't even read. For my part, I deny myself everything, and spend my nights——"

"Then, why did you ever have daughters, sir? You're surely not going to grudge them their education? Any other man, in your place, would be proud of Hortense's certificate, and of Berthe's artistic talents. Everyone to-night was charmed with the dear girl's playing of that waltz, 'Aux bords de l'Oise,' and I am sure her last water-colour sketch will delight our guests to-morrow. But you, sir, you've not even the instincts of a father; you'd rather have your daughters look after cows than send them to school!"

"Ah! and what about the insurance policy I took out for Berthe? Wasn't it you, madam, who spent the money for the fourth instalment on chair-covers for the drawing-room? Since then, you even got hold of the premiums as well."

"Of course I did, because you left us all to die of hunger. It's you who'll look foolish if your daughters become old maids!"

"Why, it's you who scare away all the likely men with your fine dresses and ridiculous parties! *I* look foolish? God blast you!"

In all his life Monsieur Josserand had never gone so far. His wife, gasping, stuttered: "*I* ridiculous—*I*!" when the door opened. Hortense and Berthe came back in petticoats and dressing-jackets, with their hair down and wearing slippers.

"Oh, the cold in our room!" said Berthe, shivering. "It freezes the very food in your mouth. Here, at least there has been a fire this evening."

And they both drew up their chairs and sat close to the stove, which still retained some heat. Hortense held the rabbit bone between her finger-tips, and adroitly picked it. Berthe dipped bits of bread in her tumbler of syrup. But their parents were so excited that they hardly noticed them enter, but went on:

"Ridiculous ,did you say, sir, ridiculous? I will be so no longer. Hang me if ever I wear out another pair of gloves in trying to get them husbands! Now it's your turn; and I hope you'll not prove more ridiculous than myself!"

"I daresay, madam; after you've trotted them about and compromised them everywhere! Whether you get them married or whether you don't, I don't care a hang!"

"And I care less still, Monsieur Josserand! So little do I care, that if you aggravate me much more I'll send them flying into the street. And you can go, too, if you like; the door is open. Lord! what a good riddance of bad rubbish that would be!"

The girls listened tranquilly. They were used to such lively discussions. They went on eating, with dressing-jackets unbuttoned and showing their shoulders, and they let their bare skin gently chafe against the lukewarm earthen sides of the stove. They looked charming in this undress, charming with their youth and healthy appetites, and their large eyes heavy with sleep.

"It's silly of you to quarrel like this," said Hortense, at length, with her mouth full. "Mamma will ruin her temper, and papa will be ill at the office to-morrow. It seems to me that we are big enough to get husbands for ourselves."

This speech created a diversion. The father, utterly worn out, pretended to go on with his wrappers, while the mother, who was pacing up and down the room like a lioness that has got loose, came and stood in front of Hortense.

"If you're alluding to yourself," she cried, "you're a precious fool! That Verdier of yours will never marry you!"

"That's my look-out," replied Hortense, bluntly.

After having disdainfully refused five or six suitors—a clerk, a tailor's son, and other young men of no prospects, as she thought, she pitched upon a lawyer, over forty, whom she had met at the Dambrevilles'. She thought him very clever, and bound to make a large fortune by his talents. The worst of it was that, for fifteen years, Verdier had been living with a mistress, who, in their neighbourhood, even passed as his wife. This Hortense knew, but did not appear to be much troubled thereat.

"My child," said the father, looking up from his work, "I have begged you to give up all idea of such a marriage. You know what the situation is."

She stopped sucking her bone and impatiently rejoined:

"Well, what of it? Verdier's promised me to give her up. She's only a fool."

"You've no right to talk like that, Hortense. And if the fellow gives *you* up, too, one day, and goes back to the very woman you made him leave?"

"That's my look-out," said the girl, drily.

Berthe listened, as she knew of the whole matter, and discussed each new development of it with her sister every day. Like her father, she sided with the poor woman, who, after fifteen years of housekeeping, was to be turned into the street. But Madame Josserand struck in:

"Oh, do leave off! Wretched women of that sort always drift back at last to the gutter whence they came. It's Verdier, though, who will never have the strength of mind to leave her. He's hoaxing you nicely, my dear. If I were you I wouldn't wait another second for him, but I'd try and find somebody else."

The girl's voice grew harsher still, and two livid spots appeared on her cheeks.

"You know what I am, mamma. I want him, and him I will

have. I shall never marry anybody else, if I have to wait for him a hundred years!"

The mother shrugged her shoulders.

'And yet you call other people fools!"

Hortense rose, trembling with anger.

"Now, then, don't pitch into me!" she cried. "I've done eating my rabbit, and I'd rather go to bed. Since you can't manage to get us husbands, you must let us try and find them ourselves in whatever way we choose!"

And she went out, slamming the door behind her.

Madame Josserand turned majestically towards her husband with the profound remark:

"There, sir; that's how you have brought them up."

Monsieur Josserand made no reply, but kept making little dots of ink on his finger-nail, while waiting to continue his writing. Berthe, who had eaten her bread, was dipping a finger in the glass to finish up her syrup. As her back was nice and warm, she felt comfortable, and was in no hurry to go back to her room, where she would have to put up with her sister's ill-temper.

"Yes, that's what one gets," continued Madame Josserand, as she walked up and down the dining-room. "For twenty years one wears oneself out for these girls, denying oneself everything, so that they may become accomplished, and then they won't even give you the satisfaction of making a marriage such as you approve. If one had ever refused them anything it would be different. But I have spent my last centime over them, and have gone without proper clothes, in my endeavours to dress them just as if our income was fifty thousand francs a year. No, it is really *too* much. When the minxes have got a careful education, learning just enough of religion and of the manners of wealthy young ladies, they turn their backs on you, and talk of marrying lawyers, forsooth, debauched adventurers, and the like."

Stopping short in front of Berthe, she shook her finger at her, and said:

"As for you, if you behave like your sister, you'll have me to deal with."

Then she resumed her march, talking meanwhile to herself, jumping from one idea to another, contradicting herself with the complacent effrontery of a woman who is always right.

"I did what I ought to have done, and if needs were I'd do it again. In life it's only the most timid who go to the wall. Money is money, and if you haven't got any you'd better shut up shop at once. For my part, whenever I had twenty sous I always pretended I had forty, for the great thing is to command envy, not pity. It is no good having a fine education if one has shabby clothes, for then people only look down on you. It mayn't be right; but, anyhow, it is so. I'd rather wear dirty petticoats than a cotton gown. Eat potatoes if you like, but put a chicken on the table if you ask people to dinner. It's only *fools* who would deny that."

She looked hard at her husband, for whom these last remarks were intended. But, utterly exhausted, he declined to enter the lists a second time, and was cowardly enough to say:

"Ah, too true! money is everything nowadays."

"You hear that," said Madame Josserand, approaching her daughter. "Go straight ahead and try and do us credit. How was it you managed to let this marriage slip through your fingers?"

Berthe felt that now it was her turn.

"I don't know, mamma," she faltered.

"An assistant manager," continued her mother, "not yet thirty, and with magnificent prospects. Money coming in every month—a regular income; there's nothing like it. I am sure you were up to some nonsense, as before."

"No, I am sure I wasn't, mamma. I expect he found out that I hadn't got a farthing."

Madame Josserand's voice rose.

"And what about the dowry that your uncle is going to give you? Everyone knows about that. No, it must have been something else; he hedged off too abruptly. After dancing with him you went into the parlour, and——"

Berthe became confused.

"Yes, mamma, and, as we were alone, he tried to do all sorts of horrid things—caught me by the waist and kissed me. And I was frightened, and—I pushed him up against the table."

Her mother, boiling over with rage, interrupted her.

"Pushed him up against the table! Oh, the vixen! She pushed him up against the table, did she?"

"Well, mamma, he caught hold of me."

"What's that? Caught hold of you? As if that mattered. A lot of good it is to send simpletons like you to school! Whatever did they teach you there, eh?"

Blushes covered the girl's cheeks and shoulders, while, in her virginal confusion, tears came into her eyes.

"I could not help it. He looked so wicked; I did'nt know what to do."

"Did'nt know what to do? She didn't know what to do! Haven't I told you a hundred times not to be so absurdly timid? You've got to live in society. When a man takes liberties, it means that he's in love with you, and there is always a way of prettily keeping him in his place. Just for a kiss behind the door! Why, I'd be ashamed to mention such a thing. And you go pushing people up against the table and spoiling all your chances of getting married?"

Then, assuming a learned air, she went on:

"I give it up in despair; you're really so silly, my child. I should have to coach you in everything, and that would be a bore. As you have no fortune, do try and understand that you've got to catch men by some other means. One ought to be amiable, give tender glances, let your hand go sometimes, and submit to a little playfulness without appearing to do so; in short, one should fish for a husband. Now, you needn't think it improves your eyes to cry like a great baby."

Berthe was sobbing violently.

"Look here, you exasperate me—do leave off crying! Monsieur Josserand, just tell your daughter not to disfigure herself by crying like that. If she loses her looks, that will really be too much."

"My child," said her father, "be good and listen to your mother's advice. You mustn't spoil your looks, my pet."

"And what annoys me is, that when she likes she can be agreeable enough," continued Madame Josserand. "Come, dry your eyes and look at me as if I was a gentleman making love to you. You must smile and let your fan drop, so that, as he picks it up, his fingers just touch yours. No, no, that's not the way! With your head stuck up in the air like that, you look like a sick hen. Throw back your head and show your neck; it's pretty enough to be looked at."

"Like this, mamma?"

"Yes; that's better. And don't be so stiff; keep your waist lissom. Men don't care about deal boards. And, above all, if they go a little bit too far, don't behave like a noodle. When a man goes too far, he's done for, my dear!"

The drawing-room clock struck two, and, excited as she was by sitting up so late, and as her desire for an immediate marriage grew frenzied, the mother, in her abstraction, began thinking aloud as she twisted her daughter about like a Dutch doll. Berthe, heavy at heart, submitted in a tame, spiritless fashion; fear and confusion half choked her. Suddenly, in the middle of a merry laugh that her mother was forcing her to attempt, she burst into tears, exclaiming:

"No, no, it's no use; I can't do it!"

For a moment Madame Josserand remained speechless with astonishment. Ever since leaving the Dambrevilles' party her hand had been itching; there were slaps in the air. All at once she boxed Berthe's ears with all her might.

"There, take that! You're positively too annoying, you great booby! Upon my word, I don't blame the men!"

The shock caused her to drop her "Lamartine." Picking it up, she wiped it, and swept majestically out of the room without another word.

"I knew it must end like that," muttered Monsieur Josserand, who was afraid to detain his daughter. She also went off to bed, holding her cheek and sobbing louder than ever.

As Berthe felt her way across the ante-room she found her brother Saturnin, barefooted, was up, listening. Saturnin was a big hulking fellow of twenty-five, wild-eyed, and who had remained childish after an attack of brain fever. Without being actually insane, he occasionally frightened the household by fits of blind fury whenever anybody annoyed him. Berthe alone was able to subdue him by a look. When she was still a little girl he had nursed her throughout a long illness, obedient as a dog to all her little caprices; and, ever since he had saved her life, he adored her with a deep, passionate devotion.

"Has she been beating you again?" he asked, in a deep, tender voice.

Surprised at meeting him, Berthe tried to send him back to his room.

"Go to bed; it has nothing to do with you."

"Yes it has. I won't let her beat you. She shouted so that she woke me up. She'd better not do it again, or else I'll give it her."

The she caught hold of his wrists, and talked to him as if he were a disobedient animal. He was at once subdued, and whimpered like a little boy:

"It hurts you dreadfully, doesn't it? Where is the place? Let me kiss it."

And when he had found her cheek in the dark, he kissed it, wetting it with his tears, as he repeated:

"Now it's well again; now it's well again."

Meanwhile Monsieur Josserand, left alone, had put down his pen, too grieved to go on writing. After a few minutes, he got up and went gently to listen at the doors. Madame Josserand was snoring. No sounds of weeping came from his daughter's room. All was dark and silent. Then, somewhat easier, he came back. He looked to the lamp, which was smoking and mechanically recommenced writing. Unconsciously, two great tears fell on to the wrappers, amid the solemn silence of the dreaming house.

III

As soon as the fish had been served (some dubiously fresh skate, with black butter, which that muddling Adèle had swamped in vinegar), Hortense and Berthe, seated on either side of the uncle Bachelard, kept urging him to drink, filling his glass up in turns, and repeating :

"Now, then, uncle, drink away; it's your fête day, you know! Here's your health, uncle!"

They had conspired together to make him give them twenty francs. Every year their thoughtful mother placed them thus, on either side of her brother, leaving him to their tender mercies. But it was up-hill work, needing all the cupidity of two girls spurred thereto by visions of Louis Quinze shoes and five-button gloves. In order to get him to give them the twenty francs, they had to make him completely drunk. In his own family circle he was furiously avaricious, though elsewhere he would squander in drunken debauchery the eighty thousand francs which he made by his commission agency. Fortunately, that evening he had arrived half-drunk, having spent the afternoon with a lady in the Faubourg Montmartre, a dyer, who used to get vermouth for him from Marseilles.

"Your health, my duckies!" he replied in his big, raucous voice, whenever he emptied his glass.

Covered with jewellery, and with a rose in his buttonhole, he filled the centre of the table—the type of a huge, boozing, brawling tradesman who has wallowed in all sorts of vice. There was a lurid brilliancy about the false teeth in his furrowed, evil face; his great red nose poised thereon like a beacon below his snow-white, close-cropped hair; while now and again his eyelids dropped involuntarily over his rheumy eyes. Gueulin, son of his wife's sister, declared that his uncle had never been sober during the whole ten years that he was a widower.

"Narcisse, may I give you some skate? It is excellent," said Madame Josserand, smiling at her brother's drunken condition, though inwardly somewhat disgusted.

She sat opposite to him, with little Gueulin on her left, and on her right, Hector Trublot—a young man to whom she was obliged to show some attention. She usually took advantage of this family dinner to pay back certain invitations which had to be returned; and so it came about that Madame Juzeur, a lady living in the house, was also present, and sat next to Monsieur Josserand. As the uncle behaved outrageously at table, and it was only the thoughts of his fortune which helped to temper their disgust, she only asked her intimate acquaintances to meet him, or else such people as she deemed it useless to hoodwink any longer. For instance, at one time she had thought of young Trublot as a son-in-law, who was then in a money-changer's office, expecting that his wealthy father would buy him a share in the business. But as Trublot displayed a calm disdain for marriage, she took no further trouble about him, even putting him beside Saturnin, who had never yet learnt how to eat decently. Berthe, who always had to sit next to her big brother, was charged to keep him in order with a look whenever his fingers found their way too frequently into the sauce.

After the fish came a pasty, and the damsels thought the moment ripe for their preliminary attack.

"Do drink, uncle dear!" said Hortense. "It is your saint's day; now aren't you going to give us something on your saint's day?"

"Oh! so it is," added Berthe, with an innocent air. "One always gives something on one's saint's day; so you must give us twenty francs."

Directly there was any mention of money, Bachelard pretended to be more tipsy still. That was his usual trick. His eyelids drooped, and he became absolutely drivelling.

"Eh, what's that?" he stuttered.

"Twenty francs. You know very well what twenty francs are; it's no use pretending that you don't," said Berthe. "Give us twenty francs; and then we'll love you—oh, ever so much!"

They flung their arms about his neck, called him the most endearing names, and kissed his inflamed face, without showing any disgust for the revolting odour of low debauchery which he exhaled. Monsieur Josserand, upset by this nauseous smell—a mixture of absinthe, tobacco and musk—was shocked to see his daughters' virginal charms in such close contact with this lecherous old blackguard.

"Do leave him alone!" he cried.

"What for?" asked Madame Josserand, as she gave her husband

a terrible look. "They are only having a game. And if Narcisse likes to give them twenty francs, he has a perfect right to do so!"

"Monsieur Bachelard is so good to them," murmured little Madame Juzeur, complacently.

Struggling thus, the uncle became more and more idiotic, as he slobbered out:

"It'sh funny thing, but, 'pon my shoul! don't know (*hic*)—don't, really!"

Hortense and Berthe exchanged glances and then let him go. No doubt, he had not had enough to drink. So they filled up his glass anew, laughing like whores who mean to pick a man's pocket. Their bare arms, delightfully plump and fresh, kept passing every moment under their uncle's luminous proboscis.

Trublot meanwhile, like a quiet fellow who prefers having his fun all to himself, kept watching Adèle as she clumsily waited on the guests. He was very short-sighted, and thought she looked pretty with her heavy Breton features and her hair the colour of dirty hemp. As she placed the roast veal on the table, she stretched right across him, when he, pretending to pick up his napkin, gave her a good pinch on the calf of her leg. The girl, not understanding, looked at him as if he had asked her for some bread.

"What's the matter?" said Madame Josserand. "Did she push against you? Oh, that girl! she is so awkward! But she's quite new to service, don't you know, and wants proper training."

"Of course she does; it's all right," replied Trublot, stroking his bushy black beard with an air as serene as that of some young Indian god.

Conversation grew brisker in the dining-room, which, icy cold at first, was gradually being warmed by the steam from the various dishes. Yet once again Madame Juzeur confided to Monsieur Josserand the whole sad story of her thirty years of solitude. She raised her eyes to heaven, and, with this discreet allusion to the drama of her life, remained content. Her husband, after ten days of connubial bliss, had left her—no one knew why. More than this she did not say.

Now she lived in quiet lodgings—oh, so comfortable they were; and the priests often popped in.

"It's so sad, though, at my age!" she simpered, cutting up her veal in an affected manner.

"A most unfortunate little woman," whispered Madame Josserand in Trublot's ear, with an air of profound sympathy.

But Trublot callously surveyed this light-eyed devotee, full of reserve and mystery. She was not at all in his line.

Then they had a sudden scare. Saturnin, whom Berthe was no longer watching, being so busy with her uncle, had begun playing with his food, making a revolting mess with it on his plate. To his mother the poor lad was a source of exasperation, for she was both afraid and ashamed of him. How to rid herself of him she knew not, her pride forbidding her to make a common workman of him after she had sacrificed him in favour of his sisters, by taking him away from a school where his slothful intelligence was all too long in becoming roused. All these years that he had lounged about the house, helpless and stupid, had been years of terror for her, especially when she had to let him appear in society. This was as gall and wormwood to her pride.

"Saturnin!" she cried.

But Saturnin grinned again with delight at the nasty mess on his plate. He had no respect for his mother, but frankly treated her as a lying old hag, with the strange intuition of idiots who think aloud. Matters, were, indeed, becoming unpleasant, and he would have thrown the plate at her head if Berthe, recalled to her duty, had not fixed him with a look. He tried to resist; then his eyes dropped, and he leant back in his chair, gloomy and depressed, as if in a trance, until dinner was over.

"Gueulin, I hope you have brought your flute?" asked Madame Josserand, trying to dissipate the uncomfortable feeling that prevailed.

Gueulin played the flute in amateur fashion, but solely at houses where he felt quite at home.

"My flute? Of course I did," replied he.

His red hair and whiskers seemed more tangled and bristly than usual as he looked on, utterly absorbed, at the girl's manœuvre to trick their uncle. Himself a clerk in an insurance office, he used to meet Bachelard directly after office hours and never left him, going the round of all the cafés and brothels in his wake. Behind the huge, ungainly figure of the one, you were sure to see the pale, wizened features of the other.

"That's it; go ahead; stick to him!" he cried, as if he were an egger-on at a fight.

Uncle Bachelard, as a matter of fact, was getting the worst of it. When, after the vegetables—French beans soaked in water—Adèle brought in a vanilla and currant ice, there was great rejoicing all round the table; and the young ladies took advantage of the situation to make their uncle drink half the bottle of champagne which Madame Josserand had bought at a grocer's round the corner for three francs. He was getting maudlin, and forgot to keep up the farce of appearing imbecile.

"Eh? twenty francs! Why twenty francs? Oh, I see! you want me to give you twenty francs? But I haven't got them, 'pon my word, I haven't! Ask Gueulin. Didn't I come away without my purse, Gueulin, and you had to pay at the café? If I'd got them, my poppets, you should have them for being so sweet and charming!"

Gueulin, with a laugh that sounded like an ill-greased cartwheel, muttered:

"Oh, the old humbug!"

Growing suddenly excited, he cried:

"Why don't you search his pockets?"

Then, losing all restraint, Hortense and Berthe flung themselves upon their uncle anew. Checked at first by their good breeding, this desire for the twenty francs suddenly got the better of them, and in their wild excitement they flung manners to the winds. The one, with both her hands, searched his waistcoat pockets, while the other thrust her fist into the pockets of his frock-coat. Assailed in this way, uncle Bachelard still struggled with his persecutors, but laughter overcame him, a laughter broken by drunken hiccups.

"'Pon m'honour! not a sou. Leave off, do; you're tickling me!"

"Look in his trousers!" cried Gueulin.

So Berthe, grown resolute, thrust her hand into one of his breeches pockets. The girls trembled with excitement as they grew rougher and rougher, and they could almost have boxed their uncle's ears. Then Berthe uttered a cry of victory; from the depths of his pocket she drew forth a handful of money, which she scattered on a plate, and there, among copper and silver, was a gold twenty-francs piece.

"I've got it!" she cried, as, with disordered hair and flushed cheeks, she tossed the coin into the air and caught it.

All the guests clapped their hands; they thought it a great joke. There was a buzz of merriment, and it was the success of the dinner. Madame Josserand smiled a smile of motherly solicitude as she watched her dear daughters. The old man, collecting his money, remarked sententiously that if one wanted twenty francs one ought to earn them. And the two girls, exhausted but content, sat panting on either side of him, their lips still quivering with the excitement of the fray.

A bell rang. They had sat a good while over dinner, and guests were now beginning to arrive. Monsieur, who had decided to laugh, like his wife, at what had occurred, would willingly have had them sing a little Béranger at table, but she silenced him; that sort of entertainment was too much for her poetic taste. She hurried on the dessert, the more so because her brother Bachelard, vexed at having to make this present of twenty francs, was becoming quarrelsome, complaining that Léon, his nephew, had not even deigned to trouble about wishing him many happy returns. Léon had only been invited to the soirée. Then, as they rose from table, Adèle said that the architect from the floor above and a young gentleman were in the drawing-room.

"Ah, yes! that young man," whispered Madame Juzeur, as she took Monsieur Josserand's arm. "So you invited him? I saw him to-day in the hall-porter's room. He is a very nice-looking young fellow."

Madame Josserand took Trublot's arm, and then Saturnin, who alone remained at table, and whom all the fuss about the twenty francs had not roused from his torpor, with eyes rolling, upset his chair in a sudden paroxysm of fury, crying:

"I won't have it, by God! I won't!"

This was just what his mother feared. She motioned to Monsieur Josserand to go on with Madame Juzeur, while she disengaged her arm from that of Trublot, who, acting on the hint, disappeared. But, apparently, he made some mistake, for he slipped off towards the kitchen, in the wake of Adèle. Bachelard and Gueulin, ignoring the "crack-pot," as they called him, stood chuckling and nudging each other in a corner.

"He was quite queer all the evening; I feared something like this might occur," muttered Madame Josserand, in great alarm. "Berthe, quick, quick!"

But Berthe was shewing her booty to Hortense. Saturnin had caught up a knife, and kept repeating: "By God! I won't have it. I'll rip their bellies up, I will!"

"Berthe!" shrieked her mother, in despair.

And as the girl came rushing up, she had only just time to prevent her brother from going straight to the drawing-room, knife in hand.

She angrily shook him, while he, insanely logical, tried to explain.

"Leave it to me; they've got to have it. It will be all right, I tell you. I'm sick of their beastly goings on. They all want to sell us."

"Stuff and nonsense!" cried Berthe. "Why, what's the matter with you? What are you shouting about?"

Confused and trembling with vague fury, he stared at her, as he stammered out:

"They've been trying again to get you married. They never shall. Do you hear? I won't let anybody harm you!"

His sister could not help laughing. How had he got hold of the notion that they were going to marry her? He nodded his head, declaring that he knew it, that he was certain of it. And when his mother interposed to soothe him, he gripped the knife so fiercely that she shrank back, appalled. It alarmed her, too, to think that others had witnessed the scene; and she hurriedly told Berthe to take him away and lock him into his room, while Saturnin meanwhile kept gradually raising his voice as he became more and more excited.

"I won't have them marry you to anybody. I won't have them hurt you. If they do, I'll rip their bellies up!"

Then Berthe put her hands on his shoulders and looked him straight in the face.

"I'll tell you what," said she; "you just be quiet, or else I won't love you any more."

He staggered back; his face wore a gentler, despairing look, and his eyes filled with tears.

"You won't love me any more? You won't love me any more? Oh, don't say that! Oh, say that you'll love me still; say that you'll always love me, and never love anybody else!"

She caught him by the wrist and led him out, docile as a child.

In the drawing-room Madame Josserand, with exaggerated cordiality, addressed Campardon as her dear neighbour. Why had not Madame Carpardon given her the great pleasure of her company? When the achitect replied that his wife was always ailing, she grew more gushing still, and declared that she would have been delighted to welcome her in a dressing-gown and slippers. But her smile had lighted on Octave, who was talking to Monsieur Josserand; all her gushing speeches were meant to reach him over Campardon's shoulder. When her husband introduced the young man to her, she displayed such effusive cordiality that Octave was actually disconcerted.

Guests now arrived—stout mothers with lean daughters; fathers and uncles only just roused from their day of somnolence at the office, driving before them their flocks of marriageable daughters. Two lamps, covered with pink paper shades, threw a subdued light over the room, hiding the shabby yellow velvet of the furniture, the dingy piano, and the three dirty prints of Swiss scenery, which formed black patches against the bare, chilly panels of white and gold. And this niggardly brilliance served to cloak the guests' shortcomings, veiling their squalid faces and their still more squalid attempts at finery. Madame Josserand wore her flame-coloured gown of the previous evening; only, in order to put people off the scent, she had spent the whole day in sewing new sleeves on to the body and embellishing it with a *pèlerine* of lace to hide her shoulders, while her daughters sat beside her in their greasy dressing-jackets, stitching away with all their might and putting new trimmings on to their only gowns, which ever since last winter they had been patching up and altering in this way.

Each time the bell rang there was a sound of whispering in the ante-room. In the bleak drawing-room people talked in an undertone, where every now and then the forced giggling of some damsel struck a discordant note. Behind little Madame Juzeur, Bachelard and Gueulin kept nudging each other as they told improper stories. Madame Josserand anxiously watched them, fearful that her brother might misbehave himself. But Madame Juzeur was ready to listen to everything, her lips trembling as she smiled angelically at all the naughty anecdotes. Uncle Bachelard was reputed to be a sad dog. His nephew, on the other hand, was chaste. However tempting the opportunity, Gueulin refused women's favours on principle; not because he despised them, but because he had doubts as to the sequel of such bliss. "Sure to have some bother or other," he would say.

At last Berthe came back. She hurriedly approached her mother.

"Well, I have had a nice job," she whispered. "He wouldn't go to bed. I double-locked the door, but I'm afraid he'll break everything in his room."

Madame Josserand tugged her daughter's frock furiously. At that moment Octave, close by, turned his head.

"My daughter Berthe, Monsieur Mouret," she said, in her most gracious manner, as she introduced her to him. "Monsieur Octave Mouret, my love."

She gave her daughter a look. The latter well knew the significance of that look—an order, as it were, to commence action, a supplementary lesson to those of the previous night. She at once obeyed, with the complacent indifference of a girl who no longer cares to pick and choose a suitor. She went through her part quite prettily, with the easy grace of a Parisienne, already a trifle bored, but completely at home with all subjects, speaking enthusiastically of the South, where she had never been. Used as he was to the starched manner of the provincial virgin, Octave was charmed by this voluble little lady, who chattered away as if she were his comrade.

Just then Trublot, who, ever since dinner, had disappeared, suddenly slipped in through the dining-room door, when Berthe, observing him, asked, thoughtlessly, where he had been. He did not answer, which embarrassed her somewhat, and, to get out of her awkward position, she introduced the two young men to each other. Her mother, meanwhile, never took her eyes off her, assuming the attitude of a commander-in-chief, and directing the progress of the campaign from her arm-chair. When satisfied that the first engagement had been thoroughly effective, she made a sign to her daughter, and whispered :

"Wait until the Vabres come before you play. And mind you play loud enough."

Octave, finding himself alone with Trublot, began to question him.

"Charming, isn't she?"

"Yes, not half bad."

"The young lady in blue is her elder sister, isn't she? She is not so pretty."

"Rather not. Why, look how much thinner she is."

Trublot, who, short-sighted as he was, could really distinguish nothing, had the build of a strapping male, stubborn in his tastes. He had come back contented, chewing little black things, which Octave, to his surprise, perceived were coffee-berries.

"I say," he asked, bluntly, "in the South the women are plump, I reckon?"

Octave smiled, and immediately he and Trublot were on the best of terms. Their similarity of ideas brought them into touch. Lolling back on the sofa, they proceeded to exchange confidences. The one talked of his manageress at "The Ladies' Paradise"—Madame Hédouin, a damned fine woman, but too frigid. The other said that he was employed as correspondent from nine to five at Monsieur Desmarquay's, the money-changer's, where there was a most awfully fine slavey. Just then the door opened, and three people came in.

"Those are the Vabres," whispered Trublot, as he leant forward to his new friend. "Auguste, the tall one, with a face like a diseased sheep, is the landlord's eldest son. He is thirty-three, and suffers continually from splitting headaches, which affect his eye-sight, and at one time hindered him from learning Latin—a bad-tempered fellow, who's gone into trade. The other, Théophile, that sandy-haired horror with a weedy-looking beard, that little old man of twenty-eight, a victim to coughs and toothache, first tried all sorts of trades, and then he married the young woman walking in front, Madame Valérie."

"I've seen her before," interrupted Octave. "She is the daughter of a neighbouring haberdasher, isn't she? But how deceptive those little veils are. At first sight I thought her pretty, but she's only striking-looking, with her dried-up, leaden complexion."

"Yes, there's another woman that's not my style at all," replied Trublot, sententiously. 'She's got splendid eyes; some fellows are satisfied with that. But, my word, what a plate-rack!"

Madame Josserand had risen to shake hands with Valérie.

"What?" cried she, "Monsieur Vabre hasn't come with you? And Monsieur and Madame Duveyrier have not honoured us by their presence either, though they promised to come. It's really most unfortunate!"

The young wife made excuses for her father-in-law on the score of his age, though he really preferred to stay at home and work in the evening. As for her brother-in-law and sister-in-law, they had charged her to offer their excuses, as they had been invited to an official reception which they were obliged to attend. Madame Josserand bit her lips. She had never missed one of the Saturdays of those stuck-up first floor people, who thought it *infra dig.* to come up to the fourth floor for her Tuesdays. Certainly, her modest tea-party was not equal to their concerts with a grand orchestra. But, wait a bit! When her daughters were both married, and she had got two sons-in-law and their relatives to fill her drawing-room, she would have choral entertainments, too.

"Get ready to begin," she whispered in Berthe's ear.

There were about thirty guests, wedged in rather tightly, as they had not thrown open the little *salon,* which now served as a cloak-room for the ladies. The new-comers shook hands all round. Valérie sat next to Madame Juzeur, while Bachelard and Gueulin made remarks in a loud voice about Théophile Vabre, whom they thought it droll to describe as "no good." Monsieur Josserand, a cipher in his own drawing-room, blotted out as completely as if he were a guest for whom everyone was looking, although he stood right in front of them—Monsieur Josserand was listening, horrified, to a story told by one of his old friends. He knew Bonnaud, didn't he?—Bonnaud, the chief accountant of the *Chemin de Fer du Nord,* whose daughter got married last spring? Well, Bonnaud, it seems, had just found out that his son-in-law, to all appearance a most respectable person, had been formerly a clown, who, for ten years, had been kept by a female circus-rider!

"Hush, hush!" murmured several obliging voices. Berthe had opened the piano.

"Well, you know," explained Madame Josserand, "it's quite an unpretentious sort of piece—a simple little rêverie. You are fond of music, Monsieur Mouret, I dare say. Won't you come closer to the piano? My daughter plays this rather well—only an amateur, you know; but she plays with feeling—a great deal of feeling.

"You're in for it!" said Trublot, under his breath. "That's the sonata dodge."

Octave was obliged to rise, and he remained standing near the piano. To see the bland attentions which Madame Josserand lavished upon him, one would have thought that she was making Berthe play simply and solely for him.

" 'The Banks of the Oise,' " she went on. "It's really very pretty. Now, my love, begin; and don't be nervous. I'm sure Monsieur Octave will make allowances."

The girl attacked the piece without the least sign of nervousness; albeit her mother never took her eyes off her, with the air of a sergeant ready to punish with a slap the least technical blunder. What mortified her was that the instrument, cracked and wheezy after fifteen years of daily scale-playing, had not the sonorous quality of tone possessed by the Duveyriers' grand piano. Moreover, as she thought, her daughter never would play loud enough.

After the tenth bar Octave, with a rapt expression, and keeping time with his head to the more florid passages, no longer listened. He watched the audience, noting the polite efforts on the part of the men to pay attention, and the affected delight of the women. He surveyed this collection of human beings left to themselves, quit of their daily harassing cares, which had deepened the gloom on their tired faces. The mothers, it was plain, cherished fond dreams of marrying their daughters, as they stood there with mouths agape and ferocious teeth, unconsciously letting themselves go. It was by the weird madness that pervaded this drawing-room—a ravenous appetite for sons-in-law—that these middle-class women were devoured, as they listened to the piano's asthmatic utterances. The girls languidly dozed; their heads drooped, and they forgot to hold themselves upright. Octave, who despised novices, gave the greater attention to Valérie. Plain she certainly was, in that extraordinary yellow silk dress, trimmed with black satin; and, half-fascinated, his eyes always wandered uneasily back to her as, unnerved by the shrill music, her features wore a vague expression—a sickly, neurotic smile.

Then came a catastrophe. The bell rang outside, and a gentleman entered carelessly.

"Oh, doctor!" said Madame Josserand, in a vexed tone.

Doctor Juillerat bowed his excuses, and remained stationary. At this moment Berthe, in die-away fashion, dwelt lingeringly upon a certain tender phrase, which her listeners greeted with a buzz of approval. "Charming!" "Delightful!" Madame Juzeur assumed a languishing attitude, as though someone were tickling her. Hortense, who stood by her sister, was turning over the pages, insensible to the surging torrent of notes, her ear alert to catch the sound of the door-bell; and when the doctor came in, her gesture of disappointment was so marked that she tore one of the leaves. Then suddenly the piano trembled beneath Berthe's frail fingers, that beat upon it like hammers. The dream had come to end in a deafening crash of furious harmonies.

There was a moment's hesitation. The hearers roused themselves. Had it really finished? Then came a shower of compliments. "Quite too lovely!" "Talent of a very superior kind."

"Mademoiselle is really an artist of the first rank," said Octave, interrupted in his observations. "No one has ever given me such pleasure before."

Once more a confused sound of voices filled the room. Berthe coolly accepted all the praise bestowed upon her performance, and did not leave the piano, waiting for her mother to relieve her from this boredom. The latter was just telling Octave of the astonishing dash with which her daughter played "The Reapers," a brilliant gallop, when a dull, far-off sound of knocking created some commotion among the guests.

Every minute the noise grew louder, as if someone were endeavouring to break open a door. The guests were silent, and exchanged questioning glances.

"What can that be?" Valérie ventured to enquire. "There was a sound of knocking like that just now as the music ended."

Madame Josserand turned quite pale. She had recognised Saturnin's lusty blows. Wretched lunatic that he was. She seemed to see him rushing into the room among her guests. If he went on thumping like that, there was another marriage knocked on the head!

"It's the kitchen door that keeps banging," said she, with a forced smile. "Adèle never will shut it. Just go and see, Berthe."

Her daughter had also understood, and, rising, she disappeared. The knocking at once ceased, but she did not immediately return. Uncle Bachelard, who had scandalously disturbed the performance of "The Banks of the Oise" by making loud remarks, succeeded in disconcerting his sister by shouting out to Gueulin that he was bored to death, and was going to get himself some grog. They both returned to the dining-room, slamming the door after them.

"Dear old Narcisse—such an original!" said Madame Josserand to Valérie and Madame Juzeur, as she sat down between them. "He's so bothered about business! You know, he made nearly a hundred thousand francs this year!"

Free at last, Octave hastened to rejoin Trublot, lolling drowsily on the sofa. Near them a group surrounded Doctor Juillerat, the old physician of the neighbourhood, a man of mediocre ability, but who, by degrees, had got a thriving practice, having attended all the mothers in their confinements, and prescribed remedies for all their daughters' ills. He made a special study of diseases of women, so that in the evening he was besieged by husbands eager to obtain advice gratis in some corner of the room. Théophile was just telling him that Valérie had had another attack yesterday; she always struggled for breath, complaining of a lump in her throat. He himself was not very well, but his symptoms were not identical. Then he talked of nothing but himself, and of his bad luck. First, he had begun to study law, had dabbled in industry at an iron-foundry, tried administrative work in the offices of the Mont-de-Piété. Then he took up photography, and believed he had discovered a patent for automatic cabs; meanwhile he got a commission on the sale of piano-flutes, invented by one of his friends. Then he returned to the subject of his wife; it was her fault if they were never successful, her perpetual nervous seizures were enough to kill him.

"Do give her something, doctor," he pleaded, with a malevolent light in his eyes, as he coughed and moaned in all the mad exasperation of impotence.

Trublot scrutinised him, full of disdain, laughing inwardly as he looked at Octave. Doctor Juillerat, meanwhile, uttered vague and soothing words; doubtless some effiacious remedy could be administered to the dear lady. At the age of fourteen she used to have similar attacks at the shop in the Rue Neuve-Saint-Augustin; he had treated her for deafness, which had terminated in bleeding from the nose. And as Théophile recollected in despair her languid apathy as a girl, while now she was a source of torture to him—flighty, fantastic, changing her mood a score of times in the day—the doctor was content to nod his head. Marriage did not agree with every woman.

"No, by Jove, it doesn't!" murmured Trublot. "A father who brutalised himself for thirty years by hawking needles and cottons, and a mother whose face was always one mass of pimples, living in that stuffy hole of a shop—how do you suppose such people could produce decent daughters?"

Octave was surprised. He had begun to lose some of his respect for this drawing-room, which he had entered with all the awe of a provincial. He again felt curious when he saw Campardon consulting the doctor in his turn, whispering, however, like a serious person who did not wish anyone to know of his domestic disasters.

"By-the-bye," said Octave to Trublot, "as you seem to know everything, do tell me what is the matter with Madame Campardon. Whenever her ill-health is mentioned I notice that everyone assumes a rueful visage."

"Why, my dear fellow," replied the young man, "she has got——"

And he whispered in Octave's ear. At first his listener smiled, then he made a long face of deep astonishment.

"Is it possible?" said he.

Whereupon Trublot declared upon his word of honour that it was so. He knew another lady who had the same thing.

"Besides," added he, "after a confinement it sometimes happens that——"

And he began to whisper again. Octave, convinced, felt sad. For a moment he had imagined all sorts of things—a regular romance; the architect attracted elsewhere, and urging him to provide amusement for his wife! At any rate, he could feel sure that her honour was safe. The young men pressed closer against each other in the excitement of disclosing all these feminine secrets, forgetful that they might be overheard.

Just then Madame Juzeur was about to impart to Madame Josserand her impressions of Octave. She certainly thought him most agreeable, but she preferred Monsieur Auguste Vabre. This gentleman stood, mute and insignificant, in a corner of the room, with his usual evening headache.

"What surprises me, my dear madam, is that you have not thought of him for your daughter Berthe. A young man established in business and extremely steady. He wants a wife, too. I know that he is desirous of getting married."

Madame Josserand listened in surprise. She had really never thought of the haberdasher. Madame Juzeur, however, insisted, for, unfortunate herself, it was her passion to work for the happiness of other women, so that she took an interest in all the romantic affairs of the house. She declared that Auguste had never once taken his eyes off Berthe. In short, she brought her own experience of men to bear upon the subject; Monsieur Mouret would never let himself be caught, whereas a match with that nice Monsieur Vabre would be both easy and advantageous. But madame, adding up the last-named with a look, felt decidedly convinced that a son-in-law of that sort would never be of any good in filling her drawing-room.

"My daughter detests him, said she, "and never will I go against her feelings."

A gawky damsel had just played a fantasia upon the *Dame Blanche*. Uncle Bachelard having fallen asleep in the dining-room, Gueulin came back with his flute and gave imitations of the nightingale. Nobody listened, however; the story about Bonnaud was going the round. It had quite upset Monsieur Josserand; fathers held up their hands in horror, while mothers gasped for breath. What! Bonnaud's son-in-law was a clown! In whom, then, could they put their trust? Thus, in their avid lust for marriage, were the parents distraught as by a nightmare, dismay written large on all their faces, like those of so many convicts in evening dress. As a matter of fact, Bonnaud had been so delighted to get rid of his daughter that the flimsiest of references had sufficed him, despite his rigid prudence as a fussy accountant-in-chief.

"Mamma, tea is ready," said Berthe, as she and Adèle opened the folding doors.

Then, as people slowly passed into the dining-room, she went up to her mother and whispered:

"I've had about enough of it. He wants me to stop and tell him stories, or else he says he'll smash up everything."

On a grey cloth, too small for the table, one of those laboriously-served teas was spread, with a *brioche* bought at a neighbouring baker's and flanked by sandwiches and little cakes. At either end of the table were flowers in profusion; roses of great beauty and great price prevented one from noticing the stale biscuits and rancid butter. More notes of admiration and more heart-burnings; those Josserands were simply ruining themselves in their attempt to marry off their daughters. And the guests, throwing sidelong glances at the flowers, gorged themselves with weak tea and injudiciously battened upon the stale buns and badly-baked *brioche;* for they had dined scantily, and their one thought was to go to bed with their bellies full. For those who did not like tea, Adèle handed round red-currant syrup in glasses. This was pronounced excellent.

Meanwhile the uncle slumbered in a corner. They did not wake him; they even politely pretended not to see him. One lady spoke of the fatigues of business. Berthe was most attentive, handing round sandwiches, carrying cups of tea, asking the men if they would like any more sugar. But she could not attend to everybody, and Madame Josserand kept looking for Hortense, whom she suddenly descried in the centre of the empty drawing-room talking to a gentleman whose back alone was visible.

"Yes, yes," she blurted out, in a sudden fit of wrath, "he's come at last!"

The guests began to whisper. It was that Verdier, who had been living with a woman for fifteen years, while waiting to marry Hortense. Everybody knew the story, and girls exchanged significant glances; but for propriety's sake they forbore to speak of it, and merely bit their lips. When Octave had been enlightened, he watched the gentleman's back with interest. Trublot knew the woman, a good soul as ever was; a reformed prostitute, as well-conducted now, said he, as the best of wives, looking after her chap and keeping all his shirts in order. He was full of brotherly sympathy for her. Whilst thus watched from the dining-room, Hortense was scolding Verdier for being so late, rebuking him after the manner of a peevish boarding-school miss.

"Hullo! there's red-currant syrup," said Trublot, observing Adèle in front of him, tray in hand. Sniffing at it, he declined. But as Adèle turned round she was pushed by a stout lady's elbow against him, when he squeezed her waist hard. She smiled, and came back with the tray.

"No, thanks," said he. "Presently."

The ladies sat round the table, while the men stood, eating, in their rear. Enthusiastic exclamations were heard, which subsided as mouths became full. The gentlemen were asked for their opinion.

Madame Josserand exclaimed:

"True; I was forgetting. Come and look, Monsieur Mouret, as you are fond of art."

"Look out! that's the water-colour dodge," muttered Trublot, who was up to the ways of the house. It was better than a water-colour. As if by chance, there was a porcelain bowl on the table, upon the bottom of which, in a mount of newly-varnished bronze, was a copy of Greuze's "Girl with Broken Pitcher," painted on in washy tints varying from lilac to pale blue. At the chorus of praise Berthe smiled.

"Mademoiselle possesses every talent," said Octave, in his most bland accents. "How well the colours are blended. Exactly like, too, exactly."

"The drawing is, I'll be bound," said Madame Josserand, exultant. "There's not a hair too many or too few. Berthe copied it at home from an engraving. At the Louvre, you know, there are really such a number of nude subjects, and such queer people, too."

In delivering this last criticism she lowered her voice, anxious to assure the young man that, although her daughter was an artist, this did not carry her to the pitch of libertinism. However, Octave, she thought, seemed indifferent; she felt, somehow, that the bowl had not made its mark, and she watched him uneasily, while Valérie and Madame Juzeur, who had got to their fourth cup of tea, were uttering faint cries of admiration as they examined Berthe's masterpiece.

"You are looking at her again," said Trublot to Octave, whose eyes were riveted on Valérie.

"So I am," he replied, somewhat confused. "A funny thing, but just now she looks quite pretty. I say, do you think one might risk it?"

Trublot puffed out his cheeks.

"She's hot enough, but you never know. Strange you should fancy her. Anyway, it's better than marrying the little girl."

"What little girl?" cried Octave, forgetting himself. "Why, do you think I am going to let myself be landed? Not I. My good fellow, we don't go in for marrying at Marseilles."

Madame Josserand, close by, overheard that last phrase. It stabbed her like a knife. Another fruitless campaign, another wasted soirée. The blow was such that she had to lean against a chair as she ruefully surveyed the table, swept clean of all refreshment, on which there only now remained the burnt top of the *brioche*. She no longer counted her defeats; but this, in truth, should be the last. And she swore a hideous oath that never again would she feed folk who simply came there to stuff themselves. And, in her exasperation, she look round the room to see what man there was at whom she could hurl her daughter, when she spied Auguste leaning against the wall, resigned, having had no refreshment.

Just then Berthe, all smiles, was moving towards Octave with a cup of tea in her hand. She was carrying on the war in obedience to her mother's instructions. The latter seized her roughly by the arm, and whispered to her as if she were some refractory animal. Then she said out loud, in her most gracious manner:

"Take the cup to Monsieur Vabre, who has been waiting a whole hour."

Then came another whisper and another war-like look.

"Make yourself agreeable, or you'll have me to deal with!"

Berthe, disconcerted for a moment, at once recovered herself. This change of front occurred as often as three times in an evening. She took the cup of tea to Auguste, together with the smile that she had begun to wear for Octave. She made herself most agreeable, talked about Lyons silks, and gave herself the airs of an engaging young lady who would look charming behind the counter. Auguste's hands trembled somewhat, and his face was red, as that evening he had a worse headache than usual.

Out of politeness, some of the guests went and sat down again for a moment in the drawing-room. They had got their food, and now it was time to go. When they looked for Verdier he had already left, and the girls in their merriment could only take away with them the blurred impression of his back. Without waiting for Octave, Campardon went away with the doctor, whom he still kept on the staircase to ask him if there was really no hope. During tea one of the lamps had gone out, exhaling an odour of rancid oil;

the other lamp, with its burnt wick, gave such a lugubrious light that the Vabres rose of their own accord, despite the profuse attentions with which Madame Josserand overwhelmed them. Octave, preceding them, had reached the ante-room, where a surprise was in store for him. Trublot, who was looking for his hat, suddenly disappeared. He could only have made his exit by the passage leading to the kitchen.

"Why, what's become of him? Does he make use of the servants' staircase?" murmured the young man.

However, he thought no more about the matter. Valérie was there, looking for her China crepe fichu. The two brothers, Théophile and Auguste, without heeding her, were going downstairs. Having found the fichu, the young man presented it to her with the air of rapture with which he served pretty customers at "The Ladies' Paradise." She looked at him, and he felt certain that her eyes, as they met his, shot forth amorous flames.

"You are too kind, sir," said she, simply.

Madame Juzeur, who was the last to leave, wrapped them both with a smile at once tender and discreet. And when Octave, greatly excited, had got back to his cold bedroom, he glanced at himself in the glass, and determined, by Jove, to have a try for it!

Meanwhile, mute, and as if swept hither and thither by a whirlwind, Madame Josserand paced up and down the deserted rooms. She shut the piano with a bang, put out the last lamp, and then going into the dining-room, began to blow out the candles with such vehemence that they trembled in their sockets. The sight of the devastated table, with its disorderly array of plates and empty tea-cups, only enraged her more, and, as she walked round, she flung terrible glances at her daughter Hortense, who sat calmly crunching the burnt top of the *brioche*.

"You're working yourself up into a rage again, mamma," said the latter. "Something gone wrong again? I'm quite happy. He's going to buy her some chemises so as to get rid of her."

The mother shrugged her shoulders.

"Ah!" continued Hortense, "you'll say that that proves nothing. All right, only mind you steer your ship as well as I steer mine. Well, that's what I call a vile *brioche*. People who can eat such filth can't be accused of squeamishness."

Worn out by these parties of his wife's, Monsieur Josserand leant back in his chair, dreading another encounter, or that Madame Josserand might sweep him away in her tempestuous career; so he joined Bachelard and Gueulin, who were sitting at the table opposite Hortense. On waking, the uncle had found a flask of rum, and, while emptying this, he returned to the bitter subject of the twenty francs.

"It's not the money I mind," he kept repeating to his nephew, "but it's the way they did it. You know how I am with women; I'd give them the very shirt off my back, but I don't like them to ask like that. Directly they begin asking it annoys me, and I wouldn't give them a farthing."

And when his sister began reminding him of his promises:

"Hold your tongue, Eléonore!" he rapped out. "I know what I ought to do for the child! But when a woman asks like that, it's more than I can stand. I have never yet been able to keep one, have I, Gueulin? And besides, such little respect is shown to me! Why, Léon has not even condescended to wish me many happy returns of the day!"

With clenched fists, Madame Josserand resumed her march. It was true; Léon had promised to come, but, like the others, had thrown her over. There was a fellow who wouldn't give up an evening even to get one of his sisters married! She had just found a little cake, which had fallen behind one of the vases, and was locking it up in a drawer, when Berthe, who had gone out to set Saturnin at liberty, brought him back with her. She was trying to soothe him, as, with a haggard look of mistrust in his eyes, he feverishly hunted about in the corners of the room like a dog that has been long shut up.

"How silly he is!" said Berthe; "he thinks that I have just been married, and he is looking for the husband! My dear boy, you may well look! Didn't I tell you that it had all come to nothing. You know very well that it never *does* come to anything!"

Then Madame Josserand burst forth:

"Ah, but it shan't come to nothing this time, that I swear!—even though I have to hook him on to you myself! It's he that shall pay for all the others. Yes, yes, Monsieur Josserand, you may stare, as if you didn't understand. The wedding shall come off; and, if you don't approve of it, you can stay away. So, Berthe, you've only got to pick him up, do your hear?"

Saturnin apparently did not understand. He looked under the table. The girl pointed to him, but Madame Josserand made a sign as if to say that they would get rid of him. And Berthe murmured:

"So it's settled, is it, that it's to be Monsieur Vabre? It's all the same to me. But I do think you might have managed to save me just one sandwich!"

IV

NEXT day Octave began to grow interested in Valérie. He watched her ways, and found out the time when he was likely to meet her on the staircase, managing to go up frequently to his room, either when lunching at the Campardons' or when he got away under some pretext from "The Ladies' Paradise." He soon noticed that every day, about two o'clock, when taking her child to the Tuileries gardens, the young woman went down the Rue Gaillon. Accordingly, he used to stand at the door and wait for her, greeting her, like a comely shopman, with a gallant smile. Every time they met, Valérie politely bowed, but never stopped, though he noticed that her dark glance was full of the fire of passion, and he found encouragement in her unhealthy complexion and the supple undulation of her hips.

He had already made his plan—the bold one of a seducer used to the chivalrous conquest of shop-girl virtue. It was merely a question of luring Valérie into his room on the fourth floor; the staircase was always quiet and lonely, and up there nobody would ever catch them. He laughed inwardly as he thought of the architect's moral advice; for having a woman who lived in the house was not the same as bringing one into it.

There was one thing, however, which made him uneasy. The Pichons' kitchen was separated from their kitchen by the passage, and this constantly obliged them to leave their door open. At nine in the morning Pichon went off to his office, whence he did not return until five o'clock. Every other night of the week he went out after dinner, from eight to twelve, to do some book-keeping. Moreover, as soon as she heard Octave's step, the young woman, shy and reserved, would push the door to, and he only got a back view of her as she fled, with her light hair tied up into a scanty knot. By such discreet glimpses he had only caught hitherto a corner of the room, the furniture, sad-looking and clean; the linen of a dull whiteness, as seen through an invisible window; the corner of a cot, at the back of the inner room—in fact, all the monotonous solitude of a woman who busies herself from morn till night with the petty cares of a clerk's household. But not a sound was heard there; the child seemed as silent and apathetic as its mother. Sometimes one could just hear her humming some tune for hours together in a feeble voice. Octave, however, was none the less furious with the scornful jade, as he called her. Perhaps she was playing the spy. In any case, Valérie could never come up to his room if the Pichons' door was always being opened in this way.

He had just begun to think that matters were going right. One Sunday, in the husband's absence, he had managed to be on the first-floor landing just as Valérie, in her dressing-gown, was leaving her sister-in-law's to return to her own apartments. She was obliged to speak to him, and they had just exchanged a few polite remarks. Next time he hoped that she might ask him in. With a woman of her temperament the rest would follow as a matter of course.

During dinner that evening at the Campardon's, the talk turned upon Valérie, as Octave tried to draw them out. But as Angèle was listening, and looking slyly at Lisa, who gravely handed round the roast mutton, the parents at first were lavish of their praise. Besides, the achitect was for ever upholding the respectability of the house, with the conceited assurance of a tenant who appeared to derive therefrom a certificate of his own moral probity.

"Most respectable people, my dear boy! You met them at the Josserands. The husband is no fool—a man full of ideas. Some day he'll make some great discovery. As for his wife, she's got a style about her, as the artists say."

Then Madame Campardon, rather worse to-day and half recumbent, though her illness did not prevent her from eating great red slices of meat, languidly murmured, in her turn :

"Poor Monsieur Théophile! He's like me; he just drags along. And there's a good deal to be said for Valérie, for it's not very lively for her to be tied to a man who's always shaking with fever, and whose ailments make him peevish and unjust."

During dessert Octave, seated between husband and wife, got to know more than he had asked. They forgot Angèle's presence, talked with hints, with winks that, as it were, underlined the double meaning of their words; and if these failed them, they whispered to him, confidentially, by turns. In short, Théophile was an impotent idiot, who deserved to be what his wife had made him. As for Valérie, she was not worth much; she would have behaved just as badly even if her husband had been able to satisfy her, being so carried away by her natural impulses. Moreover, everybody knew that, two months after marriage, in despair at finding that she could never have a child by her husband, and fearing to lose her share of old Vabre's fortune if Théophile happened to die, she had her little Camille got for her by a brawny young butcher's assistant of the Rue Sainte-Anne.

Finally, Campardon whispered in Octave's ear :

"In short, you know, my dear fellow, an hysterical woman!"

And he put into the words all the gross indecency of the middle classes, together with the loose-lipped grin of the father of a family, whose imagination, suddenly let loose, battens upon pictures of lascivious orgies. Angèle looked down at her plate, fearing to catch Lisa's eye lest she should laugh. The talk then took another turn; they spoke about the Pichons, and words of praise for them were not withheld.

"Oh, those worthy folk!" repeated Madame Campardon. "Sometimes, when Marie takes her little Lilitte out for a walk, I let Angèle go with her. And I can assure you, Monsieur Mouret, I would not trust my daughter to everybody; I must be absolutely certain that their morals are unquestionable. You're very fond of Marie, aren't you, Angèle?"

"Yes, mamma," replied the litle girl.

Then came other details. It would be impossible to find a woman better brought up than she, or who had stricter principles. And how happy her husband was! Their little home was so neat, so pretty; each adored the other, and they never had the least cross word!

"Besides, if they misbehaved themselves, they would not be allowed to remain in the house," said the architect, gravely, forgetting his disclosures anent Valérie. "We only want decent folk here. 'Pon my honour! I would give notice the same day that my daughter ran the risk of meeting disreputable people on the stairs."

That very evening he had made secret arrangements to take cousin Gasparine to the Opéra-Comique. So he at once went to fetch his hat, saying something about a business engagement, which might detain him until very late. However, Rose must have known something about this, for Octave heard her whisper, in her resigned, motherly way, as Campardon stooped to kiss her with his usual effusive tenderness :

"I hope you'll enjoy yourself—and don't catch cold coming out."

Next morning Octave had an idea. It was to make Madame

Pichon's acquaintance by doing her some trifling neighbourly service; and in this way, if she ever caught Valérie, she would keep her eyes shut. That very day an opportunity presented itself. Madame used to take out her little Lilitte, aged eighteen months, in a wicker perambulator, a proceeding which roused the righteous wrath of Monsieur Gourd, who never would allow the vehicle to be taken up by the main staircase, so that Madame Pichon had to pull it up by the servants' stairway. Moreover, as the door of her apartment was too narrow, she had to take off the wheels every time, which was quite a long business. It so happened that on this particular day, as Octave was coming home, he found Marie with her gloves on, trying all she could to unscrew the wheels. When she felt him standing close behind her, waiting until the passage was clear, her hands trembled, and she quite lost her head.

"But why do you take all that trouble, madam?" asked he, at length. "It would be far simpler to put the perambulator at the end of the passage, behind my door."

She did not reply, but remained in a squatting position, excessive timidity preventing her from rising, and under the flaps of her bonnet he noticed that her neck and ears were suffused by a burning blush. Then he insisted :

"I assure you, madam, that it will not inconvenience me in the least."

Without further delay, he lifted the perambulator and carried it off in his easy, unaffected way. She had to follow him, but felt so confused, so amazed at this startling adventure in her hum-drum every-day existence, that she watched his action, unable to do more than stammer out a few disjointed phrases :

"Dear me, sir, it's giving you too much trouble. I am so confused—you'll be putting yourself to such inconvenience. My husband will be so pleased——"

And she went in, half-ashamed, this time tightly fastening the door after her. Octave thought she must be stupid. The perambulator was very much in his way, for it prevented him from opening his door, and he had to get through it sideways. But he seemed to have won his neighbour's good will, the more so because Monsieur Gourd, owing to Campardon's influence, had graciously consented to sanction this obstruction at the end of this out-of-the-way passage.

Every Sunday Marie's parents, Monsieur and Madame Vuillaume, used to come and spend the day with her. On the following

Sunday, as Octave was going out, he perceived the whole family just about to have their coffee, and was discreetly hurrying past, when the young wife hastily whispered something to her husband. The latter at once rose, saying:

"Pray excuse me, sir. I am always out, and have not yet had an opportunity of thanking you; but I am anxious to be able to tell you how pleased I was——"

Octave, protesting, was at last obliged to go in, and, though he had already had some, was obliged to accept a cup of coffee, and the place of honour between Monsieur and Madame Vuillaume. Facing him on the opposite side of the round table, Marie had one of her sudden blushing fits, which for no apparent reason sent all the blood from her heart to her face. He noticed how she never seemed at her ease, and agreed with Trublot that she was certainly not his ideal; she looked so puny, so washed-out, with her flat bosom and scanty hair, though her features were delicate, even pretty. When she had somewhat regained her composure, she began giggling, as she enthusiastically discussed the perambulator incident.

"Jules, if you could only have seen the way that monsieur whipped it up in his arms! It was quick work, I assure you."

Pichon reiterated his thanks. He was tall and thin, mournful of mien, already bowed beneath the dull routine of office life, and his lack-lustre eyes had a look of stupid resignation, like those of a broken-down cab-horse.

"Pray, don't say any more about it," Octave at last exclaimed. "It really is not worth mentioning. Your coffee, madam, is delicious; I have never tasted any to equal it."

She blushed again, so violently this time that even her hands grew rosy pink.

"Don't spoil her, sir," said Monsieur Vuillaume, gravely. "Her coffee's good enough, but there's better than that to be got. You see how conceited she's grown all of a sudden."

"Pride had a fall," observed Madame Vuillaume, sententiously. "We have always taught her to be modest."

They were both little, shrivelled, grey-faced old people—she squeezed into a black gown, and he into an undersized frock-coat, with a large red ribbon at his button-hole.

"Yes, sir," said he, "they decorated me at the age of sixty, the day I got my pension, after thirty-nine years' service as clerk at the Office of Public Instruction. Well, sir, that day I dined just as usual, without letting pride interfere with my ordinary habits. The cross was my due; of that I was well aware. I simply felt profoundly grateful."

His record was untarnished, and he wished everybody to know as much. After five-and-twenty years' service his salary had been raised to four thousand francs. His pension amounted to two thousand. But he had been obliged to re-enter the service as *expéditionnaire,* with a salary of fifteen hundred, as little Marie had been born to them late in life, when Madame Vuillaume had given up all prospects of either a girl or a boy. Now that the child had got a home of her own, they lived on the pension-money, economising all they could, in the Rue Durantin, at Montmartre, where it was less expensive.

"And I am seventy-six years old," said he, in conclusion. "So there, now, my son, think of that."

Pichon, tired and silent, surveyed him, all eyes for the decoration at his button-hole. Yes, he would be able to tell the same tale if fortune favoured him; he, the youngest son of a greengrocer's widow, who spent all her shop earnings in enabling him to take his degree as *bachelier,* because all her neighbours pronounced him to be such an intelligent lad, and who died insolvent a week after his triumph at the Sorbonne. After three years' bullying from an uncle, he had had the good luck to get a Government appointment, which ought to lead him on to great things. He had already married upon the strength of it.

"We do our duty, and the Government do theirs," he murmured; as he mechanically calculated that he would have another thirty-six years to wait before he could be decorated and obtain a pension of two thousand francs.

Then, turning to Octave, he said :

"It's children, you know, monsieur, that are such a drag on one."

"Of course they are," remarked Madame Vuillaume. "If we had had another, we should certainly never have been able to make ends meet. Don't you remember, Jules, what I made you promise me when I gave you our Marie; one child and no more, or else we shall fall out. It's only the working classes that beget children as a hen lays eggs, regardless of what it will cost them. It's true, they turn them loose into the street like so many flocks of sheep. I declare it makes one quite sick."

Octave looked at Marie, for he thought that so delicate a subject would have brought rosy blushes to her cheeks. But her face was pale, as, serenely ingenuous, she agreed with her mother's remarks. He was bored to death, and did not know how to escape. There, in their chilly little dining-room, these people would spend the whole afternoon, making a few mild remarks every now and then, as they talked of nothing but their affairs. Even dominoes were too disturbing for them.

Madame Vuillaume now began to expound her views. After a long silence, in which, as it were, they could provide themselves with a fresh supply of ideas, she began :

"You have no child, monsieur? Ah that'll come later. Oh, it's a great responsibilty, especially for a mother! When my little girl over there was born I was forty-nine, an age when one fortunately knows how to behave oneself. A boy, you know, can shift for himself, but a girl! However, I have the consolation of knowing I did my duty by her, that I did!"

Then, she briefly set forth her method of education. Propriety first of all. No playing about on the staircase, the child always at home and closely looked after, for brats were always up to mischief. Doors and windows tightly shut; no draughts which bring with them naughty things from the street. Out-of-doors, never let go of the child's hand, and accustom it always to cast its eyes downwards so as to avoid seeing anything improper. Religion, useful as a moral check, ought not to be overdone. As she grows up, governesses must be engaged for the girl, who should never be sent to a boarding-school, where innocent children are corrupted. Then one should be present at her lessons, to see that she be kept in ignorance of certain things; all newspapers to be hidden, of course, and the bookcase locked.

"A girl always knows too much," declared the old lady, in conclusion.

While her mother thus discoursed, Marie looked vaguely, dreamily, into space. In imagination, she again saw the claustral little lodging, those stuffy rooms in the Rue Durantin, where she was not even allowed to look out of window. Hers was a long, dreary childhood; all sorts of prohibitions that she could not understand; lines in their journal of modes and fashions which her mother had scratched out with ink—black bars that made her blush; pieces cut out of her lessons which proved embarrassing to her governesses themselves when she asked them questions. But, on the whole, a sweetness about her childhood, a soft tepid growth as in a greenhouse, a waking dream in which the words and deeds of each day assumed a distorted, foolish significance. And, even now, as with a far-off look in her eyes all these memories came back to her, the smile on her lips was the smile of a child, as ignorant after marriage as she had been before.

"You will, perhaps, hardly believe it," said Monsieur Vuillaume, 'but when turned eighteen, my daughter had not read a single novel. Had you, Marie?"

"No, papa."

Then he continued: "I had a very nicely bound edition of George Sand, and, despite her mother's fears, I resolved to allow her, some months before her marriage, to read 'André,' a harmless work, ennobling, and full of imagination. I am all for a liberal education, you know. Literature certainly has claims. Well, the book had a most extraordinary effect upon her. She used to cry at night in her sleep—a proof that there is nothing like having a pure, unsullied imagination, in order to understand genius."

"It is such a beautiful book," murmured Marie, as her eyes sparkled.

But, Pichon having expounded his theory, the theory of no novels before marriage and all sorts of novels after marriage, Madame Vuillaume gave a nod of dissent. She never read at all, and was quite happy. Whereupon Marie gently alluded to her loneliness.

"Dear me! I sometimes get hold of a book to read. But Jules, you know, chooses one for me from the lending library in the Passage Choiseul. It would be another thing if I could play the piano."

For some time Octave felt anxious to put in a word.

"Why, madam, don't you play the piano?"

The question was an embarrassing one. The parents made a long excuse about unfortunate circumstances, not wishing to admit that they had been afraid of the expense. However, Madame Vuillaume declared that Maria had sung ever since she was born, while as a little girl she knew all sorts of pretty songs by heart. She had only got to hear a tune once in order to remember it; and her mother instanced the song about Spain, which told of a captive who mourned for his lady-love, a song that the child sang with such expression that she drew tears from the hardest of hearts. Marie, however, looked disconsolate. Pointing to the adjoining room, where her little child lay asleep, she cried:

"Ah, I swear that Lilitte shall learn how to play the piano, although I have to make the utmost sacrifices!"

"First think of bringing her up as we brought you up," said Madame Vuillaume, severely. "Of course I am not condemning music; it develops the sentiments. But, above all things, watch over your daughter; keep her untouched by any evil breath; and see to it that she remains ignorant."

Then she began all over again, laying further stress upon religion, stating the requisite number of confessions in each month, and to what Masses one was absolutely obliged to go—all such dicta being delivered from the standpoint of propriety. Octave could bear it no longer, but mentioned an appointment which obliged him to leave. His ears buzzed from sheer boredom; it was plain that they would go on talking like this until the evening. So he escaped, leaving the Vuillaumes and the Pichons to go on with their tedious chit-chat as they sat over their coffee-cups and slowly emptied them, just as they did every Sunday. As he made his final bow, Marie, for no reason whatever, suddenly blushed violently. After this experience, Octave on Sundays would always hurry past the Pichons' door, especially if he heard the rasping voices of the Vuillaumes. Besides, he was wholly bent upon the conquest of Valérie. Despite the burning glances, of which he believed himself to be the object, she displayed an unaccountable reserve; this was her coquetry, so he thought. One day, too, he met her by chance in the Tuileries gardens, when she began to talk calmly about the storm of the previous night; and this sufficed to convince him that she had a deuced amount of nerve. And he was always up and down the staircase, watching his opportunity to pay her a visit, being determined to come straight to the point.

Every time that he now passed, Marie, blushing, smiled at him. They nodded to each other in neighbourly fashion. One morning, about lunch-time, as he was bringing her a letter that Monsieur Gourd had entrusted to him so as to avoid the long journey up to the fourth floor, he found her in great perplexity. She had just placed Lilitte on the round table in her chemise and was trying to dress her.

"What is the matter?" asked the young man.

"Oh, it's this child!" she replied. "I was so silly as to undress her because she was fretful. And I don't know what to do next."

He looked at her in astonishment. She kept turning the child's petticoat over and over, trying to find the hooks and eyes. Then she added :

"You see, her father always helps me to dress her of a morning, before he starts. I never have to see to it all by myself. It's such a bother, it worries me so!"

The little girl, tired of being in her chemise, and frightened at seeing Octave, struggled and turned over on the table.

"Take care," cried he; "she will fall."

A catastrophe seemed imminent. Marie looked as though she dared not touch the naked limbs of her child. She gazed at her in a sort of original surprise, amazed at having been able to produce such a thing. Besides the fear of harming the child, there was in her awkwardness a certain vague repugnance to its living flesh. However, helped by Octave, who soothed Lilitte, she was able to dress her again.

"How will you manage when you have a dozen?" he asked, laughingly.

"But we are never going to have any more!" she replied, in a frightened tone.

Then he chaffed her, telling her it was a mistake to be so sure; it was so easy to make a little baby!

"No, no," she obstinately repeated. "You heard what mamma said the other day. She told Jules that she would not allow it. You don't know what she is; there would be endless squabbles if another were to come."

Octave was amused at the calm way in which she discussed this question. Though he kept drawing her out, he could not succeed in embarrassing her. Moreover, she just did as her husband wished. She was fond of children, of course, and if he wanted any more, she would not say no. And under all this complacent submission to her mother's orders, one could note the indifference of a woman whose maternal instinct had not yet been roused. Lilitte had to be looked after in the same way that her home required attention—a mere duty that must be done. When she had washed up the crockery, and had taken the child for a walk, she continued to live her old life as a girl—a somnolent, empty existence, lulled by vague expectations of a joy that never came. When Octave observed that she must find it very dull to be always alone, she seemed surprised. Oh, no, she was never dull! the days slipped by somehow without her knowing, as she went to bed, how she had employed her time. Then on Sundays she sometimes went out with her husband, sometimes her parents came, or else she had a book to read. If reading had not given her a headache, she would have read from morning till night, now that she was allowed to read every sort of book.

"The annoying thing is," she continued, "that they have got nothing at the lending library in the Passage Choiseul. For instance, I wanted to read 'André' again, just because it made me cry so when I first read it. Well, that's the very volume that has been stolen; and my father won't lend me his copy because Lilitte might tear out the pictures."

"Well, my friend Campardon has got all George Sand's works," said Octave. "I'll ask him to lend me 'André' for you."

She blushed again, and her eyes sparkled. It was really too kind of him! And when he left her she stood there, in front of Lilitte, without any idea in her head, in the same position that she was wont to remain for whole afternoons together. She hated sewing, but used to do crochet; always the same little scrap of wool, which was left lying about the room.

The following day, which was Sunday, Octave brought her the book. Pichon had been obliged to go out, to leave a card on one of his superiors. Finding her in walking dress, as she had just come back from an errand close by, Octave, just for curiosity's sake, asked her if she had been to Mass, thinking that possibly she was very religious. She said no. Before her marriage her mother used to take her to church regularly. And for six months after her marriage she used to go from sheer force of habit, being always afraid of getting there too late. Then, she hardly knew why, after missing two or three times, she left off going altogether. Her husband could not bear priests, and her mother now never mentioned the subject. Octave's question, however, was a disturbing one, as if it had roused within her emotions long since buried beneath the indolent apathy of her actual existence.

"I must go to Saint-Roch one of these days," said she. "When you stop doing something you've been accustomed to, you always feel the lack of it."

And over the pallid features of this girl, begotten out of due season by elderly parents, there came an expression of sickly regret, of longing for some other existence, dreamed of long since in shadowland. She could hide nothing; everything revealed itself in her face, with her skin as tender, as transparent as that of some chlorotic patient. Then she impulsively caught hold of Octave's hand.

"Oh, I must thank you so much for bringing me this book!

Come in to-morrow, after lunch. I will give it back to you, and tell you what effect it had upon me. That will be amusing, won't it?"

There was something droll about the woman, thought Octave, as he came away. He had begun to feel interested in her, and he thought of speaking to Pichon, so as to get him to wake her up a bit, for there was no doubt that she only wanted rousing. It so happened that he met Pichon the very next day as he was going out, and he walked some part of the way with him, though he himself risked being a quarter of an hour late at "The Ladies' Paradise." Pichon, however, appeared to be even less wide-awake than his wife, full of incipient manias, and entirely overcome by a dread of dirtying his boots, as it was rainy weather. He walked along on tip-toe, talking incessantly about his sub-director. As Octave's motive in this matter was a purely brotherly one, he left him at last in the Rue-Saint-Honoré, after advising him to take Marie as often as possible to the theatre.

"Whatever for?" asked Pichon, in amazement.

"Because it does women good. It makes them nicer."

"Do you really think so?"

He promised to think about it, and crossed the street, looking about in terror lest the cabs should splash him, this being his one and only torment in life.

At lunch-time Octave knocked at the Pichon's door to fetch the book. Marie, with her elbows on the table, was reading, her hands thrust through her dishevelled hair. She had just been eating an egg, cooked in a tin pan, which now lay on the untidy table devoid of a cloth. Lilitte, neglected, was asleep on the floor, her nose touching the fragments of a plate which, doubtless, she had smashed.

"Well?" said Octave, enquiringly.

Maria did not immediately reply. She was still in her dressing-gown, which, being buttonless, displayed her neck and breasts in all the disorder of a woman who has just got out of bed.

"I've only read about a hundred pages," she said, at last. "My parents were here yesterday."

Then she talked in a dreary, mournful way. When younger she had longed to live in the depths of the forest, and was for ever dreaming that she would meet a huntsman there sounding his horn. Approaching, he knelt down before her. All this happened in a coppice far, far away, where roses bloomed as in a park. Then, all at once, they were married, and lived on there, wandering about together eternally. She, in her perfect happiness, desired nothing more; while he, tender, submissive as a slave, remained ever at her feet.

"I had a chat with your husband this morning," said Octave. "You don't go out enough, and I have persuaded him to take you to the theatre."

But she shook her head, pale and trembling. There was a silence. The narrow, chilly dining-room once more appeared to her, and the dull, decorous figure of Jules suddenly blotted out the huntsman of her romance, the distant sound of whose horn still rang in her ears. At times she would listen; perhaps he was coming. Her husband had never taken her feet in his hands and kissed them, nor had he ever knelt down to tell her that he adored her. Nevertheless, she was very fond of him, but it amazed her that love did not possess more sweetness.

"The parts that touch me in novels," she said, coming back to the book, "are the parts where lovers tell each other of their love."

Octave at last sat down. He wanted to treat the matter as a joke, caring little for such sentimental stuff.

"I hate a lot of speechifying," he said. "If two people adore each other, the best thing is for them to prove it there and then."

But apparently she did not understand, as she looked at him with lack-lustre eyes. Stretching out his hand, he just touched hers, and leant close to her to look at a passage in the book, so closely that his breath warmed her bare shoulder. But she remained impassive, cold as a corpse. Then he got up to go, full of a contempt touched with pity. As he was leaving, she said :

"I read very slowly; I shall not have finished it until to-morrow. That's when it will be amusing; so do come in in the evening."

It is true Octave had no designs upon the woman; and yet, somehow, he was angry with her. He had felt a curious sort of attachment for this young couple, who exasperated him, just because they were content to lead such a stupid life. And he half resolved to do them a service, in spite of themselves. He would take them out to dinner, make them drunk, and then amuse himself by pushing them into each other's arms. When a good-natured fit like this came over him, he, who was loth to lend anyone ten francs, delighted to squander money in bringing lovers together and in giving them joy.

However, this coldness on the part of little Madame Pichon reminded Octave of Valérie the ardent. She surely would not want her neck to be breathed upon twice. He had made advance in her favour. One day, as she was going upstairs in front of him he had ventured to compliment her upon her leg without her showing any signs of displeasure.

At length the long-watched-for opportunity came. It was the evening that Maria had made him promise to come and talk about the novel, as they would be alone, for her husband was not coming home until very late. But the young fellow would have preferred to go out; the bare thought of this literary treat appalled him. However, about ten o'clock he thought he would try it on, when, on the first-floor landing, he met Valérie's maid, who, with a scared look, said :

"Madame is in hysterics, master is out, and everyone opposite has gone to the theatre. Do, please, come in, as I am all alone, and I don't know what to do."

Valérie was in her bedroom, stretched out in an armchair, her limbs rigid. The maid had unlaced her stays where her breasts protruded. The attack was over almost directly. She opened her eyes, seemed surprised to see Octave there, and behaved just as if he were the doctor.

"I must ask you to excuse me, sir," she murmured, in a choking voice. "This girl only came yesterday, and she lost her head."

Her perfect composure in taking off her stays and in buttoning up her dress, disconcerted the young man. He remained standing, resolved not to go like this, yet not daring to sit down. She had sent away her maid, the sight of whom seemed to irritate her, and she went to the window to breathe the cool night air, which she inhaled in long, nervous gasps, with her mouth wide open. After a pause, they began to talk. She first had these attacks when she was fourteen, and Doctor Juillerat was tired of prescribing for her; sometimes she had them in her arms, and sometimes in her loins. However, she was getting used to them; as well suffer from them as from anything else, for nobody had perfect health, you know. And as she talked thus, her limbs placid, almost lifeless, the sight of her roused his sensual appetites, and he thought her tempting, in all her disorder, with her leaden complexion and her features drawn, as if by the exhaustion of a long night of love. Behind the dark tresses of her hair, that fell all about her shoulders, he thought he beheld the puny, beardless face of her husband. Then, with outstretched arms, he roughly caught her round the waist, as he would have clipped some harlot.

"Well, what is it?" she asked, in surprise.

Now, in her turn, she looked at him, her eyes so cold, her body so impassive, that he felt frozen and awkwardly his hands dropped. The absurdity of his gesture did not escape him. Then, stifling a last nervous yawn, she slowly murmured :

"Ah, my dear sir, if you only knew !"

And she shrugged her shoulders, showing no sign of anger, but merely of overwhelming contempt and weariness of the male. Octave thought she was about to have him turned out when he saw her go towards the bell-rope, trailing her petticoats as she went. But she only wanted some tea, and this she ordered to be very weak and very hot.

Utterly nonplussed, he muttered some excuse and made for the door, while she lay back in her armchair, like some chilly woman in absolute need of sleep.

As he went upstairs, Octave stopped on each landing. So she did not care for that, then? He had just seen how indifferent she was, without desire and without resentment, as disobliging as his employer, Madame Hédouin. Why, then, did Campardon say that she was hysterical? How absurd to hoax him with such a nonsensical tale! But for the architect's lie he would never have risked such an adventure. The result of it quite bewildered him, and his ideas as to hysteria became confused as he thought of the various tales about Valérie that were afloat. Trublot's remark came back to his mind : one never knew what to expect from this sort of crazy women with eyes like burning coals.

On reaching his own floor, Octave, vexed with womankind in general, walked as noiselessly as possible. But the Pichons' door opened, and he was obliged to resign himself to his fate. Marie stood waiting for him in the little, ill-lighted room. She had drawn the cot close to the table, and Lilitte lay asleep in the yellow circle of light made by the lamp. The same plates which had done duty at lunch-time must have been used for dinner, for the closed book lay close to a dirty plate filled with the remains of some radishes.

"Have you finished it?" asked Octave, surprised at her silence.

She looked like one intoxicated, her cheeks puffy, as if just awaking from some heavy sleep.

"Yes, yes!" she exclaimed with difficulty. "Oh, I have spent the whole day poring over it! When one is absorbed like that, one hardly knows where one is. Oh, my neck *does* ache!"

So exhausted was she that she could speak no more about the novel; the emotions, the confused dreams that it had aroused in her mind, almost overwhelmed her. Still ringing in her ears she heard the faint clarion notes of her ideal huntsman, wafted to her across the dim blue landscape of her dreams. Then she suddenly said that she had been that morning to the nine o'clock Mass at Saint-Roch. She had wept much; in religion lay the one substitute for all other things.

"Oh, I am better now!" she said, as, sighing deeply, she stood still in front of Octave.

There was a pause. She smiled at him with her light-blue eyes. Never had she seemed to him so utterly useless, with her scanty hair and muddy complexion. Then, as she continued to gaze at him, her face grew very pale, and she tottered forward, so that he had to hold out his hands to save her from falling.

"My God! my God!" she sobbed out.

He looked at her in embarrassment.

"You ought to take a little *tilleul.* This comes of reading too much."

"Yes, it upset me when, on closing the book, I found myself alone. How good you are, Monsieur Mouret! Without you, I should have come to some harm."

Meanwhile, he looked about for a chair on which to place her.

"Would you like me to light a fire?"

"No, thank you; it would make your hands dirty; I have noticed that you always wear gloves."

The idea brought back that choking sensation at her throat, and, as she suddenly sank down, half swooning, she clumsily launched a kiss into the air, vaguely, as if in her dream. It just touched Octave's ear.

Such a kiss amazed him. The young woman's lips were cold as ice. Then, as she fell forward upon his breast, yielding up her whole body, he felt a sudden desire burn within him, and he was for carrying her into the room beyond. But this abrupt advance roused Marie from her swoon; her womanly instincts revolted. Struggling, she called upon her mother, forgetting her husband, who would soon come home, and her daughter, asleep at her side.

"No, no, not that! no, it is wrong."

But he kept saying, in his excitement:

"Nobody will ever know; I shall never tell."

"No, no, Monsieur Octave! You will spoil all the happiness that is mine in knowing you. I am sure it won't do us any good, and I dreamed of—oh, such things!"

Then, without another word, he felt that he must have his revenge upon womankind and as she would not go into the bedroom with him, he brutally thrust her backwards across the table. She gave in, and he enjoyed her there, midway between the dirty plate and the novel, which, when the table shook, fell on to the floor. The door had not even been shut; the solemn silence of the staircase pervaded all. Lilitte lay sleeping peacefully in her cot.

When Marie and Octave got up, she with her rumpled petticoats, neither had a word to say. Mechanically she went and looked at her daughter, took up the plate, and then laid it down again. He, too, was dumb, feeling equally ill at ease, for this had happened so unexpectedly. He recollected, too, how he had formed the brotherly plan of making husband and wife fall round each other's necks. Impelled to break this insufferable silence, he at length muttered :

"Why, you did'nt shut the door !"

She looked out on to the landing, and stammered :

"No more I did. It was open."

She seemed to walk with difficulty, and on her face there was a look of disgust. The young man began to reflect that there was nothing particularly amusing in an adventure of this sort with a helpless, lonely woman. She had not even had any pleasure from it.

"Oh, look ! the book has tumbled down !" she continued, as she picked the volume up. One of the corners of the binding was crushed and bent. This brought them together again; it was a relief. Speech came back to them. Marie appeared much distressed.

"It wasn't my fault. You see, I had put a paper cover on it, for fear it should get soiled. We must have knocked it off the table by mistake."

"It was there, then?" asked Octave. "I never noticed it. It doesn't matter a bit to me; but Campardon thinks such a lot of his books."

Each kept handing the book to the other, and trying to bend the corner straight. Their fingers touched, yet neither felt a thrill. As they thought of the consequences, they were both dismayed at the accident which had befallen the beautiful volume of Georges Sand.

"It was bound to end badly," said Marie, with tears in her eyes.

Octave felt obliged to console her. He would invent some story or other. Campardon wouldn't eat him. And, as they were about to separate, the feeling of uneasiness returned. One kind word, at least, they would like to have said to each other, but somehow it stuck in their throats. Fortunately, just then a step was heard; it was the husband coming upstairs. Silently Octave put his arms about her again, and kissed her in his turn upon the mouth. And again she complacently submitted, her lips icy cold as before. When he had noiselessly got back to his room, he remarked to himself, as he took off his coat, that apparently she didn't like that either. Then what on earth was it that she wanted? And why did she go tumbling into fellows' arms? Women were certainly queer folk.

Next day, after lunch at the Campardons', as Octave was again explaining how by his clumsiness he had damaged the book, Marie came in. She was going to take Lilitte to the Tuileries gardens, and had called to ask if they would let Angèle go with her. She smiled at Octave with perfect self-possession, and glanced innocently at the book lying on a chair.

"Why, of course," said Madame Campardon, "I shall be delighted. Angèle, go and put on your hat. With you she's quite safe."

Looking like modesty personified in her simple dark stuff dress, Marie spoke about her husband, who had come home late last night and had caught cold. She also mentioned the price of meat; soon people would not be able to afford any at all. Then, after she had left, taking Angèle with her, they all leant out of the window to see them start. There was Marie leisurely pushing Lilitte's perambulator along with her gloved hands, while Angèle, who knew that she was being watched, walked beside her, with downcast eyes.

"Doesn't she look nice!" exclaimed Madame Campardon. "So ladylike, so respectable!"

Then, slapping Octave on the back, her husband said:

"In a family, education is everything, my dear boy—everything!"

V

At the Duveyriers' that evening there was a reception and a concert. Octave had been invited for the first time, and about ten o'clock he was just finishing dressing. He was in a serious, half-irritable mood. How was it that his affair with Valérie had not come off—a woman so well connected as she was? And Berthe Josserand, ought he not to have reflected before refusing her? Just as he was tying his white tie, the thought of Marie Pichon became positively unbearable to him. Five months in Paris, and only a paltry adventure like that! He felt ashamed of himself, being well aware of the hollowness and the vanity of such a connection. And as he drew on his gloves, he vowed that he would no longer waste his time in such a way. Now that at last he had got into society, he resolved to act, for opportunities were certainly not lacking.

Marie was looking out for him at the end of the passage. As Pichon was not there, he had to go in for a moment.

"How smart you are!" she whispered.

They had never been invited to the Duveyriers'; accordingly she felt for these first-floor people excessive awe. But she was jealous of no one; for this she had neither the strength nor the will.

"I shall wait for you," she said, holding up her forehead. "Don't stay too late; and you must tell me how you enjoyed yourself."

Octave was constrained to kiss her hair. Though a relationship had been established between them which depended upon his inclination, it was not really an intimate one. At last he went downstairs, and she, leaning over the banisters, followed him with her eyes.

At the same moment quite a drama was being enacted at the Josserands'. According to the mother, this evening party at the Duveyriers' was to decide the match between her daughter Berthe and Auguste Vabre. Despite sundry vigorous onslaughts during the past fortnight, the latter still hesitated, evidently exercised by doubts as to the dowry. With a view to striking a decisive blow,

Madame Josserand had written to her brother, announcing the projected marriage, and reminding him of his promises, hoping that his reply might furnish her with something which she could use to advantage. And, at nine o'clock, as the whole family stood round the dining-room stove, in full dress and ready to go downstairs, Monsieur Gourd brought up a letter from uncle Bachelard, which had been left lying under Madame Gourd's snuff-box ever since the last delivery.

"Ah, at last!" cried Madame Josserand, as she tore open the envelope.

The girls and their father anxiously watched her as she read. Adèle, who had been obliged to dress the ladies, was moving about in her clumsy fashion as she cleared away the dinner-service. Madame Josserand turned very pale.

"Not a word!" she stuttered, "not a single clear sentence! He says that he will see later on, at the time of the marriage. And he sends his best love to us all! The wretched old humbug!"

Monsieur Josserand, in evening clothes, sank backwards into a chair. Hortense and Berthe, whose legs ached, sat down as well; the one in blue, the other in pink; those eternal frocks of theirs that they had furbished up yet once again.

"Bachelard is an impostor; I have always said so," murmured the father. "He'll never part with a sou."

Standing there in her flaming red gown, Madame Josserand read the letter over again. Then she burst forth:

"Oh, you men! Take him, for instance. One would think he was an idiot, to judge by the life he leads. But, no, not a bit of it! He may look like a fool, but he's wide-awake enough directly you mention money. Oh, you men!"

Then she turned towards her daughters, to whom this lesson was addressed.

"Look here, it's got to this, that I positively wonder why you girls are so mad to get married! Ah, if you'd been worried to death by it, as I have! A fellow who doesn't love you for yourself, nor brings you a fortune without haggling over it! A millionaire uncle, who, after living upon you for twenty years, declines even to give his neice a dowry! A husband who is incompetent—do you hear me, sir, incompetent!"

Monsieur Josserand bowed.

Adèle, not even listening, had just cleared away the things.

Madame Josserand swerved round furiously at her.

"What are you listening here for? Go back to the kitchen at once!"

Then came her peroration.

"In short, everything for these vile men, and nothing for us—not even a crust if we're starving! Depend upon it, the only thing they're fit for is to be taken in! So just mark my words!"

Hortense and Berthe nodded as though profoundly impressed by the truth of such counsel. Their mother had long since convinced them of the absolute inferiority of man, a creature whose sole mission in life was to marry and to pay. There was a long silence in that fusty dining-room that smelt of the stale food which Adèle had omitted to remove. Sitting about in their finery the Josserands forgot the Duveyriers' concert as they meditated upon life's perpetual deceptions. From the adjoining room came the sound of Saturnin, whom they had sent to bed early, snoring.

At last, Berthe spoke.

"So there's an end of that! Had we better go and take our things off?"

In an instant Madame Josserand's energy came back. What! take their things off! And why, pray? Was their family not a respectable one, or an alliance with them not as good as with other people? The marriage should come off all the same; she would die rather. And she hastily gave to each their parts. The girls were told to make themselves particularly agreeable to Auguste, and not to let go of him until he had taken the plunge. The father was entrusted with the task of conquering the sympathies of old Vabre and Duveyrier, by always agreeing with everything they said, if this proceeding were not too great a strain upon his intellect. As for herself, she would tackle the women, and knew well how to win them all over to her side of the game. Then, collecting her thoughts, and glancing round the dining-room once more, as if to make sure that no weapon had been overlooked, she assumed the terrible mien of a warrior leading forth his daughters to be massacred, as in a loud voice she cried:

"Let us go down!"

And down they went. In the solemn atmosphere of the staircase, Monsieur Josserand felt thoroughly uneasy. He foresaw many things, all too unpleasant for so straitlaced, well-meaning a man as himself.

The Duveyriers' rooms were already crowded as they entered. The huge grand piano filled one side of the panelled drawing-room;

the ladies were seated before it in rows, as if at a theatre, a dense black background being formed by the men in evening dress, which extended to the dining-room and parlour beyond. The chandelier and six bracket-lamps lighted up the white and gold apartment to a pitch of brilliancy that was positively dazzling, exhibiting in all their crudeness of tone the red silk hangings and furniture. The heat was great; and, as they regularly rose and fell, fans dispersed the pungent aroma of corsets and of naked busts.

Just at that moment Madame Duveyrier was about to sit down at the piano. With a gesture, Madame Josserand smilingly besought her hostess not to trouble herself. Leaving her daughters among the men, she took a chair between Valérie and Madame Juzeur. Monsieur Josserand found his way to the parlour, where Monsieur Vabre, the landlord, was asleep in his customary corner of the sofa. Here, too, in a group, were Campardon, Théophile and Auguste Vabre, Doctor Juillerat, and the Abbé Mauduit; while Trublot and Octave had just fled together from the music to the far corner of the dining-room. Near them, behind the sea of black coats, stood Duveyrier, tall and thin, watching his wife at the piano, and waiting for silence, At his button-hole, in a neat little rosette, he wore the ribbon of the Légion d'Honneur.

"Hush! hush! Be quiet!" murmured many sympathetic voices.

Then Clotilde Duveyrier attacked one of Chopin's most difficult nocturnes. Tall and fine-looking, with splendid auburn hair, she had a long face, pale and cold as snow. In her grey eyes alone music had lighted a flame—an exaggerated passion on which she lived without any other need, either spiritual or physical. Duveyrier continued looking at her; then, after the first few bars, his lips twitched nervously, and he withdrew to the far end of the dining-room. On his clean-shaven face, with its pointed chin and crooked eyes, large red patches showed the unhealthy state of his blood—a seething mass of scrofula, that lay just beneath the skin.

Trublot, scrutinising him, quietly remarked:

"He does not like music."

"No more do I," replied Octave.

"Ah! but for you it's not so disagreeable as for him. A man, my boy, who was always in luck. Not a bit cleverer than anyone else, but who was helped on by everybody. Comes of an old middle-class family; his father, an ex-chief-justice. Called to the bar directly he had passed his exams; appointed assistant judge at Rheims; is transferred thence to Paris, to the High Court of Appeal; gets decorated, and made counsellor before he is forty-five. Pretty sharp work, isn't it. But he's not fond of music; the piano has proved the bane of his life. Well, one can't have everything!"

Meanwhile, Clotilde was rattling away in the coolest manner possible. She managed her piano just as a circus-rider would her horse. Octave was only interested in such terrific manual dexerity.

"Only look at her fingers," said he; "it's appalling! After a quarter of an hour of that sort of thing, I should think she must feel it."

Then they both began talking about women, without paying further heed to her performance. On seeing Valérie, Octave felt rather embarrassed. How should he behave? Speak to her, or pretend not to see her? Trublot put on an air of fine disdain; not a woman among the lot that took his fancy; and, in reply to his companion's protest that there was surely somebody to suit his taste, he sagely remarked:

"Well, pick and choose, and then you'll soon see when they get up. Eh? Not that one at the back there, with feathers; nor yet the blonde person in mauve; nor that elderly female, although she, at least, is plump. I tell you, it is absurd to look for anything of that sort in society. Lots of airs and graces, but no fun!"

Octave smiled. He had his position to make in the world; he could not afford merely to follow his taste, like Trublot, whose father was so rich. Those long rows of women set him thinking, and he asked himself which of them all he would have chosen for his fortune or his pleasure if it had been allowed him to take one of them away. Suddenly, as he was appraising them all, he exclaimed, in surprise:

"Hullo! there's my employer's wife! Does she come here?"

"Yes; didn't you know that?" rejoined Trublot. "In spite of the difference in their ages, Madame Hédouin and Madame Duveyrier are old school friends, inseparables, who went by the name of the Polar Bears, as they were always twenty degrees below zero. Another pair of figure-heads for you! I pity Duveyrier, if he's no other hot-water bottle than that to warm his feet in winter!"

Octave, however, had grown serious. He now, for the first time, saw Madame Hédouin in an evening gown, cut low, showing her neck and arms, her dark hair being plaited across her forehead, and in this heated glare she seemed the realisation of his desires. A superb woman—healthy, handsome, who could but prove a benefit to a man. A thousand schemes absorbed him, when a loud noise of clapping roused him from his dream.

"What a blessing! It's over!" said Trublot.

Everyone was congratulating Clotilde. Rushing forward, Madame Josserand seized her by both hands, as the men went on talking, and the women plied their fans with greater vigour. Duveyrier then ventured to retreat to the parlour, whither Trublot and Octave followed him. Hemmed in by petticoats, the former whispered:

"Look there, on your right! The hooking process has begun."

It was Madame Josserand inciting Berthe to the conquest of young Vabre, who imprudently had gone up to them to pay his respects. That evening his headache was better, and he only felt a slight touch of neuralgia in the left eye; but he dreaded the end of the party, as there was going to be singing—the very worst thing for him.

"Berthe, tell Monsieur Auguste about the remedy which you copied for him out of that book—a sovereign cure for headache!"

And, having started them, Madame Josserand left them standing near the window.

"By Jove! they've got to chemistry," whispered Trublot.

In the parlour, Monsieur Josserand, anxious to please his wife, sat in a state of great embarrassment before Monsieur Vabre, for the old fellow was asleep, and, from motives of civility, he did not like to wake him. But when the music stopped, Monsieur Vabre opened his eyes. He was a little, stout man, quite bald, with two tufts of white hair on his ears, a red face, thick flabby lips, and goggle eyes. After a polite enquiry as to his health, Monsieur Josserand started the conversation. The ex-notary, whose four or five ideas were always expressed in the same order, began by mentioning Versailles, where, for forty years, he had had a practice. Then he spoke of his sons, as he once more lamented their incapacity to carry on the business, so that he had decided to sell it and live in Paris. Then came the whole history of his house, the building of which had been the romance of his life.

"I sank three hundred thousand francs in it, sir. A magnificent speculation, so my architect said. But to-day I find it hard work to get my money back, especially as all my children have come to live here gratis, with not the slightest intention of paying me. In fact, I should never get a quarter's rent if I did not apply for it myself on the fifteenth. However, my work consoles me, I am glad to say."

"Are you always hard at work?" asked Monsieur Josserand.

"Always, sir, always!" replied the old man, with desperate energy. "Work, to me, is life."

Then he proceeded to explain his colossal work. For ten years past, every year he had gone through the official catalogue of the Salon, writing the name of each painter and the pictures exhibited, on a slip. He alluded to this wearily, distressfully: a year was not long enough for a work so arduous; sometimes it proved too much for him. For instance, when a female artist got married and exhibited under her husband's name, how could he possibly know this?

"My work will never reach completion; that is what is killing me," he murmured.

"I suppose you take a great interest in art, do you not?" said Monsieur Josserand, with a view to flattering him.

The old man stared at him in great surprise.

"Oh, no, I don't! there's no need for me to see the pictures, it's merely a matter of statistics. Well, well! I had better get to bed, and then my head will be clearer in the morning. Good night, sir."

He leant upon a stick, which he used even indoors, and hobbled off, evidently suffering from partial paralysis of the spine. Monsieur Josserand was perplexed; it was not all quite clear to him. And he was afraid that he had not spoken of the catalogue-slips with sufficient enthusiasm.

Just then there was a faint murmur in the drawing-room, which brought Trublot and Octave back to the door. They saw a lady of about fifty coming in. She was powerfully built, still handsome, and was accompanied by a serious-looking, carefully-dressed young man.

"Oh, they go about together now, do they?" murmured Trublot. "That's right! it's no good being particular!"

The newcomers were Madame Dambreville and Léon Josserand. She had agreed to get him a wife, but meanwhile had reserved him for her own personal use, and now, as their romance was at its full, they advertised their *liaison* in every middle-class drawing-room. There was much whispering among mothers with marriageable daughters. Madame Duveyrier, however, made haste to welcome Madame Dambreville, who was useful in finding her young men to sing in her choruses. Then Madame Josserand, in turn, overwhelmed her with polite speeches, thinking that some day she might make use of her son's friend. Léon drily exchanged a word or two with his mother, who began to believe that he might really do something for himself, after all.

"Berthe doesn't see you," she said to Madame Dambreville. "I am sure you will excuse her, but she is just telling Monsieur Auguste about a cure for his headache."

"Of course. Why, they are quite happy where they are; don't let us disturb them," quoth the lady, with a meaning glance. She had understood.

With maternal solicitude, they both watched Berthe. She had contrived to push Auguste into the window-recess, and had hemmed him in there with her pretty gestures. He was growing quite vivacious, at the risk of an awful headache.

Meanwhile, in the parlour, a group of grave men were discussing politics. The day before, there had been a stormy sitting in the Chamber, when the Roman question had formed the subject of debate. Doctor Juillerat, an atheist and a revolutionary, was for giving Rome up to the King of Italy, while the Abbé Mauduit, one of the heads of the Ultramontane party, prophesied the direst catastrophes if France did not shed the last drop of her blood in protecting the temporal power of the Pope.

"Perhaps some *modus vivendi* may be found acceptable to both parties," said Léon Josserand, who had joined the group.

He was acting then as secretary to a famous barrister, one of the deputies of the Left. For two years, having nothing to expect from his parents, whose mediocrity exasperated him, he had posed in the Quartier Latin as a red-hot Radical. But since he had got to know the Dambrevilles, where he had blunted the first edge of his appetites, he had grown calmer and was gradually becoming a sapient Republican.

"No," said the priest; "no agreement is possible. The Church can come to no terms."

"Then it must disappear," cried the doctor.

And though most attached to each other, having met at all the death-beds in the Saint-Roch district, they now seemed irreconcilable—the thin, nervous physician, and the portly, affable priest. The latter smiled politely even when making the most absolute statements, like a man of the world who tolerates the ills of life, but also like a good Catholic who had no notion of abandoning his beliefs.

"The Church disappear? Bah!" said Campardon, with a show of anger, for he wanted to make up to the Abbé, from whom he expected to get work.

Moreover, all present shared his opinion; the Church could never disappear. Théophile Vabre, as he coughed and spat and shivered with the ague, dreamed of universal happiness achieved by the formation of a humanitarian republic, and alone expressed his belief that the Church would have to be transformed.

Then, in his gentle voice, the priest continued:

"The Empire is committing suicide. Wait and see next year, at election time."

"Oh! as regards the Empire, you're quite at liberty to rid us of that," said the doctor, bluntly. "That will be doing us a great favour."

Whereupon Duveyrier, who appeared to be profoundly interested, shook his head. He belonged to an Orléanist family; but he owed everything to the Empire, and thought himself bound to defend it.

"Believe me," said he, at last, severely, "it does not do to shake the bases of society, or else everything will collapse. From each catastrophe it is we who suffer."

"That is very true," remarked Monsieur Josserand, who had no opinion of his own, but who remembered his wife's instruction.

Then everybody spoke at once. None of them was in favour of the Empire. Doctor Juillerat condemned the Mexican Expedition, the Abbé Mauduit censured the recognition of the Kingdom of Italy. Yet Théophile Vabre and even Léon, felt anxious when Duveyrier threatened them with another '93. Of what use were such perpetual revolutions? Had not liberty been gained? And this hatred of new ideas, this fear of the people claiming their share, soothed the liberalism of these self-satisfied bourgeois. However, they all declared, with one accord, that they would vote against the Emperor. He had to be taught a lesson.

"Oh, dear! how they bore me," said Trublot, who for a moment had been trying to understand.

Octave induced him to return to the ladies. In the recess, Berthe was deafening Auguste by her bursts of laughter. The big, sickly fellow was forgetting his dread of women, and had grown quite flushed beneath the attacks of his bewitching companion, whose warm breath touched his face. Apparently, Madame Josserand considered that the campaign was not being conducted with sufficient despatch, for she looked hard at Hortense, who, obedient to the signal, went to her sister's aid.

"I hope you have quite recovered, madam," said Octave to Valérie.

"Quite, thank you," she coolly replied, as if she remembered nothing as to what had occurred.

Madame Juzeur asked the young man about some old lace which she wanted to show him and get his opinion on, and he had to promise to call upon her next day for a minute or two. Then, as the Abbé Mauduit came back to the drawing-room, she called him, and made him sit beside her, as she assumed an air of rapture.

The conversation continued. The ladies were discussing their servants.

"Well, yes," said Madame Duveyrier, "I am quite satisfied with Clémence; she is a very clean, active girl."

"And your footman, Hippolyte?" asked Madame Josserand. "I believe you had thoughts of discharging him?"

Just then Hippolyte, the man-servant, was handing round ices. He was tall and strong, with a ruddy complexion, and when he had passed, Clotilde replied, with some embarrassment:

"Well, we are going to keep him; changing is so disagreeable. Servants get used to each other, you see, and I like Clémence so much."

Madame Josserand hastily acquiesced, feeling they were on delicate ground. They hoped to arrange a marriage between them some day; and the Abbé Mauduit, whom the Duveyriers had consulted in this matter, gently shook his head, as if to hide a scandal well known to the whole house, but to which no one alluded. However, the ladies unbosomed other secrets. Valérie that very morning had sent away another maid—the third within a week. Madame Juzeur had decided to get a little girl of fifteen from the Foundling Hospital, and train her herself. As for Madame Josserand, she never ceased abusing Adèle, that slut, that good-for-nothing, whose extraordinary achievements she recounted at length. Seated thus, in languid fashion, amid the glare of candles and the perfume of the flowers, they wallowed in all this gossip of the scullery, as they eagerly discussed a coachman's insolence or the pertness of a parlourmaid.

"I say, have you seen Julie?" asked Trublot suddenly, in a mysterious voice.

As Octave looked at him in amazement, he added:

"My dear fellow, she is stunning. Go and have a look at her. Just pretend that you want to leave the room for a moment and then slip through into the kitchen. She is simply stunning."

It was the Duveyriers' cook to whom he alluded. The ladies' conversation had taken another turn. Madame Josserand, in the most gushing manner, was praising the very modest estate which the Duveyriers owned near Villeneuve-Saint-Georges, and which she had noticed once from the train, when going to Fontainebleau. But Clotilde did not like the country; she lived there as little as possible, only during the holidays of her son, Gustave, who was then studying rhetoric at the Lycée Bonaparte.

"Caroline is quite right not to want to have any children," she declared, turning to Madame Hédouin, who was sitting two chairs away from her. "They do so interfere with all one's habits."

Madame Hédouin said that she liked children very much. But she was far too busy for babies; her husband was always travelling about, here, there, and everywhere; and she had the entire business to look after.

As he stood behind her chair, Octave, glancing sideways, remarked the little black curls at the nape of her neck and the snowy whiteness of her bosom, lost in a wave of delicate lace. She succeeded in disconcerting him as she sat there so calmly, saying little, and with her beautiful smile. He had never met anyone so fascinating, not even at Marseilles. It was certainly worth trying for, though it would take a long while.

"Having children spoils a woman's good looks," he whispered in her ear, anxious to say something to her, yet not knowing what other remark to make.

She slowly raised her large eyes, and said simply, just as if she were giving him an order at the shop :

"Oh, no! Monsieur Octave, with me that's not the reason. One wants the time; that is all."

Madame Duveyrier here interrupted them. She had merely greeted the young man with a slight bow when Campardon had introduced him to her. Now she watched him, and listened to his conversation with sudden, undisguised interest. As she heard him talking to her friend, she could not resist enquiring :

"Please excuse my interrupting you, but—what is your voice?"

At first he hardly understood her, but ended by saying that he had a tenor voice. Clotilde at once was all enthusiasm. A tenor voice—had he really! What a lucky thing, for tenor voices were becoming so rare! Now, for the "Blessing of the Poniards," which they were going to sing directly, she had never been able to find more than three tenors among all her acquaintances, though at least five were wanted. And, as her eyes sparked with sudden excitement, she could hardly refrain from going at once to the piano to try his voice. He was obliged to promise to come in one evening and let her do so. Trublot, in his rear, kept nudging him, enjoying himself in his own stolid, animal fashion.

"So you are in for it, too, are you?" he murmured, when his hostess had moved on. "My dear fellow, at first she thought I was a baritone. Then, when that did not do, she tried me as a tenor, which was worse still. So she has decided to make use of me to-night as a bass. I'm to be a monk."

Madame Duveyrier just then called him, so he was obliged to leave Octave. They were going to sing the chorus from the *Huguenots,* the great event of the evening. There was a great bustling, and fifteen men, all amateurs, recruited from the ranks of the guests, tried with much difficulty to pass the ladies and reach their meeting point near the piano. They kept constantly stopping and begging to be excused, their voices drowned by the buzz of conversation, while fans moved more rapidly as the heat increased. Madame Duveyrier counted them at last; they were all there; and she began to distribute the parts which she herself had copied out: Campardon took the rôle of Saint-Bris; to a young auditor employed by the Council of State, De Nevers' few bars had been entrusted; and there were eight nobles, four provosts, and three monks, represented by barristers, clerks, and simple householders. Madame Duveyrier accompanied, having, moreover, reserved the part of Valentina for herself, uttering passionate shrieks as she struck crashing chords. She was resolved to have no lady among all the gentlemen, whom, in a resigned troop, she led with all the harsh vigour of a *chef d' orchestre.*

Meanwhile, the talking went on, the noise in the parlour becoming positively intolerable, where obviously the political discussion had grown more heated. So, taking a key from her pocket, Clotilde gently tapped on the piano with it. There was a murmur throughout the room, a hush of voices, the black evening coats again surged forward to the doors. Above the rows of heads one caught a glimpse of Duveyrier's blotchy face, which wore a look of anguish. Octave remained standing behind Madame Hédouin, looking downwards at the shadows about her breast swathed in filmy lace. But just as silence had been established, there was a burst of laughter, when he looked up. It was Berthe, amused by some joke of Auguste's. She had heated up his poor blood to such a pitch that he had become quite rakish. Everyone present looked at them; mothers became grave, and relatives exchanged eloquent glances.

"She's so full of her fun!" murmured Madame Josserand, fondly, yet loud enough to be heard.

With a complacent air of self-sacrifice, Hortense stood by to help her sister, echoing her laughter and pushing her up against the young man, while air from the open window behind them lightly stirred the large red-silk curtains.

Then the sound of a sepulchral voice was heard, and all eyes were turned towards the piano. With mouth agape and beard waving in a gust of lyrical fervour, Campardon declaimed the opening stave.

"Aye, by the Queen's command we gather here."

Up the scale and down again ran Clotilde; then with her eyes fixed on the ceiling, and a look of terror in her face, she screamed:

"Ah, me! I tremble!"

And then the whole thing began, as the eight lawyers, householders, and clerks, with noses glued to the score, and looking like schoolboys mumbling over a page of Greek, swore that, one and all, they were ready to deliver France. Such a beginning as this created some surprise, as the voices were deadened by the low ceiling, so that one could only hear a loud humming, like the noise of carts full of paving-stones, which, when they pass, make the window panes rattle. But when Saint-Bris' melodious phrase, "For this cause so holy," developed the leading theme, some of the ladies recognised it, and nodded to show how clever they were. The room grew hotter, and the nobles roared at random:

"We swear it! We will follow you."

Every time it was like an explosion, a blow that struck each guest full in the face.

"They are singing too loud," murmured Octave, in Madame Hédouin's ear.

She never moved. Then, being bored by the vocal explanations of De Nevers and of Valentina, the more so because the auditor attached to the Council of State was not a baritone at all, he made signs to Trublot, who was waiting for the monk's entrance, and winked significantly at the window-recess, where Berthe still kept Auguste imprisoned. The two were now by themselves, breathing the cool outdoor air, while Hortense played sentry, leaning against the curtain and mechanically twisting the loop. No one was looking at them now; Madame Josserand and Madame Dambreville even had given up watching them, after exchanging significant glances.

Meanwhile, with her fingers on the keys, Clotilde, who in her excitement dared not gesticulate, could only stretch out her neck, as she addressed to the music-stand the following vow, intended for De Nevers :

"Ah, from this day my blood shall all be yours!"

The aldermen had now entered, as well as a substitute, two solicitors, and a notary. The quatuor electrified everyone with the phrase, "For this cause so holy," which was repeated in broader style, half the chorus taking it up as the whole theme gradually expanded. Campardon, whose mouth grew ever wider, gave orders for the fray with a tremendous volley of syllables. Then all at once the monks' chant broke forth. Trublot's psalm-singing came from his stomach, so as to get at the low notes.

Octave, who had watched him singing with some curiosity, was greatly surprised on looking once more at the curtained window. As if impelled to do so by the music, Hortense had unhooked the loop by a movement which might have been unintentional, and the curtain as it fell had completely hidden Auguste and Berthe. They were there behind it, leaning against the window-bar; not a single movement betrayed their presence. Octave no longer took any interest in Trublot, who just then was blessing the poniards :

"Ye holy poniards, now by us be blessed."

What could they both be about behind that curtain? The fugal passages were beginning as, to the monks' deep tones, the chorus replies, "Death ! death ! death !" Yet the couple behind the curtain never moved. Perhaps, overcome by the heat, they were only looking out at the passing cabs. Now Saint-Bris' melodious phrase again came back; all the singers gradually uttered it at the top of their voices, progressively, in one grand final outburst of amazing force. It was like a sudden gust of wind that swept through the narrow room, making the candles flare, as the guests grew pale, and there was a rush of blood to their ears. Clotilde furiously thumped the piano, galvanising the chorus by her very glance; then the voices sank to a whisper :

"At midnight, not a sound!"

Then she went on by herself, using the soft pedal when imitating the regular footfall of the patrol as it dies away in the distance.

All at once, as the music faintly, swooningly expired, just in this pleasant lull that had followed the storm, a voice was heard to exclaim :

"Don't! You're hurting me!"

Everyone looked round towards the window. Madame Dambreville, anxious to make herself useful, was kind enough to pull the curtain aside. And the whole room beheld Auguste, looking very confused, and Berthe, very red, as they still leant against the window-bar.

"What is it, my precious?" asked Madame Josserand, eagerly.

"Nothing, mamma. Monsieur Auguste knocked my arm in opening the window. I was so hot."

And she blushed deeper still. There was some covert tittering and grimacing among the audience. Madame Duveyrier, who for a while had been trying to keep her brother out of Berthe's way, turned quite pale, especially as the incident had completely spoilt the effect of her chorus. However, after the first momentary surprise, there was a burst of applause. Congratulations were showered upon her, as well as compliments for the vocalists. How well they had sung! What pains she must have taken to make them sing with such precision! It was positively as well done as at any theatre! But under all this noisy praise she could not help hearing the whispering that went round. The girl had certainly been too greatly compromised; an engagement was inevitable.

"Well, so he's hooked!" said Trublot, on rejoining Octave. "What a fool he was not to squeeze her while we were all bellowing! I thought that he would profit by the opportunity. You know, at parties where there is singing you can pinch a lady, and if she cries out it doesn't matter, as nobody can hear her!"

Berthe, who had now completely regained her composure, was laughing again; while Hortense surveyed Auguste with the sullen air of a girl who has got her diploma. In this their conquest, one could detect the mother's tuition—the result of her lessons regarding undisguised contempt for man. All the male guests now invaded the drawing-room, mixing with the ladies, and talking in a loud voice. Annoyed at the scene in which Berthe had figured, Monsieur Josserand drew nearer to his wife. It irked him to hear her thanking Madame Dambreville for all her lavish attentions to Léon, in whom there was no doubt, she had wrought a most beneficial change. She pretended to talk in a low voice to Madame Juzeur, intending Valérie and Clotilde, who stood by, to overhear her.

"Yes, you know, her uncle only wrote to me to-day; Berthe is to have fifty thousand francs. That's not much, certainly; but still, it's a lump sum, in hard cash, you know!"

This lie absolutely disgusted her husband. He could not help lightly touching her on the shoulder. She looked up at him; so resolute was the expression on her face that his eyes fell. Then, as Madame Duveyrier turned round, she smiled a gracious smile, and asked with an air of concern about her dear father.

"Oh! papa must have gone up to bed," replied Clotilde, quite overcome by such tender solicitude. "You know, he works so hard!"

Monsieur Josserand then told her that her surmise was correct, as he had indeed retired, in order that his brain might be perfectly clear in the morning. And he stammered out a few phrases about "a most remarkable intellect, extraordinary faculties," etc., wondering all the while where on earth the dowry was coming from, and what sort of figure he should cut on the day fixed for signing the contract.

The pushing back of chairs now made a great noise in the drawing-room, and the ladies trooped into the dining-room, where tea was served. Madame Josserand, victorious, went thither, surrounded by her daughters and the Vabre family. Soon, amid the disordered array of chairs, only the group of grave debaters remained. Campardon had got hold of the Abbé Mauduit. The Calvaire of Saint-Roch, it seemed, had to undergo certain repairs. The architect declared that he was perfectly ready to undertake these, as the Evreux diocese gave him but little to do. He had only to construct a pulpit there, and put in heating apparatus, as well as new ovens in monseigneur's kitchen; besides, these were things which his surveyor could attend to. The abbé accordingly promised to submit the matter for consideration at the next meeting of the directors. They then both joined the others, who were complimenting Duveyrier upon a bill of which he confessed himself the author. The President, who was his friend, reserved for him certain work, at once easy and brilliant, which in this way should bring him to the front.

"Have you read this new novel?" asked Léon, as he turned over the pages of a copy of the *Revue des Deux Mondes,* which lay on the table. "It is well-written, but it's another adultery story; they really are getting quite improper!"

Then they began to talk about morality. Some women, said Campardon, were perfectly blameless. Everybody agreed with him. Moreover, the architect observed, married life was easy enough if one knew how to give and take. Théophile Vabre remarked that that depended upon the woman, without explaining himself further. They were anxious to have the opinion of Doctor Juillerat, who, smiling, declined to express one. He thought that virtue lay in health. Duveyrier, meanwhile, remained silent, as if dreaming.

"Why, dear me!" he murmured at last, "those novelists exaggerate; adultery is very rare among the well-educated classes. A woman, if she be of good family, has in her soul a flower——"

He took the high moral tone, and talked of ideals with such emotional fervour that his eyes were dimmed. And he seconded the Abbé Mauduit when the latter spoke of the necessity of religious beliefs for the wife and mother. The conversation was thus brought back to religion and politics, to the point where these gentlemen had left it. Never would the Church disappear, because it formed the basis of domestic life as well as the natural support of governments.

"In its capacity of police, granted," muttered the doctor.

Duveyrier did not care to have politics discussed at his house, and contented himself by remarking, as he glanced across at the dining-room where Berthe and Hortense were stuffing Auguste with sandwiches:

"Gentlemen, this fact settles everything: religion makes marriage moral."

At the same moment, Trublot, on the sofa, was leaning over and whispering to Octave.

"By the way," he asked, "would you like me to get you an invitation from a lady at whose house one has some fun?"

And, as his companion wished to know what kind of lady, he added, as he pointed to Duveyrier:

"His mistress."

"Never!" exclaimed Octave, in amazement.

Trublot slowly opened and shut his eyes. It was so. When one had married a wife who was not obliging, who appeared disgusted at the idea of having babies, and who thrashed the piano until all the dogs of the neighbourhood fell sick, why, one went elsewhere about town to find consolation.

"Let us make marriage moral, gentlemen; let us make it moral," repeated Duveyrier, stiltedly, with his inflamed visage, in which Octave now noted the traces of disordered blood, the result of secret excesses.

These gentlemen were now called away to the dining-room, and the Abbé Mauduit, who remained alone for a moment in the empty apartment, watched the crush of guests from afar. His fat, shy face wore a sad expression. As confessor to these ladies and their daughters, he knew them thoroughly from head to heel, like Doctor Juillerat. He had finally been obliged to keep an eye upon outward appearances only, as a sort of master of the ceremonies covering this corrupt bourgeoisie with the cloak of religion, trembling at the certain prospect of a final collapse, whenever the plague-spot should be unmasked in the light of day. Fears such as these sometimes troubled him, whose faith as priest was ardent and sincere. But he soon smiled again, accepting the cup of tea brought to him by Berthe, as he chatted to her for a moment, so as to cover by his priestly office the scandal of the window incident. Thus he again became a man of the world, content merely to exact decorous behaviour from his penitent flock, the members of which had strayed far from the fold, and who would have compromised the Deity himself.

"Well, that's a nice state of affairs!" said Octave to himself, whose respect for the house had received another shock.

Then, seeing that Madame Hédouin was going to find her cloak, and wishing to get there before her, he followed Trublot, who was also about to leave. Octave's idea was to see her safely home. She declined his escort, as it was barely midnight and she lived so close by. Then, as a rose fell from the bouquet at her bosom, he picked it up with an injured air and made a show of keeping it as a souvenir. For a moment her handsome brows contracted. Then she said, in her calm, self-possessed way:

"Kindly open the door for me, Monsieur Octave—thank you."

When she had gone downstairs, Octave, in his embarrassment, looked about for Trublot. But, as before at the Josserand's, Trublot had just disappeared. He must have slipped away by the servants' staircase.

So, somewhat out of humour, Octave went up to bed with the rose in his hand. At the topmost landing, leaning over the banisters, he saw Marie, just where he had left her. She was waiting to hear his step, and had run to see him coming up. She invited him in, saying:

"Jules has not yet come home. Did you enjoy yourself? Were there any pretty dresses?"

But she never stopped for his answer. She had just noticed the rose, and, with childish gaiety, exclaimed:

"Ah! that's for me, that flower, is it? You thought of me, then. How kind of you; how kind of you!"

Her eyes filled with tears, and she blushed deeply, in her confusion. Moved by a sudden impulse, Octave kissed her tenderly.

About one o'clock the Josserands, in their turn, went home. On a chair in the hall, Adéle had placed a candlestick and matches. None of them spoke as they came upstairs, but on reaching the dining-room, which they had erst quitted in such a despairing mood, they yielded to a sudden burst of mad merriment, wildly seizing each other's hands as they danced a sort of savage dance all round the table. The staid father, even, yielded to the infection; the mother cut elephantine capers, and the girls uttered little inarticulate cries, while the candle on the table flung their huge dancing shadows along the wall.

"Well, at last that's settled!" exclaimed Madame Josserand, as she sank breathlessly into a chair.

But in a sudden paroxysm of maternal tenderness, she at once got up again, and running to Berthe, kissed her effusively on both cheeks.

"I am pleased, very pleased, with you, my darling. You have just rewarded me for all my exertions. My sweet child! my sweet child! so it really is true this time."

Her voice was broken by emotion, sudden and heartfelt, as in her flame-coloured gown she collapsed at the very moment of victory, prostrated by the fatigues of her terrible campaign of three winters.

Berthe was obliged to protest that she was not unwell, for her mother thought that she was looking pale, and paid her all sorts of little attentions. She even insisted upon making her a cup of linden-tea. When Berthe had gone to bed, her mother, barefoot, went softly to her bedside, as in the far-off days of her childhood.

Meanwhile, with his head on the pillow, Monsieur Josserand awaited his wife's return. She blew out the light, and got across him to her side, nearest the wall. Then he again felt ill at ease, and the same qualms of conscience assailed him as he thought of the promise of a dowry of fifty thousand francs. And he ventured to express his scruples out loud. Why promise when one did not know if one could keep one's word? It was not honourable.

"Not honourable, indeed!" cried Madame Josserand, out of the darkness, as her voice again assumed its usual ferocity of tone. "I'll tell you what is not honourable, sir, and that is to let your daughters turn into old maids; yes, old maids, which was probably your intention. Why, good gracious me! we've lots of time to look about us; we must talk the matter over, and get her uncle to make up his mind. Moreover, *my* family, I would have you know, sir, have always acted honourably."

VI

THE next day, which was Sunday, Octave lay for an extra hour drowsing in the warm sheets. He awoke in the mood of lazy good-humour which accompanies the mental clearness that morning brings. Why should he be in any hurry? He was quite comfortable at "The Ladies' Paradise"; he was shaking off his provincial airs, and he felt absolutely certain that one day Madame Hédouin would become his, and make his fortune. The matter, however, required prudence, a long series of gallant tactics, the thoughts of which appealed pleasurably to his voluptuous feeling for the female. As he dropped off to sleep again, making plans, and giving himself six months in which to succeed, the vision of Marie Pichon served to soothe his impatience. A woman of that sort was very handy; he had only to stretch out his arm if he wanted her, and she did not cost him a sou. While waiting for the other one, surely no better arrangement than this were possible. As, in this drowsy way, he reflected upon her cheapness and utility, he became quite tender-hearted towards her, and, in her good-nature, she seemed charming to him, and he resolved to treat her henceforth with greater kindness.

"Nine o'clock, by Jove!" said he, as the clock, striking, thoroughly roused him. "I suppose I must get up."

A fine rain was falling, so he determined not to go out all day. He would accept an invitation to dine with the Pichons, an invitation which for a long while he had always refused, owing to his dread of the Vuillaumes. That would please Marie; and he would find some opportunity of kissing her behind the door. As she liked books, he even thought of taking her a whole parcelful as a surprise—some that he had left in one of his trunks in the loft. When he had dressed, he went downstairs to Monsieur Gourd to get the key of the loft, which was used in common by the different tenants for storing their superfluous and cumbersome articles.

Down below, on such a damp morning as this, it was stifling on the heated staircase, where vapour dimmed the sham marble walls, long mirrors, and mahogany doors. At the porch Mother Péron, a poorly-clad woman (whom the Gourds paid twopence an hour for doing the rough work of the house), was scrubbing the pavement as the icy air blew full upon her from the courtyard.

"Now then, old girl, just you scrub that properly, and don't let me find a single stain!" cried Monsieur Gourd, who, wearing warm headgear, stood at the door of his lodge.

And as Octave arrived, he spoke to him about Mother Péron in that brutally domineering way which shows the mad longing for revenge which ex-servants have when they, in their turn, are waited upon.

"Lazy old thing! I can do nothing with her! I should just like to have seen her at my lord duke's! They'd have made her sit up! I shall send her flying if she doesn't give me my money's worth; you see if I don't! But what was it that you wanted, Monsieur Mouret?"

Octave asked for the key. Then the porter, without hurrying himself, went on explaining that he and Madame Gourd, if they had liked, could have lived in their own house at Mort-la-Ville, only that Madame Gourd adored Paris, in spite of her swollen legs, which prevented her from getting as far as the pavement even. They were only waiting until they had got a snug income, always longing for the time when they should be able to retire upon the little fortune that penny by penny they had amassed.

"I can't be worried, you know," said he, as he drew up his majestic figure to its full height. "I've no longer any need to work for my daily bread. The key of the loft, I think you said, Monsieur? I say, wife, where did we put the key of the loft?"

Cosily ensconced in an easy-chair, Madame Gourd was drinking her coffee out of a silver cup before a wood fire, which brightened the whole room by its blaze. She didn't know where the key was —at the back of the chest of drawers, perhaps. And, while dipping her pieces of toast in the coffee, she kept her eyes fixed upon the door of the servants' staircase at the other end of the courtyard, which looked bleaker and more gloomy than ever on this rainy morning.

"Look out! there she is!" grunted Madame Gourd, as a woman came through the door in question.

Monsieur Gourd at once stood in front of his lodge to block the woman's way. She advanced at a slower pace, looking uneasy.

"We've been watching for her all the morning, Monsieur

Mouret," said Gourd, under his breath. "We saw her pass yesterday evening. She's come from that carpenter upstairs—the only working-man we have got in the house, thank God! And if the landlord would only listen to me, he'd keep the room (it's only a servants' attic) empty. For the sake of a hundred and thirty francs a year, it's really not worth while having filthy goings-on in your house——"

Interrupting himself, he roughly asked the woman:

"Where have you come from?"

"Why, from upstairs, of course," she replied, as she went on without stopping.

Then he burst out:

"We're not going to have any women here; do you understand? The man who brings you here has been told as much already. If you come back here to sleep, I'll fetch a policeman, and we'll soon see if you shall play any of your dirty games in a decent house."

"Oh, what a bother you are!" said the woman. "It's my home, and I shall come back to it when I like."

And she went off, pursued by the righteous wrath of Monsieur Gourd, who talked of going upstairs to fetch the landlord. Did you ever hear of such a thing? A creature like that among respectable folk, in a house where not the faintest immorality would be tolerated! It would seem as if this carpenter's garret were the cesspool, so to speak, of the house—a sink of iniquity, the surveillance of which was revolting to all his delicate instincts and a source of trouble to him at night.

"And the key, where is it?" Octave ventured to repeat.

But the hall-porter, furious that a lodger should have seen his authority set at naught, fell to badgering poor Mother Péron again, in his desire to show how he could command obedience. Did she mean to defy him? She had just splashed his door again with her broom. If he paid her out of his own pocket, it was because he did not want to soil his hands, and yet he had always had to clean up after her! He'd see her damned before he would give her another job just for charity's sake. She might starve first.

Worn out by such work, which was too hard for her, the old woman, without answering, went on scrubbing with her skinny arms, keeping back her tears for very awe of this alarming personage in smoking-cap and slippers.

"Now I remember, my dear," cried Madame Gourd, from the arm-chair in which she spent the whole day, warming her fat body.

"I hid the key under some shirts, so that the maid-servants should not always be messing about in the lumber-room. Pray let Monsieur Mouret have it."

"A nice set, too, those maid-servants!" muttered Monsieur Gourd, whose long life as a servant had led him to loathe his fellow-menials. "Here is the key, sir, but please let me have it back again, for one can't leave a single place open anywhere, or the maids go there to misbehave."

Not wishing to cross the wet courtyard, Octave ascended the front stairs, only going up by the back stairs when he got to the fourth floor, as the door communicating with this was close to his room. At the top was a long passage, with two turnings at right angles; it was painted in light yellow, with a darker dado of ochre, and, as in hospital corridors, the doors of the servants' rooms, also yellow, were ranged along at regular intervals. It was as cold as ice under the zinc roofing, bare and cleanly, with a sort of stale smell, like the smell of pauper lodging-houses.

The lumber-room looked out on to the courtyard at the extreme end of the left wing. But Octave, who had not been up there since the day of his arrival, went along the left-hand passage, when suddenly a sight which met his view through one of the half-open doors caused him to stop short in sheer amazement. A gentleman in his shirtsleeves stood before a small looking-glass, tying his white tie.

"What, you here?" he exclaimed.

It was Trublot. At first he seemed like one petrified. No one ever came up there at that hour. Octave, who had entered, looked first at him and then at the room, with its narrow iron bedstead and washhand-stand, where a little ball of woman's hair was floating on the dirty water in the basin. Seeing a black dress-coat still hanging up beside the aprons, he could not help exclaiming:

"So you sleep with the cook?"

"No, I don't," answered Trublot, with a wild look in his eyes.

Then, aware of the folly of telling such a lie, he began to laugh complacently.

"Well, she is rare good fun, my dear fellow; most awfully smart, I assure you."

Whenever he dined out, he used to slip out of the drawing-room and go and pinch the cooks over their ovens, and when one of them let him have her key he managed to leave before midnight, and would go and wait patiently for her in her room, sitting on her trunk in his evening clothes and white cravat. The next morning, about ten o'clock, he would leave by the front stairs, and passed the hall-porter's as if he had been calling upon one of the tenants at an early hour. As long as he kept office hours his father was satisfied. Besides, he had to be at the Bourse now every day from twelve to three. On Sundays he sometimes spent the whole day in some servant's bed, quite happy, with his nose buried under her pillow.

"You, too, who some day will be so rich!" said Octave, with a look of disgust.

Then Trublot learnedly remarked:

"My dear boy, you don't know what it is, so you can't judge."

And he spoke up for Julie, a tall Burgundian woman of forty, her big face all pock-pitted, but whose body was superbly built. One might strip all the other women in the house; they were all sticks; not one of them would come up to her knee. Then, too, she was a well-to-do girl; and, to prove this, he opened drawers and showed a bonnet, some jewellery, and some lace-trimmed skirts, all which had doubtless been stolen from Madame Duveyrier. Octave, in fact, now noticed a certain coquettishness about the room—some gilt cardboard boxes on the drawers, a chintz curtain hanging over the petticoats, and other things which testified to the cook trying to play the fine lady.

"With this one," repeated Trublot, "I don't mind admitting that I do. If all the others were only like her!"

Just then there was a noise on the back stairs; it was Adèle coming up to clean her ears, as Madame Josserand, furious, had forbidden her to touch the meat until she had washed them thoroughly with soap and water. Trublot, peeping out, recognised her.

"Shut the door, quick!" he cried, anxiously. "Hush! Not a word!"

Listening attentively, he heard Adèle's heavy footstep along the passage.

"So you sleep with her too, then?" asked Octave, astonished to see him turn so pale, and guessing that he was afraid of a scene.

This time, however, Trublot's cowardice made him answer:

"No, hang it all, not with that filth! My good fellow, what do you take me for?"

He sat down at the edge of the bed waiting to finish dressing himself, while begging Octave not to move. So they both remained perfectly quiet, as Adèle kept scrubbing her ears, an operation which lasted a good ten minutes. They heard the whirlpool in the basin.

"There is a room, though, between this one and hers," Trublot explained, in a whisper. "It is let to a carpenter, who stinks the whole place out with his onion soup. This morning, again, it almost turned me up. And, you know, they make the partitions in the servants' rooms now-a-days as thin as paper. I can't think what the landlords are about, but I don't call it decent. Why, you can hardly turn round in your bed. Most inconvenient, I assure you!"

When Adèle had gone down again, his bold air returned as he finished dressing with the help of Julie's combs and pomatum. When Octave mentioned the lumber-room, he insisted on showing him where it was, as he knew every hole and corner of that place. And, as they passed the doors, he familiarly mentioned the servants' names. At this end of the passage, after Adèle, came Lisa, the Campardon's maid, a wench who got what she wanted outside; then there was Victoire, their cook, an old whale of seventy, but the only one for whom he had any respect. Then came Françoise, who, the day before, had entered Madame Valérie's service, and whose trunk would, probably, only remain about twenty-four hours behind that squalid bed, in which such scores of maids had slept that one always had to make certain, before going thither to wait in the warm sheets. Then there was a quiet couple in the service of people on the second floor; then came their coachman, a strapping fellow, of whom he spoke jealously, as one handsome man might speak of another, suspecting him of going from door to door, and doing some fine tricks on the quiet. At the other end of the passage, there was Clémence, the Duveyriers' maid, whom her neighbour, Hippolyte, the footman, visited conjugally every night. Last of all, there was little Louise, the orphan, whom Madame Juzeur had engaged on trial, a hussy of fifteen, who must hear some queer things at night-time, if she were a light sleeper.

"Don't lock the door again, there's a good fellow, just to oblige me," said Trublot, when he had helped Octave to get out the books. "You see, when the lumber-room is open, one can hide in there and wait."

Having consented to deceive Monsieur Gourd, Octave returned with Trublot to Julie's room, as he had left his overcoat there. Then he could not find his gloves, and shook out the petticoats, turned the bed-clothes inside out, making such a dust, and such a fusty smell of dirty linen, that Octave, half-choked, opened the window. It looked on to the narrow inner courtyard, from which all the kitchens in the house got whatever light they had. And, leaning out, he looked down into this damp well, from which there rose the fœtid odours of dirty sinks, when a sound of voices made him hastily withdraw.

"That's their little morning gossip," said Trublot, who, on all-fours, was still looking under the bed. "Only listen to it."

It was Lisa, who from the Campardon's kitchen was leaning over to talk to Julie, two storeys below her.

"So it's come off this time, has it?"

"Seems so," replied Julie, looking up. "You know, she all but pulled his trousers down in her efforts to catch him. Hippolyte came back from the drawing-room so disgusted that he was nearly sick."

"If we were only to do a quarter as much!" said Lisa.

For a moment she disappeared to drink some broth that Victoire had brought her. They got on capitally together, pandering to each other's vices, the maid hiding the cook's drunkenness, and the cook helping the maid to have those outings from which she came back dead-beat—her back aching and her eyelids blue.

"Ah, my children," said Victoire, who in her turn leant out, her elbows next to Lisa's, "you're young! Wait till you see what I've seen! At old Campardon's there was his niece, a girl who had been well brought up, and she used to look at men through the keyhole."

"That's a pretty thing!" muttered Julie, with her air of a scandalised fine lady. "If I'd been the little girl on the fourth floor, I'd have fetched Monsieur Auguste such a smack on the face if he had pinched me in the drawing-room. A nice fellow, indeed!"

At these words a shrill laugh came from Madame Juzeur's kitchen. Lisa, who was opposite, soon spied Louise, who, with her precocity of fifteen, delighted to listen to the chatter of the servants.

"That brat keeps spying upon us from morning till night," she said. "What a nuisance it is to have a child like that hanging about! We soon shan't be able to talk at all!"

She did not finish her speech, for the noise of a window opening suddenly made them all vanish. There was a profound silence; then they ventured to look out again. What was it, after all? They thought it was Madame Valérie or Madame Josserand, who was going to catch them gossiping.

"It's all right," said Lisa. "They have all got their heads in the basin by this time. Too much occupied with their complexions to think about bothering us! It's the only minute in the day when one can breathe!"

"So things are always the same at your place, are they?" enquired Julie, as she peeled a carrot.

"Always the same! It's all over; she's hopeless."

"Well, what does your big idiot of an architect do, then?"

"Why, he has her cousin, of course!"

They laughed louder still, until Francoise, Madame Valérie's new maid, looked out. It was she who, when opening the window, had startled them. First of all there was an interchange of civilities.

"Oh, it is you, mademoiselle!"

"Yes, indeed, mademoiselle! I am trying to get things straight in this kitchen, but, my word, it's that filthy!"

Then came certain nauseous details.

"Ah! you'll be a marvel of patience if ever you stop there. The last servant had her arms all scratched by the child, and madame made her slave so, that we could hear her crying from here."

"Ah, well, that won't suit me very long!" said Françoise. "Thanks, all the same, for telling me."

"Where's she gone—your missus?" asked Victoire, inquisitively.

"She has just gone out to lunch with a lady."

Leaning out, Lisa and Julie exchanged glances. They knew her well, that lady. A queer sort of lunch, too, with her head down and her legs in the air! How people dared tell such shocking lies! They did not pity the husband, who deserved more than that; but, all the same, it was a disgrace to humanity when a women could not behave herself better.

"There's Dish-Clout!" cried Lisa, as she spied the Josserand's maid-of-all-work above her.

Then a volley of gross abuse broke from this hole, as dark and stinking as a sewer. One and all, looking up at Adèle, yelled violently at her, who was their scapegoat—the filthy, clumsy creature on whom all the servants vented their spite.

"Oh, look! She's washed herself, that's plain!"

"Just you throw your offal into the yard again, and I'll come and rub your face with it!"

Adèle, bewildered, looked over at them, half her body being out of the window. At last she said:

"Leave me alone, can't you?"

But the cries and laughter increased.

"You got your young mistress married last night, did you? Perhaps it's you who taught her how to get hold of the men!"

"Ah, the mean-spirited thing! She stops in a place where they don't give you enough to eat! 'Pon my word, it's that which aggravates me! What a big fool you must be! Why don't you send them all flying?"

"None of your nonsense," she blurted out. "It's not my fault if I don't get enough to eat."

And the voices grew louder, as more abuse was about to be exchanged between Lisa and the newcomer, Françoise, who took Adèle's part; when the latter, forgetting how they had abused her, and yielding to her instinct of *esprit de corps,* cried:

"Look out! Here's missus!"

Instantly all was silent as the grave. All of them went hurriedly back to their kitchens; and from the dark, narrow chasm of a courtyard only the stench of drains came up, like the fumes of family ordure, hidden out of sight but stirred up ever and anon by servants in their rancour. Here was the sewer of the house—the very dunghill of its shames; while the gentry still lounged about in slippers, and the front staircase lay revealed in all its majesty amid the stuffy silence of the hot-air stove. Octave remembered the sudden explosion which had greeted him from this inner court, on entering the Campardon's kitchen, the day of his arrival.

"How charming they are," he said simply.

And, leaning out in his turn, he looked at the walls almost as if vexed that he had not been able to see through the whole sham at once, covered up as it was by imitation marble and gilt stucco.

"Where the devil has she put them?" said Trublot once more, who had even looked in the po-cupboard for his white gloves.

At last he discovered them at the bottom of the bed; they were flattened out and quite warm. He glanced once more at the mirror, then hid the bedroom key in a place agreed upon, at the end of the passage, under an old sideboard which had been left behind by some lodger. Then he led the way downstairs, accompanied by Octave. On the front stairs, as he got past the Josserand's door, all his assurance returned as he buttoned up his overcoat up to his neck to hide his evening clothes and white tie.

"Good-bye, my dear boy," said he, raising his voice. "I felt somewhat anxious, so I just called to see how the ladies were. They have had a very good night, it seems. Ta ta!"

Octave, smiling, watching him as he went downstairs. Then, as it was almost lunch-time, he determined to return the lumber-room key later on.

At luncheon-time, at the Campardons', he watched Lisa with particular interest, as she waited at table. She looked pleasant and neat, as usual, though her vile words still echoed in his brain. His instinct for women had not deceived him with regard to this flat-bosomed wench. Madame Campardon might well continue to be delighted with her, and wonder that she did not steal anything. That was true enough, for her vice was of another kind. Moreover, the girl appeared to be very kind to Angèle, and the mother placed entire confidence in her.

That very morning, as it happened, Angèle disappeared at dessert, and they heard her laughing in the kitchen. Octave ventured to remark :

"Perhaps you are hardly wise in letting her be so familiar with the servants."

"Oh, there's no great harm in that!" replied Madame Campardon, in her languid way. "Victoire was in service when my husband was born, and I have such perfect confidence in Lisa. Then, you know, the child makes my head ache. I should go mad if she were always dancing about me all day long."

The architect sat gravely chewing the end of his cigar.

"It is I," said he, "who makes Angèle spend two hours in the kitchen every afternoon. I want her to learn housekeeping, and that is the best way to teach her. She never goes out, my dear boy; she is always under our wing. You will see what a treasure we shall make of her!"

Octave said no more. Some days Campardon seemed to him absolutely stupid; and when the architect urged him to come to Saint-Roch and hear a famous preacher, he refused, obstinately persisting in remaining at home. Having told Madame Campardon that he would not dine there that evening, he was on his way to his room, when he felt the lumber-room key in his pocket. He thought it better to return it at once.

On the landing an unexpected sight roused his attention. The door of the room let to the distinguished gentleman, whose name nobody knew, was open. This was quite an event, for it was always shut, barricaded as by the silence of the tomb. His surprise grew greater when, on looking for the gentleman's writing-table, he saw in its place the corner of a large bedstead, and perceived a graceful little lady coming out of the room. She was dressed in black, and wore a thick veil which concealed her features. The door closed noiselessly behind her.

His curiosity being roused, he followed the lady downstairs to see if she were pretty. But she timidly tripped along at a great rate, her dainty little boots barely touching the stair-carpet, and leaving no trace behind her but a faint perfume of verbena. As he got to the hall, she disappeared, and he only saw Monsieur Gourd standing in the doorway, who, cap in hand, was making her a low bow.

As Octave returned the key, he tried to draw the doorkeeper on to tell him something.

"She looks nice," he said. "Who is she?"

"A lady," replied Monsieur Gourd.

And he would not add anything further. But he was more communicative regarding the gentleman on the third floor. A man, you know, in the best society; he had taken that room just to come there and work quietly one night a week.

"Oh, he does work, does he? I wonder what at?" asked Octave.

"He was good enough to ask me to look after his room," continued Monsieur Gourd, pretending not to have heard, "and, you know, he pays down on the nail. Ah, sir! when you wait on people, you soon find out if they are all right or not. He's a thorough gentleman, he is; you could tell that from his linen."

He was obliged to stand on one side, and Octave even had to step back for a moment into the porter's lodge, so as to let the carriage of the second-floor people go by on their way to the Bois. The horses, reined in by the coachman, pawed the ground; and, as the large closed landau rolled along under the vaulted room, two handsome children were seen through the windows, their smiling faces almost hiding the indistinct profiles of their father and mother. Monsieur Gourd stood at attention, polite but cold.

"Those people don't make much noise in the house," said Octave.

"Nobody makes any noise," replied the porter, drily. "Each one lives as best pleases him, that's all. Some people know how to live, and some don't."

The folk on the second floor were rather severely criticised, because they associated with no one. They appeared to be rich, however. The husband wrote books, but Monsieur Gourd's curling lip showed that he put little faith in that sort of thing, especially as nobody knew how things went on in the household, which never seemed to want anybody, but which always appeared to be perfectly happy. That was not natural, so he thought.

Octave was opening the hall-door when Valèrie came back. He politely stood aside to let her pass.

"Are you quite well, madame?"

"Yes, thank you, monsieur."

She was out of breath, and as she went upstairs he looked at her muddy boots, and thought about the lunch alluded to by the servants. No doubt she had walked home, not having been able to get a cab. A warm, stale smell came from her damp petticoats. Fatigue and utter physical languor made her catch hold of the banisters every now and then.

"What an awful day, madame, isn't it?"

"Awful, and so close, too!"

She had reached the first floor, when they exchanged bows. At a glance he saw how haggard was her face, how heavy her eyelids were with sleep, and how her tousled hair showed underneath the hastily-tied bonnet. And, as he went along upstairs, his thoughts vexed, angered him. Why, then, would she not do that with him? He was not sillier nor uglier than anybody else.

On passing Madame Juzeur's on the third floor, he recollected his promise to her of the previous evening. He felt a sort of curiosity as to that discreet little woman with eyes like periwinkles. He rang the bell, when Madame Juzeur answered the door herself.

"Oh, my dear sir, how good of you! Do come in!"

There was a certain stuffiness about the apartments. Carpets, curtains everywhere; chairs as soft as eider-down, and the atmosphere as warm and heavy as that of a chest lined with old rainbow-coloured satin. In the drawing-room, which with its double curtains had the solemn stillness of a sacristy, Octave was asked to take a seat on a broad, low sofa.

"This is the lace," said Madame Juzeur, as she came back with a sandal-wood box full of pieces of stuff. "I want to make a present of it to somebody, and I am curious to know it value."

It was a piece of very fine old *point d' Angleterre*. Octave examined it with his professional eye, and at last declared that it was worth three hundred francs. Then, without waiting further, as they were both handling the lace, he stooped down and kissed her fingers, which were small and delicate as those of a little girl.

"Oh, Monsieur Octave, at my age! You can't think what you're doing!" exclaimed Madame Juzeur, with a pretty air of surprise, though not at all annoyed.

She was thirty-two, and gave out that she was quite an old

woman. As usual, she spoke of her troubles. Gracious goodness! after ten days' married life the cruel man had gone and left her one morning and had never returned—nobody knew why.

"You can well understand," she said, looking up to the ceiling, "that after such a shock as that, it is all over for any woman."

Octave had kept hold of her warm little hand, which seemed to melt into his own, and he kept lightly kissing it on the finger-tips. She looked down at him vaguely, tenderly, and then, in a maternal way, she exclaimed:

"Oh, you child!"

Believing himself to be encouraged, he tried to put his arm round her waist and pull her on to the sofa, but she gently slipped away from him, laughing as if she thought he were only joking.

"No, leave me alone, and don't touch me if you wish us to remain good friends."

"Then you don't want it?" he asked, in a low voice.

"What what? I don't know what you mean. Oh! you may have my hand as much as you like."

He caught hold of her hand again. But this time he opened it, kissing the palm. With half-shut eyes, she treated the process as a joke, opening her fingers as a cat puts out its claws so as to be tickled inside its paw. She would not let him go farther than the wrist. The first day a sacred line was drawn there where naughty things began.

"Monsieur le curé is coming upstairs," said Louise, abruptly, as she returned from an errand. The orphan was of the regular foundling type, with muddy complexion and insignificant features. She giggled idiotically when she caught sight of the gentleman nibbling at missus' hand. But madame extinguished her with a look.

"I fear I shall not be able to make anything of her," said Madame Juzeur. "Well, all the same, one ought to try and put one of these poor creatures on the right road. Look here, Monsieur Mouret, will you come this way?"

She took him into the dining-room, so that the other room might be left for the priest, whom Louise showed in. And as she said good-bye, she expressed a hope that Octave would come again and have a chat. It would be a little company for her; she was always so lonely and so depressed. But, happily, in religion she had her consolation.

About five o'clock that evening Octave felt it a positive relief to make himself at home with the Pichons, while waiting for dinner.

The house and its inmates bewildered himself somewhat. After having let himself feel all a provincial's awe for the grave splendour of its staircase, he was gradually becoming filled with supreme contempt for all that he imagined took place behind those big mahogany doors. He did not know what to think; these middle-class women, whose virtue at first froze him, seemed now as if they ought to surrender at a mere sign, and, if one of them resisted, it filled him with surprise and vexation.

When she saw him put down the parcel of books which he had fetched for her that morning, Marie grew crimson with pleasure.

"How good of you, Monsieur Octave!" she kept repeating. "Thank you so much. How nice of you to come so early. Will you have a glass of sugar and water, with some cognac in it? That will give you an appetite."

Just to please her, he accepted. There was something pleasant about everyone; even about Pichon and the Vuillaumes, who gossiped on in their doddering Sunday fashion. Every now and then Marie ran to the kitchen, where she was cooking a shoulder of mutton, and Octave, jokingly, followed her thither, and catching her round the waist, in front of the oven, kissed the back of her neck. Without a cry, without a start, she turned round and kissed him on the mouth with her icy lips. To the young man their coldness seemed delicious.

"Well, what about your new Minister?" he said to Pichon, on coming back to the room.

The clerk started up in surprise. What! there was going to be a new Minister of Public Instruction? He had heard nothing about it; at offices like his they never took any interest in that sort of thing.

"It's such horrid weather," he said jerkily. "It's quite impossible to keep one's trousers clean!"

Madame Vuillaume was talking about a girl at Batignolles who had gone wrong.

"You will hardly believe me, monsieur," said she. "The girl has been extremely well brought up, but she was so bored at having to live with her parents that she twice tried to jump out of the window. It's past all belief!"

"They should put gratings over the windows," remarked Monieur Vuillaume, simply.

The dinner proved delightful. Talk of this sort went on all the while, as they sat round the frugal board, which was lighted by one small lamp. Pichon and Monsieur Vuillaume, having got upon the subject of Government officials, never ceased talking about directors and sub-directors. The father-in-law obstinately upheld those of his day, and then recollected that they were dead, while Pichon, for his part, went on talking incessantly about the new ones, amid an endless muddle of names. On one point, however, the two men, as well as Madame Vuillaume, were agreed: that big lubber, Chavignat, whose wife was so plain, had had far too many children. With such an income as his, it was simply absurd. Octave, feeling happy and comfortable, smiled. For a long time he had not spent such a pleasant evening. At last he, too, had nothing for Chavignat but blame. Marie seemed to soothe him with her innocent, docile look, stirred by no emotion whatever as she saw him sitting next to her husband, and helping them both to what they liked best, in her languidly obedient way.

At ten o'clock punctually the Vuillaumes rose to go. Pichon put on his hat. Every Sunday he went with them as far as their 'bus. It was a habit which, out of deference, he had observed ever since his marriage, and the Vuillaumes would have been much hurt if he had now tried to discontinue it. They all three set out for the Rue Richelieu, and walked slowly up it, scrutinising the Batignolles omnibuses, which were always full. Pichon thus was often obliged to go as far as Montmartre, for it would never have done for him to leave the Vuillaumes before putting them into their 'bus. As they walked very slowly, it took him nearly two hours to go there and back.

There was much friendly shaking of hands on the landing. As Octave went back with Marie to the room, he said:

"It's raining. Jules won't get back before midnight."

As Lilitte had been put to bed early, he at once made Marie sit on his knee, drinking the remainder of the coffee with her out of the same cup, like a husband who is glad that his guests have gone and that he is all to himself after the excitement of a little family gathering, and able to kiss his wife at his ease, when the door is shut. A drowsy warmth pervaded the poky little room, and a faint odour of vanille from the dish of frosted eggs which they had eaten. As he was lightly kissing the young woman under the chin, someone knocked at the door. Marie did not even start up in fear. It was young Josserand, the half-witted lad. Whenever he could escape from the apartment opposite, he used to come across and chat to her, as her gentleness had an attraction for him; and they both got on very well together as they exchanged inconsequent remarks at intervals of ten minutes.

Octave, greatly annoyed, remained silent.

"They've got some people there to-night," stammered Saturnin. "I don't care a hang if they won't have me at table. I've taken the lock off and got out that way. That will make them swear."

"But they will wonder what has become of you. You ought to go back," said Marie, who observed Octave's impatience.

Then the idiot grinned with delight as, in his faltering way, he told her all that had happened at home. His visit each time seemed to be in order to relieve his memory.

"Papa has been working all night again, and mamma boxed Berthe's ears. I say, when one gets married, does it hurt?"

Then, as Marie did not answer, he excitedly continued:

"I won't go away into the country, that I won't! If they do but touch her, I'll strangle them; that is easy enough, at night-time, while they are asleep. The palm of her hand is as smooth as note-paper; but the other is a beast of a girl."

Then he began again, and got more muddled, as he could not express what he had come to say. Marie at last persuaded him to go back to his parents without his even having noticed her companion.

Fearing another interruption, Octave wanted to take the young woman across to his own room; but, blushing violently, she refused. Not understanding such bashfulness, he continued assuring her that they would be certain to hear Jules coming upstairs, and there would be plenty of time for her to get back to her room. Then, as he was pulling her along, she became quite angry, as indignant as a woman to whom violence is offered.

"No, not in your room; never! It would be too dreadful. Let us stop here." And she rushed away to the back of her apartment.

Octave was still on the landing, amazed at such unexpected resistance, when he heard a loud noise of wrangling in the courtyard below. Things were evidently all wrong to-day; it would have been better if he had gone to bed. A noise of this sort was so unusual at that hour, that at last he opened a window so as to listen. Monsieur Gourd was shouting out:

"I tell you, you shall not pass! The landlord has been sent for. He will come down himself and kick you out!"

"Kick me out? What's that for?" said a gruff voice. "Don't

I pay my rent? Go on, Amélie, and if the gentleman touches you, he'll know it!"

It was the carpenter from upstairs, who was returning with the woman they had sent off that morning. Octave leant out to look; but in the black courtyard he only saw great moving shadows thrown by the dim gaslight in the hall.

"Monsieur Vabre! Monsieur Vabre!" cried the porter, as the carpenter pushed him aside. "Quick, quick! she's coming in!"

Despite her bad legs, Madame Gourd had gone up to fetch the landlord, who, just then, was at work upon his great task. He was coming down. Octave heard him furiously reiterating:

"It is scandalous, disgraceful! I won't allow such a thing in my house!" Then, addressing the workman, who at first seemed somewhat abashed, "Send that woman away at once! At once, do you hear? We don't want any women brought in here."

"But she's my wife!" replied the carpenter, with a scared look. "She is in service, and only comes once a month, when her people let her have a day off. That's the plain truth about it. It's not your place to prevent me from sleeping with my wife, I should think!"

Then both porter and landlord lost their heads.

"I give you notice to quit," stuttered old Vabre, "and, meanwhile, I forbid you to make a brothel of my premises! Gourd, turn that person into the street. No, sir, none of your nonsense with me. If a man is married, he ought to say so. Hold your tongue, and let me have no more of your insolence!"

The carpenter, good-natured fellow as he was, and who, no doubt, had had a little too much wine, burst out laughing.

"It's a damned funny thing, all the same. Well, Amélie, as the gentleman objects, you had better go back to your employer's. We'll make our baby some other time. We wanted to make a baby, that's all we wanted. I'll take your notice with pleasure, old boy! Don't think I want to stop in your dirty show. Nice goings-on there are, too. He won't have women brought into the house—oh, no! but he lets well-dressed hussies stop on every floor, who, behind their doors, lead the life of a bitch. Oh, you bloody toffs!"

Amélie had gone away, so as not to cause her husband any more annoyance, while he continued his good-humoured banter. Meantime Gourd covered Monsieur Vabre's retreat while venturing to make certain remarks out loud. What a filthy lot the lower orders were, to be sure! One workman in the house was quite enough to infect it.

Octave shut the window. Then, just as he was returning to Marie, some one lightly brushed past him in the passage.

"Hullo! you again!" he said, recognising Trublot.

For a moment the latter was speechless; then he sought to explain his presence.

"Yes; I've been dining with the Josserands, and I was going up to——"

"To that slut, Adèle, I suppose? And you swore you didn't!"

Then, brazening it out in his usual way, Trublot said, with an enthusiastic air:

"I assure you, my dear fellow, it's rare sport! She's got a skin——you've no idea!" Then he abused the workman, who, with his damned nonsense about women, had almost caused him to be caught coming up the back stairs. He had been obliged to come round by the front staircase. Then, as he hurried away, he added: "Remember, it's next Thursday that I am going to take you to Duveyrier's mistress. We will dine together first."

The house regained its holy calm which, coming from each chaste bedchamber, seemed to pervade it. Octave had rejoined Marie in her bedroom, sitting beside her on the conjugal couch while she was arranging the pillows.

As upstairs the only chair had a basin on it and an old pair of slippers, Trublot sat down on Adèle's narrow bed and waited for her there in his evening dress. When he recognised Julie's step as she came up to bed, he held his breath, being perpetually terrified of women's quarrels. At last Adèle appeared. She was angry, and, seizing his arm, said:

"I say, why do you treat me like that when I am waiting at table?"

"What do you mean?"

"Well, you never so much as look at me, and you never say 'if you please,' when you want some bread. This evening, as I was handing the veal round, you looked as if you had never had anything to say to me. I've just had about enough of it. The whole house torments me, and it's a little bit too much if you side with the rest!"

She undressed herself in a great fury, and, flinging herself down on the old bed, which cracked again, she turned her back upon him.

Meanwhile, in the next room, the carpenter, still full of wine, was talking to himself at the top of his voice, so that the whole corridor could hear him.

"Well, that's a rum thing, ain't it; when they won't let you sleep with your own lawful wife? You won't have any women in the house, won't you, you silly old ass! Go and stick your snout at this moment under all the bed-clothes, and you'll pretty soon see!"

VII

In order to induce Uncle Bachelard to give Berthe a dowry, for the past fortnight the Josserands had asked him to dinner almost every evening, in spite of his revolting habits.

When they told him about the marriage, all he did was to pat his niece on the cheek and say :

"What! so you're going to get married? That's nice, isn't it, my girlie?"

To all hints he turned a deaf ear, exaggerating his airs of a bibulous old rake, becoming suddenly drunk whenever the subject of money was mentioned. Madame Josserand once thought of asking him to meet Auguste, the bridegroom-elect, feeling sure that the sight of the young man would bring him to the point. In this method there was something heroic, for the family did not care to exhibit their uncle, for fear it might create a false impression. However, he behaved fairly well; there was only a large stain on his waistcoat, caused, no doubt, by syrup at some café. Yet when his sister, after Auguste's departure, questioned him, and asked what he thought of the bridegroom, without compromising himself, he merely said :

"He is charming—quite charming."

The thing must be settled somehow, for time was short. So Madame Josserand determined to put matters plainly before him.

"As we are now by ourselves," she continued, "let us make the most of it. You just go away, dears, as we have to talk with your uncle. Berthe, do look after Saturnin, and see that he doesn't take the lock off the door again."

Ever since they had been busy about his sister's marriage, keeping it a secret, Saturnin wandered about the house with wild eyes, suspicious that something was going on; he imagined all sorts of awful things, to the utter consternation of his family.

"I have made all enquiries," said the mother, when she had shut herself in with the father and the uncle. "This is the Vabres' position."

Then she went into long details of figures. Old Vabre had brought half-a-million with him from Versailles. If the house had cost him three hundred thousand francs, he would have two hundred thousand left, which in the last twelve years had been producing interest. Besides, every year his rents brought him in twenty-two thousand francs, and, as he lived with the Duveyriers and hardly spent anything at all, he must consequently be worth five or six hundred thousand francs, not counting the house. In that quarter, therefore, there were handsome expectations.

"He has no vices, then?" asked Bachelard. "I thought he speculated on the Bourse."

At this Madame Josserand loudly protested. Such a quiet old man, absorbed in such important work! He, at least, had shown that he could amass a fortune! She smiled bitterly as she glanced at her husband, who bowed.

As for Vabre's three children, Auguste, Clotilde, and Théophile, they had each had a hundred thousand francs at their mother's death. Théophile, after certain ruinous enterprises, was living as best he could on the remains of this inheritance. Clotilde, whose only passion was her piano, had probably invested her share. Auguste had just bought the warehouse on the ground-floor, and had started in the silk trade with his hundred thousand francs, which he had long been keeping in reserve.

"Of course, the old fellow won't give his children anything when they marry," remarked Bachelard.

Well, no, he didn't care about giving; that was only too plain. When Clotilde married, he had undertaken to give her a dowry of eighty thousand francs; but Duveyrier had never received more than ten thousand. He did not ask for the balance, but even gave his father-in-law free board and lodging!—flattering his avarice, no doubt, in the hope of one day acquiring his whole fortune. In the same way, after promising Théophile fifty thousand francs when he married Valérie, he at first merely paid the interest, and since then had not parted with a single penny, even going so far as to exact his rent from the young couple, which they paid for fear of being struck out of his will. So that, all things considered, one could not count too much on the fifty thousand francs that Auguste was to receive when the marriage-contract was signed. It would be a lucky thing if his father let him have the ground-floor warehouse rent free for a few years.

"Well," declared Bachelard, "it's always rough on the parents, you know. Dowries are never really paid."

"Let us go back to Auguste," continued Madame Josserand. "I have told you what expectations are his; the only danger is on the side of the Duveyriers, and Berthe, when she becomes one of the family, will do well to keep a sharp look-out upon them. At the present moment, Auguste, after buying the business for sixty thousand francs, has started with the other forty thousand. Only the sum is not sufficient; then, again, he is single and wants a wife, so he means to marry. Berthe is pretty, and he already thinks how nice she would look in his counting-house; and as for her dowry, well, fifty thousand francs is a good sum, and that caused him to make up his mind."

Uncle Bachelard never moved an eyelash. At last he said, with a tender air, that he had dreamed of something much better. And he began to criticise the bridegroom-elect. A charming fellow, certainly, but too old, much too old; why, he was over thirty-three. Then, he was always out of health, racked by neuralgia; a doleful-looking wight, not half sprightly enough for a tradesman.

"Have you got anybody else?" asked Madame Josserand, whose patience was well-nigh exhausted. "I hunted all over Paris before I could find him."

However, she herself had no illusions regarding him; and in her turn she, too, picked him to pieces.

"Oh, he's not a paragon, I grant you; in fact, I think he is rather a fool. Then, I always mistrust men who have never had their fling when young, and who have to reflect for years before risking a step in life. When he left college, as bad headaches put a stop to his studies, he remained a mere clerk for fifteen years before daring to touch his hundred thousand francs; while his father, so it seems, cheated him out of the interest on it. No, he is not brilliant, I admit."

Hitherto, Monsieur Josserand had not spoken. He now ventured to remark :

"But, my dear, why insist on this marriage, if the young man is in such bad health——"

"Oh !" struck in Bachelard, "it's not bad health that need prevent it. Berthe would find it easy enough to marry again."

"But supposing he is impotent," suggested the father. "Supposing he should make our child unhappy?"

"Unhappy, indeed !" cried Madame Josserand. "Why don't you

say at once that I have thrown my girl at the head of the first-comer? Among ourselves, surely, we can discuss him, and say he is this, or he is that—not young, not good-looking, nor clever. It is only natural that we should talk the matter over like this, isn't it? However, he'll do. We shall never find anybody better! and, let me tell you, it is a most unexpected match for Berthe. I was going to give it all up as a bad job—upon my word, I was!"

She rose; and Monsieur Josserand, reduced to silence, pushed back his chair.

"I am only afraid of one thing," continued she, as she resolutely planted herself in front of her brother; "and that is, that he may break it off if the dowry is not forthcoming on the day the contract is to be signed. One can easily understand that; he wants money, you know."

Just then she heard the sound of laboured breathing close behind her, and she turned round. It was Saturnin, who had thrust his head round the door, glaring at her with wolfish eyes. They were all panic-sticken, for he had stolen a spit from the kitchen, to spit the geese, so he said. Uncle Bachelard, who had felt very uncomfortable at the turn their conversation was taking, profited by the general scare.

"Don't disturb yourselves," he called out from the ante-room. "I'm off; I have got a midnight appointment with one of my clients, who has come over expressly from Brazil."

When they had succeeded in putting Saturnin to bed, Madame Josserand, in her exasperation, declared that it was impossible to keep him any longer. He would do them some injury at last, if he were not shut up in an asylum. It was simply insufferable to have always to keep him out of the way. His sisters would never get married as long as he was there to disgust and terrify everybody.

"Let us wait a while longer," mutter Monsieur Josserand, whose heart bled at the thought of this separation.

"No, no," declared his wife. "I don't want him to finish up by spitting me. I had just got my brother into a corner, and was going to make him do something. Never mind. We will go with Berthe to-morrow, and have it out with him at his own place, and then we'll see if he has the impudence to evade keeping his promises. Besides, Berthe ought to pay her godfather a visit. It is only proper."

Next day all three—mother, father, and daughter—paid an official visit to the uncle's premises, on the ground-floor and the basement of an enormous house in the Rue d'Enghein. The entrance was blocked by large vans. In the covered courtyard numerous packers were nailing up cases, and through open doorways one caught sight of piles of goods, dried vegetables, and remnants of silk, stationery, and tallow, all accumulated in executing the thousands of commissions given by customers, and by buying in advance when prices were low. Bachelard was there, with his big red nose, his eyes still inflamed by last night's debauch, but with his intellect clear, as his business acumen and resource came back to him directly he sat down to his account-books.

"Hullo! is that you?" he said, utterly bored at the sight of them. He took them into a little office, whence he could overlook his men from a window.

"I have brought Berthe to see you," explained Madame Josserand. "She knows how much she is indebted to you."

Then, after kissing her uncle, when the girl, obedient to a wink from her mother, had gone off to look at the goods in the courtyard, Madame Josserand resolutely broached the subject.

"Look here, Narcisse, this is just how we are situated. Relying upon your kindheartedness and your promises. I have engaged to give a dowry of fifty thousand francs. If I don't do so, the match will be broken off, and, now that things have gone so far, this would be a disgrace. You cannot possibly leave us in such an awkward position."

A film came over Bachelard's eyes, and he stammered out, as if quite drunk:

"Eh? What's that? You should never promise; bad thing to promise."

Then he pleaded poverty. For instance, he had brought a whole lot of horse-hair, thinking that the price of it would go up. Not a bit of it; the price had fallen lower still, and he had been obliged to get rid of it at a loss. Rushing to his books, he opened his ledger, and insited on showing them the invoices. It was simply ruin.

"Rubbish!" exclaimed Monsier Josserand, at last, losing all patience. "I know all about your business, and that you're coining money. You would be lolling in wealth if you did not squander it as you do. Mind, I don't ask you for anything for myself. It was Eléonore who determined to take such a step. But allow me to tell you, Bachelard, that you have been fooling us, For fifteen years, every Saturday, when I went through your books for you, you always promised that——"

The uncle interrupted him, violently slapping his chest.

"*I* promise? Nothing of the sort. No, no! let me do as I like, and then you'll see. I don't like to be asked; it annoys, it upsets me. One day you'll see what I shall do."

Even Madame Josserand herself could wring nothing further from him. Shaking them by the hand, he brushed away a casual tear, spoke of his kindheartedness and of his affection for the family, and begged them to tease him no further, as, by God! they would never have cause to repent it. He knew his duty, and would do it to the uttermost. Later on Berthe would find out how much her uncle was attached to her.

"And what about the dotal insurance?" he asked, resuming his natural voice. "Those fifty thousand francs for which you had insured the girl's life?"

Madame Josserand shrugged her shoulders.

"That was all done for fourteen years ago. We've told you twenty times that when the fourth premium became due we were unable to pay the two thousand francs."

"That doesn't matter," he murmured, with a wink. "You must talk about this insurance to the family, and take your time about paying the dowry money. One never pays a dowry."

Monsieur Josserand rose in disgust.

"So that's all you have to tell us, is it?"

Pretending not to understand, the uncle insisted that such a thing was always done.

"One never pays, I tell you. You pay something on account, and then the interest. Why, look at Monsieur Vabre himself! Did my father every pay for Eléonore's dowry? Of course not. Each one sticks to his money, you bet."

"In short, you advise me to do a blackguardly thing!" cried Monsieur Josserand. "It would be a lie! I should be committing forgery if I produced the life policy of that insurance——"

Madame Josserand cut him short. At this suggestion of her brother's she became grave. It was surprising that she had never thought of this before.

"Good gracious me! how touchy you are, to be sure! Narcisse never told you to commit forgery!"

"Of course I didn't," muttered Bachelard. "There's no need to show any papers."

"The point is to gain time," she continued. "Promise the dowry, and we must manage to give it later on."

Then the worthy man's conscientious scruples drove him to speak. No, he refused; not again would he venture to approach the brink of such a precipice. They were always taking advantage of his easy-going nature, so getting him gradually to consent to things which afterwards made him quite ill, so greatly did he take them to heart. Since he had no dowry to give, it was impossible for him to promise one. Bachelard whistled and drummed on the window-pane, as if to show his utter contempt for such scruples. Madame Josserand listened, while her face grew livid with pent-up fury that suddenly burst forth :

"Very well, monsieur, since that is so, the marriage shall take place. It is my daughter's last chance. I would rather cut off my right hand than let it slip. So much the worse for the others. When you're driven to it, why you're capable of anything at last."

"Then, madame, I presume you would commit murder in order to get your daughter married?"

She drew herself up to her full height.

"So I would!" she retorted, angrily.

Then she smiled. Bachelard was obliged to quell the tempest. What was the use of wrangling? It was far better to come to some amicable arrangement. Thus, worn out and trembling from the effects of the quarrel, Monsieur Josserand agreed to talk matters over with Duveyrier, on whom, according to Madame Josserand, everything depended. In order to get hold of the counsellor when he was in good humour, Bachelard proposed to let his brother-in-law meet him at a house where he could refuse nothing.

"It is merely to be an interview," said Josserand, still protesting. "I will enter into no engagement, that I swear."

"Of course not, of course not," said Bachelard. "Eléonore does not want you to do anything dishonourable."

Then Berthe came back. She had spied some boxes of preserved fruits, and by dint of much kissing and coaxing she tried to get her uncle to give her one. But he again became afflicted by his stammer. He couldn't possibly do so; they were all counted, and had to be sent off to St. Petersburg that very night. He gradually got them out into the street, while his sister, at the sight of these huge warehouses packed to the roof with every sort of merchandise conceivable, lingered behind, mortified to think that such a fortune should have been made by a man totally devoid of principle, and comparing it bitterly with her husband's impotent honesty.

"Well, then, to-morrow night, about nine o'clock, at the Café de Mulhouse," said Bachelard, as he shook Monsieur Josserand's hand when they got into the street.

It so happened that the next day, Octave and Trublot, who had dined together before going to see Clarisse, Duveyrier's mistress, went into the Café de Mulhouse so as not to call too early, though she lived a good way off, in the Rue de la Cerisaie. It was hardly eight o'clock. On entering, they heard a loud noise of quarrelling at the further end of the room. There they saw Bachelard, drunk already, enormous in size, with flaming cheeks, who was having a row with a little pale-faced, testy gentleman.

"You've been spitting in my beer again," roared he, in a voice of thunder. "I won't stand it, sir!"

"Hold your damned row, will you, or I'll punch your head!" said the little man, standing on tip-toe.

Then Bachelard raised his voice to an exasperating pitch, without ceding an inch. "Just you dare, sir! just you dare!"

And when the other man knocked his hat off, which he always wore cocked on one side of his head, he repeated, with fresh energy:

"Just you dare, sir! just you dare!"

Then, picking up his hat, he sat down majestically, and called out to the waiter:

"Alfred, change this beer!"

Octave and Trublot, greatly astonished, had noticed Gueulin sitting beside his uncle, with his back to the wall, smoking away with utter indifference. They asked him what was the reason of the quarrel.

"Don't know," he replied, watching the cigar-smoke curling upwards. "There's always some row or other. A rare one for getting his head punched! He never gives in!"

Bachelard shook hands with the new-comers. He adored young fellows. He was delighted to hear that they were going to see Clarisse. So was he; Gueulin was coming too; only he had to keep an appointment here first with Monsieur Josserand, his brother-in-law. And the little room resounded with his strident voice as he ordered every conceivable sort of drink for his young friends, with the wild prodigality of a young man who, when out for a spree, thinks nothing about the cost. Uncouth, with glittering false teeth, and his nose like a flame below his snowy, close-cropped hair, he hob-nobbed with the waiters and ran them off their legs, while he became so unbearable to his neighbours that the proprietor twice asked him to leave if he could not be quiet. The night before, he had been turned out of the Café de Madrid.

Just then a girl came in, and went out again after walking round the room with a tired look in her eyes. This led Octave to talk of women. Bachelard, spitting sideways, hit Trublot, but he never even apologised. Women had cost him far too much; he flattered himself he had had the best to be got in all Paris. In his line of business one never bargained about such things. The dodge was to show oneself independent of one's business. But he had dropped all that sort of thing now; he wanted to be loved for his own sake. And as Octave watched this swaggerer flinging bank-notes broadcast, he thought with surprise of the uncle who put on a drunken stutter to escape domestic extortion.

"Don't you brag, uncle," said Gueulin. "One can always have more women than one wants."

"Then you, silly idiot," retorted Bachelard, "why don't you ever have any?"

Gueulin shrugged his shoulders with a look of profound disdain.

"Why don't I? Well, only yesterday I dined with a friend and his mistress. She at once began kicking me under the table. There was a chance, wasn't there? Well, when she asked me to see her home, I bolted, and haven't been near her since. Oh! I don't say but what it would not have been very pleasant for the time being. But afterwards, uncle, afterwards! Perhaps, one of those women that stick to you like glue! No, I'm not quite such a fool!"

Trublot nodded approvingly, for he, too, had given up society women, through fear of troubles that come with the morrow. Then, Gueulin, shaking off his phlegmatic manner, proceeded to cite examples. One day, in the train, a splendid brunette whom he did not know went to sleep on his shoulder; but then he thought about what he would have done with her when he got to the station. Another time, after a wedding, he found a neighbour's wife in his bed. A bit stiff, wasn't it? And he would certainly have done something foolish, had he not been haunted by the idea that she would certainly ask him to buy her some boots.

"Talk about opportunities, uncle," said he, in conclusion, "why nobody has had such opportunities as I have! But I restrained myself. For the matter of that, everyone else does, too, being far too much afraid of consequences. If it weren't for consequences, why, that would be all right. By Jingo! You'd see nothing else but that going on in the streets!"

But Bachelard, dreaming, paid no attention. His noisy mood had vanished; there was a mist before his eyes.

"If you're very good," quoth he, suddenly, "I'll let you see something."

And, after paying, he took them out.

Octave reminded him of his apointment with Monsieur Josserand. That did not matter; they would come back for him. Before leaving the room, Bachelard looked round furtively and then stole the lumps of sugar left by a customer at an adjoining table.

"Follow me," said he, when they got out. "It's close by."

He walked along, gravely meditating, without a word, and stopped before a door in the Rue Saint-Marc. The three young men were about to follow him, when suddenly he seemed to hesitate.

"No, let's go back. I don't think I will."

But they cried out at this. Why was he trying to humbug them in this way?

"Well, Gueulin mustn't come up, nor you either, Monsieur Trublot. You don't behave nicely; you'd only laugh and jeer. Come on, Monsieur Octave, you're a steady sort of fellow."

He made Octave go upstairs in front of him, while the other two laughed, and from the pavement begged to be kindly remembered to the ladies. On reaching the fourth floor he knocked, and an old woman opened the door.

"Oh! it's you, is it, Monsieur Narcisse? Fifi did not expect you this evening."

She was a fat old party, and her face was white and calm as that of a sister-of-mercy. In the narrow dining-room which they entered, a tall, fair girl, pretty and simple-looking, was embroidering an altar-cloth.

"Good-day, uncle," said she, as rising, she put out her forehead to Bachelard's thick, tremulous lips.

As the latter introduced Monsieur Octave Mouret, a distinguished young friend of his, the two women dropped him an old-fashioned curtsey, and they sat down at the table, lighted by a petroleum lamp. It was like some calm provincial interior; two regular lives lost to the outside world, supported by next to nothing. As the room looked on to an inner courtyard, even the sound of traffic was inaudible.

While Bachelard, with paternal solicitude, questioned the girl as to her employments and interests since the previous evening, her aunt, Mademoiselle Menu, confided their whole history to Octave, with the frank simplicity of an honest woman who has nothing to conceal.

"Yes, sir, I come from Villeneuve, near Lille. I am well known at Mardienne Brothers', in the Rue Saint-Sulpice, where I worked as embroideress for thirty years. Then, when a cousin of mine left me a house in the country, I was lucky enough to let it for life, at a thousand francs a year, so some people who hoped that they would bury me the next day, and who have been finely punished for their wicked thought, for I'm still alive, in spite of my seventy-five years."

She laughed, showing teeth as white as those of a girl.

"I was unable to work," she went on, "for my eyesight was gone, when my niece Fanny needed looking after. Her father, Captain Menu, died without leaving a farthing, and not a single relative to help her, sir. So I had to take the girl away from school, and I have taught her embroidery—poor sort of trade, it's true, but either that or nothing; it's always the women who have to die of starvation. Luckily, she met Monsieur Narcisse, so now I can die happy."

And with hands across her stomach, like some old seamstress who has sworn never to touch a needle again, she enveloped Bachelard and Fifi in a humid glance. Just then the old man was saying to the child :

"Now, did you really think about me? And what did you think, then?"

Fifi raised her clear eyes, without ceasing to go on with her embroidery.

"Why, that you were a good friend, and that I loved you very much."

She hardly looked at Octave, as if indifferent to the charm of such a comely young fellow. However, he smiled at her, struck by her grace, and not knowing quite what to think; while the spinster aunt, staled by a chastity that had cost her nothing, continued in an undertone :

"I could have married her to somebody, eh? A workman would beat her; a clerk would only make her bear him heaps of children. It's better that she should behave nicely to Monsieur Narcisse, who seems such a good, kind gentleman."

Then, raising her voice :

"Well, Monsieur Narcisse, it isn't my fault if you're not satisfied with her. I always tell her, 'Make yourself pleasant—be grateful.'

It's only natural that I should be glad to know that she is well looked after. When one has no relatives, it is so difficult to find a home for a young girl."

Then Octave gave himself up to the quiet enjoyment of this pleasant little home. The heavy air of the apartment was charged with an odour of ripe fruit. Only Fifi's needle, as it pricked the silk, made a slight noise at regular intervals, like the ticking of a cuckoo-clock, which might have regulated Bachelard's idyllic amours. The old spinster, however, was probity personified; she lived on her income of a thousand francs, and never touched a farthing of Fifi's money, who spent it just as she pleased. The only things she ever allowed her to pay for occasionally were roast chestnuts and white wine, when she emptied the money-box where she collected the pence given her as good-conduct medals by her kind friend.

"My little duck," said Bachelard, as he rose to go, "we have got some business on hand. I shall look in to-morrow. Be a good girl."

He kissed her on the forehead. Then, looking affectionately at her, he said to Octave:

"You may give her a kiss, too. She is but a child."

The young man's lips touched her cool skin. She smiled; she was so modest. It seemed as if he were one of the family; he had never met worthier folk. Bachelard was going away, when he suddenly came back, crying out:

"Oh, I forgot! Here's a little present for you!"

And, emptying his pocket, he gave Fifi the sugar which he had just stolen at the café. She thanked him heartily, and blushed with pleasure as she crunched one of the lumps. Then, growing bolder, she said:

"You have not any four-sou pieces, have you?"

Bachelard searched his pockets, but in vain. Octave happened to have one, which the girl accepted as a souvenir. She did not go to the door with them, no doubt for propriety's sake; and they could hear the click of her needle as she at once sat down to her altar-cloth, while Mademoiselle Menu showed them out in her good-natured, old-fashioned way.

"Well, that's worth seeing, eh?" said Bachelard, stopping short on the stairs. "You know, that doesn't cost me five louis a month. I've had enough of those hussies that fleece one. 'Pon my word! I wanted something with a heart."

Then, as Octave laughed, his misgivings came back.

"You're a steady chap, now; you won't take advantage of my

good-nature. Not a word, mind, to Gueulin; swear it, on your honour! I am waiting till he is worthy to be shown such an angel. Say what you like, virtue is a good thing; it refreshes one. I myself have always believed in the ideal!"

His old toper's voice trembled; tears filled his flabby eyelids. Down below, Trublot began chaffing him, and pretended he would take the number of the house, while Gueulin shrugged his shoulders and asked Octave, to his astonishment, what he thought of the little thing. When maudlin after a carouse, Bachelard could never resist taking people to see these ladies, feeling vain as displaying such a treasure, yet fearful lest someone should rob him of it. Then, next day, he would forget all about it, and go back to the Rue Saint-Marc with his wonted air of mystery.

"Everybody knows Fifi," said Gueulin, quietly.

Bachelard, meanwhile, was looking for a cab, when Octave exclaimed:

"What about Josserand, who is waiting for you at the café?"

The other two had forgotten all about him. Extremely annoyed at wasting his evening like this, Monsieur Josserand stood fidgeting at the door of the café, not going inside, as he never took any refreshment out-of-doors. At last they started for the Rue de la Cerisaie. But they were obliged to have two cabs, the commission agent and the cashier going in one, and the three young men in another.

Gueulin, whose voice was drowned by the rattling of the crazy vehicle, first began talking about the insurance company where he was employed. As Trublot affirmed, insurance companies were as great a bore as stocks and shares. Then the conversation turned upon Duveyrier. Wasn't it a pity that a rich man like that—a magistrate, too—should let himself be humbugged by women as he did! He also fancied keeping them in out-of-the-way neighbourhoods, beyond the limits of the omnibus routes—modest little so-called widows, who had apartments of their own, nondescript milliners, who kept shops devoid of customers; wenches picked out of the gutter, whom he rigged out and kept snug, visiting them regularly once a week, just as a clerk goes regularly to his office. Trublot took his part, affirming that, in the first place, his temperament was at fault, and then, again, everybody had not got such a wife as he had. People said that ever since their wedding-night she loathed him, his red blotches filling her with disgust. And she willingly let him have mistresses, who were good-natured enough to rid her of him; although occasionally she put up with the disgusting boredom of it, resigned like a virtuous wife who carefully fulfils all her duties.

"Then she's a virtuous woman, is she?" asked Octave, becoming interested.

"Oh, yes! she's straight enough, my dear boy. All the virtues, by Jove—pretty, serious, well-bred, clever, lots of taste, pure, and—— intolerable!"

At the bottom of the Rue Montmartre, a block in the traffic stopped the cab. The young men, having let down the windows, could hear Bachelard abusing the driver in a furious voice. Then, as they moved on again, Gueulin gave his listeners certain details about Clarisse. Her name was Clarisse Bocquet, the daughter of a man who once kept a small toy-shop, but now went about to fairs with his wife and a troop of brats in tatters. One evening, when it was thawing, Duveyrier had met her just as one of her gallants had kicked her out-of-doors. Probably this buxom wench corresponded to the long-sought ideal, for the very next day he was landed, weeping as he kissed her on the eyelids, overcome by a tender yearning to cultivate just one little blue flower of romance, apart from all his grosser sexual desires. Clarisse had consented to live in the Rue de la Cerisaie, so as not to show him up; but she led him a rare dance, had made him buy her twenty-five thousand francs' worth of furniture, sponging on him to her heart's content, together with several artists from the Montmarte Theatre.

"I don't care a damn," said Trublot, "as long as she gives us a good time. At least, she doesn't insist upon your singing, nor does she strum eternally upon her piano, like that other woman. Oh, that piano! Well, I say this: if one is deafened at home, being so unlucky as to have as wife a piano-organ which drives everybody away, why, a fellow would be a precious fool if he did not fix up some snug little corner for himself where he could receive his friends in his slippers."

"Last Sunday," said Gueulin, "Clarisse wanted me to lunch with her alone. I declined. After lunches of that sort one is apt to do something foolish, and I was afraid she might come and plant herself upon me when she left Duveyrier. She detests him, you know. She's so disgusted with him that it almost makes her ill. She does not care for pimples, either, it seems, poor girl! But she can't send him elsewhere, as his wife does; otherwise, if she could hand him over to her maid, she would jolly soon shunt the old bore."

The cab stopped. They alighted in front of a dark, silent house in the Rue de la Cerisaie. But they had to wait a good ten minutes for the other cab, Bachelard having taken his driver to have some grog, after their quarrel in the Rue Montmartre. On the stairs, assuming his respectable-tradesman air, Bachelard, when questioned once more by Josserand as to this friend of Duveyrier's, merely said:

"A woman of the world—very nice girl. She won't eat you."

The door was opened by a little rosy-faced maid, who, smiling half-tenderly, half-familiarly, helped the gentlemen off with their coats. Trublot stopped behind in the ante-room with her for a moment, whispering something in her ear which set her giggling as if she were being tickled. Bachelard had already pushed open the drawing-room door, and he at once introduced Monsieur Josserand. The latter felt momentarily ill at ease; Clarisse seemed quite plain; he could not imagaine why Duveyrier preferred her to his own wife, one of the most beautiful woman in society—this queer sort of person, very dark, very thin, and with a fluffy head like a poodle's. However, Clarisse had charm. She chattered like a true Parisienne, with her frothy, borrowed wit, and her droll ways, acquired by constant contact with men; though, if need be, she could put on her fine-lady airs when it suited her.

"Monsieur, I am charmed. All Alphonse's friends are mine as well. Pray make yourself quite at home."

Duveyrier received Monsieur Josserand most cordially, acting on a hint given to him in a letter of Bachelard's. Octave was surprised at his youthful appearance. He was no longer the severe-looking, restless individual of the Rue de Choiseul, who never looked as if he were at home in his own drawing-room. The unsightly blotches on his face had become pink; his wizened eyes sparkled with childish glee as Clarisse was telling a group of guests he sometimes paid her a flying visit during some short adjournment of the Court, having only just time to jump into a cab, kiss her, and drive back again. Then he complained of being overworked—four sittings a week, from eleven to five; always the same tangled skein of roguery to be unravelled; it positively shrivelled up all feeling.

"Among all that," said he, laughing, "one really wants a few roses. I feel the better for it afterwards."

He was not wearing his red ribbon, however, which he always took off when visiting his mistress. This was a last scruple, a certain delicate distinction which, from a sense of decency, he obstinately observed. Though she would not tell him so, this greatly offended Clarisse.

Octave, who at once shook her by the hand as if she were his comrade, listened and looked about him. The room, with its staring carpet, red satin furniture and hangings, was very much like the drawing-room in the Rue de Choiseul, and, as if to complete this resemblance, several of the counsellor's friends whom Octave had seen on the night of the concert were here also, forming the same groups. But people smoked and talked loudly; everybody seemed bright and merry in the brilliant candle-light. Two gentlemen, with outstretched legs, took up the whole of a divan; another, seated cross-wise on a chair, was warming his back at the fire. There was a pleasant, free-and-easy air about everyone—a freedom, however which did not go any farther. Clarisse never invited any women to these parties—for propriety's sake, she averred. When her guests remarked that ladies were missing from her drawing-room, she would laughingly rejoin :

"Well, and what about me? Don't you think I am enough?"

Thoroughly middle-class in her ideas, she had made a fairly comfortable little home for Alphonse, her passion being for the respectable and the proper. When she received company she declined to be addressed as "thou"; but when her guests had gone, and the doors were closed, all Alphonse's friends enjoyed her favours in succession, clean-shaven actors and painters with bushy beards. It was an ingrained habit this, the need of enjoying herself a bit behind her keeper's back. Only two out of all her friends had not been willing to comply—Gueulin, who dreaded consequences, and Trublot, whose heart lay elsewhere.

The little maid was just then handing round some glasses of punch in her engaging way. Octave took one, and whispered in Trublot's ear :

"The maid is better-looking than the mistress."

"Of course; she always is," replied Trublot, shrugging his shoulders with an air of disdainful conviction.

Clarisse came up and talked to them for a moment. She tripped about hither and thither, from one to the other, joking, laughing, gesticulating. As each new-comer lighted his cigar, the room soon became filled with smoke.

"Oh, you horrid men !" she archly exclaimed, as she went to open a window.

Bachelard, without loss of time, made Monsieur Josserand take a seat in the recess of this window, so that, as he said, they might get a breath of air. Then, by a masterly manœuvre, he brought up Duveyrier and at once plunged *in medias res.* So the two families were about to be united by a close tie; he felt extremely gratified. Then he enquired what day had been fixed for signing the contract, and this gave him the chance to broach the subject.

"We had meant to call on you to-morrow, Josserand and I, to settle everything, being well aware that Monsieur Auguste can do nothing without you. It is with reference to the payment of the dowry, and really, as we seem so comfortable here——"

Seized by fresh qualms of conscience, Monsieur Josserand looked out in the gloomy depths of the Rue de la Cerisaie, with its deserted streets and sombre facades. He was sorry that he had come. They were again going to take advantage of his weakness to involve him in some disgraceful matter which he would live to regret. In a sudden fit of repugnance, he interrupted Bachelard.

"Some other time; this is hardly the place."

"Why not?" exclaimed Duveyrier, most courteously. "We are more comfortable here than anywhere else. You were saying, sir, that——"

"We are going to give Berthe fifty thousand francs. Only, these fifty thousand francs are represented by a dotal insurance at twenty year's date, which Josserand took out for his daughter when she was four years old. It will be three years, therefore, before she can draw the money."

"Allow me," interrupted Josserand, amazed.

"No, just let me finish what I was saying; Monsieur Duveyrier understands perfectly. We do not wish the young couple to wait three years for money which they may need at once, and so we engage to pay the dowry in instalments of ten thousand francs every six months, on the condition that we repay ourselves later with the insurance money."

There was a silence. Monsieur Josserand, chilled and confused, looked out again into the dark street. The counsellor appeared to be thinking the matter over for a moment. Perhaps he scented something fishy about it, and felt delighted at letting the Vabres be tricked, whom he detested in the person of his wife.

"It all seems to me a most reasonable arrangement. It is we who ought to thank you. A dowry is seldom paid in full."

"Of course not," affirmed Bachelard, energetically. "Such a thing is never done!"

And the three shook hands, after making an appointment to meet at the notary's on the following Thursday.

When Monsieur Josserand came back into the light, he looked so pale that they asked him if he felt unwell. This was, in fact, the case, and he withdrew, not caring to wait for Bachelard, who had just gone into the dining-room, where the traditional tea had been replaced by champagne.

Meanwhile, Gueulin, sprawling on a sofa near the window, muttered:

"Oh, that old wretch of an uncle!"

He had overheard a phrase about the insurance money, and chuckled as he told Octave and Trublot the actual truth of the matter. The policy had been taken out at his office; there was not a farthing due; the Vabres were being utterly hoaxed. Then as the other two, holding their sides, roared at this splendid joke, he added, with absurd vehemence:

"I want a hundred francs. If uncle doesn't give me a hundred francs, I'll split!"

Louder grew the buzz of voices, as the champagne gradually upset the decorum upon which Clarisse delighted to insist. Her parties always became rather rowdy before they ended. Even she herself had occasional lapses. Trublot pointed her out to Octave. She was standing behind a door with her arms round the neck of a strapping young fellow with the build of a peasant, a stone-cutter from the South, whom his native town desired to transform into an artist. However, Duveyrier pushed open the door, whereupon she quickly removed her arms and introduced him to the young man—Monsieur Payan, a sculptor of charming talent. Duveyrier was delighted, and promised to get him some work.

"Work, indeed!" muttered Gueulin, under his breath, "he's got as much work as he wants here, the silly idiot!"

About two o'clock, when the young men left the Rue de la Cerisaie with Bachelard, he was completely drunk. They wanted to shove him into a hansom, but the whole neighbourhood was wrapped in solemn silence—not a sound of a wheel, nor even of some belated footstep; so they decided to hold him up. The moon had risen clear and bright; it whitened all the pavement. In the deserted streets their voices assumed a grave sonority.

"For God's sake hold up, uncle, do! You're enough to break our arms!"

Overcome by maudlin sentiment, he was now in his tenderest, most moralising mood.

"Go away, Gueulin! go away!" he spluttered out. "I don't want you to see your uncle in such a state as this! No, my lad, it's not proper you should. Go away!"

And when his nephew called him an old swindler, he said:

"Swindler? That doesn't mean anything. One must command respect. For my part I esteem women—virtuous women, that is; and if there's no feeling, why, it disgusts me. Go away, Gueulin! you're making your uncle blush. These gentlemen are sufficient help."

"Very well, then," said Gueulin, "you must give me a hundred francs. I really must have them to pay my rent, or they will turn me out."

At this unexpected demand Bachelard's drunkenness increased to such an extent that he had to be propped up against the shutters of a shop. He stuttered out:

"Eh? What? A hundred francs? Don't search my pockets—I've only got a few pence. So that you may squander the money in some brothel? No, I will never encourage you in such vicious conduct! I remember my promise to your mother on her death-bed, when she confided you to my care! Now, if you search my pockets, I'll call out!"

And he meandered on, inveighing against the dissolute ways of young men, and insisting upon virtue as a necessity.

"Well, anyhow," cried Gueulin, "I have not got so far as swindling whole families! Ah, you know what I mean! If I were to split, you would jolly soon give me my hundred francs!"

His uncle instantly became stone-deaf, as he went stumbling and grunting along. In the narrow street where they were, behind the church of Saint Gervais, only one white lamp burned feebly as a night-light, showing a huge number painted on the grained glass. A sort of muffled noise inside the house could be heard; a few thin rays of light came through the fast-closed shutters.

"I've had about enough of this!" exclaimed Gueulin, abruptly. "Excuse me, uncle; I left my umbrella upstairs."

So saying, he went into the house. Bachelard, indignant and full of disgust, declared that one ought at least to have a little respect for women. Immorality of that sort would be the ruin of France. Finally, at the Place de l'Hôtel-de-Ville, Octave and Trublot found a cab, into which they thrust him as if he were a bundle.

"Rue d'Enghien," they told the driver. "You must pay yourself. Look in his pockets."

On Thursday the marriage-contract was signed before the notary, Maître Rénaudin, Rue de Grammont. Just as they were starting, there had been another furious row at the Josserands', as the father, in a moment of supreme revolt, had told his wife that she was responsible for the lie to which they wanted him to subscribe. And once again they flung their families in each other's teeth. Where did they suppose he was going to get ten thousand francs every six months? Such an agreement was monstrous; it drove him mad. Uncle Bachelard, who was there, kept slapping his heart as he bubbled over with fresh promises, now that he had arranged things in such a way that he would not have to part with a farthing, tenderly declaring that he would never leave his dear little Berthe in a fix. But the father, exasperated, only shrugged his shoulders, asking him if he really thought him quite a fool.

However, at the notary's, the reading of the contract, drawn up from notes furnished by Duveyrier, somewhat soothed Monsieur Josserand. There was no mention of an insurance; moreover, the first instalment of ten thousand francs was only to fall due six months after the marriage. This, at any rate, left them breathing-time. Auguste, who listened most attentively, showed some signs of impatience. He looked at smiling Berthe, at the Josserands, at Duveyrier, and at last ventured to speak of the insurance, a guarantee which he thought it only reasonable should be mentioned. Then they all appeared astonished. What was the good of that? The thing was understood; and they quickly signed the paper, while Maître Rénaudin, a most obliging young man, said not a word, but handed the ladies a pen. It was not till they had got outside that Madame Duveyrier ventured to express her surprise. Not a syllable had been uttered about any insurance. The dowry, so they understood, was to have been paid by uncle Bachelard. But Madame Josserand naively remarked that her brother's name had never even been mentioned by her in connection with so paltry a sum. It was the whole of his fortune that he would eventually leave to Berthe.

That same evening a cab came to take away Saturnin.

His mother had declared that it was too dangerous to let him be present at the ceremony. It would never do, at a wedding, to turn loose among the guests a lunatic who talked of spitting people; and Monsieur Josserand, half broken-hearted, had been obliged to get the poor lad into the Moulineaux Asylum, kept by Doctor Chassagne. The cab was brought up to the porch at dusk. Saturnin came down, holding Berthe's hand, and thinking he was going into the country with her. But when he had got into the cab, he struggled furiously, breaking the windows and shaking his blood-stained fists. Monseiur Josserand went upstairs in tears, overcome by this departure in the gloom; his ears yet rang with the wretched boy's shrieks, mingled with the cracking of the whip and the galloping of the horse.

During dinner, as tears again rose to his eyes at the sight of Saturnin's empty place, his wife, not understanding, impatiently exclaimed:

"Come, that's enough, isn't it, sir? Are you going to your daughter's wedding with that funereal face? Listen! By all that I count most sacred, by my father's grave, I swear to you that her uncle will pay the first ten thousand francs. He swore solemnly to me that he would, as we were leaving the notary's!"

Monsieur Josserand did not even answer. He spent the night in addressing wrappers. By the chill daybreak he finished his second thousand, and had earned six francs. Several times he raised his head, listening, as usual, if Saturnin moved in his room close by. Then, at the thought of Berthe, he worked with fresh ardour. Poor child! she would have liked a wedding-dress of white *moiré*. Never mind; six francs would enable her to have more flowers in her bridal bouquet.

VIII

The marriage before the mayor had taken place on the Thursday. Ever since a quarter-past ten some of the lady guests were waiting in the Josserands' drawing-room, the religious ceremony having been fixed for half-past eleven at Saint-Roch. Madame Juzeur was there, in black silk as usual; Madame Dambreville, squeezed into a gown the colour of faded leaves. Madame Duveyrier was very simply dressed in pale blue. They all three were talking in a low voice among the rows of empty chairs, while Madame Josserand, in the next room, was putting the finishing touches to Berthe's toilette, assisted by the servant and the two bridesmaids, Hortense and Angèle Campardon.

"Oh, it's not that!" murmured Madame Duveyrier; "the family is an honourable one. But I confess that, for Auguste's sake, I am rather afraid of the mother's domineering spirit. One cannot be too careful, you know!"

"No, indeed!" said Madame Juzeur. "One very often not only marries the daughter, but the mother as well; and it is so disagreeable when she interferes in household matters."

At this moment the door of the next room opened, and Angèle ran out, exclaiming:

"A hook, at the bottom of the left-hand drawer! Wait a moment!"

She rushed across the drawing-room, and then ran back again; her white frock, tied at the waist by a broad blue sash, floating behind her like foam at a vessel's wake.

"You're mistaken, I think," resumed Madame Dambreville. "The mother is only too glad to get rid of her girl. The only thing she cares about is her Tuesday at-homes. Then, she has still got another victim."

Valérie now came in, wearing a red dress of extraordinary make. She had hurried up the stairs, fearing she would be late.

"Théophile will never be ready," said she to her sister-in-law. "You know, I dismissed Françoise this morning, and he is looking everywhere for his tie. I left him in such a muddle!"

"The question of health is also a very grave one," continued Madame Dambreville.

"No doubt it is," replied Madame Duveyrier. "We were careful to consult Doctor Juillerat. It seems that the girl has an excellent constitution. The mother's, as you know, is astonishing; and it was that which, in some degree, led us to making a decision, for nothing is more vexatious than sickly relatives whom you have to look after. It is always best to have sound, healthy relations."

"Especially if they have nothing to leave," said Madame Juzeur, in her dulcet voice.

Valérie had taken a seat, but not having the cue to their talk, all out of breath, she asked :

"What ! Eh ? Of whom are you talking ?"

The door was again hastily opened, when one could hear the sounds of quarrelling going on in the other room.

"I tell you the box isn't on the table."

"It's not true ; I saw it there a moment ago."

"Oh, you obstinate thing ! go and see for yourself."

Hortense, also in white, with a large blue sash, passed through the drawing-room. The snowy folds of the muslin made her look older, giving a hardness to her features and a yellowness to her complexion. She returned, furious, with the bridal bouquet, for which they had been hunting for the last five minutes in every part of the disordered room.

"Well, you see," said Madame Dambreville, by way of conclu-ion, "marriages are never made just as one would like. The wisest thing is to come to the best possible arrangement afterwards."

Angèle and Hortense now opened the folding-doors so that the bride's veil might not catch on anything, and Berthe appeared, dressed in white silk, white flowers on a white ground, a white wreath, white bouquet, and spray of white flowers across her skirt, which vanished near the train in a shower of little white buds. In this white array she looked charming, with her fresh complexion, sunny hair, laughing eyes and pretty mouth, the mouth of a girl to whom enlightenment has come.

"How sweet she looks !" cried all the ladies.

They all embraced her, in ecstasies. The Josserands had been at their wits' end to know how to get the couple of thousand francs which the wedding would cost—five hundred francs for the dress, and another fifteen hundred for their share of the dinner and dance expenses. So they were obliged to send Berthe to Doctor Chassagne's asylum to see Saturnin, to whom an aunt had just left a legacy of three thousand francs. Then Berthe, having obtained permission to take her brother out for a drive, coaxed and petted him in the carriage until he was quite dazed, and then took him upstairs to the lawyer for a moment, who, not knowing the poor lad's witless condition, had everything ready for him to sign. Thus it was that the silk dress and the profusion of choice flowers came as a surprise to all these ladies, who, appraising them critically, exclaimed : "Exquisite—most perfect taste !"

Madame Josserand came in, radiant, in a mauve gown, cruel in tint, which made her look bulkier and rounder than ever—a sort of majestic tower. She stormed at Monsieur Josserand, told Hortense to fetch her shawl, and energetically forbade Berthe to sit down.

"Mind, you will crush your flowers !"

"Don't worry yourself," said Clotilde, in her calm voice. "We have plenty of time. Auguste has to come and fetch us."

As they were all waiting in the drawing-room, Théophile suddenly burst in, without a hat, his coat all awry, and his white tie tied so tightly that it looked like a piece of cord. His face, with its scanty moustache and discoloured teeth, was livid; he was trembling all over with rage, like a feverish child.

"What is the matter with you?" asked his sister, in astonishment.

"The matter is—the matter is——"

A fit of coughing cut his sentence short, and he stood there for a minute, choking and spitting in his handkerchief, in a fury at being unable to give vent to his anger. Valérie, disconcerted, watched him, as if some instinct told her the cause for this outburst. At length, he shook his fist at her, ignoring the presence of the bride and of the other ladies.

"Yes; as I was hunting everywhere for my tie, I found a letter in front of the wardrobe."

He nervously crumpled a piece of paper between his fingers. His wife turned pale. She saw the situation at a glance, and, to avoid the scandal of a public explanation, she went out into the room that Berthe had just left.

"Oh! well," said she, quietly, "I would rather not stay, if he is going to behave like a lunatic."

"Leave me alone !" exclaimed Théophile, as Madame Duveyrier tried to pacify him. 'I want to confound her. This time I have got a proof, and there's no doubt about it—none whatever. It shan't be overlooked in that way, for I know the fellow——"

His sister, seizing his arm, shook it with a gesture of authority.

"Be quiet, do! Don't you know where you are? This is not the proper time—do you understand?"

But he began again.

"Yes, it *is* the proper time! I don't care a hang about the others. So much the worse that it has happened to-day. It will be a lesson to everybody."

He lowered his voice, however, and sank exhausted into a chair, almost bursting into tears. Everyone in the drawing-room felt thoroughly uncomfortable. Madame Dambreville and Madame Juzeur politely moved away, affecting not to understand. Madame Josserand, feeling greatly annoyed that an incident of this sort should throw a gloom over the wedding, went into the adjoining room to cheer Valérie up. As for Berthe, she kept looking at her wreath in the glass, and pretended not to hear, while questioning Hortense in a low voice. They whispered together, and the elder sister, pointing out Théophile, added sundry explanations while pretending to be busy in arranging the folds of the veil.

"Oh, that's it!" said the bride, with a chaste air of amusement, as she gazed at Théophile, perfectly self-possessed beneath her aureole of snow-white flowers.

Clotilde, under her breath, was questioning her brother. Madame Josserand came back, spoke to her for a moment, and then returned to the next room. An exchange, this, of diplomatic notes. The husband accused Octave, that bounder, whose head he would punch at church, if he dared to come there. Only the day before, he would swear that he saw him on the steps of Saint-Roch's with his wife. At first he had had his doubts, but now he was perfectly certain; everything tallied—his height, his walk. Yes, madame invented stories about luncheons with her lady friends, or else went into Saint-Roch's with Camille, by the main entrance, to pray. Then she left the child with the chair-keeper, and she and monsieur went off together by the disused way—a dirty passage, where nobody would have thought of looking for her. However, when Octave's name was mentioned, Valérie smiled. It certainly was not with him, so she swore, to Madame Josserand. It was not with anybody at all, for the matter of that, she added, but least of all with him. Feeling strong in the knowledge that truth was on her side, she, in turn, talked of confounding her husband by proving that the letter was not in Octave's handwriting, any more than he was the mysterious gentleman of Saint-Roch's. Madame Josserand, listening, watched her knowingly, merely anxious to discover some way for Valérie to deceive her husband. And she plied her with the most sapient advice.

"Let me manage things; don't you interfere. As he will have it that it is Monsieur Mouret, very well, then, it is Monsieur Mouret. There's no harm, is there, in being seen on the steps of a church with Monsieur Mouret? Only, the letter is rather compromising. It will be a triumph for you when our young friend shows him a couple of lines in his own handwriting. Above all things, mind you say exactly what I do. I can't allow him, you know, to go and spoil such a day as this for us."

When she brought Valérie back, who seemed greatly upset, Théophile was saying to his sister, in a choking voice:

"For your sake, then, I promise not to make a scene here, for it would not be right, on account of this marriage. But, at the church, I cannot answer for anything. If that bounder dares to brave me at the church, in the presence of all my family, I will do for both of them."

Auguste, carefully got up in a black evening coat, with his left eye half closed by the neuralgia that for three days past he had been dreading, now arrived to take his *fiancée* to church. He was accompanied by his father and his brother-in-law, both looking very solemn. There was some little jostling, as they were all rather behind time. Two of the ladies, Madame Duveyrier and Madame Dambreville, were obliged to help Madame Josserand to put on her shawl. It was a sort of huge tapestry shawl with a yellow ground, and she always brought it out on state occasions, albeit the fashion for such things had long since gone by. It enveloped her in folds so ample and so brilliant, that her effect in the streets was almost revolutionary. They had still to wait for Monsieur Josserand, who was looking about under the table for a cuff-link which had been swept into the dust-bin. At last he made his appearance, stammering out excuses, looking forlorn, yet happy, as he led the way downstairs, tightly holding Berthe's arm in his. Auguste and Madame Josserand followed, and the others came after, in go-as-you-please fashion, their chatter disturbing the dignified silence of the vestibule. Théophile had got hold of Duveyrier, whose dignity he upset by his grievance. Pouring out all his woes into his ear, he begged for advice, while Valérie, who had recovered her self-possession, walked modestly in front, Madame Juzeur comforting her tenderly. She appeared not to notice the awful glances hurled at her by her husband.

"Oh, your prayer-book!" cried Madame Josserand, suddenly, in accents of despair.

They had already got into the carriage. Angèle was obliged to go back and fetch the prayer-book bound in white velvet. At last they started. The whole household was there to see them, the maids and the door-keepers. Marie Pichon had come down with Lilitte, dressed as if about to go for a walk. The sight of the bride, looking so pretty and smart, touched her to tears. Monsieur Gourd remarked that second-floor people were the only ones who had not budged—a queer set of lodgers, who always behaved differently from anyone else!

At Saint-Roch both the big doors had been thrown open, and a red carpet extended as far as the pavement. It was raining, and the air was very chilly on this morning in May.

"Thirteen steps," whispered Madame Juzeur to Valérie, as they entered. "That's a bad sign."

As soon as the procession moved up the aisle between the rows of chairs towards the altar, on which the candles burned like stars, the organ overhead burst into a pæan of joy. It was a snug, pleasant-looking church, with its large white windows edged with yellow and pale blue, its dadoes of red marble on the walls and the pillars, its gilded pulpit supported by the four Evangelists, and its side chapels glittering with metal ornaments. The roof was enlivened by sundry paintings of a theatrical sort; crystal chandeliers hung from it, suspended by long cords. As the ladies passed over the broad gratings of the heating apparatus a warm breath penetrated their skirts.

"Are you sure that you have got the ring?" asked Madame Josserand of Auguste, who with Berthe had taken his seat before the altar.

He was in dismay, fearing that he had forgotten it, but subsequently discovered it in his waistcoat pocket. However, she never waited to get his reply. Ever since her entry she stood with a great air of self-importance, scrutinising everybody, watching Trublot and Gueulin, the groomsmen; uncle Bachelard and Campardon, the bride's witnesses; Duveyrier and Doctor Juillerat, witnesses for the bridegroom, and all the host of acquaintances of whom she felt so proud. She had just caught sight of Octave, who was doing his utmost to make room for Madame Hédouin to pass. She drew him aside, behind a pillar, and hastily whispered something to him. The young man did not appear to understand, but seemed bewildered. He bowed, however, with an air of polite compliance.

"I've arranged it," whispered Madame Josserand in Valérie's ear, as she returned and took a seat behind Berthe and Auguste in one of the chairs reserved for the family. Monsieur Josserand, the Vabres, and the Duveyriers were there also. The panting organ now showered forth little pearly notes in roulades, that floated along on great waves of sound. The crush grew greater, as all the seats in the chancel were filled up and people were standing in the aisles. Abbé Mauduit had reserved for himself the joy of pronouncing a blessing upon the nuptials of one of his fair penitents. When he appeared, arrayed in his surplice, he exchanged a friendly smile with the congregation, whose every face he knew.

The choir now struck up the *Veni Creator,* as the organ again rolled forth its song of triumph; and it was just at this moment that Théophile spied Octave, to the left of the chancel, standing before the Chapel of Saint Joseph.

Clotilde endeavoured to keep him back.

"I cannot," he stuttered. "I will never put up with such a thing!" And he made Duveyrier follow him, as the family's representative. The *Veni Creator* went on. A few people looked round.

Théophile, who had talked about head-punching, became so agitated on going up to Octave, that at first he could not say a word, vexed to feel that he was so short, and standing on the tips of his toes.

"Sir," said he at last, "I saw you yesterday with my wife."

The *Veni Creator* was now over, and the sound of his own voice alarmed him. Much annoyed at what was taking place, Duveyrier sought to make him understand how ill-chosen the present place was for such a discussion. The ceremony had now begun before the altar. After a touching address to the happy couple, the priest proceeded to bless the ring:

"Benedic, Domine Deus noster, annulum nuptialem hunc, quem nos in tuo nomine benedicimus."

Then Théophile, growing bolder, repeated in a low voice: "Sir, you were in this church yesterday with my wife."

Octave, still bewildered by Madame Josserand's injunctions, which he had not rightly understood, told the whole little story of their meeting in a frank, easy way.

"Yes, that's quite true. I met Madame Vabre, and we went and looked at the repairs of the Calvary, which my friend Campardon is supervising."

"You admit it!" stammered Théophile, in a fresh access of fury. "You admit it."

Duveyrier felt obliged to tap him on the shoulder in order to soothe him. A boy's voice now rang out a piercing *Amen.*

"Doubtless, you'll recognise this letter!" continued Théophile, offering Octave a piece of paper.

"I say, not here, of all places," whispered Duveyrier, completely scandalised. "You must be off your head, my good fellow."

Octave looked at the piece of paper. There was a fresh stir among the congregation, accompanied by whisperings, elbow-nudgings, and furtive glances over the tops of prayer-books. No one now paid the least attention to the ceremony. Only the bridal couple remained, grave and stiff, before the priest. Then even Berthe herself looked round, and saw Théophile, white with passion, as he talked to Octave. From that moment her thoughts were elsewhere, in the Chapel of Saint Joseph, towards which she shot brilliant glances now and again.

Meanwhile Octave, in an undertone, read as follows:

"My ducky, what fun we had yesterday. Tuesday next, at the Chapel of the Holy Angels, in the confessional."

Having obtained a "yes" from the bridegroom, the assent of a serious man, who signs nothing until he has read it, the priest addressed the bride:

"Will you promise and swear to be faithful to Monsieur Auguste Vabre in all things, as behoves a dutiful wife, and in accordance with God's holy commandment?"

But Berthe, having caught sight of the letter, was fully expecting an interchange of blows, and paid no heed, as she kept looking sideways at the two men from under her veil. There was an embarrassing silence. As last, aware that they were waiting for her, she hastily replied, "Yes, yes!" in a don't-care tone of voice.

The abbé, surprised, looked in the same direction, and guessed that something unusual was taking place in one of the side aisles, and he, in his turn, became absent-minded. The story by this time had gone the round; everybody knew about it. The ladies, pale and grave, never took their eyes off Octave. The men smiled in a discreetly rakish way. And as Madame Josserand, by slight shoulder-shrugs, sought to reassure Madame Duveyrier, Valérie alone seemed to take any interest in the ceremony, for which she was all eyes, as if overwhelmed by tender emotion.

'My ducky, what fun we had yesterday."—Octave read it over again, apparently much surprised.

Then, returning the letter to Théophile, he said :

"I don't know what you mean, sir. That is not my writing. You can see for yourself."

And taking a note-book from his pocket, in which, like a careful fellow, he always put down his expenses, he showed it to Théophile.

"What? Not your writing?" stammered the latter. "You are fooling me; it must be your writing."

The priest was about to make the sign of the cross on Berthe's left hand. As his eyes were elsewhere, he made it on her right one, by mistake.

"In nomine Patris, et Filii et Spiritus Sancti."

"Amen!" responded the choir-boy, who also stood up on tiptoe to see.

At any rate, a scandal had been avoided, Duveyrier having proved to Théophile, in his confusion, that the letter could not have been written by Monsieur Mouret. For the congregation this proved almost a disappointment. Long breaths were drawn and hasty words exchanged. Then, as everyone, still palpitating with excitement, turned round again towards the altar, behold! Auguste and Berthe had become man and wife, she apparently unaware of what was taking place, while he had not missed a single word uttered by the priest, but had given his whole attention to the subject, being merely tormented by neuralgia, which had succeeded in closing his left eye.

"Dear children!" whispered Monsieur Josserand, in a trembling voice, to Monsieur Vabre, who ever since the commencement of the ceremony had been sedulously counting the lighted candles, always making a mistake and beginning all over again.

The organ again pealed forth from the nave; Abbé Mauduit reappeared in his chasuble; the choir had begun the Mass, a choral one of a most grandiose kind. Uncle Bachelard was wandering round from chapel to chapel, reading the Latin epitaphs, which he did not understand. He was particularly interested in the Duc de Créquy's. Trublot and Gueulin, eager for details, had joined Octave, and all three were chuckling behind the pulpit. There were sudden bursts of song, like gusts of wind in a storm; choir-boys swung their censers; and then, as a bell tinkled, there came periods of silence, when one heard the priest mumbling at the altar.

Théophile could not remain in one place; he kept following Duveyrier, whom he overwhelmed by his incoherent talk, baffled for the nonce, and at a loss to comprehend how the gentleman of the assignation was not the gentleman of the letter. The whole congregation continued to observe his every gesture; the entire church, with its procession of priests, its Latin, its music, its incense, excitedly discussed the incident. When, after the *Pater,* the Abbé came down to give the newly-married pair his final benediction, he looked askance at this commotion among his faithful flock, noticing the women's excited expression and the sly merriment of the men, in all the bright light that streamed down upon them from the windows amid the rich appointments of the side chapels and the nave.

"Don't admit anything," whispered Madame Josserand to Valérie, as they moved towards the sacristy after the Mass.

In the sacristy the newly-married pair and their witnesses had, first of all, to sign the register. However, they were kept waiting some time by Campardon, who had taken several ladies to see the newly-restored Calvary at the end of the choir, behind a wooden hoarding. At last he arrived, full of apologies, and signed his name to the register with an enormous flourish. The Abbé Mauduit wished to pay both families a compliment by handing round the pen himself, pointing with his finger to the place where each one had to sign; and he smiled with his air of good-humoured urbanity as he stood in the centre of the solemn room, the woodwork of which was impregnated with the odour of incense.

"Well, mademoiselle," said Campardon to Hortense, "don't you feel tempted to go and do likewise?"

Then he regretted his want of tact. Hortense was the elder sister; she bit her lip. That evening, at the dance, she was expecting to have a definite answer from Verdier; she had been urging him to choose between herself and that creature. So she replied icily:

"There's plenty of time—when it suits me."

And, turning her back upon the architect, she flew at her brother Léon, who had only just arrived, being late, as usual.

"You're a nice fellow! Papa and mamma were in a fine way! You could not even be here in time to see one of your sisters married! At least, we thought you would have come with Madame Dambreville."

"Madame Dambreville does what she likes; I do what I can," said Léon, drily.

There was a coolness between the two. Léon considered that she was keeping him overlong for her own use, and was tired of a *liaison* the boredom of which he had consented to put up with in the sole hope of its leading to some desirable match; and for the last fortnight he had been importuning her to keep her promises. Madame Dambreville, passionately in love, had even complained to Madame Josserand about these fads on the part of her son. His mother, indeed, was all too ready to scold Léon, reproaching him with his want of family affection and regard, since he did not scruple to absent himself from the most solemn ceremonies. Then, in his supercilious voice, the young democrat offered sundry explanations, mentioning unexpected work which had to be done for the deputy whose secretary he was, alluding to a lecture which he had to prepare, and to various other things, besides important visits which he had had to pay.

"A marriage, though, is so quickly got over!" observed Madame Dambreville, without thinking what she was saying, as she looked supplicatingly at him to soften him.

"Not always," he coldly replied.

Then he went up to kiss Berthe and shake hands with his new brother-in-law; while Madame Dambreville grew pale with vexation as, drawing herself up to her full height in her dead-leaf coloured dress, she smiled vaguely at everybody coming in.

It was one long procession of friends, of mere acquaintances, and guests who had thronged the church and now filed into the sacristy. The newly-married pair stood shaking hands continually, both looking delighted yet embarrassed. The Josserands and the Duveyriers found it impossible to introduce everyone. Now and again they exchanged glances of surprise, for Bachelard had brought in people whom nobody knew, and who talked much too loud.

"Oh, look!" whispered Gueulin, "he is kissing the bride! How nice it must smell!"

At last the crowd gradually dispersed. Only the family and a few intimate friends remained. The tale about the much-wronged Théophile had continued to spread during all the hand-shaking and pretty speeches; in fact, nobody talked of anything else while exchanging the usual stereotyped, ready-made compliments. Madame Hédouin, who had just heard the story, looked at Valérie with the amazement of a woman for whom virtue is as the very breath of her being. Doubtless the Abbé Maudit must have received confidential information upon the subject also, for his curiosity seemed appeased, and his manner became more than usually unctuous amid all the secret sorrows of his flock. Here was another gaping sore, which on a sudden had begun to bleed, and over which he must needs fling the mantle of religion! And he sought to say a word in season to Théophile, discreetly dwelling upon the necessity of forgiving injuries, alluding to God's mysterious, unfathomable designs; while endeavouring above all things to quosh the scandal, embracing all his hearers in one broad gesture of pity and despair, as if to hide their shame from the very eye of Heaven itself.

"He's a good one, that parson fellow," murmured Théophile, beside himself as he listened to the homily. "He does not know what has happened."

Valérie, clinging to Madame Juzeur to keep her in countenance, listened with emotion to the conciliatory words which the Abbé Mauduit likewise deemed it his duty to address to her. Then, as all were leaving the church, she stopped short in front of the two fathers, to let Berthe go by on her husband's arm.

"You ought to feel satisfied," said she to Monsieur Josserand, desirous to show that her conscience was clear. "Allow me to congratulate you."

"Yes, yes," said Monsieur Vabre, in his guttural voice, "it's another very great responsibility off our minds."

And while Trublot and Gueulin ran hither and thither, putting all the ladies into their carriages, Madame Josserand, whose appalling shawl caused a block in the traffic, obstinately remained on the pavement to the last, as if to make a public display of her triumph as a mother.

That evening the dinner which took place at the Hôtel du Louvre was also marred by Théophile's unfortunate affair. It was like an epidemic; people talked about it the whole afternoon, and as they drove in the Bois de Boulogne; all the ladies being of the opinion that the husband ought certainly to have waited until the following day before finding the letter. At the dinner, however, only intimate friends were present. The one merry episode was a toast proposed by uncle Bachelard, whom, despite their terror, the Josserands could not help inviting. By the time they got to the joint, indeed, he was intoxicated, and raising his glass, he embarked upon a speech beginning with the phrase, "I am happy in the pleasure I feel." This he repeated over and over again, without ever getting any further, while his hearers were good enough to smile blandly. Auguste and Berthe, both of them utterly worn out, exchanged occasional glances, surprised to find themselves sitting opposite to each other. Then, remembering the reason for this, they looked down, embarrassed, at their plates.

For the dance nearly two hundred invitations had been issued. About half-past nine, people began to arrive. The large red drawing-room was lighted by three chandeliers, chairs having been placed all along the walls, while at one end, in front of the fire-place, the little orchestra was installed. There was also a buffet in an adjoining room, another apartment having been reserved for the two families, to which they could retire.

Just as Madame Duveyrier and Madame Josserand were receiving the first arrivals, that wretched Théophile, whom they had been watching ever since the morning, was guilty of most outrageous conduct. Campardon had asked Valérie for the pleasure of the first waltz. She laughed, and her husband considered that this levity was tantamount to a provocation.

"Yes, you laugh, you laugh!" he stuttered, "but tell me who sent that letter! It must have come from somebody!"

It had taken him the whole afternoon to disengage that one idea from the nebulous perplexity with which Octave's reply had filled him. Now, he was positive upon one point; if it was not from Monsieur Mouret, it was from somebody else. And the name of that somebody, this is what he absolutely *would* know. As Valérie, without answering, was moving away, he caught hold of her arm and twisted it viciously, like an infuriated child, saying:

"I'll break it, if you don't tell me who sent that letter."

Valérie, terrified, could hardly suppress a cry of pain as she turned quite white. Campardon felt her sink back on to his shoulder in one of those nervous seizures which occasionally would torture her for hours together. He had only just time to take her into the ante-room, where he placed her on the sofa. Madame Juzeur and Madame Dambreville followed him, and proceeded to unlace her, while he discreetly withdrew.

Meanwhile, in the ball-room, only two or three persons had noticed this brief scene of violence. Madame Duveyrier and Madame Josserand continued to receive the guests, who, streaming in, gradually filled the vast room with gay dresses and black coats. There was quite a murmur of pretty speeches as all their smiling faces revolved round the bride—the fat faces of fathers and mothers, the angular profiles of their daughters, and the delicate, sympathetic countenances of young married women. At the far end of the room a violinist was tuning his A string. It gave out little plaintive cries.

"Sir, I have to ask your pardon," said Théophile, accosting Octave, whose eyes had met his when he was twisting Valérie's arm. "Anyone in my place would have suspected you, would he not? But I am anxious to shake hands with you, to show you that I am sensible of the mistake that I made."

Shaking him by the hand, he took him aside, feeling constrained to pour forth his woes and to find some confidant to whom he could unbosom himself.

"Ah! sir, if I were to tell you——"

And he began to talk at length about his wife. As a girl she was delicate, and people said, jokingly, that marriage would set her right. She could not get fresh air in her parents' shop, where for three months he used to see her, when she seemed so nice, so obedient; somewhat melancholy in temperament, but, for all that, quite charming.

"Well, sir, marriage did *not* set her right—very far from it! After a few weeks she was simply awful; we could never agree about anything. Quarrels about nothing at all; changes of mood every minute; laughing, crying, without my knowing why or wherefore. Absurd sentimentalisms; ideas fit to take your breath away; an eternal mania for driving other people wild. In short, sir, my home has been turned into a perfect hell upon earth!"

"It's very odd," murmured Octave, who felt obliged to say something.

Then the husband, livid with excitement, straightened his stumpy legs, to avoid looking ridiculous and with a view to appearing dignified, as he approached the subject of what he termed his wretched wife's misconduct. Twice he had had his suspicions; but he was too generous ever to harbour such a thought. On this occasion, however, he was obliged to yield to evidence. There was absolutely no doubt about it whatever, was there? And with his trembling fingers he felt about in his waistcoat pocket for the letter.

"If she did such a thing for money I could understand it," he added, "but they don't give her any; that I'm sure, or else I should find it out. Then what the deuce possesses her to do such a thing? I am always very nice to her. She's got everything she wants at home. I can't make it out. If you can understand it, sir, pray tell me."

"It's very odd, very odd," repeated Octave, who found all these confidences embarrassing, and who sought to escape from them.

But the husband would not let him go, in his feverish anxiety to get at the whole truth. At this moment Madame Juzeur came back, and whispered in Madame Josserand's ear, who was just making her best bow of welcome to a wealthy jeweller of the Palais-Royal, and who, turning right round, hastily followed her.

"I am afraid your wife has got a very bad attack," said Octave to Théophile.

"Never mind about her," exclaimed the other, exasperated at not being taken ill, too, so that they might look after him. "She's only too glad to have hysterics; it always makes everybody sympathise with her. My health is no better than hers; but I have never been unfaithful to her, not I."

Madame Josserand did not return. Among intimate friends the rumour got about that Valérie was struggling in the most frightful convulsions. It needed men to hold her down; but, as they had been obliged partially to undress her, the proffered services of Trublot and of Gueulin were declined. Meanwhile the orchestra was playing a quadrille; Berthe was about to open the ball with Duveyrier, in his magisterial capacity, as her partner, while Auguste, not being able to find Madame Josserand, took Hortense to form their *vis-à-vis*. The news of Valérie's seizure was kept a secret from the bridal pair, for fear it might have unpleasant effects. The dance grew lively, and there was a sound of silvery laughter under the gleaming chandeliers. A polka, the measure of which the violins vigorously marked, set all the couples whirling round the room amid a maze of floating trains.

"Doctor Juillerat! Where's Doctor Juillerat?" cried Madame Josserand, rushing out.

The doctor had been invited, but no one had yet noticed his arrival. Then she no longer contained the rage that had slumbered within her ever since the morning. To Octave and Campardon she expressed herself in the most unvarnished manner.

"I've just had about enough of it. A pleasant thing, isn't it, for my daughter, all this perpetual fuss about adultery?"

She looked about for Hortense, and at last observed her talking to a gentleman of whom she could only see the back, but whom she recognised by his broad shoulders. It was Verdier. This served to increase her ill-humour. She coldly summoned her daughter, and told her in a whisper that it would be better if she remained at her mother's disposal on an occasion such as this. Hortense ignored the rebuke. She was triumphant, for Verdier had just fixed their marriage for June—in two months' time.

"Hold your tongue," said her mother.

"I assure you he has, mamma. He sleeps out three times a week, so as to accustom the other woman to it, and in a fortnight he is going to stop away altogether. It will be all over then, and I shall get him."

"Do hold your tongue; I've had far more than enough of your romance! Be good enough, please, to wait at the door until Doctor Juillerat comes, and send him to me directly he does. On no account mention a word of this to your sister!"

Then she went back into the adjoining room, while Hortense muttered something about her not wanting anybody, thank goodness, to approve of her conduct, and that they would all be nicely sold when they discovered that she had made a better match than the rest. She took her stand, however, in the doorway to watch for Doctor Juillerat's arrival.

The orchestra was now playing a waltz. Berthe was dancing with her husband's cousin, so as to get rid of her relations in turn. Madame Duveyrier had not been able to refuse uncle Bachelard, who made her most uncomfortable by puffing into her face. The heat increased; the buffet was thronged by gentlemen who mopped their brows. Two little girls hopped about together in a corner, while the mothers, sitting apart, mused dreamily upon the wedding of their own daughters that somehow never took place. Congratulations were showered upon the two fathers—Monsieur Vabre and Monsieur Josserand who sat side by side the whole evening, neither uttering a word. Everyone appeared to be enjoying themselves and declared that it was a most delightful ball. It's gaiety was of the right sort, so Campardon sententiously observed.

Though the architect gallantly professed great concern at Valérie's condition, he managed not to miss a single dance. It occurred to him that he would send his daughter Angèle, in his name, to ask for news. The girl, whose childish curiosity had been deeply excited by this lady about whom everyone was talking, was delighted at being able to go into the adjoining room; but, as she did not return, Campardon took the liberty of putting his head round the door. He saw his daughter standing by the couch intently watching Valérie, whose breasts, as spasms shook her, protruded from her unloosened stays. There were loud feminine cries of protest; he must not come in; so he withdrew, declaring that he only wanted to know how she was getting on.

"No better, I fear; no better!" he said, mournfully, to enquirers at the door. "There are four of them holding her down. What a frame the woman must have, to fling herself about like that without hurting herself!"

There was now quite a group of sympathisers. The slightest phases of the attack were discussed in an undertone. Ladies, hearing what had taken place, ran up, sympathetically, in the pauses of a quadrille, entered the little room, brought back details to the men, and then went on dancing. It became a sort of mysterious corner for the interchange of whispers and glances in the midst of the ever-increasing din of the dance.

Théophile, meanwhile, forsaken and alone, walked up and down in front of the door, tortured by this one idea that he was being made a fool of, and that he ought not to tolerate it.

Doctor Juillerat now swiftly crossed the ball-room, accompanied by Hortense, who was explaining matters. They were followed by Madame Duveyrier. Some persons appeared surprised; the air was rife with fresh rumours. No sooner had the doctor arrived than Madame Josserand came out of the room with Madame Dambreville. Her fury was increasing. She had just emptied two bottles of water over Valérie's head; never before had she seen hysterics reach such a pitch as that. Now she determined to go the round of the ball-room to put an end to all silly gossip by her presence. However, so terrible was her step, and so acid her smile, that, as she sailed past, everyone in her wake divined her secret.

Madame Dambreville never left her. Ever since the morning she had talked to her about Léon in vague terms of complaint, endeavouring to persuade her to intercede with him on her behalf, and so patch up their intimacy. She pointed to him as he was escorting a gaunt girl to her seat and pretending to pay her great attention.

"He avoids us, do you see?" she said, with a faint smile, while trembling with suppressed emotion. "Do scold him for not even looking at us."

"Léon!" cried Madame Josserand. And as he approached she said bluntly, being in no mood to wrap up her meaning: "Why are you angry with Madame Dambreville? She bears you no ill-will. Go and make it up with her. Sulking won't do any good."

And she left them thus mutually embarrassed. Madame Dambreville took Léon's arm, and they both repaired to a recess, wher they spent some time in talk, and then left the ball-room togethe in an affectionate manner. She had faithfully promised to arrange marriage for him in the autumn.

Meanwhile, Madame Josserand went along distributing smiles and as she came to Berthe, all breathless with dancing, looking ros and rumpled in her white dress, she was seized with sudden emotion She clasped the girl in her arms, appalled perhaps by a vagu association of ideas, as she recollected Valérie lying there with he face convulsed and distorted.

"My poor darling, my poor darling!" she murmured, as she gav her two resounding kisses.

"Well, how is she?" asked Berthe, coolly.

Instantly Madame Josserand's severe look returned. What Berthe knew about it, then? Why, of course, she did; everybod knew about it. It was only her husband over there, with the ol lady at the buffet, who was still ignorant of what had happened. Sh had even intended to ask someone to tell him all about it, for i made him look so silly always to be a day behind the news.

"And I, all the while, have been struggling to keep matte dark!" cried Madame Josserand, beside herself. "Well, well, shan't trouble about it further, only the thing must be put a sto to. I will not allow them to make you ridiculous."

As a matter of fact, everybody did know, though the affair wa not talked about, so as not to cast any gloom over the ball. Th first expressions of sympathy had been drowned by the orchestra and now, as the dancers became more free, they all found matte for laughter in the affair. It was growing late, and the heat became intense. Servants handed round refreshments. On a sofa overcome by fatigue, two little girls had fallen asleep in each other' arms, cheek touching cheek. Near the orchestra, to the sonorou grunting of a 'cello, Monsieur Vabre had decided to entertai Monsieur Josserand with the details of his monumental work especially mentioning a doubt which for a fortnight had harasse him, regarding the real works of two painters of the same name Close by, Duveyrier, in the centre of a group, was bitterly censurin the Emperor for having permitted the production, at the Comédi Française, of a play which attacked modern society. But wheneve the band struck up a waltz or a polka, the men had to move, a couple after couple swelled the dance, while skirts swept the polishe floor, filling the heated air with invisible dust and a vague odour of musk.

"She is better," said Campardon, running up, after another peep round the door. "One may go in now."

Certain of the sterner sex made the venture. Valérie was still lying at full length, but the hysteria had subsided, and, for decency's sake, her breasts had been covered over by a napkin found lying on the sideboard. At the window, Madame Juzeur and Madame Duveyrier stood listening to Doctor Juillerat, who was explaining that attacks of this kind were sometimes relieved by the application of hot-water compresses to the neck. Then, as the patient noticed Octave coming in with Campardon, she beckoned to him, addressing him incoherently, as if in a dream. He was obliged to sit down beside her, at the doctor's special request, who was above all things anxious to avoid annoying her. Thus, the young man listened to her disclosures, just as, earlier in the evening, he had listened to those of her husband. Trembling with fright, she took him for her lover and besought him to hide her. All at once she recognised him and burst into tears, as she expressed her gratitude to him for his lie at Mass that morning. With the greedy desire of a schoolboy, Octave thought of that other fit of hysterics, which he had tried to turn to advantage, He was now her friend, and she would tell him everything; better so, perhaps.

At this moment, Théophile, rampant at the door, tried to enter. Other men had gone inside, so why should not he? This, however, created quite a panic. At the mere sound of his voice, Valérie's trembling fits came back again. Everybody feared that she would have another seizure. As, struggling for admission, he was pushed back by the ladies, he kept doggedly repeating :

"I only ask her for the name; let her tell me that."

Then Madame Josserand, coming up at this juncture, gave reins to her wrath. Pulling Théophile aside into a little room, to avoid a scene, she faced him, furious :

"Look here, are you going to hold your tongue, sir, or are you not? The whole day long you have been bothering us to death with your nonsensical rubbish. You've no tact, sir, no tact whatever. On a wedding-day one does not continue harping on such a thing as this!"

"Excuse me, madam," he murmured, "but the matter is one that concerns me. You have nothing whatever to do with it."

"Haven't I, though! I am a member of your family now, sir,

and do you suppose I find your affair amusing because of m daughter? A nice wedding she's had, thanks to you! Not anothe word, sir; you are utterly wanting in tact!"

He looked about him, bewildered, as if to find someone to tak his part. But, by their frigid mien, all the ladies showed that the judged him with like severity. He had no tact, that was the ver word; for really there were times when one ought positively to b able to control one's temper. Even his own sister sided against hin When he again protested, he created a general revolt. No, no, a reply was futile; conduct such as his was simply monstrous.

This clamorous rejoinder silenced him. He looked so scared, s puny, with his slender limbs and his face like a stale spinster's, tha the women tittered contemptuously. When one had not the where withal to give a woman pleasure, one ought not to marry. Hortens summed him up in a single disdainful glance, and little Angéle whom they had forgotten, kept hovering about him with her sh air, as if she were looking for something, and he retreated in blush ing embarrassment before these portly women, who surrounded hin with their opulent hips. They felt, however, that the matter mus be adjusted in some way or other. Valérie had begun to sob agair while the doctor kept bathng her temples. Understanding on another at a glance, they were drawn together by one commo feeling of defence. They cudgelled their brains to try and see how t explain the letter to Théophile.

"Bah!" muttered Trublot, who had just joined Octave. "That' easy enough. Say that it was addressed to the maid."

Madame Josserand overheard his suggestion. She looked roun at him, her eyes sparkling with admiration. Then she addresse Théophile.

"Do you suppose, sir, that an innocent woman would lower her self to offer any explanation when accused in such a brutal fashio as you have accused her? I am at liberty to speak, however. Tha letter was dropped by Françoise, the maidservant whom your wif was obliged to discharge on account of her dissolute conduc There, will that satisfy you? Aren't you ashamed to look us in th face?"

At first Théophile shrugged his shoulders incredulously. But a the ladies looked so serious, and met his objections with irresistib logic. To complete his discomfiture, Madame Duveyrier angril denounced his conduct as abominable, and declared that she woul have nothing more to do with him. Then, vanquished, yearning fo someone to embrace him, he threw his arms round Valérie's neck, beseeching her to forgive him. It was positively touching. Even Madame Josserand seemed much moved.

"It is always best to come to some understanding," she observed, with relief. "The day won't end so badly, after all."

When they had dressed Valérie, and she appeared in the ballroom on Théophile's arm, the gaiety of the guests became complete. It was by this time nearly three o'clock; people had begun to leave, and still the band played quadrille after quadrille with final feverish energy. Men smiled at one another behind the backs of the reconciled pair. Some medical remark of Campardon's about poor Théophile sent Madame Juzeur into ecstasies. Girls crowded to look at Valérie, and then re-assumed their sheepish airs, as their mothers, scandalised, glared at them. Berthe, who at last was dancing with her husband, must have whispered something in his ear, for he turned his head on hearing the story about Théophile, and, without getting out of step, he watched his brother with astonishment and the superiority of a man to whom things of that sort could never happen. As a finale, there was a galop, when everybody lost all restraint in the stifling heat and the lurid light of the candles, that, flickering, caused their sockets to split.

"You are a great friend of hers, I suppose?" asked Madame Hédouin, as she whirled round on Octave's arm, having accepted his invitation to dance.

The young man almost fancied that he felt a slight shiver agitate her straight, calm figure.

"Nothing of the sort," he replied. "They mixed me up in the matter, to my great annoyance. The poor devil has swallowed everything."

"It's a great shame," she said, in her grave way.

Octave must surely have been mistaken, for, as he withdrew his arm from her waist, Madame Hédouin was not even out of breath; her eyes were untroubled, her hair as smooth as ever. But before the ball ended there was another disgraceful incident. Uncle Bachelard, who at the buffet had put the finishing touch to his carousal, now ventured upon a rare piece of merriment. He was suddenly seen dancing a grossly indecent dance in front of Gueulin. This time there was a general protest. It was all very well to earn lots of money, but really there were limits which no decent-minded man ought ever to overstep, especially when young people were present. In shame and despair, Monsieur Josserand got his brother-in-law to withdraw, while Duveyrier did not conceal his intense disgust.

At four o'clock the bridal couple returned to the Rue de Choiseul. They brought Théophile and Valérie back in the carriage. As they went up to the second floor, where an apartment had been furnished for them, they met Octave, who was also going upstairs to bed. The young man politely sought to stand aside, but Berthe made a like movement and they bumped against each other.

"Oh, I beg your pardon, mademoiselle!" said he.

At the word "mademoiselle" they were much amused. She looked at him, and he remembered the first time their eyes had met on this very staircase, her merry, bold glance, which for him again possessed something charmingly inviting. Perhaps they understood each other. She blushed; and he went on upstairs to his room alone, amid the death-like silence of the upper floors.

Auguste, with his left eye closed, and half-mad with the neuralgia, which had persecuted him all day long, had already reached the apartment, where other members of the family now assembled. Then, just as she was leaving Berthe, Valérie, in a sudden fit of emotion, impulsively embraced her, so completely crumpling her white dress, and, kissing her, she said in a low voice:

"Ah, my dear, I hope you'll be more lucky than I was!"

IX

Two days later, about seven o'clock, as Octave got to the Campardons' in time for dinner, he found Rose by herself, dressed in a cream-coloured silk dressing-gown trimmed with white lace.

"Do you expect anybody?" he asked.

"Oh, no!" she said, looking somewhat confused. "We will have dinner directly Achille comes in."

Latterly the architect had been much worried, and never came back to meals at the proper time, but at last he appeared, looking flushed and scared, abusing the business that had delayed him. Then every night he went off somewhere, making all sorts of excuses appointments at cafés, social gatherings and the like. Thus Octave often kept Rose company until eleven o'clock, for he had begun to see that the husband, in taking him as a boarder, only wanted him as a companion for his wife. She used gently to complain as she expressed her fears. Oh, yes, she let Achille do just as he liked, only she always felt anxious if he was not home by midnight!

"Don't you think he looks rather sad lately?" she asked, in her tenderly timorous way.

No, Octave had not remarked it. "I rather think he seems worried. The restorations at Saint-Roch are probably causing him a deal of bother."

But she shook her head, and made no further remark. Then she showed her kindly interest in Octave by asking him how he had spent his day, affectionately, as if she were his mother or his sister. During the whole time—nearly nine months—that he had been their boarder, she treated him thus, as if he were one of the family.

At last Campardon appeared.

"Good evening, my pet! good evening, my darling!" said he, fondly kissing her like an affectionate husband. "Another idiot again kept me standing a whole hour in the street!"

Octave, moving away, heard them exchange a few words under their breath.

"Is she coming?"

"No; what's the use? Whatever you do, don't worry about it."

"You swore that she would come?"

"Well, there she *is* coming. Are you pleased? I only did it for your sake."

Then they sat down to table. During the whole of dinner-time they talked about the English language, which little Angèle, a fortnight ago, had begun to learn. Campardon had suddenly insisted upon the necessity for a young lady to know English, and, as Lisa had come to them from an actress who had just returned from London, every meal was devoted to discussing the English names for the dishes that were brought in. On that evening, after long and ineffectual attempts to pronounce the word "rump-steak," they were obliged to send the meat away, for Victoire had left it too long at the fire, and it was as tough as boot-leather.

During dessert, a ring at the bell made Madame Campardon start.

"It is madame's cousin," said Lisa, on returning, in the injured tone of a domestic to whom one has neglected to communicate some family secret.

It was, in fact, Gasparine. She wore a plain black stuff dress, with her thin face and jaded shop-girl air. Snug in her cream-coloured dressing-gown, Rose, looking plump and fresh, got up to greet her, with tears in her eyes.

"Oh, my dear," she murmured, "this *is* nice of you! We will let bygones be bygones, won't we?"

Then, embracing her, she kissed her twice, effusively. Octave was about to withdraw discreetly, but they insisted upon his remaining; he was one of the family. So he amused himself by watching the whole scene. Campardon, at first greatly disconcerted, avoided looking at the women, but fussed about in search of a cigar; while Lisa, as she roughly removed the dinner-service, exchanged glances with the astonished Angèle.

At length the architect addressed his daughter: "This is your cousin of whom you have heard us speak. Go and give her a kiss."

Angèle kissed her in her sulky way, feeling uncomfortable beneath the scrutiny of Gasparine's governess eyes, as she said how old she was and what she was learning. Then, as they went out into the drawing-room, she slunk behind Lisa, who, banging the door, remarked, without any fear of being overheard:

"Things are coming to a pretty pitch!"

In the drawing-room Campardon uneasily began to make excuses.

"Upon my word, it was not my idea, but Rose's; she wanted to make it up. Every day, for more than a week, she kept saying, 'Do go and fetch her.' So at last I obeyed."

Then, as if he felt that he ought to convince Octave, he led him aside to the window.

"Well, well, women are just women, you know. To me the whole thing was a bore, because I dread scenes myself. With one on the right, and the other on the left, no squabbling was possible. However, I had to give in. Rose declares that we shall all be far happier. Well, we'll try it. It depends upon those two if my life is a comfortable one or the reverse."

Meanwhile, Rose and Gasparine sat on the sofa side by side. They talked of old times, of days spent with good papa Domergue, at Plassans. Rose at that time had a complexion the colour of lead, and the puny limbs of a child that has been ailing ever since its birth; while Gasparine, at fifteen already a woman, was tall and attractive-looking, with beautiful eyes. Now they hardly recognised each other—the one cool and plump in her enforced chastity, and the other dried up, consumed by the furnace of perpetual nervous passion. For a moment Gasparine felt mortified, as with her sallow face and shabby gown she formed such a contrast to Rose, arranged in silk, whose soft, white neck was swathed in filmy lace. But she mastered this touch of jealousy, at once accepting her position of poor relation grovelling before her cousin's grace and elegance.

"Well, what of your health?" she enquired, under her breath. "Achille spoke to me about it. Is it no better?"

"No, no better," replied Rose, mournfully. "I can eat, you see, and I look perfectly well. But it doesn't get any better; it never will get any better."

As she began to cry, Gasparine, in her turn, embraced her, pressing her close to her flat, burning bosom; while Campardon hastily endeavoured to console them.

"Why do you cry?" she asked, with motherly tenderness. "The great thing is that you are not in pain. What does it matter, if you always have people about you who love you?"

Rose, growing calmer, now smiled through her tears. Then, carried away by his feelings, Campardon clasped them both in one embrace, as, kissing them, he murmured :

"Yes, yes, we will all love one another; and love you, too, my poor darling. You will see how well everything will go now that we have become united."

Then, turning to Octave :

"Say what you like, my boy, there's nothing like home life, after all."

The evening ended delightfully. Campardon, who, if at home, usually went to sleep directly after dinner, got back some of the quondam gaiety of his artist days, as he rehearsed the old jokes and the loose songs of the Ecole des Beaux Arts. When Gasparine was leaving, about eleven o'clock, Rose insisted on accompanying her, in spite of the difficulty which, that day, she found in walking. Leaning over the banisters, in the solemn silence of the staircase, she called after her cousin :

"Come and see us often !"

Next day, feeling interested, Octave tried to sound Gasparine at the shop, as they were sorting a consignment of linen goods. But she gave him curt answers, and he felt that she was hostile to him, being vexed that he was a witness of the reconciliation of the previous evening. Moreover, she did not like him; even in their business relations she showed towards him a kind of spite. For a long while past she had seen through the game he was pursuing with regard to the mistress, and for his assiduous courtship she had only black looks and a contemptuous curl of the lip. This caused him occasional uneasiness. As long as this lanky devil of a girl put out her bony fingers to part them, he had the impression, at once firm and unpleasant, that Madame Hédouin would never become his.

Octave, however, had given himself six months. Four had hardly passed, and he was growing impatient. Every morning he asked himself whether he should not hasten matters somewhat, since he saw such slight advance towards gaining the affection of this woman, always so icy and so gentle. However, she showed real esteem for him, taken by his large ideas, by his dreams of huge modern warehouses, unloading millions of bales of merchandise in the streets of Paris. Often, when her husband was not there, as she and the young man opened the letters of a morning, she detained him and consulted him, glad of his advice. Thus a sort of commercial intimacy was established between the two. Their hands met amid piles of invoices; as they counted rows of figures, each felt the other's warm breath touching their cheeks in moments of excitement over the cash-box after unusually lucky receipts. Of such moments he even sought to take advantage, his plan now being to touch her affections through her tradeswoman instinct, and to conquer her on some day of weakness when excited by the good news of some unlooked-for sale. So he kept waiting for some surprising stroke of luck, that thus should deliver her up to him. However, whenever she did not keep him talking business to her, she at once resumed her quiet tone of authority, politely ordering him to do this or that, just as she would the other shopmen. In fact, she superintended the whole establishment, coldly beautiful, with a man's little cravat round her classic neck, and girt in her demure, tightly-fitting bodice of eternal black.

About this time, as Monsieur Hédouin became ill, he went to take a course of the waters at Vichy, much to Octave's undisguised delight. Though as cold as marble, Madame Hédouin, during this term of widowhood, would, as he thought, relent. But vainly did he watch for a single shiver, a single languorous symptom of desire. Never had she seemed so active, her head so clear, her eye so bright. Rising at day-break, she herself received the consignments of goods in the basement, looking as busy as a clerk with her pen behind her ear. She was ubiquitous; upstairs, downstairs, in the linen department, in the silk warehouse, superintending the window-dressers and the saleswomen, moving noiselessly about among the piles without getting so much as one speck of dust. When meeting her in some of these narrow gangways between walls of woollen stuffs and piles of napkins, Octave would stand aside awkwardly, on purpose, so that for a second she might be crushed close against his breast. But so busy did she seem, that he hardly felt her dress brush past him. Moreover, he was much embarrassed by Mademoiselle Gasparine's cold eyes, which were ever steadily fixed upon them at such moments as these.

However, the young fellow did not despair. At times he thought he had reached the goal of his desire, and was already mapping out his life for the day, so close at hand, when he would be the lover of his employer's wife. He had kept Marie on merely as an aid to his patience; nevertheless, though obliging and cheap, she might eventually prove troublesome with her fidelity of the whipped-cur species. And, while always going to her on nights when he was dull, he bethought himself of some method of breaking off their intimacy. To do this abruptly seemed inexpedient. One holiday morning, when bound for the bed of his neighbour's wife, while his neighbour was taking an early constitutional, the idea possessed him of giving Marie up to her Jules, and of letting them fall into one another's arms, so amorous that, with conscience clear, he could retire. A kind action, after all; so touching, indeed, that it left him quit of all remorse in the matter. Nevertheless, he waited, not wishing to be without female consolation of some kind.

At the Campardons' another complication gave Octave matter for reflection. He felt that the moment was coming for him to get his meals elsewhere. For three weeks Gasparine had been making herself thoroughly at home there; her authority, day by day, increased. First she began by coming every evening, then she made her appearance at lunch, and, in spite of her work at the shop, she began to undertake everything, whether it was Angèle's education, or the purchase of provisions for the house. Rose never ceased saying to Campardon: "Ah, if Gasparine only lived with us!" Yet every time the architect, conscientiously scrupulous, blushed, as he shame-facedly replied:

"No, no; that would never do! Besides, where could she sleep?"

And he explained that he should have to give up his study to Gasparine as a bedroom, he moving his table and plans into the drawing-room. Certainly, it would not inconvenience him at all, and one day, perhaps, he would agree to the alteration, for he did not want a drawing-room, and his study was too small for all the work that he now had in hand. Yet, Gasparine, after all, had better stay where she was. It was no good living in such hugger-mugger style.

About that time he was obliged to go to Evreux for a couple of days. The work for the archbishop worried him. He had acceded to the wishes of monseigneur, though no credit had been opened for the purpose, to construct new kitchens and heating apparatus; the expenses for this seemed likely to be very heavy, far too heavy to include in the cost of repairs. Besides this, the pulpit, for which there was a grant of three thousand francs, would cost ten, at the very least. For safety's sake, he desired to come to some arrangement with the archbishop.

Rose did not expect him home before Sunday night; but he arrived in the middle of lunch, and his sudden appearance quite scared them. Gasparine was at table, sitting between Octave and Angèle. They pretended to be perfectly at their ease, but there was evidently something mysterious in the air. Lisa had just shut the drawing-room door, obedient to a despairing gesture of her mistress, while Gasparine kicked certain pieces of paper out of sight which lay about here and there. When he talked of changing his things, they stopped him.

"Do wait a moment. Take some coffee, as you lunched at Evreux."

Then, as he noticed how embarrassed Rose was, she flung her arms round his neck.

"Don't scold me, dear. If you had not come until this evening you would have found everything straight."

She tremblingly opened the folding-doors, and took him into the drawing-room and the study. A mahogany bedstead, brought in that morning from a furniture dealer's, stood in the place of his drawing-table, which had been moved into the middle of the next room. But nothing had been put straight yet; portfolios were jumbled up with some of Gasparine's clothes, while the Virgin of the bleeding Heart was leaning against the wall, propped up by a new wash-hand basin.

"It was to be a surprise!" murmured Madame Campardon, as, with swelling heart, she hid her face in the folds of her spouse's waistcoat.

Much moved, he looked at her in silence, while he avoided meeting Octave's eyes.

Then Gasparine, in her dry voice, asked:

"Will it put you out, cousin? Rose pestered me so to have it done. But, if you think I shall be in your way, of course, I can go."

"No, cousin!" cried the architect, at last; "whatever Rose does is right."

Then, as his wife burst out sobbing on his breast, he said:

"There, there, darling; it's silly to cry. I am very pleased. You want to have your cousin with you; very well, so you shall. It won't disturb me in the least. Now, don't cry any more! See, I'll kiss you like I love you—oh, such a lot!"

And he devoured her with kisses. Then Rose, who, at a word, became dissolved in tears, smiling again directly afterwards, took comfort while she wept. She, in her turn, kissed him on his beard, saying gently:

"You were rather hard upon her. Give her a kiss, too."

Campardon embraced Gasparine. Angèle was called, who looked on from the dining-room with mouth and eyes agape; she,, too, had to kiss the cousin. Octave stood aloof, having come to the conclusion that in this family they were really getting rather too affectionate. He had noticed with surprise Lisa's respectful manner and smiling attentiveness towards Gasparine. A sharp girl, evidently, that strumpet with blue eyelids!

Meanwhile the achitect had taken off his coat, whistling and singing like a merry schoolboy, and spent the whole afternoon in arranging the cousin's room. She helped him to push the furniture into its place, unpack the bed-linen and shake out the clothes, while Rose, who sat down for fear of tiring herself, made various suggestions for putting the wash-stand here or the bed there, so that everyone might find it convenient. It was then that Octave became aware that he damped such genial effusiveness; he felt out of place in a household so closely knit together. Accordingly he told them that he was going to dine out that evening, being determined, moreover, that the next day he would express his thanks to Madame Campardon for her hospitality, and invent some tale or other for not trespassing upon it further.

About five o'clock, as he was regretting that he did not know where to find Trublot, he suddenly thought he would invite himself to dinner at the Pichons', so as not to spend the evening by himself. No sooner had he got to their rooms, however, than he found himself in the midst of a deplorable family scene. The Vuillaumes were there, indignant and trembling.

"It is disgraceful, sir!" said the mother, standing erect as she apostrophised her son-in-law, prone upon a chair. "You gave me your word of honour."

"And you," added the father, making his trembling daughter retreat in terror to the sideboard—"don't make any excuses; you're just as much to blame. I suppose you both want to starve, eh?"

Madame Vuillaume had put on her bonnet and shawl again, saying solemnly:

"Good-bye! we, at least encourage your concupiscence by our presence. Since you no longer pay the least attention to our wishes, we have nothing more to do here. Good-bye!"

And as Jules, from force of habit, rose to accompany them, she added:

"Never mind; we are quite able to get a 'bus without you. Go on, Monsieur Vuillaume. Let them eat their dinner, and much good may it do them, for they won't always have one!"

Octave, astonished, stood aside to let them pass. When they had gone, he looked at Jules, prostrate in his chair, and Marie standing by the sideboard, pale as death. Both were speechless.

"What is the matter?" he asked.

But, without answering him, the young woman dolefully began to scold her husband.

"I told you how it would be. You ought to have waited until you could break the matter to them gently. There was no hurry about it; nothing can be noticed so far."

"Why, what is it?" asked Octave, again.

Then, not even looking away, she blurted out, in her emotion, "I am in the family-way."

"Oh! they're a damned nuisance!" cried Jules, indignantly, as he rose from his chair. "I thought it right to tell them straight off about this bother. Do they think it amuses me? Not a bit of it. I am far worse off than they are, more especially as it's through no fault of mine. We can't think where the likes of that came from, can we, Marie?"

"No, indeed!" said the young woman.

Octave made a calculation. She was five months gone—from the end of December to the end of May. His calculation was correct; it quite affected him. Then he preferred to doubt; but, as his emotion became deeper, he felt a longing to do the Pichons a kindness of some sort. Jules went on grumbling. They would look after the child, of course they would; but, all the same, it had far better have stopped where it was. Marie, usually so quiet, got into a temper, too, siding with her mother, who never forgave disobedience. A quarrel seemed imminent, each blaming the other for the youngster's appearance, when Octave gaily interposed:

"Come, come, it's no use quarrelling, now that it's on the way. I vote we don't dine here; it's too dismal by half. I'll take you both to a restaurant. Will you come?"

Marie blushed. Dining at a restaurant was her delight. But she mentioned her little girl, who always prevented her from getting out to enjoy herself. However, they settled that this time Lilitte should come too. They had a most pleasant evening. Octave took them to the "Bœuf à la Mode," where they had a private room, as that would be more comfortable, so he said. Here he lavishly plied them with all sorts of food, never thinking about the bill, but only gratified at seeing them eat. When dessert came, and they laid Lilitte down on two sofa-cushions, he even called for champagne, and they sat dreaming there, with elbows on table and humid eyes, sentimentally drowsy in the suffocating atmosphere of the dining-room. At eleven o'clock, however, they talked of going home; the cool night-air, as it touched their flushed cheeks, seemed intoxicating. Then, as Lilitte, utterly fagged out for want of sleep, declined to walk, Octave, anxious to do the whole thing handsomely, insisted on having a cab, though the Rue de Choiseul was close by. In the cab he scrupulously avoided squeezing Marie's legs between his own. Only, upstairs, while Jules was tucking Lilitte up, he kissed the young woman's forehead; the parting kiss, this, of a father surrendering his daughter to her husband. Then, as he saw them looking amorously at each other in a maudlin way, he sent them to bed, wishing them through the door a very good night and lots of pleasant dreams.

"Well," thought he, as he slipped in between the sheets, "it's cost me fifty francs, but I owe them every bit as much as that. My own wish, after all, is that her husband may make her happy, poor little woman!"

And quite overcome by a sense of good-nature, before going to sleep he resolved to make his grand attempt the very next evening.

Every Monday, after dinner, Octave helped Madame Hédouin to check the orders of the week. For this purpose they both withdrew to a little parlour at the back, a narrow room which only contained a safe, a bureau, two chairs, and a sofa. It so happened that on this particular Monday the Duveyriers were going to take Madame Hédouin to the Opéra-Comique. Accordingly, she sent for the young man about three o'clock. In spite of the bright sunshine, they had to burn the gas, as the room was only faintly lighted by windows overlooking the dismal inner courtyard. He bolted the door, and noticing her surprised look, he said, gently:

"Now nobody can come and disturb us."

She nodded assent, and they commenced work. The summer novelties were going splendidly; business was always increasing. That week, in particular, the sale of little woollen goods had looked so promising that she heaved a sigh.

"Ah, if we only had enough room!"

"But you know," said he, beginning the attack, "that depends upon yourself. For some time past I have had an idea, and I should like to talk to you about it."

It was a bold stroke of this kind that he had been awaiting. He thought of buying the adjoining house, in the Rue Neuve-Saint-Augustin, giving the umbrella-maker and the toy-shop man their notice to quit, and then of enlarging the warehouses, to which several extensive departments could be added. And he talked enthusiastically of it all, full of disdain for the old way of doing business at the back of damp, dark shops, with no display in their window-fronts. With a single gesture he was for creating another style of commerce on new lines, harbouring every kind of luxury for women in huge palaces of crystal, amassing millions in the broad light of day, being at night-time brilliantly illuminated as if for some princely festival.

"You will paralyse all the trade in the Saint-Roch neighbourhood," said he, "while securing all the petty custom. For instance, Monsieur Vabre's silk warehouse does you harm at present; but if you enlarge your shop-front and start a special department for the sale of silks, you will make a bankrupt of him in less than five years' time. Then, again, there is always a talk of opening the Rue du Dix-Décembre leading from the new Opera House to the Bourse. My friend Campardon sometimes mentions it. That might make business hereabouts ten times brisker."

With her elbow on the ledger, Madame Hédouin listened, resting her beautiful grave face on her hand. She had been born at "The Ladies' Paradise," founded by her father and her uncle. She loved the house, and imagined it expanding, engulfing the adjoining buildings, and displaying a broad, magnificent frontage. The dream suited her keen, active intelligence, her unwavering integrity, her woman's intuition of the Paris of the future.

"Uncle Deleuze would never consent to such a thing," she said, slowly. "And, then, my husband is too unwell."

Noticing her irresolution, Octave assumed his seductive voice—the voice of an actor, sweet and musical. At the same time he looked ardently at her with his eyes, the colour of old gold, and which some women pronounced irresistible. But, though the flaring gas-jet was close to the back of her neck, she felt no thrill of sexual warmth, relapsing into a reverie, half dazed by the young man's eloquence. He had got as far as figures, counting up the probable cost with the passionate air of a page making a romantic declaration of long-hidden love. Roused from her reverie suddenly, she found herself in his arms. He thrust her on to the sofa, believing that now at last she would succumb.

"Dear, dear! so that was why, was it?" she said, sadly, as she shook him off as if he were some tiresome child.

"Well, yes; for I'm in love with you!" he exclaimed. "Don't repulse me. With you, I might do such great things——"

So he went on to the end of his grand speech, which somehow rang false. She did not interrupt him, but stood turning over the leaves of the ledger. Then, when he had done, she replied:

"I know all that; I've heard it all before. But I thought that you, Monsieur Octave, had more sense than the others. I am really very sorry, for I had counted upon you. However, all young men are unreasonable. A house like this needs a deal of order, and you begin by wanting things which would unsettle us from morning to night. I am not a woman here; there's far too much for me to do. Come, now, how is it that you, with all your intelligence, could not see that I would never do such a thing as that: first, because it is silly; secondly, because it is useless; and thirdly, because, luckily for me, I don't care the least bit about it!"

He would like to have seen her full of wrath and of indignation, overflowing with exalted sentiments. Her calm voice, her quiet way of reasoning like a practical, self-possessed woman, disconcerted him. He felt that he was becoming ridiculous.

"Pity me, madam," he stammered. "You see how miserable I am!"

"Nonsense! you're not miserable at all. Anyhow, you'll soon get over it. Listen! there's somebody knocking; you'd far better go and open the door."

Accordingly, he was obliged to draw back the bolt. It was Mademoiselle Gasparine, who wanted to know about some chemises. She had been surprised to find the door bolted. But she knew Madame Hèdouin too well, and as she saw her, frigid and erect, confronting Octave, who looked thoroughly ill at ease, there was in her smile something that seemed to mock him. It exasperated him and he vaguely ascribed his failure to her.

"Madam," said he, suddenly, when Gasparine had gone, "I leave your employ this evening."

Madame Hèdouin looked at him in surprise.

"What for? I did not dismiss you. Oh, that won't make any difference! I am not afraid."

This last speech drove him frantic. He would leave that very moment, refusing to endure his martyrdom an instant longer.

"Very well, Monsieur Octave," she continued, in her calm way. "I will settle with you directly. All the same, the firm will be sorry to lose you, for you were a good assistant."

Once in the street, Octave saw that he had acted like a fool. It was striking four, and the bright May sunshine lighted up a whole corner of the Place Gaillon. Furious with himself, he strolled at haphazard down the Rue Saint-Roch, internally debating how he ought to have acted. First of all, why had he not pinched that Gasparine's buttocks? Probably that was what she wanted, but, unlike Campardon, he did not care for haunches when they got as lean and scraggy as that. Perhaps, too, he might have made á mistake in that quarter as well, for she looked like one of those squeamish persons who are strictly virtuous with Sunday gentlemen when they happen to have a week-day friend. Then, again, what a stupid idea to try and become his mistress's lover! Could he not have earned his money in the firm, without exacting at one and the same time both bread and bed? So upset was he that at the moment he was on the point of returning to "The Ladies Paradise" and admitting his error. But the thought of Madame Hédouin, proud and calm, roused his wounded vanity, and he went along in the direction of Saint-Roch's. A bad job; but the thing was done now. He would go ana see if Campardon were in the church, and take him to the café and have a glass of Madeira. It would divert his thoughts. He went in by the vestibule into which the door of the sacristy opened. It was a dark, dirty passage, like that of a brothel.

"You are, perhaps, looking for Monsieur Campardon?" said a voice close beside him, as he stood hesitating, gazing intently along the nave.

It was the Abbé Mauduit, who had just recognised him. The architect being away, he insisted on showing Octave the Calvary restorations himself; he was quite enthusiastic about them. He took him behind the choir, first showing him the Chapel of the Holy Virgin, with its walls of white marble, its altar being surmounted by the manger group, a rococo presentment of Jesus between Saint Joseph and the Virgin Mary. Then, further back still, he took him through the Chapel of Perpetual Adoration, with its seven golden lamps, gold candelabra, and gold altar shining in the dim light that came through the gold-coloured windows. There, to right and left, wooden hoardings fenced off the further section of the apse; and amid the silence, above the black kneeling phantoms mumbling prayers, the blows of pickaxes resounded, the voices of workmen, all the loud voices of a dockyard.

"Come in," said the Abbé Mauduit, lifting up his cassock. "I will explain it to you."

On the other side of the hoarding plaster kept falling from a corner of the church open to the outside air; it was white with lime, and damp with water that had been spilt here and there. To the left the Tenth Station could still be seen, with Jesus nailed to the Cross, while, on the right, there was the Twelfth, showing the women grouped round Christ. But the Eleventh Station, the group with Jesus on the Cross, had been removed and placed against a wall; it was here that the men were at work.

"Here it is," continued the priest. "It was my idea to light up the central group of the Calvary by means of an opening in the cupola. You see the effect I wanted to get?"

"Yes, yes," murmured Octave, who, as he was thus shown round, forgot his troubles.

Talking at the top of his voice, the abbé seemed like a stage carpenter-in-chief, directing the artistic arrangement of some gorgeous set.

"It must look absolutely bare, you know; nothing but stone walls, never a touch of paint, not the least vestige of gold. We must imagine that we are in a crypt, in some desolate subterranean chamber. The great effect, of course, will be the Christ on the Cross, with the Virgin Mary and Mary Magdalene at His feet. I shall place the group on the summit of a rock, the white statues sharp against a grey background; while the light from the cupola, like some invisible ray, will illuminate them with such brilliancy that they will stand out as if palpitating with the breath of supernatural life! Ah, you will see—you will see!"

Then he turned round and called out to a workman:

"Move the Virgin—do! You'll be smashing her thigh directly."

The workman called one of his mates. Between them they caught the Virgin round her loins and carried her off, as if she were a tall white wench, stiff and prostrate through some nervous seizure.

"Mind what you're about!" repeated the priest, who followed them amid all the rubbish; "her robe is cracked already. Wait a moment!"

He gave them a hand, seized the Virgin Mary round the waist, and then, all white with plaster, relinquished his embrace. Then, turning to Octave, he said:

"Now, just imagine that the two bays of the nave there, in front of us, are open, and go and stand in the Chapel of the Holy Virgin. Above the altar, through the Chapel of Perpetual Adoration, right at the back, you will see the Calvary. You can think what an effect that will make, those three great figures, this bare simple drama in the dim tabernacle, beyond the mysterious twilight from painted windows, mid candelabra and lamps of gold. Ah, I think it will be irresistible!"

He was waxing eloquent, and smiled gleefully, being very proud of this idea of his.

"The most unbelieving will be touched," said Octave, just to please him.

"So they will," he exclaimed. "I am anxious to see everything put straight."

On coming back to the nave, he still forgot to lower his voice, as he spoke swaggeringly, like some successful theatrical manager, alluding to Campardon in terms of high praise, as a fellow who, in the Middle Ages, would have had very remarkable religious feeling. He led Octave out through the small doorway at the back, keeping him for a moment longer in the courtyard of the vicarage, from which one could see the main body of the edifice buried amid the surrounding buildings. This was where he lived, on the second floor of a lofty house, the facade of which was all decayed. All the clergy of Saint-Roch lived in it. An odour as of discreet clerics and the hushed whisperings of the confessional seemed to come from the vestibule, adorned by an image of the Holy Virgin; its spacious windows were veiled by thick curtains.

"I shall come and see Monsieur Campardon this evening," said the Abbé Mauduit as they parted. "Please ask him to wait in for me. I want to have a fine talk to him about some other restorations."

And he bowed with the easy grace of a man of the world. Octave was calmer; Saint-Roch with its cool vaulted aisles had soothed his nerves. He looked with curiosity at this entrance to a church through an ordinary house, at this porter's lodge, where at night the latch had to be lifted to let the Almighty pass, at all this convent corner lost in the black, seething neighbourhood. On reaching the pavement, he once more looked up at the bare frontage of the house with its barred, curtainless windows. The window-sills on the fourth floor were bright with flowers, while below were little shops which the clergy found handy—a cobbler's, a watch-makers, an embroiderer's, and even a wine-shop where mutes were wont to meet whenever there was a funeral. Octave, still smarting from his repulse, felt in a mood to renounce the world, and thought regretfully of the peaceful existence which the priests' servants must lead up there in those rooms bedecked with verbena and sweet-peas.

That evening, at half-past six, as he went into the Campardons' flat without ringing, he suddenly caught the architect and Gasparine kissing in the ante-room. She had only just got home from the shop, and had not even shut the door. They both looked rather foolish. "My wife—er—is combing her hair," stammered the architect, merely to make a remark of some sort. "You go in and see her."

Octave, feeling as uncomfortable as they did, hastily knocked at the door of Rose's bedroom, which he was wont to enter in his capacity of relative. He certainly could not continue to board there any longer, now that he caught them kissing like this, behind the door.

"Come in!" cried Rose. "Oh! it's you, Octave? That won't matter."

She had not yet put on her dressing-gown, and her soft, milk-white shoulders and arms were bare. Carefully scrutinising herself in the mirror, she was twisting her golden hair into tiny curls. Every day she sat for hours thus, busied with minute details of her toilet, thinking of nothing but the pores of her skin, of beautifying her person. Then, when her adornment was achieved, she would recline at full length in an easy-chair, luxurious and lovely, like some idol devoid of sex.

"You're making yourself a great swell again to-night, I see," said Octave, smiling.

"Well, there! it's my only amusement," she replied. "It's something to do. I never cared about housekeeping, you know; and now that Gasparine is here——these little curls suit me, eh? It's a sort of consolation to be nicely dressed, and to feel that I look pretty."

As dinner was not ready, he told her how he had left "The Ladies' Paradise." He invented a story about some other situation which he had long been looking out for, and this gave him a pretext for his intention of taking his meals elsewhere. She was surprised at his leaving a firm like that, where he had such good prospects. But she was far too busy at her looking-glass to listen carefully.

"Do you see that red spot behind my ear? I wonder if it is a pimple?"

He was obliged to examine her neck, which she held out to him with the beautiful repose of a woman whose chastity is sacred, inviolate.

"It's nothing," said he. "I expect you rubbed yourself too hard with the towel."

Then, after he had helped her to put on her dressing-gown of blue satin and silver, they went into the dining room. Before the soup had gone, Octave's departure from "The Ladies' Paradise" was fully discussed. Campardon expressed great surprise, while

Gasparine smiled her usual affected smile. Both seemed to be thoroughly at their ease. Octave even felt touched at last by the tender attentions which they lavished on Rose. Campardon poured out her wine, while Gasparine carefully chose the nicest pieces from the dish for her. Did she like the bread? If not, they would go to another baker's. Would she like to have a cushion for her back? Rose, full of gratitude, begged them not disturb themselves in this way. She ate a great deal, throned there between them, with her soft, white neck and queenly dressing-robe, having on the right her husband, short of breath and lean of body, while on her left sat her stale, sallow cousin, with shrunken shoulders covered by a black dress, and flesh dissolved by the fires of secret passion.

At dessert, Gasparine sharply scolded Lisa, who had answered rudely when her mistress enquired about a piece of cheese that was missing. The maid became very meek and mild. Gasparine had soon taken the household matters in hand, and kept the servants in their place; a word from her was enough to set even Victoire shaking among her saucepans. Rose gave her a humid glance of gratitude; they respected her, now that Gasparine was there, and her one desire was for her cousin to leave "The Ladies' Paradise" as well, and superintend Angèle's education.

"Come, now," she said, coaxingly, "there's quite enough for you to do here. Angèle, beg your cousin to come; tell her how pleased you would be.

The child entreated her cousin to come, while Lisa nodded approvingly. Campardon and Gasparine, however, looked grave. No, no; it was better to wait; one ought not to take a leap of that sort without having anything to hold on to.

Evenings in the drawing-room had become delightful. The architect never went out now. That evening, as it happened, he was going to hang up some engravings in Gasparine's bedroom. They had just come back from the framer's; one was of Mignon yearning for Heaven, together with a view of the Fountain of Vaucluse, and others. His merriment was as that of a portly burgess, with his yellow beard blown hither and thither, and cheeks flushed from excess of food—a fellow of excellent good-humour since he could gratify all his appetites.

He called Gasparine to give him a light, and they heard him hammering in the nails as he stood on a chair.

Octave, finding himself alone with Rose, went on to explain

that, at the end of the month, he would be obliged to board elsewhere. She seemed surprised, but her head was full of other things, and she at once began listening to the laughter of her husband and Gasparine in the other room.

"What fun they are having—hanging those pictures! Well, Achille never stops out now; he's not left me alone for a single evening during the last fortnight. No more appointments at cafés, no more business engagements now! You remember how anxious I used to be if he were out after midnight. Oh! it's such a relief to me now! At last I have got him all to myself!"

"Of course, of course," muttered Octave.

Then she began to talk about the economy of this new arrangement. Everything in the house went on far better; they were all as merry as the day was long.

"When I see Achille happy," she continued, "why, I am happy, too."

Then, suddenly reverting to the young man's affairs, she added:

"So you are really going to leave us? You ought to stay, now that we are all going to be so happy."

He began once more to explain. She understood at last, and looked down; the young fellow, after all, would rather interfere with their tender outbursts of domestic affection. She herself was somewhat relieved that he was going, since now she no longer needed him to keep her company in the evenings. He was obliged to promise that he would often come and see her.

"There's your 'Mignon' for you!" cried Campardon, gaily. "Wait a minute, cousin, and I will help you down."

They heard him take her up in his arms and deposit her somewhere. Then there was silence, followed by a suppressed laugh. The architect, all at once came back to the drawing-room, and held out his flushed cheek to his wife.

"It's done, my darling. Kiss your old poppet for working so hard."

Gasparine came in with some embroidery, and sat down near the lamp. Campardon, for fun, began cutting out a gilt cross of the Legion of Honour, which had come off some label. He blushed deeply when Rose tried to pin this paper decoration to his coat. Someone, in fact, had promised him the cross, but there was some mystery somewhere. On the other side of the lamp, Angèle, learning her Scripture history, kept looking across with her puzzled air of a well-brought-up young person, taught to be silent, and whose real thoughts are unrevealed.

A quiet evening, verily, in this homely, patriarchal nook.

But, suddenly, Campardon's sense of propriety met with a violent shock. He noticed that, instead of studying her Scripture history, the child was reading the *Gazette de France,* which lay on the table.

"Angèle!" said he, sternly. "What are you doing? This morning I crossed out that article with red pencil. You know quite well that you are not to read what is crossed out."

"I was reading the piece next to it, papa," said the girl.

However, he took away the newspaper, as in a low tone he complained to Octave of the utter demoralisation of the Press. That very day there was another report of some abominable crime. If the *Gazette de France* could no longer be admitted into respectable family circles, what paper, then, could they take in? And as he was turning his eyes heavenwards, Lisa announced the Abbé Mauduit.

"Oh! of course," said Octave. "He asked me to tell you he was coming."

The abbé came in smiling. Campardon had forgotten to take off the paper cross, and the cleric's smile confused him. The Abbé Mauduit, as it happened, was the very person about whom there was all this mystery, and whose name had to be kept secret. It was he who had undertaken to get the decoration.

"The ladies did it, silly things!" murmured Campardon, as he sought to take off the cross.

"No, no! Keep it on," replied the priest, pleasantly. "It's in the right place where it is, and we will find a more substantial substitute for it before long."

He at once enquired after Rose's health, and highly approved of Gasparine having made her home among relatives; young unmarried ladies living alone ran such risks in a city like Paris. He said all this in his sleek way, like a good churchman, though he was perfectly aware how matters really stood. Then he spoke of the Saint-Roch restorations, and suggested an important alteration. It seemed as if he had come to bless the sweet unity and concord of this family, and thus cover a somewhat delicate situation, which might give rise to local gossip. The architect of the Saint-Roch Calvary was, of a truth, bound to command respect from all righteous persons.

When the abbé came in, Octave bade the Campardons good

evening. As he crossed the dark ante-room he heard Angèle's voice, for she, too, had managed to slip away.

"Was it about the butter that she made all that row?" asked she.

"Yes, of course, it was," replied another voice, which was Lisa's. "She's as spiteful as some old cat. You saw how she went on at me during dinner! Much I care! One has to pretend to obey with a person of that sort, and it doesn't prevent our having our own little jokes, all the same."

Then Angèle must have flung her arms about Lisa's neck, for her voice sounded muffled, as if by the maid's bosom.

"There, there! I don't care what happens, but it's you, you, I love!"

Octave was about to go upstairs to bed, when a desire to get some fresh air led him out-of-doors. It was barely ten o'clock; he would take a stroll as far as the Palais Royal. Now he was single again, with no woman whatever in tow. Neither Valérie nor Madame Hédouin would have anything to say to his courtship, and he had been in too great a hurry to give up Marie to Jules—Marie, his only conquest, and whom he had been at no pains to win. He endeavoured to laugh at it all, but at heart he felt sad, bitterly recollecting his successes at Marseilles. In the repeated failure of all his attempts at seductions, he saw an evil omen, an actual blow aimed at his good-fortune. The atmosphere about him seemed so chilly with no petticoats hovering near. Even the lachrymose Madame Campardon had let him go without a tear. Surely a terrible revenge, this. Was Paris going to deny him her favours, after all? No sooner had he got into the street than he heard a woman's voice calling him. It was Berthe, standing at the door of the silk shop. A man was just putting up the shutters.

"Oh, Monsieur Mouret!" she asked, "is it true that you have left 'The Ladies' Paradise'?"

He was surprised to find that people already knew it in the neighbourhood. Berthe called her husband. He had meant to have a talk next day to Monsieur Mouret; well, he might just as well do so at once. And there and then Auguste, in his sulky way, offered the young man a post in his employ. Taken aback, Octave hesitated, and was on the point of refusing, as he reflected upon the insignificance of such an establishment. But when he saw Berthe's pretty face and welcoming smile, the same bright glance that twice had met his, once on the day of his arrival, and again on her wedding-day, he said, with decision:

"All right; I'll come."

X

Octave now found himself brought into closer contact with the Duveyriers. As often as Madame Duveyrier came through the shop on her way home she would stop and talk to Berthe for a moment; and the first time she saw the young man behind one of the counters, she good-humouredly scolded him for not keeping his promise of long standing to come and see her one evening and try his voice. She was going to give another performance of the *Benediction of the Poniards* at one of her first Saturday parties in the ensuing winter, with two more tenors this time—something thoroughly complete.

"If it is not inconvenient," said Berthe one day to Octave, "could you go upstairs after dinner to my sister-in-law? She expects you."

The attitude she maintained towards him was that of a mistress who desires to be studiously polite.

"Well, the fact is," said he, "I thought of putting these shelves in order this evening."

"Never mind about them," she rejoined; "there are plenty of people to do that. You can have the evening off."

About nine o'clock Octave found Madame Duveyrier waiting for him in her large white and gold drawing-room. Everything was ready, the piano open, the candles lit. A lamp, placed on a small table near the instrument, lighted half the room, and the other half remaining only in shadow. Seeing that she was alone, Octave thought it behoved him to ask after Monsieur Duveyrier. He was in excellent health, she said; his colleagues had entrusted him with the drawing up of a report concerning a most serious matter, and he had just gone out to obtain certain information respecting it.

"You know, it is the affair of the Rue de Provence," she said, naively.

"Oh! he has to deal with that, has he?" exclaimed Octave.

It was a scandal that had become the talk of all Paris—a story of wholesale traffic in children, little girls procured for personages of exalted station. Clotilde continued :

"Yes, it gives him a great deal to do. For the past fortnight, every evening has been taken up with it."

He looked at her, knowing from Trublot that Bachelard had invited Duveyrier to dinner that evening, and they were afterwards to make a night of it at Clarisse's. She seemed quite serious, however, and talked gravely about her husband, relating, in her eminently respectable way, various singular stories as to the why and wherefore of the counsellor's perpetual absence from the conjugal hearth.

"He has charge of so many human souls," said Octave, somewhat out of countenance by her frank gaze.

She seemed to him very handsome, seated there alone in the empty room. Her reddish hair heightened the pallor of her somewhat long face, which wore an expression of dogged resignation, the tranquil look of a woman wholly immersed in her duties. Dressed in grey silk, her waist and bosom tightly encased in a whalebone corset, she treated him with cold civility, as if separated from him by a triple coat of mail.

"Well, monsieur, shall we begin?" she went on. "You will excuse my importunity, won't you? Let yourself go, and sing as loud as you like, for Monsieur Duveyrier is not here. I daresay you have heard him boast that he does not like music, have you not?"

She threw such contempt into this last sentence that Octave ventured to laugh gently. It was, in fact, the only sarcasm levelled at her husband which at times escaped her before strangers, when exasperated by his perpetual chaff about her piano, although she had sufficient force of character to hide the hatred and the physical repulsion with which he inspired her.

"How is it possible not to like music?" said Octave, with an enraptured air, wishing to make himself agreeable.

Then she sat down at the piano. A collection of old airs lay open before her. She chose the one from Grétry's *Zémire et Azor*. As Octave could barely read his notes, she went through it with him first, he humming the tune. Then she played the prelude, and he began to sing :

"When Love lights up the heart,
Life becomes passing sweet !"

"That's perfect !" she cried, in rapture. "A tenor, not a doubt about it—a tenor ! Pray go on !"

Octave, quite flattered, sang the two next lines :

"And I, who feel his dart,
Lie swooning at your feet !"

She beamed with delight. For the last three years she had been looking for a tenor! And she recounted all her vexatious disappointments—Monsieur Trublot, for instance. It was positively worth while studying the causes which led to such a dearth of tenors among young men about town; no doubt, smoking had something to do with it.

"Now, then, are you ready?" she continued. "We must put some expression into it : make a bold start."

Her cold face wore a languorous expression as her eyes turned towards him with a die-away look. Thinking that she was growing excited, his animation increased, and she seemed to him full of charm. Not a sound could be heard in the adjoining apartments; the weird gloom of the large room seemed to envelop them both in drowsy voluptuousness. As, bending over her to see the music, his chin touched her chignon, he gave a thrill of passion to the lines :

"And I, who feel his dart,
Lie swooning at your feet !"

But having delivered this melodious phrase, she dropped her passionate expression as if it were a mask. The frigid woman lay beneath. He shrank back in alarm, not wishing for an adventure such as the one with Madame Hédouin.

"You will soon manage it very nicely," she said. "Only you must mark the time more—like this; do you see?"

And she herself sang the line for him, twenty times over, bringing out each note with the austerity of a woman who knows not sin, whose passion for music was shallow—a delight in mere mechanism. By degress her voice grew louder, and filled the room with shrill cries, until they both heard someone loudly calling out behind them :

"Madam! madam!"

Starting up, she saw Clémence, her maid.

"Well, what is it?"

"Oh, madam, Monsieur Vabre has fallen forward on his writing-desk, and he doesn't stir! We are all so frightened!"

Then, without exactly grasping the maid's meaning, she rose from the piano in astonishment, and went out with Clémence. Octave, who did not venture to follow her, remained walking up and down the drawing-room. Then, after some moments of awkward hesitation, as he heard the sound of hurrying footsteps and anxious voices, he determined to see what was the matter. Crossing the next room, which was quite dark, he reached Monsieur Vabre's room. All the servants had hastened thither—Julie, in her kitchen apron; Clémence and Hippolyte, their minds still full of a game of dominoes from which they had just got up. And there they all stood in bewilderment round the old man; while Clotilde, stooping down, shouted in his ear and implored him to speak. But still he never moved, his face buried in his catalogue-tickets. His forehead had struck the ink-stand. There was a splash of ink over his left eye, which was trickling slowly down towards his lips.

"He is in a fit," said Octave. "It won't do to leave him there. We must put him on to the bed."

Madame Duveyrier, however, grew terribly excited. Her callous nature was gradually stirred to its depths. She kept repeating:

"Do you think it is? Do you think it is? Goodness gracious! Oh, my poor dear father!"

Hippolyte, the footman, was in no hurry to move. He felt a kind of repugnance to touch the old man, vaguely afraid that he might die in his arms. Octave was obliged to call upon him for assistance. Between them, they laid him down on the bed.

"Bring some warm water," said the young man to Julie. "We must wash his face."

Clotilde now became incensed against her husband. Ought he ever to have been away? If anything happened, what would become of her? It was as if done on purpose; he was never at home when wanted, and the Lord knew that was not very often! Octave, interrupting, advised her to send for Doctor Juillerat. No one had thought of that before. Hippolyte started off at once, glad to get away.

"Leaving me all alone like this!" Clotilde went on. "I don't know, myself, but there must be all sorts of things to settle. Oh, my poor dear father!"

"Would you like me to inform the other members of your family?" said Octave. "I can fetch your two brothers. It might be as well."

She did not answer. Two large tears filled her eyes, while Julie and Clémence endeavoured to undress the old man. But she stopped Octave; her brother Auguste was away, having an appointment that evening, and as for Théophile, it was better that he should not come up, as the mere sight of him would be enough to kill the old man. Then she told how her father had gone personally to Théophile to get rent from him, which was overdue, but they had both given him a most brutal reception, especially Valérie, refusing to pay one penny, and claiming the sum which at the time of their marriage he had promised to let them have.

This seizure was doubtless the result of such a scene, for he had come back in a most deplorable state.

"Madame," said Clémence, "one side of him is already quite cold."

This only served to increase Madame Duveyrier's indignation. She was afraid to say anything more before the servants. Her husband obviously did not care a rap about their interests! Ah, if she had but had some knowledge of law! And she could not keep still, but walked up and down before the bed. Octave, noticing the catalogue slips, was led to look at the vast preparations which covered the table. There, in a large oak box, was a whole series of cardboard tickets, carefully classified, the foolish result of a whole lifetime of work. Just as he was reading on one of these tickets the inscription:

"ISIDORE CHARBOTEL. *Salon* 1857 *Atalanta; Salon* 1859 *Androcles and the Lion; Salon* 1861 *Portrait of Monsieur P——.*"

Clotilde stood before him, saying resolutely, in an undertone:

"Go and fetch him."

And as he seemed surprised, she, as it were, with a shrug disposed of the tale about drawing up a report of the Rue de Provence affair—one of those perpetual fictions with which she had to supply the outside world. In her emotion, she kept nothing back.

"You know, Rue de la Cerisaie. All our friends know where it is."

He made a feint of protesting. "I assure you, madam, that——"

"Don't take his part," she went on. "I am only too glad; he may stop there, if he likes. Oh, good gracious! it's only because of my poor dear father!"

Octave bent down as Julie was wiping Monsieur Vabre's eye with the corner of a towel; the ink had dried on to the skin, leaving a livid mark. Madame Duveyrier advised her not to rub so hard, and then she turned back to Octave, who had already got to the door.

"Not a word to anyone," she murmured. "It is useless to upse the whole house. Take a cab, knock at the door, and be sure and bring him back with you."

When Octave had gone she sank into a chair near the sick man' pillow. He had not recovered consciousness; his long-drawn, pain ful breathing alone broke the lugubrious silence of the chamber Then, as the doctor did not come, and seeing herself alone with tw terrified maidservants, she burst into tears, sobbing violently in paroxysm of grief.

It was at the Café Anglais that Bachelard had invited Monsieu Duveyrier to dine, though one hardly knew why. Perhaps it wa for the pleasure of having a distinguished magistrate as his guest and of showing him that tradespeople knew how to spend thei money. He had asked Trublot and Gueulin as well—four men and no women; women don't know how to appreciate a good dinner They prevent one from enjoying the truffles, and ruin one's diges tion. Bachelard, in fact, was well known all along the Boulevard for his sumptuous dinners whenever some customer of his turned up from the depths of India or Brazil—dinners at three hundred franc a head, by which he nobly upheld the prestige of French com mission agencies. A mania for spending money possessed him; he insisted upon having the most expensive dishes, gastronomica rarities that were at times uneatable: sterlets from the Volga; eels from the Tiber; grouse from Scotland; bustards from Sweden bears' feet from the Black Forest; bison-humps from America turnips from Teltow; gourds from Greece. Then, too, he must have everything that was not in season, such as peaches in December, or partridges in July, with flowers in profusion, silver plate, cut-glass, and such constant waiting-upon, that the whole restaurant was turned topsy-turvy; besides wines for which the cellar had to be ransacked. He always required unknown vintages, nothing being old enough nor rare enough for him, who was for ever dreaming of unique bottles of wine at two louis the glass.

That evening, as it was summer-time, a season when everything is in abundance, he had found it rather difficult to run up a bill. The menu, which had been arranged the day before, was, however, a noteworthy one—asparagus cream soup; *timbales à la Pompadour;* two *relevés;* trout *à la genevoise,* and fillet of beef *à la Chateaubriand;* two *entrées;* ortolans *à la Lucullus* and a crayfish salad; then, a haunch of venison, with artichokes *à la jardinière,* followed by a chocolate *soufflé* and various fruit. It was simple in its grandeur, being made more imposing by a positively princely choice of wines—old Madeira with the soup, Château-Filhot '58 with the *hors-d'-œuvres,* Johannisberger and Pichon-Longueville with the *relevés,* Château-Lafite '48 with the *entrées;* sparkling Moselle with the roast, and iced Rœderer with the dessert. He keenly regretted a bottle of Johannisberger, a hundred and five years old, which had been sold, only three days before, to a Turk for ten louis.

"Drink away, sir, drink away!" he kept perpetually telling Duveyrier; "when wine is good it never gets into your head. It's like food, which never does you any harm if it's choice."

He, however, was on his best behaviour, posing as a fine gentleman, carefully groomed, with a rose at his button-hole, refraining from smashing the dishes, as was his wont. Trublot and Gueulin ate of everything. The uncle's theory appeared to be the correct one, for Duveyrier, whose digestion was none of the best, drank quantities of wine, and then had another helping of crayfish salad without feeling at all uncomfortable; the red blotches on his face merely turned purple.

At nine o'clock the dinner was still in progress. The candles, which flared as the breeze blew in from an open window, made the silver plate and the glass sparkle, while, amid the wreckage of the feast, stood four large baskets filled with exquisite, fast-fading flowers. Besides the two *maîtres d'hôtel,* each guest had a waiter behind his chair, whose special business it was to supply him with wine and with bread, and change his plates. Despite the cold breeze from the boulevard, it was very oppressive. A sense of repletion became general, amid the spicy aroma of the dishes and the vanilla-like perfumes of the precious wines.

Then, when coffee had been served, with liqueurs and cigars, and all the waiters had withdrawn, uncle Bachelard, throwing himself back in his chair, heaved a sigh of content.

"Ah, I feel just about right!" he ejaculated.

Trublot and Gueulin, stretching themselves, leant back in their chairs as well.

"Full up!" said the one.

"Up to the eyes!" added the other.

Duveyrier, puffing, gave a nod of assent and murmured:

"Oh, those crayfish!"

All four of them looked at each other and chuckled. With bellies distended to bursting point, they slowly, selfishly proceeded to digest, like four worthy citizens who had just been stuffing themselves, aloof from family worries. It had cost a lot of money; nobody else had partaken of it with them; no girl was there to take advantage of their tender mood; so they could unbutton and, as it were, lay bare their paunches on the board. With half-closed eyes, they at first refrained from speech, each absorbed in his own solitary bliss. Then, being perfectly at liberty, and glad that no women were there, with elbows on table, they put their red faces close together and talked about women, and women only.

"I'm thoroughly disillusionised!" declared uncle Bachelard. "There's nothing like virtue, after all." Duveyrier nodded in sign of assent.) "And I've bid good-bye to fun of that sort. At one time I used to go it pretty hot, I confess. Why, in the Rue Godot-de-Mauroy, I know them every blessed one—fair girls, dark ones, and red-haired ones, who occasionally have got good limbs; not often though. Then there are those dirty holes at Montmartre—furnished lodgings, you know; filthy little streets in my part of the world, where one can pick up the most amazing creatures——"

"Oh—bitches!" broke in Trublot, in his contemptuous manner. "What utter rot! You don't catch me at that sort of game; with them you never get your money's worth."

By bawdy talk of this kind Duveyrier was deliciously tickled. He drank his *Kummel* in sips, his stiff magistrate's features distorted now and again by little sensual thrills.

"For my part," said he, "I cannot stand vice; it disgusts me. In order to love a woman, you must respect her, mustn't you? It would be quite impossible for me to have anything to do with one of those unfortunates, unless, of course, she appeared ashamed of her way of living, and had been rescued from it with a view to making her become a decent woman. Love could not have a more noble mission than that. In short, a respectable mistress—you understand? In that case I do not say that I should be able to resist."

"But I've had no end of respectable mistresses," cried Bachelard. "They are a damned sight worse than the others, and such sluts, too! Bitches that behind your back go on the loose, and then pox you up to your eyes! My last one, for instance—a most respectable-looking little lady that I met at a church-door. I took a milliner's shop for her at Ternes, just to give her a position, you know. However, she never had a single customer. Well, sir, would you believe it?—she used to have the whole street in to sleep with her!"

Gueulin chuckled, his red hair growing more bristly than usual, while the hot air brought beads of perspiration to his brow. Sucking his cigar, he mumbled :

"And the other one, that tall girl at Passy, who had a sweetmeat-shop? And the other one in a room yonder, with her outfits for orphans? And the captain's widow, do you remember, who used to show the mark of a sword-cut on her belly? They all of them, every one, made a fool of you, uncle! It does not matter my telling you now, does it? Well, one evening I had to be on my guard against the lady with the sword-mark on her belly. She wanted me to——; but I was not such a fool! You never know how far women like that may lead you."

Bachelard seemed vexed. Recovering himself, however, he screwed up his great eyelids and winked hideously.

"My boy, you may have them all if you like. I've got something better than that."

And he refused to explain himself, delighted to have roused the others' curiosity. Yet he burned to be indiscreet, to let them guess his treasure.

"A little girl," said he at last; "but the real thing, upon my honour!"

"Impossible!" cried Trublot. "They no longer make such articles."

"Respectably connected?" asked Duveyrier.

"Most respectable as regards family," affirmed Bachelard. "Imagine something stupidly chaste—a mere chance—I just had her like that. I firmly believe she thinks nothing has happened——!"

Gueulin listened in astonishment. Then, with a sceptical gesture, he muttered :

"Ah, yes! I know."

"Eh? What? You know?" said Bachelard, angrily, "You know nothing whatever, my boy; no more does anybody else. She's Bibi's property; she is not to be looked at, not to be touched—a case of 'Hands off!' "

Then, turning to Duveyrier, he said :

"You, sir, being kindhearted, can quite understand my feelings. It has a softening influence, somehow, to go and see her; it almost makes one feel young again. Anyhow, there I've got a nice quiet little nook where I can rest after all the old whore-shop business. Ah, and if you knew how sweet and clean she is, such a soft white skin, with proper little bubbies and thighs on her—not a bit scraggy, but round and firm as a peach!"

The counsellor's red blotches glowed again as, in a wave, the blood rushed to his face. Trublot and Gueulin looked at Bachelard, feeling half inclined to hit him as he sat leering there, with his row of glittering false teeth, and saliva dribbling down from either side of his mouth. What! this old carcass of an uncle, this worn-out debauchee, this wreck, whose flaming nose alone kept its place between his blubbered, flabby cheeks—so he had got, stored up discreetly, out of ken, some flower of innocence, some soft budding body, whose virginal flesh he tainted with the stench of his stale fornications, masking his lechery by a false air of drunken benevolence!

Meanwhile, growing tender, he continued the subject, as he licked the edge of his liqueur glass:

"After all, my one dream is to make the dear child happy! But, you know, her belly has begun to swell; I shall soon be a papa! 'Pon my honour! if I could come across some steady young chap, I'd give her to him—marry her to him, mind you; nothing else."

"By so doing you would make two people happy," murmured Duveyrier, sentimentally.

The atmosphere in the little room had become stifling. A glass of chartreuse had been upset, making the table-cloth sticky, which was all blackened by cigar-ash. What these gentry needed was fresh air.

"Would you like to have a look at her?" asked the uncle, rising abruptly.

They looked at one another, enquiringly. Oh, yes! they would like to do so very much, if it gave him any pleasure; and in their feigned indifference there lurked a sort of epicure's contentment at the idea of putting a finish to their dessert by inspecting the old fellow's little wench. Duveyrier merely observed that Clarisse was expecting them. Then Bachelard, pale and agitated since he had made the proposal, declared that they would not even stop to sit down. They would merely have a look at her and then go off at once. Going down, they stood outside for a few moments on the boulevard, while their host paid the bill.

When he reappeared, Gueulin pretended not to know where the damsel in question resided.

"Now, let's be off, uncle! Which way is it?"

Bachelard became grave, tortured by the vanity which prompted him to exhibit Fifi, and the dread that he might let her be stolen from him. For a moment he looked to the left, then to the right, anxiously. At last he blurted out :

"Well, no, I won't."

And he obstinately refused, caring nothing for Trublot's chaff, not even deigning to invent a pretext for thus suddenly changing his mind. They had to go to Clarisse, and as it was a lovely evening they decided, from hygienic motives, to walk thither, as it would help digestion. So they set off along the Rue de Richelieu, fairly steady on their legs, but so chock-full that the pavement hardly seemed to them broad enough. Gueulin and Trublot went in front. Behind them came Bachelard and Duveyrier, deeply engaged in an interchange of fraternal confidences. The former was earnestly assuring the latter that it was not he whom he distrusted; he would have shown her to him, for he knew his delicate feeling; but it was always unwise to expect too much from young people, was it not? And the other agreed with him, admitting that he, too, had had his fears respecting Clarisse. At first he had kept all his friends away, and then it had pleased him to invite them thither and make the place into a charming little retreat for himself after she had given him singular proofs of her fidelity. Oh, she was a woman with brains, incapable of forgetting herself; full of heart and with healthy ideas! Of course, there were certain little things in her past with which she could be reproached, things owing to want of guidance. Since she had loved him, however, she had returned to the path of honour. The counsellor talked on in this strain all along the Rue de Rivoli, while the uncle, vexed at not being able to put in another word or two about his own little girl, strove hard not to inform Duveyrier that his paragon Clarisse slept with everybody.

"Yes, yes, no doubt!" he murmured. "But depend upon it, there is nothing like virtue."

The house in the Rue de la Cerisaie seemed fast asleep amid the solitude and silence of the street. Duveyrier was surprised at not seeing any lights in the third-floor windows. Trublot gravely observed that no doubt Clarisse had gone to bed to wait for them. Or, perhaps, added Gueulin, she was playing a game of bézique in the kitchen with her maid. They knocked. The gas on the stairs burnt with the straight motionless flame of a lamp in some chapel. Not a sound, not a whisper. But as the four men passed the hall-porter, he rushed out of his room, saying :

"Sir, sir, the key!"

Duveyrier stopped short on the first step.

"Is madame not at home, then?" he asked.

"No, sir. And wait a moment; you will want a light."

As he handed him the candlestick, the porter, despite the look of exaggerated respect on his pallid face, could not repress a brutal grin. Neither the uncle nor the two young men said a word. So, in silence, with back bent, they filed up the stairs, the ceaseless beat of their footsteps echoing along the gloomy passages. Duveyrier, trying to understand it all, led the way, moving his limbs mechanically, like one that walks in a dream, while the candle that he held in his trembling hand flung the four shadows of this weird procession on the wall, like a march of broken marionettes.

On the third-floor he suddenly grew faint and could not find the key-hole. So Trublot was obliging enough to open the door for him. The key, as it turned in the lock, made a hollow, reverberating sound, as if beneath the vaulted roof of some cathedral.

"By Jove!" muttered he, "the place does not look much as if anybody lived in it!"

"Sounds pretty empty," said Bachelard.

"Like a regular little family vault," added Gueulin.

They entered. Duveyrier went first, holding the candle aloft. The ante-room was empty; even the hat-pegs had vanished. The drawing-room was empty; so, too, was the parlour; not a single piece of furniture, not a curtain at one of the windows; not even a brass rod. Petrified, Duveyrier glanced down at his feet and then looked up at the ceiling, and then went round examining the walls as if to discover the hole through which everything had disappeared.

"What a clean sweep!" said Trublot, involuntarily.

"Perhaps they are having the place done up," remarked Gueulin gravely. "Let's look in the bedroom; they may have moved the furniture in there."

But this room was equally bare, deserted, hideous in its nudity as plaster walls from which the paper had been stripped. Where the bed had stood, the iron supports of the canopy, being removed, had left gaping holes; one of the windows was half open, and the air from the street gave the room the damp, stale smell of a public square.

"My God! my God!" stammered Duveyrier, as at last he wept, overcome by the sight of the place where the mattresses had chafed the wall, rubbing off some of the paper.

Uncle Bachelard became fatherly, as he repeated:

"Courage, sir! The same thing happened to me, and I am not dead from it. Damn it all, your honour is safe!"

Duveyrier shook his head and passed on to the dressing-room, and thence into the kitchen. More disastrous revelations! The oilcloth in the dressing-room had been removed, as well as all the hooks in the kitchen.

"No, really, that is a little bit too much!" said Gueulin. "What utter caprice! She might have left the hooks behind her!"

Tired out by the dinner and the walk, Trublot began to find this solitude far from diverting. But Duveyrier never relinquished his candle, and went roaming about as if bound to dive into the uttermost depths of his abandonment. The others were forced to follow him. He went once more through every room, wishing to re-inspect drawing-room, parlour, and bedchamber, looking carefully into each corner, light in hand, while behind him these gentry in single file continued the procession of the staircase, with their huge dancing shadows which fantastically decorated the barren walls. In this melancholy atmosphere the noise of their footsteps on the boards was grimly sonorous; and, to put the finishing touch to the general dreariness, the whole flat was thoroughly clean, without a piece of paper or straw lying about, clean as a well-scrubbed bowl, for the hall-porter had been cruel enough to sweep the whole place thoroughly.

"Do you know, I can't stand any more of this," cried Trublot, at last, as they were inspecting the drawing-room for the third time. "I'd give ten sous for a chair—I would, really!"

"All four of them stood still.

"When did you see her last?" asked Bachelard.

"Yesterday, sir," exclaimed Duveyrier.

Gueulin shook his head. By Jove! she had not been long about it; she had done it rather neatly. Troublot suddenly called out. He had just spied on the mantleshelf a dirty collar and a damaged cigar.

"You must not complain," said he, laughing; "she has left you a keepsake. It's always something."

Duveyrier, suddenly touched, looked at the collar. Then he murmured:

"Twenty-five thousand francs' worth of furniture; there was twenty-five thousand francs' worth! Oh, well, it's not that which I regret—no, no!"

"Won't you have the cigar?" asked Trublot, interrupting. "Very well, if you will allow me. It's broken, but I can stick some cigarette paper round it."

He lighted it at the candle which Duveyrier still held; then, sliding into a sitting posture against the wall, he said:

'This is better than nothing! I must sit on the floor for a bit; I am ready to drop!"

"Well," asked Duveyrier, "can any of you tell me where she can possibly have gone?"

Bachelard and Gueulin looked at each other. It was a delicate matter. However, the uncle manfully decided to act as spokesman, and he told the poor fellow everything—all about Clarisse's high jinks, her perpetual tumblings, and the lovers that at every one of her parties she used to pick up behind his back. No doubt, she had gone off with her latest, that big fellow, Payan, the mason, whom his townsfolk in the South desired to turn into an artist. Duveyrier listened to these abominable revelations with a horrified air. At last he exclaimed in despair:

"There is no such thing as honesty in this world!"

Then, growing suddenly communicative, he told them all that he had done for her. He spoke of his kindheartedness, accused her of having shaken his belief in all that was best in human life, thus ingeniously hiding beneath such lackadaisical lamentation all the disorder of his fleshly appetites. Clarisse had become a necessity to him. But he would find her out, merely to make her blush for her perfidy, so he said, and to see if her heart were destitute of all noble feeling.

"Don't do anything of the sort!" cried Bachelard, secretly delighted at the counsellor's trouble; "she will only fool you again. There's nothing like virtue, you know. Get hold of some little girl without any tricks about her, and innocent as a new-born child; then there's no danger, and one can sleep in peace."

Trublot, meanwhile, went on smoking, with his back to the wall and his legs stretched out, gravely taking his ease. The others had forgotten him.

"If you particularly wish for it, I can find out the address for you," said he. "I know the maid-servant."

Duveyrier turned round, astonished at hearing this voice that appeared to come out of the floor, and when he saw Trublot smoking all that remained of Clarisse, blowing great clouds of smoke, in which he seemed to see his twenty-five thousand francs' worth of furniture evaporating, with an angry gesture, he cried:

"No; she is unworthy of me! She must beg for pardon on her knees!"

"Hullo! here she is, coming back!" said Gueulin, straining his ears to listen.

Some one, indeed, was walking in the hall; and a voice cried: "Hullo here, what's up? Is everybody dead?" And then Octave appeared. These empty rooms and open doors astonished him. But his amazement increased as, in the centre of the bare drawing-room, he saw the four men—one on the floor, and three standing—in the dim light of a single candle, which the counsellor carried like a church taper. A few words sufficed to explain all to him.

"Impossible!" he exclaimed.

"Didn't they tell you anything down below?" asked Gueulin.

"No, nothing at all; the porter calmly watched me go upstairs. So she's bolted, has she? I am not surprised. She had such funny eyes and hair!"

He asked for details, and talked for a little while, forgetful of the sad news of which he was the bearer. Then suddenly he turned towards Duveyrier.

"By the way, it was your wife who sent me to fetch you. Your father-in-law is dying."

"Oh, is he?" said Duveyrier, simply.

"What, old Vabre?" muttered Bachelard. "I expected as much."

"Bah, when one has got to the end of one's tether!" quoth Gueulin, philosophically.

"Yes, it's best to kick the bucket," added Trublot, in the act of sticking another cigarette-paper round his cigar.

At last these gentlemen decided to quit the deserted apartment. Octave kept saying that he had given his word of honour that he would bring Duveyrier back with him at once, no matter what state he was in. The latter carefully closed the door, as if he were leaving behind him all his dead affections; but downstairs shame suddenly overcame him, and Trublot had to return the key to the hall-porter. Then, in the street, there was a silent interchange of vigorous hand-shakes; and, as soon as Duveyrier and Octave had driven off in a cab, Bachelard said to Gueulin and to Trublot, as they stood there in the deserted street:

"Damn it all! I must let you see her!"

For a minute or so he kept walking up and down, greatly excited at the despair shown by the big idiot of a Duveyrier, and bursting at his own particular happiness, due, as he thought, to his own deep cunning—a joy that he could no longer contain.

"Well, you know, uncle," said Gueulin, "if you're only going to take us as far as the door again and then chuck us, why——"

"No, damn it all! You shall see her! I should like you to. It's nearly midnight, but never mind; she shall get up if she's gone to bed. You know, she is the daughter of a captain—Captain Menu, and she's got a most respectable aunt, born at Villeneuve, near Lille; upon my honour, she has! You can get any references at Mardiennes Brothers', in the Rue Saint-Sulpice. Ah, damn it all! It will do us good! You shall just see what virtue is like!"

He took their arms, Gueulin being on the right and Trublot on the left, as he hurried along in search of a cab, so as to get there quicker.

Meanwhile, as they drove along, Octave briefly described Monsieur Vabre's seizure to his companion, without concealing the fact that Madame Duveyrier knew the address in the Rue de la Cerisaie.

After a pause, the counsellor asked, in a doleful voice:

"Do you think that she will forgive me?"

Octave was silent. The cab went rumbling along, as every now and then a ray of light from some gas-lamp shot across its gloom. Just as they arrived, Duveyrier, full of anguish, asked another question.

"The best thing I can do at present is to make it up with my wife; don't you think so?"

"Perhaps that would be the wisest plan," said Octave, obliged to make some sort of reply.

Then Duveyrier felt that he ought to show regret for his father-in-law. A man of great intelligence, he said, with quite incredible capacity for work. However, very likely they might succeed in pulling him round. In the Rue de Choiseul they found the house-door open and quite a group of people in front of Monsieur Gourd's little room. Julie, on her way to the chemist's, was abusing the middle-classes who let one another die when ill; it was only working-folk, she said, who took each other soup or warm towels when there was sickness. The old fellow might have swallowed his tongue twenty times over before ever his children took the trouble to shove a bit of sugar into his mouth. A hard-hearted lot, said Monsieur Gourd—folk that did not know how to use their ten fingers, and who would have thought themselves disgraced if they had had to give their father an enema. Hippolyte, to cap everything, told them about madame upstairs, and how silly she looked with her arms a-flop in front of the poor old gentleman, while the servants were running about doing all they could. But they all held their tongues directly they saw Duveyrier.

"Well?" enquired he.

"The doctor is just putting on mustard-plasters," said Hippolyte. "Oh, I had such a job to find him!"

Upstairs, in the drawing-room, Madame Duveyrier came forward to meet them. She had been crying a good deal; her eyes shone beneath their reddened lids. The counsellor, greatly embarrased, held out his arms and embraced her, murmuring:

"My poor Clotilde!"

Surprised at such unwonted effusiveness, she shrank back. Octave had kept behind; but he heard the husband say, in a low voice:

"Forgive me! Let us forget our quarrels on this sad occasion. You see, I have come back to you and for always. Oh, I have been well punished!"

She made no reply, but disengaged herself. Then, assuming before Octave her attitude of a woman who wishes to ignore everything, she said:

"I should not have disturbed you, my dear for I know how urgent that report about the Rue de Provence scandal is. But I was all alone, and I felt that your presence was necessary. My poor father is dying. Go in and see him; the doctor is there."

When Duveyrier had gone into the adjoining room, she approached Octave, who, in order to keep in countenance, was standing by the piano. The instrument was still open, and the air from *Zémire et Azor* lay there as they had left it on the desk. He pretended to be studying it. The soft light from the lamp illuminated a part of the large room, as before.

Madame Duveyrier looked at the young man for a moment without speaking, tormented by an anxiety which led her to throw off her habitual reserve.

"Was he there?" she asked, briefly.

"Yes, madam."

"Then, what is it? What is the matter with him?"

"That person has left him, madam, taking all the furniture with her. I found him in the bare walls with only a candle!"

Clotilde made a gesture of despair. She understood. Her handsome face wore an expression of discouragement and disgust. It was not enough that she had lost her father, but the mischance must needs serve as a pretext to bring about a reconciliation between herself and her husband! She knew him well; he would always be on top of her, now that that there was nothing elsewhere to protect her, and, with her respect for all duties, she trembled at the thought that she could not refuse to submit to the abominable nuisance. For a moment she looked at the piano. Great tears filled her eyes as she said, simply:

"Thank you, sir."

Then, in their turn, they both went into Monsieur Vabre's bedroom. Duveyrier, looking very pale, was listening to Doctor Juillerat, who was explaining something in a low voice. It was a very bad attack of apoplexy. The patient might possibly linger until the next day, but there was no hope whatever. Clotilde just at that moment entered; she overheard this last statement, and sank down into a chair, wiping her eyes with her tear-drenched handkerchief, which she had nervously twisted into a ball. However, she had strength enough to ask the doctor if her poor father would regain consciousness. The doctor had his doubts; and, as if he had divined the motive for such a question, he expressed a hope that Monsieur Vabre had long since put his affairs in order. Duveyrier, whose mental faculties had apparently remained behind in the Rue de la Cerisaie, now appeared to wake up. He looked at his wife and then observed that Monsieur Vabre had confided in no one; so he knew nothing, except that certain promises had been made in favour of their son Gustave, whom his grandfather often spoke of helping as a reward for their having taken him to live with them. At any rate if there was a will, it would be found.

"Has the family been told?" asked Doctor Juillerat.

"No," murmured Clotilde. "It was so dreadfully sudden. My first thought was to send Monsieur Mouret for my husband."

Duveyrier gave her another look; now they understood each other. Slowly approaching the bed, he examined Monsieur Vabre straight and stiff as a corpse, his rigid features streaked with yellow spots. One o'clock struck. The doctor spoke of leaving, as he had tried all the usual remedies, and could no nothing more. He would call early in the morning. He was going off at last with Octave when Madame Duveyrier called the latter back.

"Let us wait till the morning," said she. "You can make some excuse to send Berthe to me, and I will call Valérie, and they shall break the news to my two brothers. Poor things! let them sleep in peace for to-night at least. It's enough for us to keep watch in tears."

And there, beside the old man, whose death-rattle echoed through the room, she and her husband stayed alone.

XI

When, next day at eight o'clock, Octave came downstairs, he was much surprised to find that the whole household knew about Monsieur Vabre's seizure of the previous night, and of their landlord's desperate condition. The household, however, was no-wise concerned as to the sufferer, but rather as to what he was going to leave behind.

In their little dining-room the Pichons sat before their cups of chocolate. Jules called Octave in.

"I say! what a nice muddle it will be if he dies like that! We shall see some queer things. Do you know if he has made a will?"

The young man, without answering, asked them where they had heard the news. Marie had brought it along with her from the baker's; in fact, it had got about from floor to floor, even to the end of the street, through the servants.

Then, after slapping Lilitte for putting her fingers into the chocolate, Marie said, in her turn :

"And all that money, too! If he had only thought of leaving us as many sous as there are five-franc pieces! Not much fear of that, though."

And, as Octave was going, she added :

"I have finished your books, Monsieur Mouret. Do come and fetch them, won't you?"

He hurried downstairs, remembering that he had promised to send Berthe to her before there was any gossip, when on the third floor he met Campardon coming out.

"Well," said the latter, "so your employer is going to inherit a fortune. As far as I can make out, the old boy has got close upon six hundred thousand francs, besides this place. Well, you see, he spent nothing at the Duveyriers', and he had a good bit left out of his Versailles property, without counting the twenty and odd thousand francs from house-rents here. Well, it's a fine cake to divide when there are only three to share it."

Thus chatting, he walked downstairs behind Octave. On the

second floor they met Madame Juzeur, who had come down to see what her little servant girl, Louise, could be doing all the morning, wasting over an hour in fetching four sous' worth of milk. She naturally joined in the conversation, being thoroughly well posted.

"It is not known how he has arranged his affairs," said she, in her quiet way. "There will probably be some bother about it."

"Well, well, said the architect, gaily, "I should like to be in their place. It would not take long. Divide the whole into three equal parts; each takes his share, and the thing's done."

Madame Juzeur leant over the banisters, and then looked up to be sure that no one was on the stairs. Then, lowering her voice, she said:

"And what if they shouldn't find what they expect?"

Campardon opened his eyes wide. Then he shrugged his shoulders. Bah! that was all bosh. Old Vabre was a regular miser, who hid his savings in worsted stockings. So saying, he went off, having an appointment at Saint-Roch with the Abbé Mauduit.

"My wife was complaining about you," said he to Octave, as, after going down three steps, he stopped and looked back. "Do go and have a chat with her, some time."

Madame Juzeur detained the young man for a moment.

"And me, too! How you neglect poor me! I did think that you liked me a little bit. When you come, I'll let you taste a liqueur from the West Indies—something quite too delicious!"

He promised to come, and then hurried down into the hall. Before reaching the little shop-door under the arch, he had to pass a whole group of servants. They were engaged in distributing the dying man's possessions. There was so much for Madame Clotilde so much for Monsieur Auguste, and so much for Monseiur Théophile. Clémence stated the figures boldly; she knew well enough what they were, for she had them from Hippolyte, who had seen the money in a drawer. Julie, however, disputed these. Lisa told how her first master, an old gentleman, had done her out of her wages by dying without even leaving her his dirty linen; while, with dangling arms and mouth agape, Adèle listened to these tales of inheritance until she fancied she saw gigantic piles of five-franc pieces toppling over into her lap. And in the street, Monsieur Gourd, pompous as ever, was talking to the stationer over the way. For him the landlord was already dead.

"What I'm interested about," quoth he, "is to know who will get the house. They'll divide everything—well and good! But what about the house? They can't cut that up into three."

At length Octave entered the shop. The first person he saw sitting at the cashier's desk was Madame Josserand, laced, combed and smartened up to the nines, in full battle array. Berthe was next to her, who, no doubt, had come down in a hurry. She looked greatly excited, but charming in her loosely-fitting dressing-gown. But on seeing him they stopped talking. The mother gave him an awful look.

"So, sir," she said, "it is in this way that you show your attachment to the firm! You take part in the conspiracies of my daughter's enemies!"

He sought to make some defence, to explain the facts of the case. But she would not allow him to speak, accusing him of having spent the night with the Duveyriers in looking for the will so as to insert certain clauses therein. And, when he laughingly enquired what possible interest he could have had in doing such a thing, she rejoined:

"Your own interest—your own interest! In short, sir, it was your duty to have come and told us, since God willed it that you should be a witness of the sad event. Only to think that, but for me, my daughter would still have been ignorant of the matter! Yes, they would have robbed her if I had not rushed downstairs directly I heard the news. Eh—what? Your interest; yes, your interest, sir! How can I tell? Though Madame Duveyrier has lost her looks, yet there are some folk, not over-particular, for whom she is good enough!"

"Oh, mamma!" cried Berthe, "Clotilde, who is so thoroughly proper!"

Madame Josserand shrugged her shoulders, commiseratingly.

"No matter! you know perfectly well that people will do anything for money!"

Octave was obliged to tell them all the particulars of the seizure. They exchanged glances. Obviously, to use the mother's phrase, there had been manœuvres. It was really too considerate of Clotilde to wish to spare her family any unnecessary emotion! However, they allowed the young man to go about his work, whilst they still had their doubts as to his behaviour in the matter. And they continued their animated discussion.

"And pray who is going to pay the fifty thousand francs agreed upon in the contract?" asked Madame Josserand, "Once he's under ground, we may whistle for them, eh?"

"Oh, the fifty thousand francs!" murmured Berthe, embarrassed. "You know that, like yourself, he only agreed to pay ten thousand francs every six months. The time is not up yet; we had better wait."

"Wait? oh, yes! wait till he comes to life again and brings them to you, I suppose? Why, you great noodle, then you want to be robbed, do you? No, no! you must claim them at once from the estate. As regards ourselves, we are alive, thank God, and it is not certain if we shall pay or not; but he is dead, and consequently he will have to pay."

And she made her daughter swear not to give in, for she herself was not going to be made a fool of by anybody. Working herself up by degrees, she now and again bent her ear as if to hear what was going on overhead at the Duveyriers'. The old fellow's bedroom was just above her. On hearing what had happened, Auguste at once had gone upstairs to his father. But that did not pacify her; she longed to be there herself, and imagined all sorts of intricate schemes.

"You go up, too!" she cried, at last, in a heart-felt outburst. "Auguste is too weak; I am sure they will let him in for it again."

So Berthe went upstairs. Octave, who was dressing the window-front, listened to what they were saying. When he saw that he was alone with Madame Josserand, and that she was going to the door, he asked her whether it would not be the proper thing to close the shop, hoping to get a day's holiday.

"Why, what for?" she asked. "Wait till he's dead. It's not worth while losing a day's business."

Then, as he was folding up a remnant of crimson silk, she added, in order to soften her harsh speech:

"Only, I think you had, perhaps, better not put anything red in the window."

On the first floor Berthe found Auguste with his father. The room had not altered since the evening before; it was still damp, silent, filled with the same noise of long, difficult breathing. The old man lay on the bed completely rigid, having lost all feeling, all movement. The oak box, full of tickets, still lay on the table; none of the furniture seemed to have been moved, nor a drawer to have been opened. The Duveyriers looked more exhausted, however, worn out by a sleepless night; their eyelids twitched convulsively;

something appeared to be weighing on their minds. As early as seven o'clock they had sent Hippolyte to fetch their son Gustave from the Lycée Bonaparte, and the lad, a thin, precocious boy of sixteen, was there, bewildered by this unlooked-for holiday, which was to be spent at the bedside of a dying man.

"Oh, my dear, what a dreadful blow!" said Clotilde, as she went up to embrace Berthe.

"Why didn't you tell us?" replied the latter, with her mother's sour pout. "We were ready to help you to bear it."

Auguste with a look begged her to be silent. The moment for squabbling had not yet come. They could afford to wait. Doctor Juillerat, who had already been once, was to pay a second visit, but he could give no hope; the patient would not live through the day. Auguste was telling all this to his wife, when Théophile and Valérie arrived in their turn. Clotilde at once came forward, saying again, as she embraced Valérie:

"What a dreadful blow, my dear!"

But Théophile seemed greatly put out.

"So now, it seems," said he, without even lowering his voice, "when one's father dies, it's through the coal-heaver one first hears of it! I suppose you wanted time to rifle his pockets!"

Duveyrier indignantly rose. But Clotilde motioned him aside, while, speaking very low, she replied to her brother.

"Miserable man! is not our father's death-agony even sacred to you? Look at him; see your handiwork; it is you, yes! you who brought on the attack by refusing to pay your back-rents."

Valérie began to laugh.

"Come, now, you're not in earnest!" she said.

"What? Not in earnest?" rejoined Clotilde, in a tone of disgust. "You knew how fond he was of collecting his rents. If you had made up your mind to kill him, you could not have acted in any better way."

Then they came to high words, and mutually accused each other of wishing to get hold of the inheritance, when Auguste, sullen and impassive as ever, called them to order.

"Be silent! There is plenty of time for that. It is not decent at the present moment!"

Accordingly, the others, admitting the justice of this remark, stationed themselves round the bed. There was dead silence in the damp room, only broken by the death-rattle. Berthe and Auguste stood at the foot of the bed; Valérie and Théophile, having come in last, had been obliged to remain some way off, near the table; Clotilde sat at the head of the bed, her husband standing beside her, while close up to the edge of the mattresses she had pushed her son Gustave, whom the old man adored. They now all looked at one another, without uttering a word. But their shining eyes and compressed lips spoke of hidden thoughts, and of all the anxiety and rancour which filled the heads of these next-of-kin, as they waited there, pale-faced and heavy-eyed. The two young couples were particularly furious at the sight of the schoolboy close to the bed, for, obviously, the Duveyriers were counting on Gustave's presence to influence his grandfather in their favour if he regained consciousness.

This manœuvre, moreover, was a proof that no will existed; and the Vabres furtively glanced at the old iron safe, which their father had brought from Versailles and had had fixed in a corner of his room. He had a mania for keeping all kinds of things in it. No doubt, the Duveyriers had carefully ransacked this safe during the night. Théophile conceived a trap for them, to make them speak.

"I say," he whispered at last in the counsellor's ear, "suppose we send for the notary? Papa may wish to make some alteration in his will."

At first Duveyrier did not hear. As he found waiting up in the bed-chamber extremely tedious, all night long his thoughts had gone back to Clarisse. Decidedly the wisest plan would be to make it up with his wife. And yet the other woman was so quaint when, with the gesture of a little street boy, she tossed her chemise right over her head; and, as he gazed dreamily at the dying man, it was as if she reappeared to him thus in a vision, and he would have given anything just to enjoy her again, even if it were but once. Théophile had to repeat his question.

"I asked Monsieur Renaudin," replied the counsellor, in bewilderment. "There is no will."

"But here?"

"Neither here nor at the notary's."

Théophile looked at Auguste. That was plain enough, wasn't it? The Duveyriers must have searched the drawers. Clotilde saw the look, and felt annoyed with her husband. What was the matter with him? Had grief robbed him of his senses? And she added:

"Papa will be sure to have done what he ought to have done. Goodness knows, we shall hear everything soon enough!"

She began to weep. At the sight of her grief, Valérie and Berthe commenced sobbing gently also. Théophile went back on tiptoe to his chair. He had found out what he wanted to know. No doubt, if his father regained consciousness, he would not allow the Duveyriers to make their brat of a son a means of turning matters to their own advantage. But, as he sat down, he saw his brother Auguste wiping his eyes, and that affected him so much that he became tearful in his turn. The idea of death possessed him; perhaps he would die of a similar seizure; it was awful. Thus the whole family became dissolved in tears. Gustave was the only one who could not weep. He was alarmed by it all, and looked on the floor, breathing in time with the dying man's death-rattle, in order to have something to do, just as at their gymnastic lessons he and his fellow-pupils were made to keep step.

Meanwhile, the hours passed quickly. At eleven o'clock it was some distraction when Doctor Juillerat again appeared. The patient had become worse; it was now doubtful whether he would be able to recognise his children before he died. Then the sobbing recommenced, when Clémence ushered in the Abbé Mauduit. Clotilde, rising to meet him, was the first to receive his consolations. He seemed deeply affected by this family misfortune, and gave to each a word of encouragement. Then, with much tact, he spoke of the rites of religion, hinting that this soul should not be allowed to pass away without the succour of the Church.

"I had thought of this," murmured Clotilde.

But Théophile raised objections. Their father paid no heed to religion; at one time he had held most advanced views, for he read Voltaire. The best plan would be to abstain from doing anything, as they could not consult him. In the heat of the argument, he even remarked:

"It is as if you were to administer the sacrament to that table."

The three women compelled him to be silent. They were all overcome by emotion, declared that the priest was right, and made excuses for not having sent for him owing to the confusion occasioned by this sad event. Had Monsieur Vabre been able to speak, he would certainly have consented, said they, for he did not like to make himself conspicuous in any way. Moreover, the entire responsibility should rest with them.

"If only on account of our neighbours," said Clotilde, "it ought to be done."

"Of course," said the Abbé Mauduit, who strongly approved of this remark; "a man in your father's position ought to set a good example."

Auguste could give no opinion. But Duveyrier, roused from his meditations upon Clarisse, of whose method of putting on her stockings with one thigh in the air he was just then thinking, vehemently urged the administration of the sacraments. They were a necessity, and no member of his family should die without them. Doctor Juillerat, who had discreetly stood aside, not even showing his freethinker's disdain, then went up to the abbé and whispered familiarly, as to a colleague whom he was often wont to meet upon occasions of this kind :

"You must make haste, for there is no time to lose."

The priest hurried away, saying that he would bring the sacrament and the extreme unction, so as to be prepared for emergencies. Then Théophile, obstinate as ever, muttered :

"Oh, yes; so now, apparently, they force the dying to take the sacrament in spite of themselves !"

Suddenly all were greatly startled. On going back to her place, Clotilde found the dying man with his eyes wide open. She could not check a slight cry. They all rushed to the bedside, and the old man's gaze slowly wandered from one to another, his head remaining motionless. Doctor Juillerat, seemingly astonished, leant over his patient to watch this final crisis.

"Father, it is we who are here. Do you know us?" asked Clotilde.

Monsieur Vabre stared at her; then his lips moved, but they uttered no sound. They all pushed one another aside in their eagerness to catch his last word. Valérie, in the rear, was obliged to stand on tiptoe, saying bitterly :

"You're suffocating him; do stand back ! If he wanted anything, no one could tell what it was."

So the others had to stand back. Monsieur Vabre's eyes were, indeed, wandering round the room.

"He wants something, that is certain," murmured Berthe.

"Here is Gustave," said Clotilde. "You can see him, can't you? He has come from school to kiss you. Kiss your grandfather, my boy."

As the lad drew back in dismay, she held him forward with her arm, waiting for a smile to light up the dying man's distorted countenance. But Auguste, following the direction of his eyes, declared that he was looking at the table. No doubt, he wanted to write. This caused great excitement, and everyone hastened to bring the table close to the bedside, and to fetch some paper, an inkstand and a pen. Then they raised him, propping him up with three pillows. The doctor authorised all this by a wink.

"Give him the pen," said Clotilde, trembling, as she still held Gustave out towards him.

Then there came a solemn moment. Crowding round the bed, all the family waited anxiously while Monsieur Vabre, who did not seem to recognise anyone, let the pen slip through his fingers. For a moment his eyes strayed across the table, on which was the oak box full of tickets. Then, sliding off the pillows, he fell forward like a bundle of rags, and, stretching out his arm in a supreme effort, he began dabbling about in the box of tickets with the gesture of a baby delighted at playing with dirt. He beamed, and tried to speak, but only could stammer out one syllable over and over again, one of those monosyllabic cries into which babies in swaddling-clothes can put a whole host of meanings.

"Ga—ga—ga—ga——"

It was to the work of his life, this immense study in statistics, that he was saying good-bye. Suddenly his head rolled forward. He was dead.

"I feared as much," muttered the doctor, who, seeing the general bewilderment, carefully straightened the dead man's limbs and closed his eyes.

Was it possible? Auguste took away the table, and all remained chilled and mute. Soon they broke forth into sobs. Well, since all hope of recovery was gone, they would still try what they could do to share the fortune. And Clotilde, after hastily sending Gustave away, to spare him so harrowing a spectacle, wept unrestrainedly, leaning her head on Berthe, who, with Valérie, was also sobbing. Théophile and Auguste, at the window, kept rubbing their eyes. But Duveyrier's grief seemed to be the most inconsolable of all, as he stifled loud sobs with his handkerchief. No, he really could not live without Clarisse; he would rather die at once, like Vabre, lying there; and thus the loss of his paramour, coming in the midst of all this mourning, gave immense bitterness to his grief.

"Madam," said Clémence, entering, "the holy sacraments."

Abbé Mauduit appeared on the threshold. Behind his back one caught sight of a choir-boy's inquisitive face. Seeing them all sobbing, the abbé glanced questioningly at the doctor, who held out his arms as if to say that it was not his fault. Then, after murmuring sundry prayers, the priest withdrew in embarrassment, taking the sacraments with him.

"That is a bad sign," said Clémence to the other servants, who were grouped round the door of the ante-room. "The *bon Dieu* is not disturbed for nothing. You see if he does not come back to the house before the year is out!"

Monsieur Vabre's funeral did not take place for two days. Notwithstanding, on the circulars announcing his death, Duveyrier caused the words to be printed, "Provided with the Holy Sacraments of the Church." The shop being closed, Octave was free, and felt delighted at getting such a holiday, as for a long while he had wanted to rearrange his room, move the furniture, and put his books together in a little bookcase that he had picked up second-hand. He had risen earlier than usual, and had just finished his alterations about eight o'clock, on the morning of the funeral, when Marie knocked at the door. She had brought him a bundle of books.

"As you don't come and fetch them," said she, "I've got to take the trouble to return them myself."

But, blushing, she refused to come in, shocked at the idea of being in a young man's room. Their intimacy, however, had completely ceased in the most natural manner possible, as he had no longer run after her. But she was as affectionate as ever, always greeting him with a smile when they met.

Octave was in high spirits that morning; he began teasing her.

"So it's Jules, is it, who won't let you come to my room?" he kept saying. "How do you get on with Jules now? Is he amiable? You know what I mean. Now, tell me."

She laughed, not being the least shocked.

"Why, of course, whenever you take him out, you go and treat him to vermouth, and tell him things that make him come home like a madman. Oh, he is far too amiable! You know, I don't want as much as all that. But I'd rather it happened at home than elsewhere, that is very certain!" She became serious again, and added: "Look, I have brought back your Balzac; I could not finish it. It's too sad; he has nothing but disagreeable things to tell one, has that gentleman."

And she asked him for tales in which there was plenty of love, all about adventures and travels in foreign lands. Then she talked of the funeral. She was going to the church, and Jules would get as far as the cemetery. She had never felt frightened of corpses; when twelve years old, she sat up a whole night with an uncle and aunt who had died of the same fever. Jules, on the other hand, hated talking of dead people, so much so that he had actually forbidden her, two days ago, to mention the landlord lying on his back downstairs. But she could find no other subject for conversation, neither could he; so that for a whole hour they barely exchanged a dozen words, and did nothing else but think of the poor gentleman. It was becoming tiresome, and, for Jules' sake, she would be glad when they fetched him away. And, happy at being able to talk about it at her ease, she satisfied her taste, overwhelming Octave with questions. Had he seen him? Was he very much altered? Was it true that something horrible had occurred as he was being placed in his coffin? Were not his relatives ripping up all the mattresses in their eagerness to search everywhere? So many tales were afloat in a house of this sort, overrun by servants! Death, after all, was the only thing that everybody was interested in.

"You're giving me another one of Balzac's," said she, looking over the fresh batch of books that he was lending her. "No, take it back; his tales are too much like real life!"

As she held the volume out to him, he caught hold of her wrist and tried to pull her into the room. She amused him with all her curiosity about death; she suddenly seemed to him droll, full of life, desirable. But she understood his meaning, and blushed scarlet. Then, freeing herself from his grasp, she ran away, saying:

"Thank you, Monsieur Mouret; we shall meet by-an-by, at the funeral."

When Octave was dressed, he recollected his promise to go and see Madame Campardon.

He had two whole hours before him, as the funeral was fixed for eleven o'clock, and he thought of utilising his morning by making a few calls in the house. Rose received him in bed; he apologised for disturbing her, but she herself called him into her room. They saw so little of him, and she was so glad to have anyone to chat to!

"Ah, my dear boy," cried she all at once; "it is I who ought to be lying down below, nailed up between four planks!"

Yes, the landlord was very lucky; he had done with existence! And as Octave, astonished to find her a prey to such melancholy, asked her if she felt worse, she replied:

"No, thank you. It is always the same thing, only there are times when I feel as if I had had enough of it. Achille has had to put up a bed in his workroom, as it annoyed me whenever he moved about at night. And, you know, we have persuaded Gasparine to leave the shop. I am so grateful to her for doing this, and she looks after me with such tenderness! Ah, if it were not for being surrounded by so much affection and kindness, I could never live!"

Just then Gasparine, with her submissive air of a poor relation turned servant, brought in the coffee. Helping Rose to raise herself, she propped her up against some cushions and gave her the coffee on a little tray covered with a napkin. Rose, in her embroidered jacket, covered up in lace-edged linen, ate with a hearty appetite. She looked so fresh—younger than ever; very pretty with her white skin and little blonde curls.

"Oh, my stomach's all right; there's nothing wrong with my stomach!" she kept saying, as she soaked her slices of bread and butter.

Two tears fell into the coffee. Then Gasparine chid her:

"Now, if you cry, I shall call Achille. Aren't you satisfied to be sitting there like a queen on a throne?"

By the time Madame Campardon had finished and again found herself alone with Octave, she became wholly comforted. Coquettishly, she once more began to talk about death, but with the languid gaiety of a woman whiling away a whole morning in warm bed-clothes. Well, she'd have to go, too, when her turn came. No, they were right; she was not unhappy, and could bear to go on living, since they saved her from all the main worries of existence. So she rambled on in her selfish, sexless-idol manner.

Then, as the young man rose to go, she said:

"Now, do come oftener, won't you? Go and enjoy yourself; don't let the funeral sadden you too much. One dies a little every day. The thing is to get used to it."

On the same floor, Louise, the little maid at Madame Juzeur's, let Octave in. She took him into the drawing-room, looked at him for a moment, grinning sheepishly, and at last said that her mistress was dressing. Madame Juzeur, however, at once made her appearance, wearing black, and in this mourning she seemed gentler, more refined, than ever.

"I was sure that you would come this morning," she sighed, languidly. "All night long I kept dreaming about you. Quite impossible to sleep, you know, with that corpse in the house!"

And she confessed that she had got up three times in the night to look under the furniture.

"Why, you ought to have called me," said the young man, gallantly. "Two in a bed are never afraid."

She affected a charming air of shame.

"Be quiet; it's naughty!"

And she held her hand over his lips. Of course, he was obliged to kiss it. Then she spread out her fingers, laughing as if she were being tickled. Excited by this game, he sought to push matters further. He caught her in his arms and pressed her close to his breast without her offering any resistance. Then he whispered:

"Come, now, why won't you?"

"Oh, in any case, not to-day!"

"Why not to-day?"

"What, with that dead body downstairs? No, no it's impossible!"

He tightened his embrace, and she yielded. Their warm breaths mingled.

"When will you, then? To-morrow?"

"Never."

"But you're quite free; your husband behaved so badly that you owe him nothing."

He sought to force her consent. But in her supple way she slipped from him. Then putting her arms round him, she held him tightly so that he could not move, and murmured caressingly:

"Anything you like except that! Do you understand me! Not that, never, never! I would rather die! It's an idea of mine, that's all. I've sworn to Heaven I wouldn't, but you need not know anything about that. So you're just as selfish, it seems, as other men, who are never satisfied as long as one refuses them anything? Yet I am very fond of you. Anything you like, only not that, my sweetheart!"

She allowed him to caress her in the warmest, most secret way, only repulsing him by a sudden movement of nervous vigour when he sought to perform the one forbidden act. Her obstinacy had in it a sort of Jesuitical reserve, a fear of the confessional, a certitude of pardon for petty sins, while so gross a one might cause over-much trouble with her spiritual pastor. Then there were other unavowed sentiments, a blending of honour and of self esteem, the coquetry of always having an advantage over men by never satisfying them, together with a shrewd personal enjoyment of getting kisses in abundance from everybody without the final, humiliating touch of the male. This she thought better, and stubbornly persisted in it. Not a man could flatter himself that he had had her since her husband's cowardly desertion. She was an honest woman.

"No, sir, not one! Ah, I can hold my head up, I can! How

many unfortunate women in my position would have gone wrong!"

She gently moved him aside and rose from the sofa.

"Let me alone. That corpse downstairs worries me dreadfully. The whole house seems to smell of it!"

Meanwhile, the time drew near for the funeral. She wished to get to the church before they started, so as not to see all the funeral trappings. But, on going to the door with him, she suddenly remembered telling him about her liqueur from the West Indies. So she made him come back, and brought the bottle and two glasses herself. It was creamy and very sweet, with a scent of flowers. When she had drunk it, a sort of girlish greediness gave a look of languid rapture to her face. She could have lived on sugar; sweets scented with vanilla and with rose troubled her senses as greatly as the touch of a lover.

"That will keep us up," said she.

And, when in the ante-room he kissed her on the mouth, she shut her eyes. Their sugary lips semed to melt like bon-bons.

It was nearly eleven o'clock. They had not yet been able to bring down the coffin, for the undertaker's men, after dawdling away their time at a wine-shop, never seemed to have done putting up the draperies. For curiosity's sake, Octave went to look at them. The porch was already closed at the back by a large black curtain, but the men had still to nail up hangings over the door. And on the pavement outside a group of servants were gossiping with their noses in the air, while Hippolyte, in deep mourning, hurried on the work with an air of dignity.

"Yes, madam," Lisa was saying to a withered widow-woman, who had been a week in Valérie's service, "it has done her no good at all. The whole neighbourhood knows the story well. To make sure of her share of the old man's money, she got that child made for her by a butcher in the Rue Sainte-Anne, as her husband looked as if he might go off the hooks any minute. But her husband is alive, and it's the old boy that's gone. A lot of good she's done herself with her filthy brat!"

The widow nodded her head in disgust.

"Serves her right!" she answered. "All her swinish tricks have done her no good. You needn't think I shall stop with her! I gave her a week's notice this morning. Why, her little brute of a Camille went wetting all over my kitchen!"

Just then Julie came downstairs to give Hippolyte an order. Lisa ran to question her, and then, after a few moments' conversation she came back to Valérie's servant.

"It's a regular mess," quoth she, "and nobody can make anything out of it. It seem to me your mistress need not have got a baby made, but could have let her husband kick the bucket, as it appear that they are still hunting for the old chap's brass. The cook say they do look a wry faced lot in there—as if they'd come to blow before the day was out."

Adèle came up, with four sous' worth of butter under her apron Madame Josserand having ordered her never to show any food tha she went to fetch. Lisa wanted to see what she carried, and then roundly abused her for being such a big fool. Who ever heard o anyone being sent to fetch four sous' worth of butter! Ah, well she would very soon have made those skin-flints feed her better or else she would have fed herself before they got anything; yes eat the butter, the sugar, the meat, everything! For some time pas the other servants had thus been inciting Adèle to rebel. She wa gradually becoming perverted. She munched off a corner of the butter, and ate it up without any bread, to show the others how little she cared.

"Shall we go up?" said she.

"No," replied the widow, "I want to see him brought down; have delayed an errand on purpose for that."

"So have I," added Lisa. "They say he weighs twelve stone If they drop him on their beautiful staircase, there will be a joll smash-up, eh?"

"Well, I'm going up, for I'd rather not see him," said Adèle "I don't want to dream again, as I did last night, that he wa pulling me out of bed by the heels, and pitching into me for making a mess."

She went off amid the laughter of her two companions. All nigh long Adèle's nightmare had been a source of merriment on the servants' floor. The maidservants, moreover, in order not to b alone, had left their doors open, whereupon a waggish coachman pretended to be a ghost, for fun, and little screams and stifled laughter were heard all along the passage until daylight. Biting he lips, Lisa declared that she would never forget it. A rare piece o fun, and no mistake!

But Hippolyte's wrathful voice brought their attention back t the hangings. Oblivious of his dignity, he was shouting out:

"Look out, you drunken fool! You're putting it on wrong sid up!"

It was true; the man was about to hook the escutcheon bearing the deceased's monogram upside down. The black hangings, edged with silver lace, were now in their proper place, and only a few curtain-rests had yet to be put up, when a truck, laden with some poor person's chattels, drew up at the door. A lad was pulling it along, while a tall, pale girl followed, and helped to push behind. Monsieur Gourd, who was talking to his friend, the stationer opposite, rushed forward, forgetful of his grand mourning, and exclaimed:

"Now, then! now, then! what's he after? Can't you see, you blockhead?"

The tall girl interposed.

"Sir, I am the new lodger, you know. These are my things."

"It's impossible! To-morrow!" cried the hall-porter, in a fury.

She looked at him and then at the funeral draperies, half-dazed. It was plain that this door, muffled up with black, bewildered her. But, recovering herself, she explained that she could not very well leave her furniture out in the street. Then Monsieur Gourd began to bully her.

"You're the bootstitcher, aren't you? The party that's taken the little room up at the top? Another bit of the landlord's obstinacy! Just for the sake of a hundred and thirty francs, and after all the bother we had with the carpenter! He promised me, too, that he would never let rooms to working-folk any more. And now, blast it! the whole thing's going to begin again, and this time with a woman!"

Then he remembered that Monsieur Vabre was dead.

"Yes, you may look. The landlord is just dead, and if it had happened a week ago you would not be here; that's quite certain. Come, hurry up, before they bring him down!"

And in his exasperation he himself gave the truck a shove, pushing it through the hangings, which opened and then slowly closed again. The tall, pale girl disappeared behind the mass of black drapery.

"She's come at a nice time!" said Lisa. "A cheerful thing to do your shifting while a funeral's going on! If I'd been in her place, I'd have let the old devil have it!"

But she was silent as she saw Monsieur Gourd reappear, for he was the terror of the servants. His ill-temper was due to the fact that, as people said, the house would fall to the share of Monsieur Théophile and his wife. He would willingly have given a hundred francs, said he, to have Monsieur Duveyrier as landlord; he, at least, was a magistrate. This was what he was explaining to the stationer. Meanwhile, people now began to come downstairs. Madame Juzeur passed, smiling at Octave, who had met Trublot outside on the pavement. Then Marie appeared, and watched them placing the trestles for the coffin with great interest.

"What extraordinary people they are on the second floor," hemarked Monsieur Gourd as he looked up at their closed shutters. "One would think that they always managed to avoid doing like anybody else. Yes, they went off on a journey three days ago."

At this moment, Lisa hid behind her friend the widow, on catching sight of Gasparine, who was bringing a wreath of violets, a delicate attention on the part of the architect, who desired to keep on good terms with the Duveyriers.

"My word!" exclaimed the stationer, "the other Madame Campardon do get herself up, don't she?"

He called her thus innocently by the name given to her by all the neighbouring tradespeople. Lisa smothered her laughter. Then suddenly the servants discovered that the coffin had been brought down, which proved a great disappointment. How silly, too, to have stopped all that while in the street, looking at the black curtains! They quickly went indoors just as the coffin, carried by four men, was being brought out of the vestibule. All the hangings darkened the porch, and at the back one could see the pallid daylight of the courtyard, which that morning had been thoroughly washed. Little Louise, who had followed Madame Juzeur, stood on tiptoe, wide-eyed and pale with curiosity. The coffin-bearers puffed and gasped at the foot of the staircase, which, with its gilding and sham marble, wore an air of frigid pomp in the faint light that fell from the ground-glass windows.

"There he goes, without his quarter's rent!" muttered Lisa, with the rancorous wit of a landlord-hating Parisienne.

Madame Gourd, who, owing to her bad legs, had remained riveted in her arm-chair, now rose with difficulty. As she could not get as far as the church, Monsieur Gourd had instructed her not to let the dead landlord go past their room without saluting him. It behoved her to do this. She came as far as the door in a black cap, and as the coffin passed she curtsied.

During the service at Saint-Roch, Doctor Juillerat ostentatiously remained outside the church. There was, moreover, a great crowd, and several of the men preferred to stay in a group on the steps. It was very mild—a glorious day in June. Since they could not smoke, they talked politics. The central door was left open, and at intervals bursts of organ-melody issued from the church, all hung with black and ablaze with tapers.

"I suppose you know that Monsieur Thiers is going to stand for our district next year," remarked Léon Josserand, in his grave way.

"Oh! is he?" replied the doctor. "Of course, you, being a Republican, will not vote for him, eh?"

The young man, whose Radical opinions under Madame Dambreville's tutelage had become milder, drily answered :

"Why not? He is the avowed enemy of the Empire."

Then ensued a violent discussion. Léon spoke of tactics; Doctor Juillerat obstinately clung to principles. The middle-classes, so he averred, had had their day; they only blocked the pathway of revolution, and now, being wealthy, they opposed progress more stubbornly and blindly than the old nobility.

"You are afraid of everything; no sooner do you believe yourself threatened than there comes a violent reaction!"

Suddenly Campardon struck in angrily :

"I, sir, at one time was a Jacobin and an atheist, like yourself. But, thank Heaven, I came to my senses. I certainly should not deign to vote for such a fellow as your Monseiur Thiers—a muddle-pate, full of wild and insane ideas!"

However, all the Liberals present—Monsieur Josserand, Octave, Trublot, who did not care two pins—all declared that they would vote for Monsieur Thiers. The official candidate, Monsieur Dewinck, was a great chocolate manufacturer of the Rue Saint-Honoré, and they made very merry about him. This same Dewinck had not even the support of the clergy, who felt uneasy at his relations with the Tuileries. Wholly on the clerical side, Campardon, at the mention of his name, grew reserved. Then he inconsequently exclaimed : "Look here! the bullet that wounded your Garibaldi on the foot ought, by rights, to have struck his heart!"

And to avoid being seen any longer in such company, he went into the church, where the Abbé Mauduit's harsh voice made answer to lamentations of the choir.

"He simply lives in the place now," muttered the doctor, shrugging his shoulders. "Ah, what a clean sweep ought to be made of the whole show!"

In the Roman question he was deeply interested. Then, as Léon reminded them of what the Cabinet Minister had said to the

Senate, viz.: that the Empire had sprung from the Revolution solely in order to keep this latter in check, they again began to talk about the coming elections. All agreed that it was necessary to give the Emperor a sound lesson; but they felt anxious—divided in opinion respecting the various candidates, whose names even conjured up grisly visions of the Scarlet Woman. Hard by, Monsieur Gourd, as sprucely dressed as any diplomat, listened to their debate with icy scorn. He believed in the powers that be—a simple creed.

The service, however, was just coming to an end. A long, melancholy wail from the depths of the church silenced them.

"Requiescat in pace."

"Amen!"

At the Père-la-Chaise Cemetery, while the coffin was being lowered into the grave, Trublot, still arm-in-arm with Octave, saw him smile once more at Madame Juzeur.

"Ah, yes!" muttered he; "that's the little woman who's awfully unhappy. 'Anything-you-like-except that!' "

Octave started. What? Had Trublot tried it on, too? Then, with a gesture of disdain, the latter explained that he had not, but a friend of his had. Lots of other fellows, too, who went in for that sort of rot.

"Excuse me," he added; "now that the old boy has been stowed away, I must go and see Duveyrier about something that I had to do for him."

The relatives, silent and doleful, were now departing. Then Trublot, detaining Duveyrier, told him that he had seen Clarisse's maid, but he could not find out the address, as the maid had left the day before Clarisse moved, after a wild row. Thus the last ray of hope vanished, and Duveyrier, burying his face in his handkerchief, rejoined the other mourners.

That evening quarrelling began. The family had made a disastrous discovery. With that sceptical carelessness that notaries sometimes display, Monsieur Vabre had left no will. Cupboards and drawers were all searched in vain, the worst of it being that not a stiver of all the hoped-for six or seven hundred thousand francs was forthcoming, neither in the shape of money, title-deeds, nor shares. All that they found was the sum of seven hundred and thirty-four francs, in ten-sou pieces—the hidden store of a drivelling dotard. Moreover, there were undeniable traces, a note-book filled with figures and letters from stockbrokers—which convinced his relatives, id with rage—of the old man's secret vice, an ungovernable ssion for gambling, an inept, furious craving for dabbling in ocks and shares, which he hid behind his innocent mania for mpiling his masterpiece of statistical research. Everything had en sacrificed; his Versailles savings, his house-rents; even the oneys squeezed out of his children. During recent years, indeed, had even mortgaged the house for a hundred and fifty thou-nd francs, at three different periods. The family, dumbfounded, ood round the wonderful safe in which they believed the fortune as locked up. All that it contained, however, was a lot of odds d ends—scraps picked up about the house, old bits of iron and ass, tags of ribbon, and broken toys stolen long since when Gus-ve was a baby.

Then came violent abuse. They called the old man a swindler; was scandalous to fool away his money in this way, like a sly gue who cares not a straw for anybody, but who acts out his famous comedy so as to get people to pet and coddle him. The uveyriers seemed grieved beyond measure that they had boarded m for twelve years, without ever once asking him for the eighty ousand francs of Clotilde's dowry, ten thousand of which they d only received. Never mind; that was always ten thousand ancs, as Théophile angrily remarked. He had not yet got a penny the fifty thousand francs promised at the time of his marriage. uguste, however, complained more bitterly, reproaching his other with having, at any rate, been able for three months to cket the interest on that sum, whereas he would never see a rthing of the fifty thousand francs specified in his contract. Then erthe, spurred on by her mother, made various cutting remarks, d appeared to be highly indignant at having become connected ith a dishonest family, while Valérie, bewailing the rent which she d continued paying for so long through fear of being disinherited, as at a loss to comprehend it all, regretting the money as though had been used to promote debauchery.

For a whole fortnight these matters were excitedly discussed by e whole house. Finally it appeared that all that remained was the ilding, valued at three hundred thousand francs. When the mort-ge had been paid off, there would be about half that sum to vide between Monsieur Vabre's three children. Fifty thousand ancs apiece! a meagre consolation, truly, but with which they ust needs be content. Théophile and Auguste had already settled hat to do with their shares. It was agreed that the building should be sold. In his wife's name Duveyrier undertook all arrangemen First of all, he persuaded the two brothers not to have a pub auction; if they were willing, the sale could take place at notary's, Maître Renaudin, a man for whose integrity he cou answer. Then, acting on the notary's advice, he slyly hinted them that it would be best to put up the house at a low figure, or a hundred and forty thousand francs, to begin with. A very knowi dodge, this, which would bring crowds of people to the sale; t bids would mount rapidly, and they would realise far more th they expected. Full of happy confidence, Théophile and Augu chuckled again. However, on the day of the sale, Maître Renaud abruptly knocked the house down to Duveyrier for a hundred a forty thousand francs. There was not even enough to pay off t mortgage!

Never were the details disclosed of the fearful scene which to place at the Duveyriers' that same evening. The house's solen walls muffled the shouts of the combatants. Théophile denounc his brother-in-law as a scoundrel, openly accusing him of havi bribed the notary by promising to appoint him a justice of t peace. As for Auguste, he actually talked of the assize court, a declared that he would drag Maître Renaudin into it as well, wh roguery was the talk of the neighbourhood. But it never transpir how the good people, as rumour said, got at last to blows; th parting words on the threshold were overheard—words that am the austere decorum of the staircase rang out with disagreeal force.

"Dirty blackguard!" cried Auguste. "You sentence people penal servitude who have not done half as much!"

Théophile, coming last, kept the door opened as, half choked fury and a fit of coughing, he yelled:

"Thief! thief! Yes, thief! You, too, Clotilde, do you hea You're a thief!"

Then he slammed the door so violently that all the adjoining or shook again. Monsieur Gourd, who was listening, grew alarme He glanced up enquiringly at the several floors, but all that could see was Madame Juzeur's delicate profile. With back be he returned on tiptoe to his room, at once reassuming his dignifi mien. One could deny having heard any disturbance. Personally, was delighted, and sided with the new landlord.

A few days afterwards there was a reconciliation betwe Auguste and his sister. It surprised everybody. Octave had be een going to the Duveyriers'. The counsellor, ill at ease, had lecided to charge no rent for the ground-floor shop for five years hus shutting one of the inheritors' mouths. When Théophile heard his, accompanied by his wife, he went downstairs to his brother's ind made another scene. So he, too, had sold himself, and had oined the gang of thieves! However, Madame Josserand happened o be in the shop at the time, and she soon extinguished him. She rankly advised Valérie not to sell herself any more than her laughter had done. And Valérie, forced to retreat, exclaimed:

"So we're the only ones who are to grin and bear it, are we? Damned if I'll pay any more rent. I've got a lease, and that gaol-bird will never dare to turn us out. And as for you, my little Berthe, ne day we shall see what it will take to have you."

Once more there was a banging of doors. A deadly feud now xisted between the two families. Octave, who had been of service, vas present on this occasion, just as if he were one of the family. Berthe almost swooned in his arms, while Auguste made sure that none of his customers had overheard. Even Madame Josserand put aith in the young man. On the Duveyriers, however, she was very evere.

"The rent is something," said she, "but I want those fifty thou-and francs."

"Of course you do, if you pay yours," Berthe ventured to re-mark.

Her mother, seemingly, did not understand.

"I tell you, I want them, do your hear? Well, well, that old rip of a Vabre must be chuckling in his grave. I'm not going to let him boast of having made a fool of me, though. What scoundrels there are in this world, to be sure! Fancy promising money that one hasn't got! Wait a bit, my girl; they shall pay you, or else I'll go and dig him out of his grave just to spit in his face!"

XII

One morning, when Berthe was at her mother's, Adèle came in looking very scared, to say that Monsieur Saturnin was there with a man. Doctor Chassagne, the director of the Moulineaux Asylum, had repeatedly informed the Josserands that he could no keep their son, he not being a patient in whom the symptoms o insanity were sufficiently marked.

Having got to know about the papers making over the three thousand francs, which Berthe had cajoled her brother into signing he feared being compromised in the matter, and suddenly sen Saturnin home.

The news was alarming to all. Madame Josserand, who feared she might be throttled, sought to reason with the attendant. Bu he curtly said :

"The director wished me to tell you that when a person is san enough to give money to his parents, he is sane enough to live with them." "But he is mad; he will murder us !"

"Not so mad that he can't sign his name, anyhow !" rejoined th man, as he went away.

However, Saturnin came in very quietly, with his hands in hi pockets, just as if he were returning from a stroll in the Tuilerie gardens. As to his stay in the asylum, he said not a word.

He embraced his father, who wept, and he gave hearty kisses t his mother and Hortense, who both trembled with fright. Then, a he saw Berthe, he became delighted, caressing her with the charm ing impulsiveness of a schoolboy. She at once took advantage of hi tender mood to tell him of her marriage. He showed no signs c anger, and at first hardly seemed to understand, as if forgetful c his former fits of rage. But when she was about to go downstairs, h began to yell; married or not married, he did not care, so long a she stayed where he was, always with him, always close to him Seeing how her terrified mother rushed away to lock herself ir Berthe thought of taking Saturnin to her own home. They would make use of him in some way, in the basement of their shop, ever if it were but to tie up parcels.

That same evening, Auguste, despite his evident repugnance, consented to his wife's wish. They had hardly been married three months, yet insensibly were becoming estranged. It was the collision of two individuals widely different from each other in temperament as in education—a husband glum, crotchety, and devoid of passion, and a wife reared in the hothouse of specious Parisian luxury, bent on getting all the enjoyment she could out of life, though for herself alone, like a selfish, spoilt child. Thus he was at a loss to understand her desire for gaiety and movement, her perpetual goings-out to shop, to take walks, or pay visits; her racing hither and thither to theatres. exhibitions, or other places of amusement. Three or four times a week Madame Josserand came to fetch her daughter, stopping out till dinner-time, delighted to let herself be seen in her company, and in getting a borrowed glory from Berthe's handsome dresses, for which she no longer paid. Auguste's rebellion, indeed, was mainly due to these flashy gowns, for which he could see no sort of use. Why dress above one's means and station? What reason was there to spend in such a way money that he so urgently needed in his business? He used often to observe that when one sold silks to other women one ought to wear stuff oneself. Then Berthe, assuming her mother's ferocity of accent, would ask if he meant to let her go about stark naked. She, moreover, helped to discourage him yet further by the doubtful cleanliness of her petticoats and her contempt for all linen that was not displayed, having always a set of stock phrases ready wherewith to silence him if he persisted in his objections.

"I would rather excite envy than pity. Money is money, and when I had only twenty sous I always pretended I had forty."

After marriage Berthe gradually began to resemble her mother in figure. She grew stouter, sturdier. No longer was she the careless, lissom girl, submissive to maternal slaps; she was a woman of ever-increasing obstinacy, dominated by a desire to bend all things to her pleasure. Auguste sometimes looked at her, amazed at such prompt maturity. At first she had taken a vain delight in enthroning herself at the cashier's desk in a modest toilet of studied elegance. Then she had quickly conceived an aversion to trade; so sedentary a life disagreed with her; indeed, it almost made her ill, yet she resigned herself to it, posing as a victim, content to secure domestic prosperity at the sacrifice of her life. And ever since that time a perpetual warfare had been going on between herself and her husband. She shrugged her shoulders behind his back, just as her mother did behind her father's; she began with him all the petty domestic bickerings of her own childhood; she treated him simply as a person whose business it was to pay, showing him how profound was her contempt for the creature man, a contempt upon which her entire training had been based.

"Oh, mamma was right, after all!" she would exclaim after every one of their disputes.

At first, however, Auguste had endeavoured to please her. Being fond of peace, he dreamed of possessing a quiet little home—for he was already as crotchety as some old fogey, having thoroughly got into the grooves of his chaste and thrifty bachelor life. As his old lodging on the *entresol* was too small, he took a flat on the second floor, facing the court-yard, and thought it a piece of wild extravagance to spend five thousand francs in furniture. Berthe, delighted at first with her room—all polished wood and sky-blue silk—showed utter contempt for it later on, after visiting a friend of hers, a banker's wife. The first quarrels, too, had arisen touching servants. Used as she was to deal with half-witted maids-of-all-work, whose very bread was doled out to them, the young wife forced her servants to perform such tasks as set them sobbing in their kitchen for whole hours. Auguste, not usually too tender-hearted, once foolishly ventured to comfort one such tearful Phyllis, but, in an hour's time, was forced to send her flying, amid the sobs of his spouse, who furiously besought him to choose between herself and that creature. After this a strapping girl came, who apparently had made up her mind to stay. Her name was Rachel—a Jewess, no doubt, although she denied it, and concealed her nationality. Aged about five-and-twenty, she had a hard face, a big nose, and coal-black hair. At first Berthe said that she would not put up with her for a couple of days, but the newcomer's mute obedience, her air of understanding all yet of saying nothing gradually satisfied her. It looked as if the mistress, in her turn, had been subjugated, who ostensibly kept the girl for her merits, though, at the same time, vaguely afraid of her. Rachel, who, unmurmuring, consented to do all sorts of work, however hard, for dry bread alone, was gradually getting possession of the household, with her eyes open and her mouth shut, like a wily servant waiting for the fatal moment when madame would be able to refuse her nothing.

Meanwhile, from top to bottom, a great calm reigned throughout the house, after the commotion caused by Monsieur Vabre's sudden death. The staircase once more became peaceful as a chapel, not a sound escaped from behind those mahogany doors, which for ever shut in the profound respectability of the several families. A rumour was afloat that the breach between Duveyrier and his wife had been healed. As for Valérie and Théophile, they spoke to no one, as they stalked by with a stiffly dignified air. Never before had the house seemed the very hotbed of all that was most strict and severe in principle. Monsieur Gourd, in cap and slippers, went about the building like some solemn beadle.

One evening, about eleven o'clock, Auguste kept continually going to the shop door and looking up and down the street with ever-increasing impatience. Berthe, whom her mother and sister had fetched at dinner-time, not letting her finish her dessert even, had not yet come back, though she had been gone more than three hours, and had promised to return before closing time.

"Oh, good gracious me!" he exclaimed at last, as he clasped his hands until the fingers cracked again.

Then he stopped short in front of Octave, who was ticketing some remnants of silk on the counter. At that late hour, no customer came to this out-of-the-way corner of the Rue de Choiseul. The shop was only kept open so as to put things in order.

"I am sure that you know where the ladies have gone, don't you?" asked Auguste.

Octave looked up with an air of innocent surprise.

"Why, sir, they told you—to a lecture."

"A lecture, indeed, a lecture!" grumbled the husband. "Their lecture was over at ten o'clock. Respectable women ought to be home long before this, I should think!"

Then he resumed his walk, giving side glances at Octave, whom he suspected of being the ladies' accomplice, or, at least, of wishing to make excuses for them. Octave, feeling ill at ease, watched him furtively also. He had never seen him in such a state of nervous excitement. What could have happened? Turning his head, he saw Saturnin at the other end of the shop, cleaning a mirror with a sponge soaked in spirit. By degrees, they had begun to set the madman to do house-work, so that at least he might earn his food. That evening Saturnin's eyes glittered strangely. He crept up close behind Octave and said to him in an undertone:

"Look out! He's found a paper. Yes, he's got a paper in his pocket. Look out, if it's anything of yours!"

Then he hurriedly continued rubbing his glass. Octave could not make it out. For some time past the lunatic had shown singular affection for him, like the caress of an animal beneath whose keen, unerring instinct lay a deeper, more subtle sentiment. What made him mention a paper? He had not written any letter to Berthe, but only allowed himself to look tenderly at her now and again, while waiting for a chance of making her some little present. This was the line of tactics which, after mature reflection, he had resolved to adopt.

"Ten minutes past eleven—damn it all!" exclaimed Auguste, who never swore, as a rule.

At that moment, however, the ladies came in. Berthe wore a charming costume of pink silk embroidered with white jet, while her sister, always in blue, and her mother, always in mauve, kept to their gaudy, elaborate gowns, which every season they furbished up anew. Madame Josserand came first, large and imposing, to stop her son-in-law from making any complaints. These the three had foreseen when holding council together at the top of the street. She even condescended to explain their delay by saying that they had dawdled along, looking in at shop-windows. Auguste, however, grew very pale, and made no remonstrance, speaking in a dry tone of voice. Evidently, he was restraining himself until later on. For a moment, Madame Josserand, used as she was to family jars, felt disposed to intimidate him; then being obliged to withdraw, she was content to say:

"Good-night, my girl, and sleep well if you want to live long."

Instantly Auguste, no longer master of himself and oblivious of the presence of Octave and Saturnin, pulled a crumbled piece of paper out of his pocket, which he thrust into Berthe's face, as he stuttered:

"What—what—what is this?"

Berthe had not even taken off her bonnet. She grew very red.

"That?" she replied. "Why, it's a bill."

"Yes, it's a bill, and for false hair, too! For false hair, of all things; as if you hadn't got any on your head! But that's not the point. You've paid this bill; now, tell me, what did you pay it with?"

Becoming more and more embarrassed, Berthe at last rejoined:

"With my own money, of course!"

"Your own money! Why, you haven't got any. Somebody must have given you some, or else you took it from here. Yes; and look here, I know everything. You've been running into debt!

I'll put up with anything you like, but I won't have debts, do you hear? I won't have debts—never!"

He said this with all the horror of a prudent fellow whose commercial integrity consists in owing no one a farthing. He now aired all his grievances, reproaching his wife for continually gadding about all over the town, complaining of her toilettes and all the luxuries that he could not supply. Was it right that people in their position should stay out till eleven o'clock at night, dressed up in pink silk gowns embroidered with white jet? Folk who had such tastes as those ought to provide themselves with a dowry of five hundred thousand francs. However, he knew well enough who was to blame; it was that idiot of a mother, who only taught her girls how to squander fortunes without having so much as a rag to put on their backs the day of their wedding.

"Don't abuse mamma!" cried Berthe, who at last became exasperated. "She's not to blame; she did her duty. And your family! They're a nice set! People that killed their father!"

Octave went on with his work of ticketing the silks, and pretended not to hear. But he furtively kept watching the dispute, and had his eye on Saturnin, who had stopped polishing the mirror and, with clenched fists and flashing eyes, stood there trembling, ready to make a spring at Auguste's throat.

"Bother our families!" rejoined the latter. "We've got enough to do at home as it is. Look here, you'll have to change your ways, as I won't pay another sou for all this tomfoolery. I've made up my mind about that! Your proper place is here, at your desk, dressed simply, like a woman who has some respect for herself. And if you run up debts, you'll see!"

Berthe was aghast at this marital hand thus roughly laid upon her pet amusements, her pleasures, her frocks. It was as if all had been wrenched from her—all that she liked, all that she had dreamed of when getting married. But, with a woman's tactics, she hid her real wound, finding a pretext for the wrath that flushed her face as she indignantly exclaimed:

"I will not permit you to insult mamma!"

Auguste shrugged his shoulders.

"Your mother, indeed! You look just like her—just ugly when you work yourself up into such a state! I shouldn't know it was you; it's your mother over again! Bah! it gives one quite a turn!"

Berthe instantly grew calm, and looked him straight in the face.

"Go and tell mamma what you said just now, and see how she'll send you to the right-about!"

"Would she?" cried Auguste, in a fury. "Then I'll just go and tell her this very minute. See if I don't!"

He went out forthwith, and not a moment too soon, for Saturnin, with wolfish eyes, was coming up on tiptoe to strangle him from behind. Berthe sank into a chair, murmuring:

"There's a man I wouldn't marry again if I had the chance, by God!"

Upstairs, Monsieur Josserand opened the door in great surprise, as Adèle had gone to bed. He was just getting ready to spend the night in addressing wrappers, in spite of the indisposition of which for some time he had complained. Thus, feeling embarrassed, and fearful of being found out, he took his son-in-law into the dining-room, alluding to some urgent work which he had to finish—a copy of the inventory of the Saint-Joseph Glass Works. But when Auguste roundly accused his daughter of running into debt, and told him of the quarrel occasioned by the incident of the false hair, the poor man trembled in every limb; he stammered incoherently, and tears filled his eyes. His daughter was in debt, and led a life of household bickering just like his own! All his own misfortunes had begun anew for his child! Another fear possessed him, and this was that his son-in-law would broach the subject of money, claim the dowry and denounce him as a swindler. No doubt the fellow knew everything, or he would never have knocked them up in this way at nearly midnight.

"My wife has gone to bed," he stuttered, in confusion. "It is no good waking her up, is it? Really, I am surprised to hear all this! My poor dear Berthe is not a naughty girl, that I assure you! Do be indulgent towards her. I'll speak to her myself. As for ourselves, my dear Auguste, I don't think we have done anything to displease you——"

He looked at him enquiringly, feeling reassured; Auguste evidently knew nothing as yet. Then Madame Josserand appeared outside her bedroom door. She stood there in her night-dress, white and appalling. Infuriated though he was, Auguste recoiled. She must have been listening at the door, for she at once delivered a blow straight from the shoulder.

"I don't suppose you've come for your ten thousand francs, have you? The instalment is not due for two months and more. We will pay you in two months, sir. We are not in the habit of dying to avoid keeping *our* promises."

Her astounding assurance completely over-powered Monsieur Josserand. Having once begun, she went on making the most extraordinary statements, to the utter bewilderment of Auguste, whom she would not give time to speak.

"You are utterly wanting in common-sense, sir. When you've made Berthe ill, you'll have to send for the doctor, and then you'll have a chemist's bill to pay. I went away just now because I saw that you had determined to make a fool of yourself. Pray do so. Beat your wife, if you like; my mother's heart is easy, for God sees all, and punishment is never far behind!"

At last Auguste was able to explain his grievances. He complained once more of the perpetual gadding about, the expensive dresses and all the rest of it, having even the hardihood to condemn the way that Berthe had been brought up. Madame Josserand listened with an air of supreme contempt. Then, when he had finished, she said:

"All that you tell me, my good fellow, is so nonsensical that it does not deserve an answer. My conscience is my own; that is enough for me. A man like that, to whom I entrusted an angel! As I am only insulted, I shall have nothing more to do with your quarrels. Settle them as best you can!"

"But your daughter will end by deceiving me, madam!" cried Auguste, in a fresh burst of rage.

Madame Josserand, about to withdraw, turned round and looked him full in the face.

"Sir," said she, "you're doing all you possibly can to make her."

Then she went back to her room, majestic as some colossal triple-breasted Ceres robed in white.

The father detained Auguste for a few minutes longer. He sought to conciliate him, pointing out that with women it is best to put up with everything; and at last sent him away pacified and resolved to forgive Berthe. But as the poor old man found himself once more alone in the dining-room, before his little lamp, he burst into tears. All was over; all happiness at an end for him. He would never find time at night to address wrappers enough to help his daughter secretly. The thought that she might run into debt overwhelmed him as if with a sense of personal shame. He felt quite ill at receiving this fresh blow; one of these nights his strength would fail him. At last, checking his tears by an effort, he went on with his work,

Downstairs in the shop, Berthe remained motionless for moment, her face buried in her hands. One of the men, having pu up the shutters, went below into the basement, and it was then tha Octave thought he might approach the young woman. Ever sinc Auguste had gone, Saturnin kept making signs over his sister' head, inviting Octave to comfort her. Now, looking radiant, he re doubled his winks, and fearing that he was not understood, h emphasised his hints by blowing kisses with childish impulsiveness

"What? Do you want me to kiss her?" Octave asked him, b signs.

The madman vigorously nodded assent. Then as he saw Octav smilingly approach Berthe, who had observed nothing, he sat o the floor behind a counter, out of sight, so as not to be in their way The gas-jets still were burning—tall flames in the silent, empt shop. There was a sort of death-like peace, and a stuffy smell fron all the bales of silk.

"Madame, let me beg you not to take it too much to heart," sai Octave, in his caressing voice.

She started on seeing him so near her.

"I must ask you to excuse me, Monsieur Octave, but it was no my fault if you were present at this painful scene. And pray mak allowances for my husband, who must be unwell this evening. I all families, you know, little unpleasantnesses occur——"

Sobs here choked her utterance. The mere thought of extenuatin her husband's faults to outsiders brought on a violent fit of weeping which completely unnerved her.

Saturnin peeped anxiously over the counter, but he bobbed dow again as soon as he saw Octave take hold of Berthe's hand.

"Let me beg of you, madam, to be brave and not to give way."

"But I cannot help it!" sobbed Berthe. "You were there, so yo heard it all. All about ninety-five francs' worth of hair! As if ever woman didn't wear false hair now-a-days! But he knows nothin and understands nothing! He knows no more about women tha the Grand Turk. He's never had one in his life, Monsieur Octave never! Oh, poor wretched me!"

In her furious spite, she blurted out everything. A man whom sh thought had married her for love, but who very soon would leav her without a chemise to her back! Didn't she do her duty b him? Could he charge her with the least neglect? If he had no flown into a rage when she asked him to get her some false hair, sh would never have been obliged to buy some with her own pocket money. For the least thing there was always the same fuss; she could never express a wish or say that she wanted some trivial article of dress, without meeting with such sullen, ferocious opposition. Naturally, she had some pride; she now asked for nothing and preferred to go without necessaries, rather than humiliate herself to no purpose. For instance, the last fortnight she had been longing for some ornaments that she had seen, with her mother, in a jeweller's window in the Palais Royal.

"You know, three paste stars to put in the hair. A mere trifle—a hundred francs, I fancy. Well, it was no good my talking about them from morning till night; my husband wouldn't see it!"

Octave could never have hoped for a more favourable opportunity. He resolved to come straight to the point.

"Oh, yes, I remember! I often heard you speak about them. Well, madam, your parents have always shown me such kindness, and you yourself have been so extremely obliging towards me, that I thought I might venture to——"

Hereupon he drew from his pocket a long box containing the three stars, which sparkled on cotton-wool. Berthe excitedly rose from her seat.

"But, sir, it's impossible for me to—I cannot, really—it was most wrong of you!"

With mock ingenuousness he invented various excuses. In the South such things were done every day. Besides, the ornaments were of no value at all. Her face bacame suffused with blushes; she ceased sobbing and looked with sparkling eyes at the contents of the cardboard box.

"Pray do me the favour, madam, just to show me that you are satisfied with my work."

"No, Monsieur Octave, really, you must not insist. I am sorry that you should have——"

At this moment, Saturnin came back and examined the jewellery with as much rapture as if they were holy relics. Soon his sharp ear detected Auguste's returning footsteps. He apprised Berthe of this by a slight click of his tongue. Just as her husband was about to enter she made up her mind.

"Well, look here," she hurriedly whispered, thrusting the box into her pocket, "I'll say that my sister Hortense made me a present of them."

Auguste ordered the gas to be turned out, and then went upstairs with his wife to bed, without saying a word about their quarrel, being secretly glad to find that Berthe had recovered her spirits as if nothing had ever taken place. The shop became wrapped in darkness, and, just as Octave was leaving also, he felt two hot hands squeezing his in the gloom. It was Saturnin, who slept in the basement. "Friend, friend, friend!" reiterated the lunatic, in an outburst of wild affection.

Thwarted somewhat in his scheme. Octave by degrees began to conceive for Berthe a virile and vehement desire. If at first he had followed his usual plan of seduction, and his wish to make women a means of self-advancement, he now no longer regarded Berthe merely as his employer, whom to possess was tantamount to gaining control of the entire establishment. What he desired, above all, was to enjoy this little Parisienne, fascinating in all her luxury and grace, a dainty creature such as he had never tasted at Marseilles. He felt a sudden hunger for her tiny gloved hands, her tiny feet in their high-heeled boots, her soft bosom concealed by lace frippery, though maybe some of her under-linen was of doubtful cleanliness, its shabbiness being hidden by magnificent dresses. This sudden impetus of passion even served to sway his parsimonious temperament to such a degree that he began to squander in presents, and the like, all the five thousand francs which he had brought with him from the South, and which by financial speculations he had already contrived to double.

But that which annoyed him more than anything was that he had become timid by falling in love. He lacked his wonted decision, his haste to reach his goal, desiring now, on the other hand, a certain languid enjoyment from not being too abrupt in his manœuvres. Moreover, this passing weakness in so thoroughly practical a nature as his, led him to conclude that the conquest of Berthe would be a campaign fraught with great difficulties, needing much delay and exquisite diplomacy. His two failures, with Valérie and with Madame Hédouin, doubtless made him the more fearful of yet another rebuff. But, beneath all his uneasiness and hesitation, there lurked a fear of the woman he adored, an absolute belief in Berthe's virtue, and all the blindness of a desperate love paralysed by desire.

Next day, Octave, pleased that he had prevailed upon Berthe to accept his present, thought that it would be expedient to stand well with her husband. Accordingly, when taking his meals with him—for Auguste always boarded his assistants so as to have them close at hand—he paid him the utmost attention, listened to him during dessert and loudly approved all that he said. He specially pretended to share his discontent with regard to Berthe, feigning to play the detective and report various little incidents to him from time to time. Auguste was much touched. One evening he confessed to Octave that he had been upon the point of dismissing him, believing him to be in league with Madame Josserand. But when Octave professed the utmost horror for that good lady, this helped at once to bind them together by a community of ideas. At heart, indeed, the husband was a good fellow; he was only bad-tempered, yet easy-going enough so long as no one put him out by spending his money or shocking his morals. He vowed that he would never lose his temper again, for after the quarrel he had suffered from a most fearful headache, which for three days had made him absolutely idiotic.

"You see what I mean, don't you?" he would observe to Octave. "All that I want is my peace of mind. Beyond that, I don't care a pin, my honour always excepted, and provided my wife does not go off with the cash-box. That's reasonable enough, isn't it? I don't exact anything very extraordinary from her, do I?"

Then Octave praised his sagacity, and they both extolled the joys of a dull existence such as this—each year exactly like the last, and all of them spent in measuring yards of silk. To please his employer, the young man was content to give up all his ideas of trade on a grandiose scale. One evening, indeed, he had frightened Auguste by his dream of huge modern bazaars, advising him, as he had advised Madame Hédouin, to purchase the adjoining house so as to enlarge his shop. Auguste whose four counters were in themselves sufficient to drive him crazy, looked at Octave with the terrified look of a shopman used to chopping farthings into four, so that the young man hastily withdrew his proposition and went into ecstasies over the sound integrity of small shopkeepers.

Days passed; Octave was building his nest in the house—a downy nest, which he found snug and warm. The husband esteemed him; and Madame Josserand herself, though he avoided being too polite to her—even she looked encouragingly upon him. As for Berthe, she treated him with delightful familiarity. His great friend, however, was Saturnin, whose mute affection he watched increasing—a devotion as of some faithful dog, which became more fervent as his desire for Berthe grew more ardent. Of everyone else the madman appeared grimly jealous; no man could go near his sister but he at once became restless, with teeth set, as if ready to bite. If, on the other hand, Octave bent over her unrestrainedly, making her laugh with the soft velvety laugh of a merry mistress, Saturnin would laugh for glee as well, while his face in part reflected their sensual delight. For this poor witless fellow, love was incarnate in this soft woman's flesh, that instinctively he felt belonged to him, while for the chosen lover he felt nothing but ecstatic gratitude. He would stop Octave in all sorts of corners, looking about him suspiciously; and then, if they chanced to be alone, he would talk about Berthe, always repeating the same tales in disjointed phrases.

"When she was little, she had tiny legs as big as that! She was so fat, so rosy, so merry! She used to crawl about on the floor then. Then whack! whack! whack! she used to kick me in the stomach. That's what I liked! Oh, I liked it awfully!"

In this way Octave got to know the entire history of Berthe's childhood, of her babyish accidents, her playthings, of her gradual growth as a charming, uncontrolled animal. Saturnin's empty brain carefully treasured up facts of no importance, which he alone had remarked, such as the day she pricked herself and he sucked the blood; the morning he held her in his arms when she wanted to get on to the table. But he always harked back to the supreme episode, the episode of the girl's illness.

"Ah, if you had only seen her! At night-time I used to be all alone with her. They beat me in order to make me go to bed. But I used to creep back barefoot. All by myself. It made me cry, she was so white. I used to feel her to see if she were growing cold. Then they let me be, for I nursed her better than they did; I knew about her medicine, and she took whatever I gave her. Sometimes, when she complained very much, I laid her head on my breast. It was so nice being together. Then she got well, and I wanted to go back to her, but they beat me again!"

His eyes sparkled, he laughed and wept, just as if the whole thing had happened only the day before. From these broken phrases of his, the whole story of this strange attachment could be made clear; this devotion of a poor half-witted fellow, keeping watch at the little patient's bedside after all the doctors had given her up; devoted body and soul to his beloved sister, who lay there dying, and whom he nursed in her nakedness with all a mother's tenderness—all his affection and all his virile impulses stopping short there, being checked once and for all by this episode of suffering, from the shock of which he had never yet recovered. Ever since that time, despite the ingratitude which had followed such devotion, Berthe became his all in all, a mistress in whose presence he trembled; at once a daughter and a sister whom he had saved from death; his idol, whom he jealously adored. Moreover, her husband he pursued with the wild hatred of a thwarted lover, being lavish of his abuse when unbosoming himself to Octave.

"His eye is still bunged up! What a nuisance that headache of his is! Did you hear how he shuffled about yesterday? Look! there he is, gaping out of window. Was there ever such a fool! Oh, you dirty brute, you dirty brute!"

Auguste could hardly move without angering him. Then he would make horrible proposals.

"If you like, we'll both of us bleed him like a pig!"

Octave sought to soothe him. Then, on his quiet days, Saturnin would go from Octave to Berthe, delighted to repeat what one had said about the other, running errands for them, and constituting himself a perpetual bond of tenderness. He would willingly have flung himself down as a carpet for their feet.

Berthe made no further allusion to the present. She appeared not to notice Octave's trembling attentions, treating him quite unconcernedly as a friend. Never before had he taken such pains with his dress, and he was for ever gazing languishingly at her, with his eyes of the colour of old gold, whose velvety softness he considered irresistible. But she was solely grateful for him for the lies that he told on her behalf when helping her to escape from the shop now and again. The two thus became accomplices, and he favoured her going-out with her mother, hoodwinking her husband if ever he showed the slightest suspicion. Her mania for such frivolous excursions at last made her absolutely reckless, and she relied entirely upon his tact and intelligence to screen her. Then, on her return, if she found him behind a pile of goods, she rewarded him with the hearty handshake of a comrade.

One day, however, she was greatly upset. She had just come back from a dog-show, when Octave beckoned her to follow him downstairs into the basement, where he gave her an invoice which had been presented during her absence—sixty-two francs for embroidered stocking. She turned quite pale, exclaiming:

"Good gracious! Did my husband see this?"

He hastened to reassure her, telling her what trouble he had had to smuggle the bill away from under Auguste's very nose. Then, in an embarrassed tone, he added:

"I paid it."

She at once pretended to feel in her pockets, and, finding nothing, merely said :

"I will pay you back. Oh, I am ever so much obliged to you, Monsieur Octave! I should simply have died if Auguste had seen that!"

And this time she took hold of both his hands, and for an instant pressed them in her own. But the sixty-two francs was never mentioned again. Hers was an ever-increasing desire for liberty and for pleasure—all that as a girl she had expected marriage would yield her, all that her mother had taught her to exact from man. She brought with her an appetite as yet unappeased, taking her revenge for her needy youth spent under the parental roof; for all the inferior meat; for all the economy in butter, which enabled her to buy boots; for all the shabby gowns that had to be tinkered up a dozen times; for the falsehood of their social position, maintained at the price of squalid misery and filth. Most of all did she now desire to make up for those three winters spent in traipsing about in ball-slippers through all the mud of Paris, trying to hook a husband; evenings of right deadly dullness during which she strove to stay her empty stomach with draughts of syrup, bored to extinction by having to show off all her virginal airs and graces to stupid young men, and inwardly exasperated at being obliged to affect ignorance of everything while she well knew all. Then, too, she must make up for all those awful home-comings in pouring rain without a cab; for the chill discomfort of her ice-cold bed, and the maternal smacks that gave her cheeks a glow. At the age of twenty-two she still despaired of getting married, humble as a hunchback, looking at herself in her nightgown to see if anything were missing. But now she had at last got a husband, and, like the sportsman who brutally despatches at a blow the hare that he has breathlessly pursued, so towards Auguste she showed herself merciless, treating him like her vanquished foe.

Thus by degrees the breach grew ever wider between the two despite the husband's efforts, who desired to lead a placid existence. He made desperate attempts to preserve the drowsy monotony of his little home, closing his eyes to trivial irregularities, and even tolerating grosser ones, being perpetually afraid of making some appalling discovery which should exasperate him to the utmost pitch of fury. All Berthe's lies respecting little gifts which, as she alleged, were tokens of sisterly or motherly affection, he now calmly accepted, nor did he even grumble overmuch if she went out of an evening. Thus Octave was able to take her twice to the theatre, in company with Madame Josserand and Hortense—delightful jaunts, which caused the ladies to agree that Octave was eminently companionable, and knew how to live.

Hitherto, at the slightest word, Berthe would always flaunt her virtue in her husband's face. She, at least, led a virtuous life, and he might deem himself lucky, for, in her opinion, as also in that of her mother, a husband was only within his right to show ill-temper when his wife had proved herself unfaithful. Such chastity as this, genuine enough at first, when greedily indulging her appetite for frivolous amusement, cost her no great sacrifice. She was by nature cold, sheer love of self predominating over passion, and she preferred to have her pleasures all to herself, independently of others. After all her rebuffs as a marriageable young lady, who thought that men would have nothing to say to her, she was merely flattered by Octave's homage, but she took care to profit thereby in various ways, calmly reaping pecuniary advantage from it, for she had been trained to worship money. One day she allowed her clerk to pay a five hours' cab fare for her; another time, when just going out, she induced him to lend her thirty francs behind her husband's back, saying that she had forgotten her purse. She never repaid anything. There was no harm in the young man, she argued; she had no designs upon him; she merely made use of him, without premeditation, just to minister to her various amusements. And all the while she posed as an ill-used wife, as a martyr who vigorously fulfilled all her duties.

One Saturday a fearful quarrel occured between the young couple, owing to a deficit of twenty sous in Rachel's household accounts. As Berthe used to pay this account, Auguste always doled her out the requisite money to meet the household expenses of each week. That evening the Josserands were coming to dinner, and the kitchen was littered with provisions—a rabbit, a leg of mutton, and cauliflowers. Near the sink Saturnin squatted, blacking boots. The quarrel arose out of a long enquiry respecting the twenty-sou pieces. What could have become of it? How could one lose twenty sous? Auguste wanted to check the bill, to see if it were added up correctly. Meanwhile Rachel, hard of face but willowy of figure, kept calmly putting her piece of mutton on the spit, with mouth shut and eyes for ever on the watch. At last Auguste disbursed the sum of fifty francs, and was going downstairs, when he suddenly came back, tormented by the thought of the lost coin.

"It will have to be found," said he. "Perhaps you may have borrowed it from Rachel and forgotten all about it."

Berthe at once became greatly annoyel. "So you accuse me of falsifying the accounts, do you? Thank you, I am obliged by the compliment."

This was the starting-point; high words soon followed. Auguste, despite his desire to pay dearly for peace, became aggressive, exasperated at the sight of the rabbit, the leg of mutton, and the cauliflowers—all that pile of provisions that his wife was going to stuff under her parents' noses. He looked through the account-book, exclaiming at every item. Good heavens! it was monstrous! she must be in league with the cook to make a profit on the marketing.

"What!" cried Berthe, beside herself with anger, "you accuse *me, me* of being in league with the cook? Why, it is you, sir, who pay her to spy upon me! Yes, I always feel her dogging me; I can't move a step but her eye is on me. Ah, she may look through the keyhole as much as she likes when I am changing my underlinen; I don't do anything I'm ashamed of, and I don't care a hang for all your detectives! Only don't carry your audacity to such a pitch that you actually accuse me of being in league with my cook!"

For a moment this unlooked-for onslaught completely dumbfounded Auguste. Without relinquishing her leg of mutton, Rachel turned round, and with hand on heart protested.

"Oh madame, how can you believe such a thing? And about me, who respect madame so highly!"

"She's mad!" exclaimed Auguste, shrugging his shoulders. "Don't trouble to make any excuse, my good girl. She's mad!"

Suddenly a noise from behind startled him. It was Saturnin, who had hurled away one of the half-cleaned shoes and was coming to his sister's help. His face wore a furious expression, and his fists were clenched as, stammering, he declared that he would throttle the dirty beast if he dared to say she was mad again. Auguste, terror-striken, rushed behind the filter, exclaiming:

"This is positively too much! I can no longer say a word to you but this fellow interferes! It's true I took him in, but on the condition that he behaved properly. He's another nice present from your mother! She was terrified of him, and so she saddled me with him, preferring to let me be murdered in her stead. I'm greatly obliged to her! Look, he's got hold of a knife. For God's sake, stop him!"

Disarming her brother, Berthe pacified him with a look, while

Auguste, turning deadly pale, continued muttering incoherently. Always flourishing knives! So easy to get wounded. In the case of a madman one got no redress whatever. In short, it was not fair to keep a brother like that as a body-guard, ready to maim one's husband at any minute, paralysing him if he sought to give vent to his just indignation, and forcing him to swallow his wrath.

"Look here, sir! you are utterly wanting in tact!" cried Berthe, scornfully. "No gentleman discusses matters of this sort in the kitchen!"

She withdrew to her room, banging the door after her. Rachel went back to her spit, as if she had heard nothing of this altercation between her superiors. Like a maid, who, though aware of all that went on, yet knew her place, she discreetly forbore to look at madame as she left the room; and when her master stamped about, she never moved a muscle. Very soon, however, Auguste rushed out after his wife, and then Rachel, impassive as before, put the rabbit on to boil.

"Pray understand, my dear," said Auguste, on joining Berthe in her bedroom, "it was not about you that I made that remark. I meant it for that girl who is robbing us. Those twenty sous will have to be found somehow."

Berthe shook with nervous exasperation as, pale and resolute, she glared at him.

"Look here! how much longer are you going to worry me about your twenty sous? It's not twenty sous I want—it's five hundred francs. Yes, five hundred francs to dress on. It's all very fine; you talk about money in the kitchen before the cook. Very well, then, I'm determined to talk about money, too! I've been keeping myself in for a long while; I want five hundred francs!"

At such a request as this he stood aghast. Then forthwith she embarked upon the battle royal, just as her mother had wrangled with her father every fortnight for twenty years. Did he intend her to go barefoot? When a man married a wife, he should, at least, manage to clothe and feed her properly. She would rather beg than consent to lead such a poverty-stricken existence. It was not her fault if he was incapable of managing his business; yes, incapable, wanting in ideas, in enterprise, knowing merely how to split farthings into four. A man whose delight it should have been to amass a fortune as rapidly as possible, so as to clothe her like a queen, and make the "Ladies' Paradise" people expire with rage! Nothing of the sort! With such a feeble pate as his, bankruptcy was bound to come ere long. In this tirade one perceived her veneration, her furious appetite for money, the cult for lucre, as taught to her by her own relations, when she saw to what base tricks they would stoop merely to appear to possess it.

"Five hundred francs?" said Auguste, at last. "I'd rather shut up shop at once."

She looked at him coldly.

"You refuse? Very well then, I'll run into debt."

"What? More debts, you miserable creature?"

He roughly caught her by the arms and pushed her violently against the wall. Choking with passion, she uttered no cry, but rushed forward and flung the window open as if she meant to jump into the street. But she came back, and in her turn pushed him out of the room, stammering :

"Go away, or I shall do myself some injury !"

And she noisily bolted the door in his face. For a moment, hesitating, he stood still to listen. Then he hurried downstairs to the shop, scared afresh at the sight of Saturnin, whose eyes glittered in the gloom. The noise of the brief wrangle had brought him out of the kitchen.

Octave, downstairs, was selling some *foulard* to an old lady. He at once noticed Auguste's agitation, and furtively watched him restlessly pacing up and down in front of the counters.

As soon as the customer had gone, Auguste's feelings brimmed over.

"My dear fellow, she's going mad !" he said, without mentioning his wife. "She has locked herself in. Will you oblige me by going up and speaking to her? I really am afraid of some accident; upon my word, I am !"

Octave pretended to hesitate. It was such a delicate matter ! However, out of pure devotion, he consented. Upstairs, he found Saturnin keeping guard outside Berthe's door. Hearing footsteps, the madman grunted menacingly. But on recognising Octave his face brightened.

"Oh, yes, you !" he murmured. "You are all right. She mustn't cry. Be nice to her, and comfort her. And stop with her, you know. There's no fear of anybody coming. I'm here. If the servant tries to peep, I'll hit her."

And, sitting down, he mounted guard before the door. As he had a boot in his hand, he began polishing it just to pass the time away.

Octave determined to knock. No answer, not a sound. Then he called out his name. The bolt was at once drawn back. Berthe, half opening the door, begged him to come in. Then she nervously bolted it again.

"I don't mind *you,*" said she, "but I won't have *him!*"

She paced up and down in a whirlwind of fury, from the bed to the window, which was still open. She muttered disconnected phrases: he might entertain her parents himself, if he chose: yes, and explain her absence to them as well, for she wouldn't sit down to table—not she; she'd rather die first! No, she preferred to go to bed. In fact, she excitedly flung back the coverlet, shook up the pillows and turned down the sheets, being so far forgetful of Octave's presence as to begin unhooking her dress. Then she went off at a tangent to something else.

"Would you believe it? He beat me, yes, beat me! And merely because I was ashamed of always going about in rags and asked him for five hundred francs."

Standing midway in the room, Octave sought to find words that might conciliate her. She ought not to let the matter upset her like that. Everything would come all right. Then he timidly ventured to make an offer of help.

"If you are bothered about any bill, why not apply to your friends? I should be most happy. Merely a loan, you understand, and you can pay me back."

She looked at him. After a pause, she replied:

"No, it would never do. What would people think, Monsieur Octave?"

So firm was her refusal, that the question was no longer one of money. Her anger, however, seemed to have subsided. Breathing heavily, she bathed her face, and became very pale, very calm, looking somewhat languid with her large, resolute eyes. As he stood there before her he felt overcome by amorous bashfulness, stupid though he deemed such emotion to be. Never before had he loved with such ardour; the very vehemence of his desire gave an awkwardness to his charms as a comely shopman. All the while he was uttering vague commonplaces about the advisability of making it up he was really debating in his own mind whether he should not take her in his arms. But the fear of another rebuff made him hesitate. She sat mute, watching him with her resolute air and slightly contracted brow.

"Well, well," he falteringly continued, "you must have patience. Your husband's not a bad sort of fellow. If you know how to manage him he'll let you have what you want."

Beneath hollow talk such as this, they felt the same thought seize them both. There they were, alone, free, secure from being surprised, the door bolted. Such safety as this and the tepid atmosphere of the room touched their senses. And yet he did not dare; the feminine side of him, his womanly instinct, in that moment of passion so far refined him as to make of him the woman in their encounter. Then, as if mindful of her early lessons, she dropped her handkerchief.

"Oh, thanks, so much!" said she to the young man as he picked it up.

Their fingers touched; ,such momentary contact brought them closer to each other. Now she smiled fondly; her waist grew willowy and supple, for she remembered that men hate boards. One must not behave like a ninny; one must submit to a little playfulness without seeming to do so, if one would land one's fish.

"It is getting quite dark," she said, as she went to close the window.

He followed, and in the shadow of the curtains she allowed him to take her hand. She began to laugh louder—a silvery laugh that almost dazed him; importuning him with all her pretty gestures. Then, as he at length grew bold, she flung back her head, disclosing her ripe, soft bosom, all palpitating with merriment. Distracted by such a vision, he kissed her under the chin.

"Oh, Monsieur Octave!" said she, confusedly, making a feint of gracefully keeping him in his proper place.

Then, catching hold of her, he threw her backwards upon the bed, which she had just been opening; and, as his desire was slaked, all the brute within him reappeared—his ferocious disdain for the female under his gentle air of adoration. She submitted tacitly, without pleasure. When she rose up, with limp wrists and her face drawn by a spasm of pain, all her contempt for the male was apparent in the black look which she flung at him. Then for a while came silence. One only heard Saturnin outside the door cleaning the husband's boots, and the regular beat of his brush.

Meanwhile Octave, in the flush of his triumph, kept thinking of Valérie and of Madame Hédouin. At any rate, he was now something more than little Madame Pichon's lover! It was as if he were rehabilitated in his own eyes. Then, noticing Berthe's movement of pain, he felt somewhat ashamed, and kissed her with great tenderness. She soon recovered her composure, however, as her face resumed its resolute, don't care expression. With a gesture she seemed to say, "It can't be helped; the thing's done." Yet she felt constrained to express the sad thoughts within her.

"Ah, if only you had married me!" she murmured.

The speech surprised, almost troubled him; but, kissing her again, he answered:

"Yes, how nice that would have been!"

That evening, the dinner given to the Josserands proved perfectly charming. Berthe had never seemed so sweet and gentle. She never said a word to her parents about the quarrel, and met her husband with a becoming air of submission. The latter, delighted, took Octave aside on purpose to thank him, doing this with such warmth, and squeezing his hands so vigorously in sign of gratitude, that the young man felt quite embarrassed. In fact, they all were profuse in their affectionate attentions to him. Saturnin, who at table behaved excellently, also looked at him with loving eyes, as if he had shared in the sweetness of his sin. Hortense even deigned to listen to him; while Madame Josserand, full of motherly zeal, kept filling his glass.

"Why, yes," said Berthe, during dessert. "I mean to take up my painting again. I have long wanted to decorate a cup for Auguste."

By so touching a thought on the part of his wife, Auguste was greatly moved. Meanwhile, under the table, Octave had kept his foot on Berthe's all through dinner—a token of possession, so to speak, at this little bourgeois festival. Berthe, however, was not without a certain uneasiness before Rachel, whom she always caught watching her with a searching gaze. Obviously, she was a girl that must be dismissed or else bought.

Good Monsieur Josserand, sitting next to his daughter, managed to soothe her by slipping nineteen francs, wrapped up in paper, into her hand under the tablecloth. Bending down, he whispered in her ear:

"That's out of my own little work, you know. If you've any debts, you ought to pay them."

Thus, between her father, who nudged her knee, and her lover, who kept gently chafing her boot, she felt thoroughly happy. Life was going to be full of charm for her. One and all they let themselves go, determined to enjoy so pleasant a family gathering, unspoiled by dispute of any sort. It was really almost too good to be true; something must be going to bring them good luck. Auguste alone suffered from a splitting headache, which, however, he had expected after such a conflict of emotions. And about nine o'clock he was actually obliged to go to bed.

XIII

For some time past Monseiur Gourd had gone prowling about, looking mysteriously ill at ease. One met him moving noiselessly along with eyes and ears on the alert, as he for ever went up and down both staircases, where even the lodgers had met him going his nightly rounds. It was clear that the morality of the house troubled him; a breath as of scandalous things had come to disturb the courtyard in its frigid nakedness, ruffling the claustral serenity of the vestibule, and menacing the spotless virtue of every hearth on every floor.

One evening Octave found the doorkeeper standing immovable and without a light, at the end of his passage, just against the door opening on the back stairs. Being surprised, he asked him the reason.

"I want to find out something, Monseiur Mouret," replied Gourd, shortly, as he shuffled off to bed.

The young man was greatly alarmed. Had the doorkeeper any suspicion as to his relations with Berthe? Perhaps, he was playing the spy. To their intrigue perpetual obstacles existed in a house so carefully supervised as this, whose inmates all professed to be so strictly moral. Thus he could only be near his mistress on rare occasions; and, if she went out in the afternoon without her mother, his sole joy was to quit the shop on some pretext and join her at the end of some out-of-the-way street, where he would walk about with her arm-in-arm for an hour. Moreover, ever since the end of July, Auguste slept away from home every Tuesday, as he went to Lyons, where he had been foolish enough to take a share in a silk manufactory which was in difficulties. Up to the present, however, Berthe had refused to profit by this night of liberty. The thought of Rachel made her tremble, and she feared that some forgetfulness on her part might put her in this girl's power.

It was precisely on a Tuesday evening that Octave caught Monsieur Gourd on the watch near his room. This redoubled his fears. For a whole week he had been vainly imploring Berthe to come upstairs to his room at night when everybody was asleep. Is this what Gourd suspected? Octave went back to bed in grievous discontent, tortured alike by passion and by fear. His amour was growing troublesome; it was turning to an insane passion; and he angrily saw himself becoming guilty of every sort of sentimental absurdity. As it was, he could never meet Berthe in these same side-streets without buying for her whatever took her fancy in a shop-window. For instance, only the day before, in the Passage de la Madeleine, she looked so avidly at a little bonnet, that he went into the shop and bought it for her as a present—plain white chip, with just a wreath of roses—something delightfully simple, but—two hundred francs! A trifle stiff, that, so he thought.

Towards one o'clock he fell asleep, after feverishly tossing about for a long while between the sheets.

Then he was roused by a gentle tapping at his door.

"It is I," faintly whispered a woman's voice.

It was Berthe. Opening the door, he clasped her passionately to him in the dark. But she had not come upstairs for that. Having lit a candle, he saw that she was in a great state of mind about something. The day before, as he had not had enough money about him, he could not pay for the bonnet at the time, while she was so delighted that she actually gave her name; and accordingly they had just sent her in the bill. Then, trembling lest they might call on her husband for the amount in the morning, she had ventured to come upstairs, emboldened by the profound silence of the house and feeling certain that Rachel was asleep.

"To-morrow morning, without fail!" she said, cajolingly, while trying to escape. "It must be paid to-morrow morning!"

But he again wound his arms about her.

"Stay here, do!"

Half awake and shivering, he whispered the words close to her bosom as he drew her nearer to the warm bed. Half clad, she wore only a petticoat and a dressing-jacket; to his touch she seemed as if naked, with her hair already knotted up for the night, and her shoulders still warm from the *peignoir* she had flung round them on coming out.

"I promise to let you go in an hour. Do stay!"

She stayed. Slowly the clock chimed the hours in the voluptuous warmth of the room; and at each stroke he held her back, pleading so tenderly that all strength forsook her. She succumbed. Then, about four o'clock, as she at last was going, they both fell sound asleep in each other's arms. When they opened their eyes, broad daylight streamed through the window. It was nine o'clock. Berthe uttered a cry of despair.

"Gracious heavens! I'm lost!"

Then came a moment of confusion. She leaped out of bed, her eyes half closed with sleep and weariness, groping about vaguely, blindly, putting her clothes on upside down, amid stifled cries of terror. Himself equally desperate, Octave stood before the door, to stop her from going out in such a dress at such an hour. Was she mad? People might meet her on the stairs; it was far too dangerous. They must think out some plan by which she could get downstairs unobserved. But she obstinately persisted in trying to leave the room there and then, endeavouring to push past him as he barred the doorway. At last he bethought himself of the back staircase. Nothing could be more convenient, and she might hurry back to her own room through the kitchen. Only as Marie Pichon was always in the passage of a morning, Octave thought it best, for safety's sake, to go and engage her in conversation while Berthe made good her escape. He hurriedly put on his trousers and an overcoat.

"My goodness! What a time you are!" muttered Berthe, to whom the bedroom had become a veritable furnace.

At last, Octave went out in his quiet, everyday fashion. To his surprise, he found Saturnin with Marie; he was calmly watching her put the place in order. The madman was glad to escape hither as once he used to do, since she left him entirely alone; and here he was sure not to get pushed about. Marie did not find him in her way, but willingly tolerated his presence, albeit he was somewhat wanting in conversation. Still, he was company in a way; and she went on singing her song in a low, mournful voice.

"Hullo! there you are with your sweetheart!" said Octave, as he dexterously contrived to keep the door behind him closed.

Marie grew purple. Poor Monsieur Saturnin! Was it likely? Why, if one only touched his hand it seemed to hurt him! The idiot was irate, as well. He would never have a sweetheart, never, never! Anybody who told his sister such a lie as that would have him to deal with. Surprised at his sudden irritability, Octave had to pacify him.

Meanwhile Berthe slipped out by the servant's staircase. She had to go down two flights of stairs. On the very first step she stopped short at the sound of a harsh laugh which came from Madame Juzeur's kitchen below, and tremblingly she caught hold of the railing of the open window overlooking the narrow court. Then, all at once, there was a babel of voices; the morning sewage surged up in waves from this foetid drain. It was the maids, who were furiously abusing little Louise for spying upon them through the keyhole as they were undressing. A fine thing for a dirty brat like that, not yet fifteen, to do. Louise only laughed the louder. She did not deny it. With Adèle's rump she was well acquainted. Wasn't it just a sight. Lisa was awfully skinny. Victoire's belly was bashed in like an old cask. To make her stop, the others all drenched her with disgusting language. Then, annoyed at having been thus stripped naked before each other, and longing for some method of self-defence, they with one accord fell foul of their mistresses, stripping these naked in their turn. Ah, yes, Lisa might be skinny, she said, but not so skinny as the other Madame Campardon, a regular dried shark; quite a tasty morsel for an architect. Victoire merely wished that all the Vabres, Duveyriers, and Josserands in the world might possess as well-preserved a belly as hers when they reached her age. As for Adèle, she certainly would not exchange her behind for such wretched little things as those of the young ladies and of madame. Thus Berthe, standing motionless and amazed, received these kitchen-rinsings full in the face. She had never dreamed of such a cesspool as this; it was her first revelation of maidservants washing all their dirty linen in public; just as their masters were busy shaving. Suddenly a voice exclaimed :

"There goes the bell for master's hot water."

At once windows were closed and doors slammed. A silence as of the grave ensued. Not yet did Berthe dare to move. As she, at last, went down, it occurred to her that Rachel might be in the kitchen waiting for her. This heightened her fears. She dreaded going in now; she would rather have got out into the street, and have rushed away, never to return. However, she pushed the door half open, and was relieved at not finding the servant. Then, gleeful as a child at seeing herself home again safe, she hurried to her room. But there, beside the unrumpled bed, stood Rachel, silent and impassive. She glanced first at the bed, then at madame. In her first confusion Berthe stammered out, as an excuse, something about her sister being unwell upstairs. Then, appalled at such a miserable falsehood, and aware that all was discovered, she burst into tears. Sinking into a chair, she sobbed bitterly.

This lasted a whole minute. Not a word was exchanged; the sound of weeping alone broke the deep silence of the room. In her excess of discretion, preserving her stolid mien of a girl who, knowing all, says nought, Rachel turned about and pretended to smooth the pillows, as if she had just finished making the bed. Then, as the silence seemed only to distress madame yet more, Rachel said respectfully, while she went on with her dusting :

"Madame should not take on so, as monsieur is not over nice to her."

Berthe stopped crying. She would tip the girl; that was the best thing to be done. So she at once gave her twenty francs. Then, somehow, that seemed rather mean, and feeling uneasy when she fancied she saw the girl's lip curl disdainfully, she went after her into the kitchen and brought her back to make her a present of a nearly new dress.

Meanwhile Octave, on his part, felt fresh misgivings with regard to Monsieur Gourd. On coming away from the Pichons, he found him standing mute in the same place as on the previous night, spying behind the door of the servants' staircase. He followed him, without even venturing to speak. Gourd gravely went down the front staircase. On the floor below he took out a key, and went into the flat which was let to the personage of distinction who came there one night a week to work. Through the half-open door Octave got a good view of this room, which always remained as closely shut as a tomb. That morning it was in a terrible state of disorder, as, no doubt, the gentleman had been working there the night before—a large bed with the sheets stripped off it, an empty wardrobe with a glass door, the remains of a lobster and two half-empty bottles, two basins full of dirty water, one near the bed and the other on a chair. With a mien as calm as that of a retired magistrate, Monsieur Gourd proceeded to empty the basins and rinse them out.

While hurrying to the Passage de la Madeleine to pay for the bonnet, Octave's fears of discovery still haunted him. On coming back, he determined to draw out the doorkeeper and his wife. Recumbent in her spacious armchair, Madame Gourd was taking the air which came in through the open window, flanked by flower-pots. Near the door Mother Péron, looking humble and abashed, stood waiting.

"Have you no letter for me?" asked Octave, by way of a start.

Just then Monsieur Gourd came down from the third-floor flat. To keep this place in order was the only work in the house that he deigned to do, and he appeared flattered that the gentleman should confide in him, paying him liberally as well, on the condition that the washing-basins did not pass through other hands.

"No, Monsieur Mouret, nothing at all!" he replied.

Though perfectly aware of old Mother Péron's presence, Gourd pretended not to see her. On the previous day he had sent her flying, in his fury at her having spilt a pail of water in the vestibule. Now she had come for her money, trembling all over at the very sight of him, and cringing close to the wall.

While Octave lingered to make pretty speeches to Madame Gourd, the doorkeeper suddenly turned round upon poor Madame Péron, saying harshly:

"So you've come for your money. How much is it?"

But Madame Gourd interrupted.

"Look, lovey; there goes that girl again, with her nasty little beast of a dog."

It was Lisa, who, a few days ago, had picked up a stray spaniel in the street. Ever since there had been continual quarrels with Gourd and his wife. The landlord would not have any animals in the house. No; no animals and no women! The little beast was not allowed to go into the courtyard; it could quite well do what it had to do in the street. As it had been raining that morning, the dog's paws were all wet, so Monsieur Gourd, rushing forward, exclaimed:

"I won't have it run upstairs! do you hear? Carry it in your arms!"

"Oh, yes! and make myself all in a mess!" said Lisa, insolently. "What a dreadful thing if he dirties the back-stairs! Trot along, doggie!"

Monsieur Gourd tried to seize the animal, but nearly slipped in doing so, as he vented his fury upon all those filthy servants. He was for ever at war with them, cantankerous as any retired footman who now desires to be waited upon in his turn. All at once, Lisa turned back, and, with the volubility of some girl reared in the gutters of Montmartre, she shouted out:

"Now, then, you dirty old flunkey, can't you leave me alone? Why don't you go and empty the duke's piss-pots?"

It was the sole taunt which could silence Monsieur Gourd, and all the servants made use of it *ad libitum*. He withdrew, fuming, muttering incoherent threats, and saying that, for his part, he had been proud to serve monsieur le duc, and that she would not have remained as long as a couple of hours in *his* employ, rotten baggage that she was. Then he fell upon Mother Péron, who trembled.

"Well, how much do we owe you: Eh, what? Twelve francs sixty-five? That can't be. Sixty-three hours at twenty centimes an hour. Oh, you reckon the extra quarter of an hour! Not if I know it. I've told you already—I never pay for extra quarters of an hour."

And he did not even give the poor woman her money then, but left her in dismay, and began to join in the talk between his wife and Octave. The latter dexterously hinted at all the worries that a house like this must cause them, endeavouring in this way to make them talk about the various tenants. Some rare goings-on at times behind those doors, eh? Then the hall-porter gravely observed:

"There are things that concern us, Monsieur Mouret, and things that don't. Now, just look there. That, for instance, is enough to madden me! Just look at it, do!"

He pointed to the boot-stitcher, who was passing, the tall, pale girl who had arrived in the middle of old Vabre's funeral. She walked with difficulty, weighed down by her enormous belly, which seemed even huger in contrast to her narrow chest and spindle legs.

"What do you mean?" asked Octave, naïvely.

"Why, can't you see? That belly of hers, that belly!"

It was that belly which so exasperated Monsieur Gourd. A single woman with a paunch like that, which she had got the Lord knows where, for she was quite flat when she first came! And now her belly had begun to swell beyond all bounds, beyond all reasonable and decent proportion!

"You can well understand how annoyed I was, sir," said the porter, "and the landlord, too, when I first noticed the thing! She ought to have told us about it, ought she not? One does not go and lodge in a respectable house with a thing like that hidden under one's skin! But at first it was hardly noticeable; perhaps she was in for it; but I couldn't be certain, and I hoped that at any rate she would use discretion. Well, I kept watching her, and you could see her swelling so fast, too, that it quite alarmed me. Now look at her to-day? She doesn't hide matters, but sticks out her guts anyhow. Why, the portico's scarcely wide enough for her to pass!"

He kept tragically pointing at her as she made for the back-stairs. This belly of hers seemed to him to stain the frigid cleanliness of the courtyard, and throw its sinful shadow athwart the sham marble and gilded zinc decorations of the Hall. It seemed to bring disgrace to the whole building, tainting the very walls, and, as it swelled, brought trouble to the placid virtue of each flat.

"Upon my word! sir, if this sort of thing goes on, we would rather retire to Mort-la-Ville; wouldn't we, Madame Gourd? For thank goodness, we've got enough to live on, and depend upon nobody. A house like ours to be made the talk of the place by a paunch like that! For it *is* the talk of the place! Everybody stares when she comes in now!"

"She looks very ill," said Octave, following her with his eyes, and afraid to pity her overmuch. "She always seems so sad, so pale, so forlorn. She must have a lover, I expect!"

Hereupon Gourd started violently.

"That's where it is. Do you hear, Madame Gourd? Monsieur Mouret also thinks that she has got a lover. Such things don't come of themselves, that's quite plain! Well, sir, I've been watching her for a couple of months, but I've never yet seen the shadow of a man! What a bad lot she must be! Only let me catch her chap; won't I just chuck him out! But I can't spot him; and that's what worries me!"

"Perhaps nobody comes to see her?" Octave ventured to suggest.

The porter looked at him in amazement.

"That would not be natural. Oh, I'm determined to catch him yet! I've got another six weeks, and she's had notice to quit in October. Fancy her being confined here! And you know, though Monsieur Duveyrier indignantly insisted on her clearing out before that comes off, I can hardly sleep myself at night for thinking that she may play us all a dirty trick yet, and not wait till then. Well, all these misfortunes would have been avoided if it had not been for that old miser of a Vabre! Just for the sake of an extra hundred and thirty francs, and in spite of my advice. The carpenter ought to have been a lesson to him. But no, not a bit of it; he must needs take in this boot-sticher as a lodger! All right! go and stink your house out with labouring folk, and let lodgings to a set of filthy work-people. When you get the lower orders into your house, sir, that's what you may expect!"

And once more he pointed to the poor woman's belly, as with painful gait she went up the back-stairs. Madame Gourd was obliged to soothe her spouse; such zeal for the chastity of the house might make him ill. Then, as Mother Péron gave sign of her presence by coughing discreetly, he fell foul of her once more, calmly deducting the sou she had charged for her extra quarter of an hour. Having at last got her twelve francs sixty, she was going way, when he offered to take her back, but at the rate of only three sous an hour. She began to cry, and accepted.

"I can always get someone to do the work," he said. "You're no longer strong enough for it. You don't even do two sous' worth."

Going up to his room for a moment, Octave felt reassured. On the third floor he caught up with Madame Juzeur, who was returning home. Every morning now she had to come down and look for Louise, who loafed about when sent to the different shops.

"How proud we are" she said, with her subtle smile. "It's plain that they are spoiling you somewhere."

The remark once more aroused the young man's fears. He followed her into her drawing-room, pretending to joke with her. Only one of the curtains was drawn aside; the carpets and *portières* softened the daylight, and in this room, as soft as eiderdown, one scarcely caught a sound from the world without. She made him sit next to her on the low, wide sofa. But, as he did not take her hand and kiss it, she asked, coquettishly :

"So you don't love me any more?"

Blushing, he declared that he adored her. Then, smothering a nervous giggle, of her own accord she gave him her hand. He was obliged to raise it to his lips, so as to quash any suspicions that possibly she might have. But she at once withdrew it.

"No, no! don't pretend to get excited. It doesn't give you any pleasure at all. I can feel that it doesn't. Besides, it's only natural."

Whatever did she mean by that? He caught her by the waist; he overwhelmed her with questions. But she would not answer, yielding to his embrace as she shook her head. In order to make her speak, he at last began tickling her.

"Why, it's because—because you're in love with somebody else," she murmured.

She mentioned Valérie, and reminded him of the evening at the Josserands', when he devoured her with his eyes. Then, when he swore that he had never had her, she laughingly replied that she was only teasing him. Only there was another whom he had enjoyed, and this time she named Madame Hédouin, growing ever merrier at all his energetic disclaimers. Who was it, then? Was it Marie Pichon? Well, he could not deny having had her. Yet he did do so; but she shook her head, and assured him that her little finger never belied her. Then, to get the names of these women from her, he had to redouble his caresses and make all her body shiver before she would speak.

However, she had not yet mentioned Berthe's name. He was about to let her go when she said :

"Then there's the last one of all."

"What last one?" he anxiously enquired.

Tightening her lips, she obstinately refused to say more until he had unsealed these with a kiss. She really could not mention the person's name, for it was she who had first suggested her marriage. Without naming her, she related Berthe's whole history. Then, on her soft bosom, he made confession of all, experiencing a certain cowardly pleasure in such an avowal. How silly of him to hide from her! Perhaps, he thought, she would be jealous? Why should she be? She had granted him no favours, had she? Oh! nothing but a little childish fun, as at present, but not that, oh, not that! For, after all, she was a virtuous woman, and she almost felt vexed that he should have thought her likely to be jealous.

All the while she lay back languidly in his arms, and referred to her cruel husband, who, after one week of matrimony, had thus basely deserted her.

A wretched woman like herself knew all too much about the tempests of the heart! For a long while she had had an idea that Octave was up to some little game or other, for not a kiss could be given in the house without her hearing it. Then, ensconced in the broad sofa, they both had a quiet little talk, unconsciously interrupted by pattings and strokings of various parts of their persons. She dubbed him a great stupid, for it was all his fault that he had not succeeded with Valérie; she could have helped him to have her at once, if he had merely asked her advice. Then she questioned him about little Marie Pichon—hideous legs and nothing between them, eh? Yet she always came back to Berthe, whom she pronounced to be charming—a lovely skin and the foot of a marchioness. But the game of patting and stroking reached such a pitch that she had to repulse him before long.

"No, no, leave me alone! For shame! How can you be so rude! And it doesn't give you any pleasure either. Ah, you say so; but I know better! It's all your nonsense just to flatter me! It would be too dreadful if it did give you any pleasure. You keep that for her. Now, be off, you naughty man!"

And she sent him away after making him solemnly promise to come and confess himself often to her, hiding nothing if he wished her to undertake the governance of his love affairs.

On leaving her, Octave felt more at ease. She had restored his good-humour, and her intricate notions with regard to virtue positively amused him. As soon as he entered the shop below, he gave Berthe a reassuring nod, who, with her eyes, interrogated him as to the bonnet-bill.

Thus the whole dreadful adventure of the morning was forgotten. When Auguste came back, shortly before lunch, he found them both as usual—Berthe bored to death at the cashier's desk, and Octave gallantly measuring silk for a lady.

Henceforth, however, the lovers' assignations became less frequent still. He, in his ardour, grew despairing, and followed her about into every nook and corner, entreating her to make some appointment, whenever and wherever she liked. She, on the other hand, with the indifference of a girl reared in a hothouse, took no pleasure in such guilty passion, except for the secret outings, the presents, the forbidden enjoyments and the hours of luxury spent in cabs, theatres and restaurants. All her early education now cropped up anew, her lust for money, for dress, for squandering; and she had soon grown tired of her lover, just as she had grown tired of her husband, deeming him all too exacting for what he gave her in return, and endeavouring, with calm unconsciousness, not to yield him his full, just measure of love. Then, exaggerating her fears, she kept constantly refusing him. Never again in his room; oh, no! she would die of fright! And to her apartment he could not possibly come, for they might be surprised. Then, as he begged her to let him take her to a hotel for an hour, she began to cry, saying that he really could not have much respect for her. However, the expenditure on her account went on, and her caprices only increased. After the bonnet, she conceived a desire for a fan of *point d' Alençon,* not counting the many little trifles that took her fancy here and there, in the shop-windows. Though as yet he did not dare say nay, his sense of thrift was once more roused as he saw all his savings frittered away in this fashion. Like the practical fellow he was, it at length seemed to him silly always to be paying, when all that he got from her in return was her foot under the table. Decidedly, Paris had brought him bad luck; first, rebuffs, and then this stupid love affair, which was draining his purse. Of a truth, he could not be accused of succeeding through women. By way of comfort, he sought to find something honourable about the whole thing, in his hidden anger at a scheme which, so far, had proved such a dismal failure.

Auguste, however, did not embarrass them much. Ever since

the bad state of affairs at Lyons, he had been racked more than ever by his neuralgic headaches. Berthe had felt a sudden thrill of delight as, on the first of the month, she saw him one evening put three hundred francs under the bedroom clock for her dress. And, despite the reduction in the sum demanded, as she had never hoped to get a farthing, she flung herself into his arms, all warm and palpitating with gratitude. On this occasion the husband had a night of endearments such as the lover never obtained.

September thus passed amid the great calm of the house, devoid during summer of its inmates. The second-floor people had gone to a watering-place in Spain, which caused Monsieur Gourd to shrug his shoulders contemptuously. How absurd! As if the most genteel folk were not content to go to Trouville! Ever since the beginning of Gustave's holidays, the Duveyriers had been staying at their country-house at Villeneuve-Saint-Georges. Even the Josserands had gone to stay for a fortnight with friends near Pontoise, while letting it be rumoured that they were about to start for some fashionable seaside resort. The house being thus empty, the flats deserted, and the staircase wrapped in yet drowsier silence, Octave seemed to think that there would be less danger, and he importuned Berthe until, from sheer weariness, she consented to let him stay with her for one night when Auguste was away at Lyons. But this meeting was like to have had an unlucky sequel. Madame Josserand (who had returned two days before) was seized with such violent indigestion after dining out, that Hortense, in alarm, went down stairs to fetch her sister. Fortunately, Rachel was just finishing cleaning her pots and pans, so she was able to let Octave escape by the servants staircase. After this scare, Berthe took advantage of it to refuse him everything, as she had already done. Then, again, they were foolish enough not to bribe the servant. She waited upon them with her coldly-respectful air, like a girl who sees nothing, who hears nothing. However, as madame was for ever hankering after money, and as Monsieur Octave had already spent far too much in presents, she curled her lips yet more in her scorn for a hole like that, where the lady's lover did not even tip her ten sous when he slept there. If they thought that they had bought her for all eternity with twenty francs and a old gown, they were vastly mistaken. Not she; she was not as cheap as all that! From this time forward she was less obliging, no longer shutting the doors after them as before, although they were never aware of her ill-humour; for one never thinks of giving tips when, eager to find some cuddling-place, one even quarrels about where this shall be. The silence of the house grew only deeper; and Octave, in his search for some safe corner, was for ever meeting Monsieur Gourd, on the watch for shameful things that made the very walls blush, as in stealth he crept hither and thither, eternally haunted by the paunches of pregnant females.

With this lovesick youth who could only view his mistress from afar, Madame Juzeur was often wont to condole, giving him, as promised, the very best advice. At one time Octave's desire reached such a pitch, that he thought of asking her to lend him her rooms for an assignation. No doubt, she would not have refused, but he feared to shock Berthe by such indiscretion. He also thought of making use of Saturnin; the madman might, perhaps, like a faithful dog, mount guard over them in some lonely room. But latterly his mood had been somewhat strange, at one time displaying exuberant affection for his sister's lover, and at another sulking with him, regarding him suspiciously, giving him fiery glances of sudden hatred. One would have said he was jealous—nervously, violently jealous as a woman. He had seemed like this—especially, on mornings when he met Octave laughing and joking with little Marie Pichon. As a matter of fact, Octave never passed Marie's door now without going in, drawn thither by some strange fancy, some sudden, unbowed touch of passion. He adored Berthe and madly desired to possess her, and of this very longing for her there was begotten for Marie an infinite tenderness, and a love the sweetness of which he had never tasted at the time of their intrigue. There was a perpetual charm in looking at her, in touching her, in joking with her, and teasing her—the playful dalliance of a man who wants to repossess a woman while secretly embarrassed by another love affair. At this time, therefore, when Saturnin caught him hovering round Marie's petticoats, the madman glared at him wolfishly, ready to bite; nor would he forgive him and kiss his hand like some tame animal, until he saw that he was back at Berthe's side, her loving, faithful slave.

As now September touched its close, and residents were about to return, Octave, in the midst of all his torment, conceived a mad idea. It so happened that Rachel, whose sister was to be married, had asked leave to stay away for a night during her master's absence at Lyons. The idea was that they should sleep together in the servants' room, where no one would ever dream of looking for them. Offended by such a proposal, Berthe at first appeared greatly disgusted but, with tears in his eyes, he besought her to comply, and spoke of leaving Paris, where he suffered too much unhappiness. At last, bewildered and exhausted by all his arguments and entreaties, she at length consented, scarcely knowing what she did. All was then arranged. On Tuesday evening, after dinner, they had tea at the Josserands' to allay any suspicion. Trublot, Gueulin and uncle Bachelard were all there. Duveyrier even came in, very late, as he occasionally slept in town now, because of early business appointments, so he averred. With all these gentlemen Octave pretended to converse freely; and then, at the stroke of midnight, he slipped away and locked himself into Rachel's room, where Berthe was to join him an hour later, when everybody was asleep.

Upstairs, he was busy for the first half-hour in setting the room straight. In order to conquer Berthe's disgust, he had promised her that he would change the sheets and bring all the necessary linen himself. Thus he proceeded to make the bed, slowly and clumsily, fearing that someone would hear him. Then, like Trublot, he sat down on a trunk and endeavoured to wait patiently. One by one the servants came up to bed, and through the thin partitions he could hear the sounds of women undressing themselves and relieving themselves. It struck one o'clock, then a quarter-past, then half-past. He grew anxious, why was she so late? She must have left the Josserands at one o'clock, at the very latest; and it would not take her more than ten minutes to get back to her flat, and leave it again by the servants' staircase. When it struck two, he imagined all sorts of mischances. At last, thinking that he recognised her footstep, he heaved a sigh of relief. And he opened the door to show her a light, when from sheer surprise he stood motionless. Outside Adèle's door Trublot, bent double, was looking through the keyhole; and, scared by this sudden light, he started back.

"Hullo! You here again?" said Octave, in a tone of annoyance.

Trublot began to laugh, without seeming the least astonished at finding Octave there at that time of night.

"Just imagine," said he, under his breath, "that idiot Adèle didn't give me her key, and now she's gone down to Duveyrier's room."

"Well, what's the matter?"

"Why, didn't you know that Duveyrier slept with her? That is so, my dear fellow. He has quite made it up with his wife, who now and then submits to his embraces; however, as she keeps him on short commons, he has to fall back upon Adèle. It's convenient for him, you see, when he comes up to Paris."

Then, breaking off, he stooped again to have another look, and then muttered between his teeth :

"No, there's nobody there! He's keeping her longer this time. What a blasted numskull that Adèle is! If she had only given me the key, I might have waited for her in bed, in the warmth."

Then he went back to the attic where he had been hiding, taking Octave with him, who was eager to question him as to how the evening had ended at the Josserands'. But Trublot never gave him a chance of opening his mouth, for he at once went on talking about Duveyrier, in this inky darkness and stuffy atmosphere, close to the rafters. Yes! the brute wanted to have Julie, at first, but she was a bit too clean for that sort of thing, and besides, in the country, she had taken a fancy to little Gustave, a lad of sixteen, who seemed promising. Being baulked thus, Duveyrier, who dared not try it on with Clémence because of Hippolyte, thought it more expedient to choose someone outside his own household. How on earth he had ever managed to get hold of Adèle nobody knew—behind some door, no doubt, in a draught; for the great slut siffened her back and took it up her as easily as a slap in the face; and to the landlord she would surely never have dared to be uncivil.

"For the last month he has never missed one of the Josserands' Tuesdays," said Trublot. "It makes me quite uncomfortable. I shall have to find Clarisse for him, so as to make him leave us in peace."

At last, Octave managed to ask him how the evening had ended. Berthe had left before midnight, apparently quite composed. No doubt she was waiting for him in Rachel's bedroom. But Trublot, delighted to have met him like this, would not let him go.

"It's too idiotic of her to keep me dawdling about all this while," he resumed. "I'm half asleep as it is. My boss has put me into the liquidation department. Up all night three times a week, my dear boy! If only Julie were here, I know she'd make room for me; but Duveyrier has only brought up Hippolyte with him from the country. By-the-way, you know Hippolyte, that hulking lout that keeps company with Clémence? Well, I just caught him in his shirt, sneaking into Louise's bedroom—that ugly brat whose soul Madame Juzeur is so anxious to save! A fine success, eh? for Madame Anything-you-like-except-that! That lump of fifteen, a bundle of filth picked up on a doorstep—there's a dainty morsel for that strapping, big-boned fellow, with his damp hands and his bull neck! I don't care a damn myself, only it's disgusting all the same!"

Bored as he was, Trublot that night seemed full of philosophical insight. He went on muttering:

"Well, well, like master, like man! When landlords set the example, the flunkeys may well be depraved in their tastes as well. There's no doubt about it, France is just one big bed!"

"Good-bye. I must be off," said Octave.

But Trublot still kept him back, telling him all the servants' rooms in which he might have slept if the summer season had not emptied so many of them. The worst of it was that they all double-locked their doors, even when they just went along to the end of the passage, as each was so frightened of being robbed by the other. There was nothing to be done with Lisa, who seemed to have rather queer tastes. Victoire hardly tempted him, though ten years ago she might have been a bit spicy. What he most deplored was Valérie's mania for changing her cook; it became positively unbearable. He counted them on his fingers—a regular string of them. One that would have her chocolate of a morning; one who left because her master did not eat in a proper way; one whom the police fetched away just as she was roasting a piece of veal; one who was so powerful that she could not touch a thing without breaking it; one who had a maid to wait on her; one who went out in her mistress's gowns, and who smacked her mistress's face when she ventured to remonstrate. All those within a month! Why, there wasn't even time to go and pinch them in their kitchen!

"Oh! and then," added he, "then there was Eugénie. You must have noticed her— a tall, fine girl, a regular Venus, my dear fellow, and no hum-bug about it! People used to turn round in the street and look at her. Well, for ten days the whole house was upside down. All the women were furious; the men could hardly contain themselves. Campardon licked his chops, and Duveyrier's dodge was to come up here and see if there was a leakage in the roof. A regular revolution—a flame that lit up the damned shanty from cellar to attic! But I had my doubts. She was a bit too smart. Depend upon it, my dear chap, it's the ugly, stupid ones for choice, as long as you get a good armful; that's my opinion, and what I like myself. Well, see what a nose I had! Eugénie was sent flying at last when madame found out, by her sheets, which were black as soot, that every morning she entertained the charcoal seller of the Place Gaillon—nigger's sheets, the washing of which must have cost a small fortune. Well, and what happened? Why, the charcoal man became very ill, while the coachman of the second-floor people, who had left him behind, that stallion of a chap who rootles them all—well, he had a dose of it, too, so that he could hardly drag one leg after another. But I don't pity him a bit, as he's such a nuisance."

At last Octave managed to escape, and as he was leaving Trublot there in the deep gloom of the attic, the latter suddenly exclaimed, in surprise;

"But, I say, what are you after up here among the maids? Ah, you rogue! so you come up, too?"

And he laughed gleefully. Promising not to tell, he sent him off and wished him a pleasant night's amusement. He himself was determined to wait for that slut of an Adèle, who, when she was with a man, never knew when to go. Duveyrier would surely never dare to keep her till the morning.

On getting back to Rachel's room Octave was once more disappointed. Berthe had not come. He now grew angry; she had simply fooled him, making such a promise in order to be quit of his entreaties. While thus he fumed and chafed, she was calmly sleeping, glad to lie alone and have the broad marriage-bed to herself. However, instead of going back to sleep in his own room, he stubbornly lay down in his clothes on the bed, meditating revenge at such an hour. This bare, cold servants'-room irritated him, with its dirty walls, its squalor, and its insufferable smell of an unwashed wench; he shrank from recognising to what depths his frenzied passion had lowered him in his craving to appease it. Far away in the distance he heard it strike three. Strapping maidservants snored away to the left of him; at times bare feet made the boards creak, and then the splashing as of a fountain resounded along the floor. But that which most unnerved him was a perpetual wailing on his right, the cry of one in pain, who for fever could not sleep. At last he recognised the voice—it was that of the boot-stitcher. Was she in labour? Poor woman, there she lay alone in her agony, close to the roof, cooped up in one of those miserable closets hardly big enough for her belly.

About four o'clock Octave was again disturbed by hearing Adèle come to bed and Trublot join her. They very nearly had a quarrel. She declared that it was not her fault; the landlord had kept her, and she couldn't help it. Then Trublot accused her of being conceited, when she began to cry. She was not conceited at all. What had she done that God suffered all the men to run madly after her like this? When one was off the other was on; there seemed no end to it. But she never tried to excite them, and their tomfoolery afforded her so little pleasure that she preferred to look sluttish on purpose, so as not to give them any encouragement. Yes, but they only ran after her more than ever, and her work kept always increasing. It was killing her, and she had had enough of Madame Josserand, for ever bullying her to scrub the kitchen every morning.

"Yes, yes!" she stammered out between her sobs, "folk like you can sleep as long as you like afterwards. But I have to work like a slave. No, no! there's no justice in this world. I am worried out of my life!"

"There, there, don't take on so," said Trublot, in a sudden access of fatherly pity. "Mind you, some women would be glad to be in your place. Since fellows like you, you great silly, why, you should let yourself be liked."

At daybreak Octave fell asleep. There was deep silence everywhere. Even the boot-sticher no longer groaned, as half-dead she lay holding her belly with both hands. The sun was shining in through the narrow window as the door being suddenly opened woke the young man. It was Berthe, who had just come up to see, driven to do so by an irresistible impulse. At first she had scouted the idea, and then had invented pretexts—the necessity of putting the room straight if, in his rage, he had left it in disorder. Nor had she ever expected to find him there, As she saw him rise from the little iron bedstead, pale and threatening, she was taken aback, and, with head lowered, listened to his furious scolding. He urged her to reply, to offer some sort of explanation. At last she murmured:

"At the last moment I could not; it was too revolting. I love you—on my oath, I do! but not here, not here!"

Then, as he approached her, she drew back, fearing that he might want to profit by the opportunity. This, indeed, he desired to do. It struck eight; all the servants had gone down, and Trublot also. Then, as he caught hold of her hands, saying that when one loves a person one doesn't mind anything, she complained of the smell of the room, and went to open the window. But he again drew her to him, and, bewildered by his persistence, she was about to give in when from the courtyard below there rose up a turbid wave of filthy talk.

"Oh, you sow! you slut! Shut up, do! Your beastly dish-cloth has fallen on my head again!"

Berthe, trembling, broke away from his embrace as she murmured:

"There! do you hear that? Oh, no, not here, I entreat you! I should feel too much ashamed of myself. Do you hear those girls? They make my very blood run cold. The other day they quite upset me. No, no! leave me alone, and I promise you that you shall have it next Tuesday in your own room."

Standing there motionless, the two lovers were forced to overhear everything.

"Just let me catch sight of you," Lisa angrily continued, "and I'll chuck it back in your face."

Then, leaning out of her kitchen window, Adèle retorted:

"What a row about a little bit of rag! Why, I only used it yesterday for washing up with, and it fell over quite by accident."

Thereupon a truce was declared, and Lisa asked her what they had had for dinner the night before. What! another *ragoût*? A nice set of skinflints! If she lived in a hole like that she'd buy herself cutlets, see if she wouldn't! And she kept on urging Adèle to crib the sugar, the meat, and the candles, just to show her independence. For her own part, never being hungry, she let Victoire rob the Campardons, without even claiming her share.

"Oh!" cried Adèle, who by degrees was becoming corrupted, "the other night I hid some potatoes in my pocket, and they burned my thigh. Oh, it was fun! And don't I just like vinegar! I don't care a bit? I drink it out of the cruet-stand now!"

Victoire then leant out, in her turn, after finishing a glassful of cassis and brandy, to which Lisa sometimes treated her of a morning, as a reward for kindly concealing her nocturnal and diurnal escapades. As, standing at the back of Madame Jeuzeur's kitchen, Louise put out her tongue at them, Victoire at once fell foul of her.

"Wait a bit, you gutter-snipe; I'll shove that tongue of yours somewhere in a minute!"

"Come on, then, you old drunken cow!" cried Louise. "I saw you yesterday, being sick all over your plates."

Then once more the flood of excrement surged up against the walls which shut in this pestilent hole. Even Adèle, who had now caught the Parisian patter, abused Louise; while Lisa cried out:

"I'll shut her up if we've any of her cheek! Yes, yes, you little bitch, I'll tell Clémence. She'll soon settle you. Isn't it sickening?

Going with men at her age! But hush! there's the chap himself; and a filthy beast, too!"

Hippolyte at that moment looked out of the Duveyriers' window. He was cleaning his master's boots. In spite of everything the other servants were very civil to him, for he belonged to the aristocracy; and he despised Lisa, who in turn despised Adèle with greater haughtiness than gentry who are rich look down on gentry who are hard-up. They asked him for news of Mademoiselle Clémence and Mademoiselle Julie. Good Lord! they were bored to death down there in the country, but they were both pretty well. Then, changing the subject, he said:

"Did you hear that girl last night writhing about with her stomach-ache? Precious nuisance, wasn't it? It's a good job she's going to leave. I'd half a mind to call out, 'Let fly and have done with it!' "

"Monsieur Hippolyte is just about right," said Lisa. "Nothing gets on your nerves more than a woman who's always got the belly-ache. Thank God, I don't know what it is; but I think I should try and bear it so that other folk might sleep."

Then Victoire waggishly turned to Adèle.

"I say, pot-belly, up there! When you had your first baby, did it come out in front or behind?"

As such coarse jesting all the kitchens were convulsed with merriment, while Adèle, looking scared, rejoined?

"A baby? no, none of that! It's not allowed; and besides, I don't want one."

"My girl," said Lisa, gravely, "everybody may have a baby, and I don't suppose the Lord made you different from anyone else!"

Then they talked of Madame Campardon, who, at any rate, had no fears on that score; it was the only pleasant thing in her existence. Then all the ladies of the house were discussed in succession. Madame Juzeur, who took her own precautions; Madame Duveyrier, who was disgusted with her husband; Madame Valérie, who got her babies made for her out-of-doors, because her precious husband wasn't man enough to make the tail of one even. Then from the foetid hole there came gross bursts of laughter.

Berthe again grew pale. Waiting thus, she was afraid to leave the room. She looked down in confusion, as if outraged in Octave's presence. Indignant with these servants, he felt that their talk was becoming too filthy, and that to embrace her was impossible. His desire ebbed away, leaving him weary and extremely sad. Then Berthe trembled. Lisa had just mentioned her by name.

"Talking of high jinks, I know someone who seems to go it pretty hot! I say, Adèle, isn't it true that your Mademoiselle Berthe was up to all sorts of games when you used to wash her petticoats?"

"And now," said Victoire, "she gets her husband's clerk to turn her over, and shake out all the dust."

"Hush!" cried Hippolyte, gently.

"What for? Her pig of a cook isn't there to-day. Sly devil, she is, that looks as if she'd eat you if you mention her mistress! She's a Jewess, you know, and they say she murdered somebody once at her place. Perhaps the handsome Octave gets her in a quiet corner too. His governor must have engaged him just to make babies for him, the great booby!"

Then Berthe, evidently suffering unutterable anguish, looked at her lover, imploringly, as she stammered out:

"Good God! good God!"

Octave caught hold of her hand and pressed it. He too, was choking with impotent wrath. What was to be done? He dared not show himself and silence those hussies. The foul talk went on, talk such as Berthe had never yet heard, while the cesspool brimmed over, as each morning it had done, close to her, although she had no suspicion of its existence. Their amour, so carefully concealed, was now trailed through all the garbage and slops of the kitchen. Though none had spoken of it, these wenches knew all. Lisa related how Saturnin played the pander. Victoire jeered at the husband's headaches. And even Adèle abused her mistress's young lady, whose ailments, soiled underlinen, and toilet secrets she did not scruple to lay bare. Thus were their kisses smirched by such filthy talk; their meetings, too; in fact, all that was sweet and subtle in their love.

"Look out, below there!" cried Victoire, suddenly. "There goes them stinkin' carrots of yesterday. They'll do for that old crack-pot, Gourd!"

For sheer spite the servants used to throw down offal into the courtyard, which the hall-porter had to sweep up.

"And there goes a lump of rotten kidney!" cried Adèle, in her turn.

All the dregs of their saucepans, all the rinsings of their pots, were flung out in this fashion, while Lisa, went on reviling Berthe and Octave, commenting on all the falsehoods by which they sought to hide their barefaced adultery. Hand in hand and face to face, the lovers stood there aghast. Their hands grew icy cold, their eyes bore witness to the uncleanliness of their amour. So that was to what it all had come, to fornication amid a pelting rain of rotten vegetables and putrid meat!

"And, you know," said Hippolyte, "the young chap don't care a damn for his missis. He's only got hold of her to help him on in the world. At heart he's a regular miser, a fellow without any scruples whatever, who, while pretending to make love to women, wouldn't mind giving them a jolly good smack in the eye!"

Berthe, looking at Octave, saw him turn pale; so changed, so upset did his face seem that it frightened her.

"My word! they're a nice couple!" rejoined Lisa. "I wouldn't give much for her, either. Badly brought up, her heart as hard as a stone, caring for nothing but her own amusement, sleeping with chaps for money; yes, for money! I know the kind of woman, and I wouldn't mind betting that she doesn't even get any pleasure with a man!"

Berthe's eyes overflowed with tears. Octave remarked her confusion. It was as if they both had been beaten until the blood came—laid bare before each other, ruthlessly and without a chance of protest. Then the young woman, stifled by the stench of this open cesspool, sought to flee. He did not attempt to keep her; mutual self-disgust made their society excruciating; and they longed for the relief of no longer seeing each other.

"Then Tuesday next, you promise, in my room!"

"Yes, yes!"

Covered with confusion, she fled. He stayed behind, walking hither and thither, his hands twitching nervously as he rolled the bed-linen up into a bundle. He no longer listened to the servants' gossip. Suddenly one phrase caught his ear.

"I tell you Monsieur Hédouin died last night. If only the good-looking Octave had foreseen that, he might have gone on keeping Madame Hédouin warm, for she's got the money-bags."

To hear news such as this in that sewer touched him to the core. So Monsieur Hédouin was dead! Profound regret took possession of him, as, thinking aloud, he could not forbear replying:

"Yes, by Jingo! I *was* a fool!"

When Octave at last went downstairs, he met Rachel coming up to her room. A few minutes earlier she would have caught them. Below she had found her mistress in tears again; however, this time she had got nothing out of her, neither a confession nor a sou. She was furious, being positive that they profited by her absence to meet, and thus cheated her of her little perquisites. She gave Octave a black, threatening scowl. A strange schoolboy bashfulness prevented him from giving her ten francs, while, anxious to show that he was completely at his ease, he went into Marie Pichon's, jokingly. Then suddenly a grunt from a corner made him turn round. Saturnin got up, exclaiming, in one of his jealous fits :

"Look out ! We're deadly enemies !"

That very morning happened to be the 8th of October, and the boot-stitcher had to go out before noon. For a week past Monsieur Gourd had been watching her belly with every-increasing uneasiness. That belly would surely never wait until the 8th. The poor woman had begged the landlord to let her stay a few days longer, so as to get over her confinement, but she had met with an indignant refusal. At every moment she was seized with pains : the last night of all she was afraid she would be delivered all by herself. Then about nine o'clock she began to move her things away, helping the lad, who had his truck in the courtyard below, leaning against the furniture or sitting down on the staircase when bent double by some excruciating pang.

Monsieur Gourd, however, had found nothing out—no man, after all. He had been regularly hoaxed. All that morning he went wandering about, wrathful and glum. When Octave met him the thought that he knew of his intrigue filled him with dread. Perhaps he did know about it. Yet his bow was no whit less polite, for what did not concern him did not concern him, as he had already observed. That morning, too, he had doffed his cap to the mysterious lady as she noiselessly hurried away from the gentleman's flat on the third floor, leaving only a faint perfume of verbena behind her. He had also saluted Trublot, as well as the other Madame Campardon and Valérie. Those were all gentry. If the young men were caught coming out of the maidservants' bedrooms, or the ladies tripping downstairs in tell-tale dressing gowns, why, that was none of his business. What concerned him did concern him, and he kept his eye on the few miserable bits of furniture belonging to the boot-stitcher, as if the long sought male were escaping in one of the drawers.

At a quarter to twelve the girl appeared, her face as white as wax, looking as sad, as despondent as ever. She could hardly walk, and until she got out into the street, Monsieur Gourd was all in a tremble. Just as she was giving up her key, Duveyrier came through the hall, so heated by his night that the red blotches on his brow looked as if they were bleeding. He put on a haughty air, an air severely, implacably moral, as the poor thing went past him. Shameful and resigned, she bowed her head, and walked out after the little truck with the same despairing gait as she had come on the day that the black funeral hangings had enveloped her.

It was then only that Monsieur Gourd had his triumph. As though it was the work-girl's belly that had removed all unhealthiness from the house, all those shameful things that caused the very walls to blush, he exclaimed to the landlord :

"Well, it's that's a good riddance! We shall be able to breathe now, for, upon my word, it was getting positively disgusting! It's like a hundred-weight off my chest. In a respectable house like this, you see, sir, there oughtn't to be any women, least of all, work-women."

XIV

Next Tuesday Berthe did not keep her promise. She had, in fact, told Octave beforehand not to expect her, when they had a hurried interview that same evening after closing time. She sobbed bitterly, for she had been to confession the day before, feeling the need of religious solace, and being still overcome by the Abbé Maudit's dolorous counsel. Ever since her marriage she had given up going to church; but after the gross language with which the maids had bespattered her, she had become so sad, so forlorn, so sullied, that for an hour she went back to her childish beliefs, ardently yearning to be made pure and good. On her return, after the priest had wept with her, she grew quite horrified at her sin. Octave shrugged his shoulders, powerless and enraged.

Then, three days afterwards, she again promised to see him on the following Tuesday. Meeting him one day by appointment in the Passages des Panoramas, she had noticed some shawls of Chantilly lace, and of these she talked incessantly, her eyes full of desire. Thus, on the Monday morning, the young man told her, laughingly, with the idea of tempering the brutality of such a bargain, that if she really kept her word she would find a little surprise waiting for her in his room. She guessed what he meant, and again began to cry. No, no, it was impossible for her to come now; he had spoilt all her pleasure in their projected meeting. She had talked about the shawl without thinking, and she did not want it now; in fact, she would throw it into the fire if he made her a present of it. Nevertheless, on the following day they arranged matters satisfactorily; at half-past twelve that night she was to knock three times very gently at his door.

That day, as Auguste was starting for Lyons, Berthe thought that he looked somewhat strange. She had caught him whispering with Rachel behind the kitchen-door; in addition to that, his face was all yellow, he trembled violently, and one of his eyes was closed up. But, as he complained of neuralgia, she thought he must be unwell, and assured him that the journey would do him good. No sooner had he gone than she went back to the kitchen, and, feeling uneasy, tried to sound Rachel, who, however, maintained her demeanour of discreet respect, being as stiff in manner as when she first came. Berthe, somehow, felt certain that she was dissatisfied, and she thought how extremely foolish she had been first to give the girl twenty francs and a dress, and then suddenly to stop all further gratuities, though she was obliged to do so, as she was always in want of a five-franc piece herself.

"My poor girl," said she, "I've not been over generous to you, have I? But that isn't my fault. I haven't forgotten you, and I mean to reward you some day."

Rachel coldly replied :

"Madame owes me nothing."

Then Berthe went to fetch two of her old chemises, just as a proof of her good intentions. But when the servant took them from her, she said they would do for kitchen-cloths.

"Much obliged, madam, but calico gives me pimples; I only wear linen."

However, so polite did she seem, that Berthe was reassured, and she spoke familiarly to the girl, telling her she was going to sleep out; asking her even to leave a lamp alight in case she came back. The front door was to be bolted, and she would go out by the back-stairs and take the key with her. Rachel took her instructions as calmly as if she had been told to cook some beef *à la mode* for the following day.

That evening, by a fine touch of diplomacy, as Berthe was dining with her parents, Octave accepted an invitation from the Campardons. He thought of staying there till ten o'clock, and then of going up to his room and of waiting as patiently as might be until half-past twelve.

The meal at the Campardons' proved quite patriarchal. Seated between his wife and her cousin, the architect lingered lovingly over the food—plain, homely fare as he termed it, wholesome and copious. That evening there was a boiled fowl and rice, a joint of beef and some fried potatoes. Ever since cousin Gasparine had taken to managing everything, the whole household lived in a perpetual state of indigestion, for she was so good at marketing, paying less money and getting twice as much meat as anybody else. Campardon was helped three times to the fowl, while Rose stuffed herself with rice. Angèle reserved herself for the beef; she liked blood, and

Lisa slily helped her to spoonfuls of it. It was only Gasparine who hardly touched anything; her stomach was shrunken, so she said.

"Eat away!" cried the architect to Octave. "You never know if some day you may not be eaten yourself!"

Madame Campardon, in a whisper, once more told the young man how delighted she was at the advent of her cousin, and of all the happiness which she had brought to the house—a saving of quite a hundred per cent., the servants made respectful, Angèle well brought up, with the advantage of a good example.

"In short," she murmured, "Achille's always as happy as a trout in a pool, whilst I have now nothing to do—absolutely nothing. Just fancy! she actually washes and dresses me now. I don't have to lift a finger; she's taken charge of the entire management of the household."

Then the architect related how he had let "those chappies at the Ministry of Public Instruction" have it.

"Just imagine, my dear boy, they caused me no end of bother about my Evreux job. Of course, I wanted to please monseigneur above all—only natural, eh? However, the new kitchens and heating apparatus came to more than twenty thousand francs. There was no vote of credit, and it wasn't easy to squeeze twenty thousand francs out of the slender sum allowed for repairs. Then, again, the pulpit, for which I had a grant of three thousand francs, came to nearly ten thousand—making another seven thousand to be got somehow. So this morning they sent for me to attend at the Ministry, where a big lanky chap began to blow me up sky-high. But I wasn't going to stand that sort of thing—not I! So I flatly told him that I would send for the bishop himself, who would soon explain matters. He at once became so awfully polite; it was quite absurd, and it makes me laugh now when I think of it! Just now they're in a dreadful funk at bishops. If I'd got a bishop to back me, why, I could demolish Notre-Dame and rebuild it, if I liked, and snap my fingers at the Government!"

Then they all grew merry over this sneer at the Ministry, alluding to it disdainfully, with their mouths chock-full of rice. Rose declared that it was best to be on the side of religion. Ever since his restoration of Saint-Roch, Achille had been overwhelmed with work; the highest families clamoured for his services; he could not get through it all, but had to sit up at night. God certainly was well-disposed towards them, and they gave Him thanks both morning and evening.

During dessert, Campardon suddenly exclaimed:

"By the way, my dear fellow, I suppose you know that Duveyrier has found——" He was going to say Clarisse. But he recollected that Angèle was present, so with a side glance at his daughter, he added: "Has found his—relative, don't you know."

By biting his lip and winking, he at last made Octave understand, who at first quite failed to catch his meaning.

"Yes, it was Trublot who told me so. The day before yesterday, when it was raining in torrents, Duveyrier stood up under a doorway, when, lo! and behold, there was his—relative, just opening her umbrella. For the last week Trublot had been on the look-out for her, so as to restore her to him."

Angèle modestly looked down at her plate, filling her mouth with food. The family were most careful that the conversation should never transgress the bounds of decency.

"Is she pretty?" asked Rose of Octave.

"That's a matter of taste," replied he. "Some people might admire her."

"She had the impertinence to come to the shop one day," said Gasparine, who, thin as she was, detested skinny people. "She was pointed out to me—a regular scarecrow!"

"Never mind," said the architect; 'Duveyrier's landed again. His poor wife, you know——"

He was going to say that the poor wife was, probably, much relieved and delighted. But he again remembered that Angèle was there, so he dolefully remarked:

"Relations don't always get on together. Well, well, every family has its troubles!"

Lisa, napkin on arm, looked across the table at Angèle, who, bursting with laughter, hastily began to take a long drink, concealing her face with her glass.

Shortly before ten o'clock, Octave professed to be so tired that he was obliged to go up to bed. Despite Rose's tender attentions, he felt ill at ease in this worthy family, aware of Gasparine's ever-increasing hostility. He had done nothing, however, to provoke this. She merely hated him because he was a good-looking fellow, who, as she suspected, had all the women in the house; and this exasperated her, although she herself did not desire his embraces in the least. It was merely the thought of his enjoyment that instinctively roused her feminine wrath, now that her own comeliness had withered all too soon.

Directly he had left, the Campardons talked of going to bed. Every evening, before getting into bed, Rose spent a whole hour over her toilet, using face washes and scents, doing her hair, manipulating her eyes and mouth and ears; even putting a little patch under her chin. At night she replaced her sumptuous dressing-gowns by equally sumptuous nightcaps and chemises. On this particular evening she chose a night-dress and cap trimmed with Valenciennes lace. Gasparine had been helping her, holding basins for her, mopping up the water she had spilt, drying her with a face-towel, showing her various little attentions with far greater skill than Lisa.

"Ah! now I feel comfortable," said Rose, at last, lying full length in bed, while her cousin tucked in the sheets and raised the bolster.

She smiled contentedly as she lay there alone in the middle of the large bed. With her plump, soft body swathed in lace, she looked like some amorous siren about to welcome the lover of her choice. When she felt pretty, she could sleep better, so she said. Well, it was the only pleasure she had.

"Everything all right, eh?" asked Campardon, as he came in. "Well, good-night, my puss."

He pretended that he had got some work to do. He would have to sit up. Whereupon she was vexed, and begged him to have a rest; it was so foolish of him to fag himself to death in this way!

"Now, listen to me; you just go to bed! Gasparine, promise me you'll make him go to bed!"

Gasparine had just put a glass of sugar and water and one of Dickens's novels by the bed. She looked at Rose, without replying, and then, bending over her, whispered:

"You do look nice to-night!"

Then she kissed her on both cheeks, with arid lips and bitter mouth, with the subdued air of a poor, plain relation. Flushed, and suffering from frightful indigestion, Campardon surveyed his spouse as well. His moustache quivered slightly as, in his turn, he stooped to kiss her.

"Good night, my poppet!"

"Good night, my love! Now, mind you go to bed at once."

"Don't be afraid, said Gasparine; "if he's not in bed and asleep by eleven o'clock, I'll get up and turn the lamp out."

About eleven o'clock, after yawning over some plans for a Swiss cottage that a tailor in the Rue Rameau had taken into his head to have built, Campardon slowly undressed, thinking meanwhile of

Rose, lying there so smart and pretty. Then, after turning down his bed, because of the servants, he went and joined Gasparine in hers. It was most uncomfortable for them, as there was no elbow-room, and he in particular had to balance himself on the edge of the mattress, so that the next morning one of his thighs was quite stiff.

Just then, as Victoire, after washing up, had gone to bed, Lisa came in to see if mademoiselle were in want of anything. Angèle was waiting for her in bed; and then it was that, unknown to the parents, they played interminable games at cards on the counterpane. And as they played, their talk for ever reverted to Gasparine, that dirty beast, whom the maid coarsely reviled before little Angèle. In this way they made up for their humble, hypocritical demeanour during the day; and Lisa took a certain base pleasure in corrupting Angèle thus, satisfying the girl's morbid curiosity now that she was on the verge of puberty. That night they were furious with Gasparine because for the last two days she had locked up the sugar with which the maid was wont to fill her pockets and afterwards empty them out on the child's bed. Nasty old cow! They couldn't even get a lump of sugar to munch when they went to sleep!

It struck midnight. Campardon and Gasparine were moaning in all the discomfort of their narrow bed, while Rose, supine in the centre of hers, stretched out her limbs and read Dickens till tears suffused her eyes. Deep silence covered all; the chaste night threw her pall over this eminently virtuous family.

On going upstairs, Octave found that the Pichons had company. Jules called to him, declaring that he must come in and have a glass of something with them. Monsieur and Madame Vuillaume were there; they had made their peace with Jules and Marie on the occasion of the latter's churching. Her confinement had taken place in September. They had even consented to come to dinner on Tuesday to celebrate the young woman's recovery. She had only been out the day before for the first time. Being desirous to appease her mother, whom the very sight of the baby, another girl, annoyed, Marie had put it out to nurse, not far from Paris. Lilitte was asleep with her head on the table, having imbibed a tumblerful of wine, which had upset her, her parents having forced her to drink to her little sister's health.

"Well, one can manage with two," said Madame Vuillaume, after clinking glasses with Octave. "Only no more of it, son-in-law, do you hear?"

They all began to laugh, but the old woman remained perfectly grave, saying :

"I can't see what there is to laugh at. We'll put up with this baby, but I swear that if another comes——"

"Oh, if another comes," cried Monsieur Vuillaume, completing her speech, "you will prove yourselves to be devoid of heart and of brains. What the devil do you think? Life's a serious thing, and one must exercise restraint when one hasn't got a fortune to spend in amusing oneself."

Then, turning to Octave, he added :

"Listen to me, sir. I have been decorated, don't you know. Well, I can assure you that, in order not to spoil too many ribbons, I never wear my decorations when I'm at home. Now, if I am ready to deprive my wife and myself of the pleasure of being decorated at home, I am sure that our children can deprive themselves of the pleasure of begetting babies. No, sir, it's not merely a question of economy."

The Pichons declared that they would obey. It wasn't likely that they'd be up to that game any more.

"Why, rather than go through what I've gone through," cried Marie, pale as death——

"I'd sooner have my leg cut off," declared Jules.

The Vuillaumes gave a nod of satisfaction. Since they had promised, they would forgive them. Then, as it was just striking ten, they all embraced one another affectionately, and Jules put on his hat to see them into their omnibus. So touching, indeed, was this return to their old habits, that on the landing they kissed yet once again. When they had departed, Marie, who, with Octave, leant over the banisters to see them go, took him back with her to the parlour, saying :

"Mamma doesn't mean to be unkind; and, after all, she's right. Children are no joke !"

Having shut the door, she began to remove the glasses, which were still on the table. The small room, with its smoking lamp, was still quite warm from this little family festival. Lilitte still slumbered, her head resting on a corner of the oilcloth.

"I'm going to bed," said Octave.

"What ! so early as this?" she replied. "You don't often keep such respectable hours, I know. Perhaps you have got something to do early tomorrow morning, have you?"

"No, I haven't," said he. "I'm sleepy, that's all. But I can stop another ten minutes or so."

Then he remembered that Berthe would not be coming untill half-past twelve. There was plenty of time. Consumed as he had been for weeks past by this thought of having her in his arms for one whole night, it now no longer roused within him carnal thrills. The feverish impatience of that day, his torments of desire, as he counted every moment which brought him nearer and nearer to his long-coveted delight—all this now vanished, being dissipated by such wearisome delay.

"Will you have another glass of cognac?" asked Marie.

"Well, I don't mind if I do."

He thought that it might stimulate his powers. As she took the glass from him he seized her hands and held them in his, she laughing meanwhile, unafraid. Pale as she was after physical suffering, he found her full of charm, and all his latent affection for her surged up again within him. As, one evening, he had given her back to her husband, after imprinting a parental kiss upon her brow, so now he felt impelled to repossess her—a sudden, sharp desire, which extinguished all his longing for Berthe. That passion now seemed remote.

"Then you're not afraid to-day?" he asked, as he squeezed her hands tighter.

"No, as henceforth it is impossible. But we shall always be good friends."

Hereupon she let him perceive that she knew everything. Saturnin must have told her. Moreover, she always noticed on which nights Octave received a certain person in his room. Observing his pallor and confusion, she hurriedly assured him that she would never tell anyone. She was not displeased; on the contrary, she wished him every sort of happiness.

"Why, I'm married, you know," she said; "so I couldn't bear you any ill-will."

Taking her on his knee, he exclaimed:

"But it's you I love!"

He spoke the truth, for at that minute it was she that he loved, with deep, with overmastering passion. All his new intrigue, and the two months spent in hankering after another woman, had vanished. Once more he saw himself in the little flat, kissing Marie on the neck when Jules' back was turned, she being gentle and complacent as ever. That was real happiness. Why had he ever disdained it? It filled him with regret. He still desired Marie; if he no longer had her, he felt that he would be eternally unhappy.

"Leave me alone," she murmured, endeavouring to get away from him. "You're unreasonable, and you want to grieve me. Now that you are in love with somebody else, where's the good of teasing me?"

Thus did she try to offer resistance in her gentle, languid way, feeling actual disgust for what afforded her no sort of amusement. But he lost his head, and squeezed her more vigorously, kissing her breast through her coarse woollen bodice.

"It's you I love; can't you see that? I swear by all that's sacred that I'm not telling you a lie. Open my heart, and you'll see. Now, please, do be nice! Just this once, and then never, never again, if you don't want to. You really are too cruel; if you don't let me, I shall die!"

Then Marie became powerless, paralysed by the dominating force of this man's will. In her, good-nature, fear and folly were about equally blended. She moved away, as if anxious first of all to carry the sleeping Lilette into the other room. But he held her fast, fearing that she would wake the child. Then she surrendered herself, in the same place where a year ago she had fallen into his arms like a woman that must obey. There was a sort of buzzing silence throughout the little apartment as the whole house lay merged in midnight peace. Suddenly the lamp grew dim, leaving them nearly in darkness, when Marie rose and just turned up the wick in time.

"You aren't cross with me?" asked Octave, still exhausted by pleasurable thrills such as he had never yet experienced.

She stopped winding up the lamp, and with her cold lips gave him one last kiss, as she said:

"No, because you enjoy it. But, all the same, it's not right, on account of that person. Doing that with me is no good whatever now."

Her eyes were wet with tears, and, though not annoyed, she seemed sad. After leaving her he felt dissatisfied with himself, and as if he should like to go straight to bed and to sleep. He had gratified his passion, but it had left a disagreable after-taste; a touch of lechery that brought merely bitterness in its wake. The other woman was now coming, and he would have to wait for her; it was a thought that weighed terribly upon his mind, and he hoped that by some accident she might be prevented from coming. This, too, after hot nights of wild scheming to possess her, to harbour her, if for but one hour, in his room. Perhaps she would again fail to keep her word. He dared not venture to solace himself with such a hope.

It struck midnight. Tired as he was, Octave sat up and waited, dreading to hear the rustle of her skirts along the narrow passage. By half-past twelve he became positively anxious, and at one o'clock he thought he was safe, though there was a kind of vague irritation mixed with his relief, the vexation of a man who had been fooled by a woman. Then, just as, yawning vigorously, he was about to undress, there came three gentle knocks at the door. It was Berthe. Half cross, half flattered, he met her with outstretched arms, but she shrank aside trembling, and listened at the door, which she hastily closed behind her.

"What is it?" he asked, speaking low.

"I don't know," she stammered, "but I'm frightened. It's so dark on the staircase; I had an idea someone was following me. What nonsense all these adventures are, to be sure! I am certain that something horrid's going to happen."

On both this speech had a chilling effect. They did not even kiss each other. However, she looked captivating in her white dressing-gown with all her golden hair twisted up into a coil at the back of her head. Gazing at her, she seemed to him far prettier than Marie; but he no longer desired to possess her; the whole thing was a bore. Being out of breath she sat down, and gave a sudden feigned start of annoyance at noticing a box on the table, which she felt positive contained the lace shawl about which she had talked for the last week.

"I shall go," said she, without moving from her chair.

"What's that for?"

"Do you suppose that I'm going to sell myself; you always manage to wound my feelings. Now, to-night, you've entirely spoilt all my pleasure. Whatever did you buy it for, after I told you not to do so?"

However, she got up and finally consented to look at it. So great was her disappointment on opening the box, that she could not forbear indignantly exclaiming:

"Why, it's not Chantilly, at all; it's llama!"

Growing less liberal as regarded present-giving, Octave this time had yielded to a niggardly impulse. He sought to explain to her that some llama was splendid—quite as handsome as Chantilly—and he extolled the beauties of the shawl just as if he were standing behind the counter, making her finger the lace, while assuring her that it would last for ever. But she shook her head disdainfully, saying:

"The fact is, this only cost one hundred francs, while the other would have come to three hundred."

Then, noticing that he turned pale, she sought to mend matters by adding:

"Of course, it's very kind of you, and I am much obliged. It's not what a gift costs, but the spirit in which it is given that makes it valuable."

Then she sat down again, and there came a pause. After a while he asked if she were not coming to bed. Of course she was; but she still felt so upset by her silly fright on the stairs. Then she disclosed her fears as to Rachel, telling how she had caught Auguste whispering with her behind the door. Yet it would have been so easy for them to bribe the girl by giving her a five-franc piece now and again. One had to get the five-franc pieces first, though; she never had a single one herself. As she spoke her voice grew harsher; the despised llama shawl exasperated her to such a pitch that at last she started the everlasting quarrel with her lover that she was wont to pick with her husband.

"Now, I ask you, is this a life? Never to have a farthing; always to be under an obligation for the least thing! Oh, I'm sick to death of it all!"

Octave, who was walking up and down the room, stopped short, and said:

"What's the point of your telling me all this?"

"The point, sir? the point? Well, there are certain things which sense of delicacy ought to prompt one to do; and merely to hint at such matters makes me blush. Don't you think that ever so long ago you ought to have made me feel easy by bribing that girl?"

She paused, and then ironically added:

"It wouldn't have ruined you, I'm sure!"

There was another pause. Octave went on walking up and down. At last he said:

"I am sorry for your sake that I am not rich."

Then their altercation grew more vehement, assuming the proportions of a conjugal dispute.

"Say that I like you for your money!" she cried, with all the effrontery of her mother, whose very words seemed to leap to her lips. "I'm a mercenary woman, am I not? Well, I admit it. I am mercenary because I'm a sensible woman. It's no use your denying it; money is money; and when I only had twenty sous I always said that I had got forty, as it is better to be envied than pitied."

Here he interrupted her, saying wearily, like a man who was anxious for peace :

"Look here, as you're so discontented with the llama shawl, why, I'll get you a Chantilly one !"

"Your shawl, indeed !" she went on, in a fury, "I've forgotten all about such a thing! It's not that which exasperates me, do you hear? Now there! You're just like my husband! I might walk about barefoot; you wouldn't care the least bit! Yet, if one's fond of a woman, mere good-nature ought to make one feel bound to clothe and feed her. But that's what no man will ever understand. Why, between the pair of you, you would let me go about with nothing on but my chemise, if I did not object !"

Worn out by this domestic quarrel, Octave determined not to make any reply, having noticed that Auguste sometimes got rid of her in this way. He slowly undressed himself and let the storm pass over, reflecting meanwhile how unlucky he had been in his love affairs. Yet for Berthe he had felt passionate desire, so passionate, indeed, that it had interfered with all his plans, and now that she was here in his bedroom, all that she did was to quarrel with him, and give him a sleepless night, just as if they have been married for six months.

"Let's go to bed, eh?" said he, at last. "We thought we were going to be so happy together. It's too silly to waste our time in wrangling like this !"

Then, anxious to make it up, feeling no desire, yet wishing to be polite, he sought to kiss, her. But she pushed him aside and burst into tears. Then, seeing that reconciliation was hopeless, he began taking off his boots in a fury, and determined to get into bed whether she came with him or not.

"That's right! Complain of my goings-out, as well !" she sobbed out. "Tell me, do, that I cost you too much! Ah, I see it all now! It's all because of that rubbishy present! If you could shut me up in a box, you'd do it. Going out to see my girl-friends is no crime. And as for mamma——"

"I'm going to sleep," said he, jumping into bed. "I wish you'd undress, and leave that mother of yours alone. She's given you a damned nasty temper, allow me to inform you."

Mechanically, she began undressing herself, growing more and more excited as she raised her voice.

"Mamma has always done her duty. It's not for you to discuss her here. How dare you mention her name? Upon my word, that's the climax, to begin abusing my family!"

Her petticoat-string had got into a knot, and she snapped it viciously. Then, sitting down on the bed to pull off her stockings, she exclaimed:

"How sorry I am for ever having been so weak! If one only could foresee things, how carefully one would reflect beforehand!"

She had now nothing on but her chemise; her legs and arms were naked—the nakedness of a soft, plump little woman. Her breasts, heaving in anger, peeped out of their covering of lace. He, who pretended to lie with his face to the wall, suddenly turned abruptly round, exclaiming:

"What's that? You're sorry you ever loved me?"

"Of course I am. A man like you, incapable of understanding a woman's feelings."

As they glared at each other their faces assumed a hard, loveless expression. She was resting one knee on the edge of the mattress, her breasts tense, her thigh bent, in the pretty attitude of a woman just getting into bed. But he had no eyes for her rosy flesh and the supple, fleeting outline of her back.

"Good God! If only it could all happen again!"

"You mean you'd have somebody else, I suppose?" he brutally ejaculated.

Lying beside him at full length under the bed-clothes, she was just about to reply in the same exasperated tone, when suddenly there came a knocking at the door. They started up, hardly knowing what it might mean; then they both remained motionless, as if frozen.

A faint voice was heard saying:

"Open the door! I can hear you, up to your filthy tricks! Open the door, or I'll smash it!"

It was Auguste's voice. Yet the lovers did not move; in their ears there was such a buzzing that they could think of nothing. They felt very cold lying there next to each other—as cold as corpses. At last Berthe jumped out of bed, instinctively feeling that she must escape from her paramour; while Auguste, outside, kept exclaiming:

"Open the door! Open the door, I say!"

Then there was a moment of terrible confusion—of unspeakable anguish. Berthe rushed about the room, distracted, trying to find some passage of escape, her face white through the fear of death. Octave's heart was in his mouth at each blow on the door, against which he leant mechanically, as if to strengthen it. The noise grew unbearable, the idiot would soon rouse the whole house; they would have to open. But when she perceived his intention, Berthe clung to his arms, imploring him in terror to desist. No, no; for mercy's sake! He would rush in upon them, armed with a knife or a pistol! Growing as pale as she, for her alarm affected him also, he hurriedly slipped on his trousers, while begging her in a low voice to get dressed. She sat there naked, doing nothing, being unable even to find her stockings. Meanwhile, Auguste grew ever more furious.

"Ah, so you won't open and you won't answer! Very well, you shall see!

Ever since last quarter-day Octave had been asking the landlord to have two new screws fixed to the staple of his lock, as it had become loosened. All at once the wood cracked, the lock gave way, and Auguste, losing his balance, fell sprawling into the middle of the room.

"Blast it all!" he cried.

He had only got a key in his hand, which, grazed by his fall, was bleeding. Then he got up, livid with shame and fury at the thought of so absurd an entry. Waving his arms wildly about, he sought to spring upon Octave. But the latter, albeit embarrassed at being caught bare-foot with trousers buttoned awry, caught him by the wrists, and, being the stronger held these as in a vice.

"Sir," cried he, "you are violating my domicile. It is disgraceful, it is ungentlemanlike!"

And he very nearly struck him. During their brief scuffle, Berthe rushed out over the shattered door in her chemise. In her husband's bloody fist she thought she saw a kitchen knife, and between her shoulders she seemed to feel the cold steel. As she fled along the dark passage she fancied she heard the sound of blows, though unable to tell by whom these were dealt or received. Voices, half unrecognisable, exclaimed: "Whenever you please, I am at your service!" "Very good; you shall hear from me."

She reached the back-stairs at a bound. But after rushing down two flights as if pursued by tongues of flame, she found her kitchen door locked, and that she had left the key upstairs in the pocket of her dressing-gown. Besides, there was no lamp, not the least light within; the maid had evidently betrayed them in this way. Without stopping to get her breath, she flew upstairs again and passed along the corridor leading to Octave's room, where the two men were still heard wrangling furiously.

They were still at it; perhaps, she would have time. And she ran down the front staircase, hoping that her husband had left the door of their flat ajar. She would lock herself into her bedroom and not open to anybody. But yet once more she found herself confronted with a closed door. Being thus naked and an outcast, she lost her head, and rushed from floor to floor like some poor hunted animal in search of a hiding-place. On no account dared she knock at her parents' door. For an instant she thought of taking refuge in the porter's lodge, but the shame of it made her turn back. Then, leaning over the banisters, she stopped to listen, her ears deafened by the beating of her heart in that great silence, and her eyes dazzled by lights that seemed to start up out of the inky darkness. The knife, that awful knife in Auguste's bloody fist! This is what terrified her. Its icy blade was about to be buried in her flesh! Suddenly, there was a noise. She fancied he was coming after her, and she shivered to the very marrow of her bones for fright. Then, being just outside the Campardons' door, she rang wildly, desperately, with energy enough to break the bell.

"Goodness gracious! Is the house on fire?" cried a voice anxiously from within.

The door was instantly opened by Lisa, who had only just left mademoiselle's bedroom, on tiptoe, carrying a candlestick. The furious tug at the bell had made her jump, just as she was crossing the hall. The sight of Berthe in her chemise utterly amazed her.

"Whatever is the matter?" asked she.

Berthe came inside, slammed the door, and leaning, breathless, against the wall, gasped:

"Hush! Don't make a noise! He wants to murder me!"

Lisa could get no more rational explanation from her before Campardon, looking very anxious, appeared upon the scene. This extraordinary noise had disturbed Gasparine and himself in their narrow bed. He had only put on his drawers, his puffy face was all over sweat, his yellow beard being crushed out of shape, and covered with white fluff from the pillow, as he breathlessly sought to show the bold front of a husband who always sleeps by himself.

"Is that you, Lisa?" he cried, from the drawing room. "What folly is this? Why are you not upstairs?"

"I was afraid that I had not locked the door properly, sir, and the thought of it prevented me from going to sleep, so I just came down to make sure. But here's Madame——"

At the sight of Berthe in her chemise, leaning against the wall Campardon was as one petrified also. A sudden sense of decency caused him to feel if his drawers were properly buttoned. Berthe seemed to forget that she was naked while repeating :

"Oh, sir, do let me stop here with you! He wants to murder me!"

"Who does?"

"My husband."

And now Gasparine made her appearance in the background. She had taken time to put on her dress, her unkempt hair was covered with fluff as well, her breasts were flaccid and pendulous, her bony shoulders stuck out under her gown as she approached, full of wrath at her interrupted pleasure. The sight of Berthe, soft plump and nude only served to exasperate her yet more.

"Well, whatever have you been doing to your husband?" she asked.

At this simple question Berthe was covered with confusion. She grew conscious of her nakedness, and she blushed from head to foot Convulsed with shame, she held both arms across her bosom, as if to shield herself from scrutiny, and faltered :

"He found me—he caught me——"

The other two undertood, and glanced at each other, profoundly shocked. Lisa, who with her candle lighted up the scene, affected to share in the indignation of her betters. However, all explanation was cut short, for Angèle came running thither, pretending to have been just woke up, and rubbing her eyes all heavy with sleep. This lady in her night-dress brought her to a sudden halt, as every muscle quivered of her slender girlish frame.

"Oh!" cried she, in surprise.

"It's nothing; go back to bed!" exclaimed her father.

Then, aware that he must invent some tale or other, he said the first thing that came into his head—an utterly ludicrous fib, as it happened.

"Madame's sprained her ankle coming downstairs, and has asked us to see after her. Go back to bed; you'll catch cold."

Lisa almost laughed as her eyes met Angèle's eager stare, and the child went back to bed, flushed and rosy, feeling delighted that she had seen such a sight. At that moment Madame Campardon was heard calling to them from her room. Being so engrossed by Dickens, she had not yet put her light out, and she wanted to know what was the matter. What had happened? Who was there? Why didn't they come and tell her?

"Come this way, madam," said Campardon, as he led Berthe in. "Just wait a moment, Lisa."

Rose lay there in the broad bed, throned luxuriously, like a queen, looking tranquil and serene as some idol. She had been greatly affected by what she had read, and had placed the volume of Dickens on her bosom, and as she breathed it rose and fell. When Gasparine briefly explained matters, she also appeared to be extremely shocked. How could anyone go and sleep with a man who wasn't your husband! She felt disgust for a thing to which she had now grown unaccustomed. Then the architect, in confusion, glanced furtively at Berthe's breasts, until Gasparine began to blush.

"I can't have this," she cried. "Really, madam, it's too disgraceful! Cover yourself up, do!"

She herself flung one of Rose's shawls round Berthe, a large knitted shawl which was lying about. It hardly reached to her thighs, and Campardon, in spite of himself, kept contemplating her legs.

Berthe still trembled from head to foot. Though safe enough where she was, she still glanced at the door and shuddered. Her eyes filled with tears as she begged the lady who looked so calm and comfortable, to protect her.

"Oh, madam, hide me! save me! He's going to murder me!"

There was a pause. They all looked questioningly at each other, without attempting to conceal their disapproval of such scandalous conduct. Imagine rushing in like that after midnight in your chemise and waking people up! No, such things were not done; it showed a want of tact, and placed them in a far too embarrassing position.

"We have a little girl in the house," said Gasparine at length. "Pray consider our responsibility, madam."

"The best thing would be for you to go to your parents," suggested Campardon. "If you will allow me to accompany you, I——"

Berthe started back in terror.

"No, no! he's on the stairs; he'll kill me!"

And she begged to be allowed to stay, anywhere, on a chair, till morning came, when she would quietly slip out. To this the architect and his wife were inclined to consent, he being fascinated by such plump charms, and she being interested in such a dramatic adventure at midnight. Gasparine, however, remained inexorable. Yet her curiosity was roused, and she at length enquired :

"Wherever were you?"

"Upstairs, in the room at the end of the passage, you know."

Campardon instantly threw up his arms, exclaiming :

"What! With Octave? Impossible!"

With Octave, that cad, such a pretty, plump little woman! The thought of it vexed him. Rose, too, felt annoyed, and she became at once severe. As for Gasparine, her fury knew no bounds, stung to the quick by her instinctive hatred of that young fellow So he'd been at it again! He used to have all the women, she was convinced that he did; but she wasn't going to be such a fool as to keep them warm for him in her own apartment.

"You should put yourself in our place," said she, sternly. "As I said before, we have a little girl in the house."

"Then there's the house," Campardon chimed in. "There's your husband, too, with whom I have always been upon the best of terms. He would have a right to be astonished. We cannot appear thus publicly to approve of your conduct, madam—conduct that I do not presume to judge, yet which, perhaps is, shall I say, somewhat—er—thoughtless, don't you think?"

"Most assuredly it is not we who are going to throw stones at you," continued Rose. "Only the world is so spiteful! People might say that you used to meet here. And my husband, you know, does work for such straitlaced folk. The least stain on his good name, and he would lose everything. But, madam, if you will allow me to ask you, how is it that religion did not restrain you doing such a thing? Only the other day the Abbé Mauduit was talking to us about you in terms of fatherly affection."

Berthe looked first at one, then at another, as they spoke, utterly dazed and bewildered.

In her terror she had begun to understand, and was surprised to find herself there. Why had she rung the bell? Why had she disturbed them all at that time of night? Now she saw plainly who they were—the wife, prone in the big bed, the husband in his drawers, their cousin in a thin petticoat, both covered with white feathers from the same pillow. They were right; it did not do to come bursting in upon people like that. Then, as Campardon gently pushed her towards the hall, she departed without even replying to Rose's religious ejaculations.

"Would you like me to accompany you as far as your parents' door?" asked Campardon. "Your proper place is with them."

She refused, with a terrified gesture.

"Then wait a moment; I'll just see if there's anybody on the stairs, as I should be grieved if anything happened to you."

Lisa had stayed in the hall holding a light. This he took from her, and went outside on to the landing, coming back instantly.

"There's no one there, I assure you. Make a bolt of it."

Then Berthe, who so far had not uttered another word, roughly took off the woollen shawl and flung it on the floor, saying:

"Look! that's yours. He's going to murder me—so what's the good?"

Then, in her chemise, she ran out into the dark, just as she had come. Campardon, furious, double-locked the door.

Then, as Lisa, behind him, sniggered, he added:

"It's true; they'd be coming here every night if we only chose to take them in. One has to look out for oneself. I wouldn't mind giving her a hundred francs, but my good name—no, not if I know it!"

In the bedroom, Rose and Gasparine sought to regain their composure. Was there ever such a bold-faced jig as that! Running up and downstairs stark-naked! True, some women there were, no doubt, who, if the fit were on them, threw aside all self-respect. But it was nearly two o'clock, they must get to sleep. Then they all kissed again. "Good night, my love." "Good night, my poppet." Ah, how nice it was to live thus in perfect love and concord when one saw what awful things happened in other homes! Rose took up Dickens, which had slipped down to her belly. He sufficed her; she would read another page or two and then fall asleep, exhausted by emotion, letting the book slide under the sheets as she did every night. Campardon followed Gasparine, making her get into bed first. Then he lay down beside her, and they both grumbled, for the sheets had got cold and they felt most uncomfortable, as it would take them a good half-hour to get warm.

Meanwhile, Lisa, before going upstairs, went back to Angèle's room and said to her.

"The lady sprained her ankle. Just you show me how she did it!"

"Why, like this, like this!" replied the child, as she flung her arms round the maid's neck and kissed her on the lips.

On the staircase Berthe shivered. It was cold there, as the hot-air stoves were never lighted before the 1st November. However, her terror subsided. She had gone down and listened at the door of her flat—nothing, not a sound. Then she had come up again, not daring to go as far as Octave's room, however, but listening at a distance. All was quiet as the grave; not a sound, not a whisper. Then she squatted down on the mat outside her parents' door, with a vague intention of waiting for Adèle. The thought of having to confess all to her mother agitated her as much as if she were still a little girl in disgrace.

Then gradually the solemn staircase tortured her afresh; it was so black, so austere. No one could see her; and yet confusion overcame her at sitting there in her chemise amid such respectable gilt and stucco. The broad mahogany doors, the conjugal dignity of these hearths, seemed one and all to load her with reproaches. Never had the house appeared to her so saturated with purity and virtue. Then, as a ray of moonlight streamed through on the windows on the landing, it was as if one were in a church; from basement to attic, peace pervaded all, the fumes of middle-class virtue floated everywhere in the gloom, whilst in that eerie light her naked body gleamed. The very walls were scandalised, and she drew her chemise closer about her, covering up her feet, terrified lest she should see the spectre of Monsieur Gourd emerge in velvet cap and slippers.

All at once a noise made her jump up in a fright; and she was about to thump with both fists at her mother's door, when the sound of someone calling stopped her.

It was a voice faintly whispering:

"Madam! madam!"

She looked over the banisters, but could see nothing.

"Madam, madam; it is I!"

And Marie appeared, in her night-dress also. She had heard the disturbance, and had slipped out of bed, leaving Jules fast asleep, while she stopped to listen in her little dining-room in the dark.

"Come in. You're in distress, and I am your friend."

Then she gently comforted her, telling her all that had happened. The two men had not hurt each other. Octave, cursing horribly, had pushed the chest of drawers in front of his door, so shutting himself in; while the other had gone down carrying a bundle with him

—some of her things that she had left, her shoes and stockings, which probably he had rolled up in her dressing-gown on seeing them lying about. Anyhow, the whole affair was over. Next day they would soon prevent their fighting a duel.

But Berthe stopped short on the threshold, still frightened and abashed at entering a stranger's house. Marie had to take her by the hand.

"See, you shall sleep here, on the sofa. I will lend you a shawl, and I'll go and see your mother. Dear, dear; what a dreadful thing! But when one's in love, one never stops to think of consequences!"

"Not much enjoyment, though, for either of us!" said Berthe, as she heaved a sigh of regret for all the emptiness and folly of her night. "I don't wonder he cursed and swore. If he's like me, he must have had more than enough of it!"

They were both going to speak about Octave, when suddenly they stopped, and, groping in the darkness, embraced each other, sobbing bitterly. Each clasped the other's naked limbs convulsively, passionately, crushing their breasts all wet with scalding tears. It was a sort of final collapse, an overmastering sorrow—the end of everything. No other word was spoken, but their tears kept falling, falling ceaselessly in the gloom, while, lapped in decency, the chaste house slumbered on.

XV

THAT morning, as the house awoke, it wore its most majestic air of middle-class decorum. Not a trace was on the staircase of all the scandals of the night; the stucco panellings preserved no reflection of a lady scampering past in her chemise, nor did the mat reveal the spot whereon the odour of her white body had evaporated. Only, Monsieur Gourd, on going his rounds, about seven o'clock, sniffed vaguely as he passed the walls. However, what did not concern him did not concern him, and when, as he came down, he saw Lisa and Julie discussing the scandal, no doubt, for they seemed so excited, he fixed them with an icy stare, separating them at once. Then he went out, to be sure that everything was quiet in the street. There all was calm. However, the maids must already have been gossiping, for the female neighbours kept stopping, and tradesmen stood at their shopdoors looking up, agape, at the different floors, just as folk stare at houses where some crime has been committed. Before so handsome a façade, however, onlookers were silent, and soon politely passed along.

At half-past seven Madame Juzeur appeared in her dressing-gown; she was looking for Louise, so she said. Her eyes glittered; her hands were feverishly hot. She stopped Marie, who was coming upstairs with her milk, and tried to make her talk. But from her she got nothing, not even learning how the mother had received her peccant child. Then, pretending to wait a moment for the postman, she stopped at the Gourds', asking, at last, why Monsieur Octave had not come down. Perhaps he was not well? The porter said that he did not know; Monsieur Octave, however, never came down before ten minutes past eight. Just then the other Madame Campardon passed by, pale and stiff; they all made obeisance to her. Being now obliged to go upstairs again, Madame Juzeur, at last, was lucky enough to catch Campardon just coming out, buttoning his gloves. At first, they exchanged rueful glances; then he shrugged his shoulders.

"Poor things!" she murmured.

"No, no! it serves them right!" said he, viciously. "They deserve to be made an example of. A fellow whom I introduced into a respectable house, begging him not to bring in any women, and who, to show how little he cares, goes to bed with the landlord's sister-in-law! It makes me look such a fool!"

Nothing further was said. Madame Juzeur went back to her rooms while Campardon hurried downstairs in such a rage that he tore one of his gloves.

As it struck eight, Auguste, worn out, and with features distorted by acute neuralgia, crossed the courtyard on his way to the shop. He had come down by the back-stairs, so ashamed was he and so afraid of meeting anyone. However, give up business he could not. At the sight of Berthe's empty desk in the middle of the counter, his feelings almost overcame him. The porter was taking down the shutters, and Auguste proceeded to give orders for the day, when Saturnin appeared, coming up from the basement, and gave him a dreadful fright. The madman's eyes flamed; his white teeth glittered like those of some ravenous wolf. With clenched fists, he came straight up to Auguste.

"Where is she? If you dare to touch her, I'll bleed you like a pig." Auguste, exasperated, recoiled.

"Now there's this one," he gasped.

"Be quiet, or else I'll bleed you!" cried Saturnin once more, as he made a rush at him.

Deeming discretion the better part of valour, Auguste hereupon preferred to withdraw. He had a horror of lunatics; there was no arguing with such people. After shouting out to the porter to shut Saturnin up in the basement, he was going out into the porch, when he suddenly found himself face to face with Valérie and Théophile. The latter, having a violent cold, was swathed in a thick red comforter, and he kept coughing and groaning. They both must have heard what had happened, for they both looked sympathisingly at Auguste. Since the quarrel about their inheritance, the two families were no longer on speaking terms, being deadly enemies.

"You've still got a brother," said Théophile, after a paroxysm of coughing, as he shook Auguste by the hand. "Remember this in your distress."

"Yes," added Valérie, "this ought to pay her out for all the beastly things she said to me, eh? But we're awfully sorry for you, for we're not utterly heartless."

Greatly touched by their kindness, Auguste took them into the back-shop, while keeping his eye on Saturnin, who was prowling about. Here their reconciliation became complete. Berthe's name was never mentioned; Valérie merely remarked that that woman had been at the bottom of all their dissension, for there had not been so much as a single disagreeable word in the family until she entered it, and brought them dishonour. Auguste, listening, looked down and nodded. A certain merriment underlay Théophile's pity, for he felt delighted that he was not the only one, and scrutinised his brother to see how people looked when in that predicament.

"Well, what do you mean to do?" asked he.

"Why, challenge him, of course!" said the husband, with decision.

Théophile's joy was spoilt. At such courage as Auguste's both he and his wife shuddered. Then their brother described the awful encounter of the previous night; how, having foolishly hesitated to buy a pistol, he had been forced to content himself with punching the gentleman's head. True, the gentleman had returned the blow; but all the same, he had got a precious good smack in the eye. A wretch who for the last six months had been humbugging him, pretending to side with him against his wife, and who actually had the impertinence to report upon her goings-out. As for her, the wretched creature had taken refuge with her parents; and there she might stop, if she liked, as he would never take her back.

"Would you believe it? Last month I let her have three hundred francs for her dress!" cried he. "I've always been so good-natured, so tolerant towards her, ready to put up with anything rather than be made ill! But that's more than anyone can stand, I can't put up with that—no!"

Théophile was thinking of death. He trembled feverishly as he stammered, choking:

"It's ridiculous; you'll only get spitted. I shouldn't challenge him."

Then, as Valérie looked at him, he sheepishly added:

"If such a thing happened to me."

"Ah, that wretched woman!" exclaimed his wife. "To think that two men are going to kill each other on her account! If I were she, I could never sleep again."

Auguste's resolve was unalterable. He was going to fight. Moreover, he had already made his arrangements for this. As he insisted on having Duveyrier as his second, he was now about to go up and tell him what had happened, and send him to Octave forthwith.

Théophile could act as the other second, if he consented. This Théophile was obliged to do; but his cold at once seemed to become worse, and he put on his peevish air, like a sickly child that wants to be cosseted. However, he offered to accompany his brother to the Duveyriers. They might be thieves; very likely they were; but in certain circumstances one forgot everything. Both he and his wife seemed anxious to bring about a general reconciliation, having doubtless reflected that it did not serve their interest to sulk any longer. In order to oblige Auguste, Valérie offered to take charge of the cashier's desk, to give him time to find some suitable person.

"Only," said she, "I shall have to take Camille for a walk in the Tuileries gardens about two."

"Never mind, just this once," said her husband. "Besides, it's raining."

"No, no; the child wants air. I must go out."

At last the two brothers went upstairs to the Duveyriers. Théophile had to halt on the first step, overcome by a frightful fit of coughing. He caught hold of the balustrade and finally gasped out:

"You know, I'm quite happy now, as I feel perfectly sure about her. No; can't blame her for that. Besides, she's given me proofs."

Auguste, not understanding, looked askance at his brother's yellow, jaded face and the sparse bristles of his beard, which showed up on his flabby flesh. Théophile was annoyed at this; his brother's temerity quite disconcerted him, and he continued:

"I'm speaking about my wife, you know. Poor old chap, I pity you with all my heart! You remember what a fool I made of myself on your wedding-day. But in your case the thing's a certainty, for you saw them."

"Bah!" cried Auguste, to show how valiant he was. "I'll soon put a bullet through him. 'Pon my honour, I should not care a damn about the whole thing, if only I'd not got this confounded headache!"

Just as they rang at the Duveyriers', Théophile suddenly bethought himself that very probably the counsellor would not be at home, for ever since he had found Clarisse he let himself go completely, and slept out from time to time. Hippolyte, who opened the door, avoided giving any information as to his master's whereabouts; the gentlemen, said he, would find madame playing her scales. They went in. There sat Clotilde, tightly-corseted, at her piano, her fingers running up and down the keyboard with regular precision. While indulging in this exercise for two hours daily, to preserve her lightness of touch, she used her brain at the same time by reading the *Revue des Deux Mondes,* which lay open on the desk before her, and her fingers lost nothing of their mechanical velocity of movement thereby.

"Ah, it's you!" she exclaimed, as her brothers rescued her from the hailstorm of notes. She showed no surprise at seeing Théophile, who, for the matter of that, bore himself very stiffly, as one who had come on another man's business. Auguste had a fib all ready, for he suddenly felt ashamed to tell his sister of his dishonour and afraid to frighten her about his projected duel. But she gave him no time for a falsehood, and, after looking fixedly at him, said, in her quiet way:

"What do you intend doing now?"

He started back, blushing violently. So everybody knew about it apparently. And he replied in the same tone of bravado whereby he had already silenced Théophile:

"Why, fight, of course!"

"Oh!" said she, this time in a tone of great surprise.

However, she did not express her disapproval. True, it would only increase the scandal, but honour must be satisfied. She was content merely to remind him of her original dislike to the marriage. One could not expect anything from a girl who, apparently, was profoundly ignorant of all a woman's duties. Then, as Auguste asked her where her husband was:

"He is travelling," she replied, without a moment's hesitation.

At this news he appeared much distressed, not wishing to do anything until he had consulted Duveyrier. She listened, never mentioning the new address, as she did not wish her relatives to share in her domestic disillusions. At last she thought of a plan, and advised him to go to Monsieur Bachelard, in the Rue d'Enghien; he might know something. Then she went back to her piano.

"It was Auguste who asked me to come with him," said Théophile, who hitherto had kept silence. "Shall we kiss and be friends, Clotilde? We're all of us in trouble."

Holding out her cold cheek she said:

"My poor fellow, only those are in trouble who bring it upon themselves. I'm always ready to forgive everybody. Now, you ought to take care of yourself, for you seem to me to have got a nasty cough!" Then, calling Auguste back, she added: "If the thing's not settled, let me know, as I shall feel very anxious about it."

Then the hailstorm of notes began again, lapping her round, drowning her, and her fingers mechanically ran up and down, hammering out scales in every key, while she gravely continued reading the *Revue des Deux Mondes*.

On getting downstairs Auguste for a moment debated whether to go to Bachelard's or not. How could he say to him: "Your niece has cuckolded me?" At last he determined to get Bachelard to give him Duveyrier's address without acquainting him with the whole sad history.

All was arranged. Valérie was to stay in the shop, while Théophile was to look after the house until his brother's return. Auguste sent for a cab and was just about to leave, when Saturnin, who had momentarily vanished, suddenly rushed up from the basement, brandishing a large kitchen knife, and crying:

"I'll bleed him! I'll bleed him!"

This proved a fresh scare. White as a sheet, Auguste hastily jumped into the cab and shut the door, exclaiming:

"He's got hold of another knife! Where on earth does he find them all, I wonder! For goodness sake, Théophile, do send him home and don't let him be here when I come back. As if I hadn't got worry enough as it is!"

The porter of the shop caught hold of the madman's shoulders. Valérie gave the address to the cabman, a hulking dirty fellow, with a face the colour of raw beef. He was recovering from last night's drinking-bout and did not hurry himself, but leisurely took up the reins after comfortably seating himself on the box.

"By distance, sir?" he asked, in a hoarse voice.

"No, by the hour, and look sharp. There'll be a good tip for yourself."

Off went the cab, an old landau, huge and dirty, which rocked fearfully on its worn-out springs. The gaunt white scarecrow of a horse ambled along with a quite surprising waste of energy as it shook its mane and flung up its hoofs. Auguste looked at his watch; it was nine o'clock. By eleven the duel might be arranged. At first, the dawdling cab annoyed him. Then drowsiness gradually overcame him; he had not had a wink of sleep all night, and this dreadful cab only heightened his depression. Rocked thus in it, all by himself, being deafened by the rattling of the cracked panes, the fever which all that morning had sustained him, now grew calmer. What a stupid affair it was, after all!

His face grew grey, as he put both hands to his head, which ached horribly.

In the Rue d'Enghien there was more to worry him. To begin with, Bachelard's doorway was so blocked up by vans, that he was all but crushed; then, in the glass-roofed courtyard, he happened on a gang of packers lustily nailing up cases. Not one of them knew where Bachelard was; and their hammering almost split his skull. However, he had just decided to wait for the uncle when an apprentice, touched by his suffering look, whispered an address in his ear—Mademoiselle Fifi, Rue Saint-Marc, third floor. In all probability, Bachelard was there.

"What d'ye say?" asked the cabman, who had fallen asleep.

"Rue Saint-Marc; and drive a bit quicker, if you can."

The cab jogged on at its funereal pace. On the boulevards, one of the wheels caught in an omnibus. The panels cracked, the springs uttered plaintive cries, and dark melancholy ever more oppressed the wretched husband in search of his second. However, the Rue Saint-Marc was reached at last.

On the third floor, a white, plump little old woman opened the door. She seemed greatly upset; and when Auguste asked for Monsieur Bachelard, she at once admitted him.

"Oh, sir, I'm sure you're one of his friends! Do try and pacify him. Poor man, he's just been put out about something. No doubt, you know who I am; he will have mentioned me to you; I am Mademoiselle Menu."

Bewildered, Auguste found himself in a narrow room overlooking the courtyard; a room which had the cleanliness and the deep peace of some country cottage. There was here an atmosphere of work, of order, of the pure, glad existence of humble folk. In front of an embroidery frame, on which was a priests' stole, a pretty, fair-haired girl of innocent mien was weeping bitterly, while uncle Bachelard, his nose aflame and eyes bloodshot, stood foaming with fury and despair. So upset was he that Auguste's entrance did not appear to surprise him. He at once appealed to him as a witness, and the scene went on.

"Now, look here, Monsieur Vabre, you're an honest man; now, what would you say in my place? I got here this morning rather sooner than usual, went into her room with my lumps of sugar from the *café,* and three four-sou pieces as a surprise, and I found her in bed with that pig Gueulin! Now, tell me, frankly, what would you say to such a thing?"

Auguste grew scarlet with confusion. At first he imagined that Bachelard knew of his trouble and was jeering at him. However, without waiting for a reply, the uncle went on :

"Ah, my girl, you don't know what you've done, that you don't! I, who was growing young again, and felt so glad at having found a nice, quiet little place where I thought I should be happy! To me you were an angel, a flower, in short, something sweet and pure, which consoled me for a heap of filthy women. And here you go and sleep with that beast of a Gueulin."

Genuine emotion choked his utterance; his voice quavered with the intensity of his grief. All seemed shattered; and with the hiccoughs of last night's carouse he bemoaned his lost ideals.

"I didn't know, uncle dear," stammered Fifi, whose sobs grew louder. "I didn't know that it would grieve you so much."

And, as a matter of fact, she did not look as if she knew. Her eyes, with their ingenuous look, her odour of chastity, her naïveté, all seemed to belong to a little girl incapable as yet of distinguishing a gentleman from a lady. Moreover, auntie Menu declared that at heart she was quite innocent.

"Pray be calm, Monsieur Narcisse. She's very fond of you, all the same. I was sure that you wouldn't like it. I says to her, I says: 'If Monsieur Narcisse hears about it he'll be angry.' But she don't know what life is yet, she don't, nor what pleases, and what doesn't please. Don't cry any more, for it's you that in her heart she loves."

As neither Bachelard nor Fifi listened to her, she turned to Auguste to inform him how deeply anxious such an occurrence made her for her niece's future. It was so difficult to find a respectable home for a young girl now-a-days. She, who for thirty years had worked at Messrs Mardienne Brothers', the embroiderers, of the Rue Saint-Sulpice, where any enquiries concerning her might be made, she well knew how hard a work-girl in Paris found it to make both ends meet if she wanted to keep herself respectable. Good-natured though she was, and though she had received Fifi from the hands of her own brother, Captain Menu, on his death-bed, she could never have managed to bring the child up on her thousand-francs life annuity, which now allowed her to put aside her needle. And, seeing her cared for by Monsieur Narcisse, she had hoped to die happy. Not a bit of it. Fifi had gone and made her uncle angry, just for a silly thing like that.

"I daresay you know Villeneuve, near Lille?" she wound up. "That's my home. It's a biggish town——"

Auguste lost all patience. Shaking off the aunt, he turned to the uncle, whose boisterous grief had now become somewhat subdued.

"I came to ask you for Duveyrier's new address. I expect you know it."

"Duveyrier's address? Duveyrier's address?" stammered Bachelard. "You mean Clarisse's address. Just wait one minute!"

And he opened the door of Fifi's room. To his great surprise Auguste saw Gueulin coming out, whom Bachelard had locked in, so as to give him time to dress himself, and also in order to detain him until he had settled what to do with him. At the sight of the young man, looking thoroughly sheepish, with rumpled hair, Bachelard's wrath revived.

"Ah, you wretch!" cried he; "so it's you, my own nephew, who dishonours me thus! So it's you who smirch your family's good name, and trail my white hairs through the mud! Ah, but you'll come to a bad end, and one day we shall see you in the dock!"

With bowed head Gueulin listened, half embarrassed and half furious.

"Look here, uncle," he muttered, "this is a little bit too much. There's a limit to everything. Not much fun for me, I can tell you. Why did you take me to see the girl? I never asked you to do so. It was you who dragged me here. You drag everybody here!"

Then Bachelard, sobbing afresh, went on:

"You've taken everything from me. I'd only got her left. You'll be the death of me, that you will, and I won't leave you a sou—not a single sou!"

Then Gueulin, mad with rage, burst out:

"For God's sake shut up! I've had enough of it. What did I always tell you? One always pays for these kind of things! Look what luck I've had, when, just for once in a way, I thought of profiting by an opportunity. The night was pleasant enough of course, but afterwards there's the very devil to pay!"

Fifi had dried her tears. She at once felt bored at having nothing to do, so, taking up her needle, she set to work at her embroidery, raising her large, guileless eyes now and again to look at the two men, being apparently dazed at their anger.

"I am in a great hurry," Auguste ventured to remark. "If you could kindly give me the address—only the street and the number—nothing else."

"The address?" said Bachelard. "Let me see! Oh, in one minute!"

Then, overcome by emotion, he seized Gueulin by both hands.

"You thankless fellow, you; I was keeping her for you; upon my honour, I was! I said to myself, Now, if he's good, I'll give her to him, with a nice little dowry of fifty thousand francs. But, you dirty pig, you couldn't wait, but must needs go and get hold of her all of a sudden like that!"

"Hands off!" cried Gueulin, touched by the old fellow's kind-heartedness. "It's plain that I shan't get out of this mess in a hurry."

But Bachelard led him up to the girl, asking her:

"Now, Fifi, look at him, and tell me if you would have loved him."

"Yes, uncle, if it pleased you," she replied.

This soft answer touched him to the core. He rubbed his eyes and blew his nose, being nearly choked by emotion. Well, well, he would see what could be done. All he had wanted was to make her happy. Then he hurriedly dismissed Gueulin.

"Be off with you! I'll think the matter over!"

Meanwhile, auntie Menu had taken Auguste aside, in order to explain her ideas to him. A workman, she argued, would have beaten the little girl; a clerk would have gone on begetting babies without ceasing. With Monsieur Narcisse, however, there was the chance of having a dowry, which would allow her to make a suitable marriage. Thank God, theirs was a respectable family, and she would never have let her niece go wrong, nor fall from the arms of one lover into those of another. No, no; it was her wish that Fifi should have a respectable position.

Just as Gueulin was about to go, Bachelard called him back.

"Kiss her on the forehead; I allow you to do so."

He himself let Gueulin out; and then came back and stood in front of Auguste, holding his hand to his heart.

"I'm not chaffing," said he. "Upon my honour, I meant to give her to him later on!"

"Well, what about that address?" asked the other, losing all patience.

Bachelard seemed surprised, as if he thought he had answered that question already.

"Eh? What's that? Clarisse's address? Why, I don't know it!"

Auguste started back in anger. Everything was in a muddle, and there seemed to be a sort of plot to make him look foolish! Seeing how upset he was, Bachelard made a proposal to him. Trublot, no doubt, knew the address, and he was to be found at Desmarquay's, the stockbroker, his employer. And the old fellow, with all the alacrity of a gay town spark, offered to accompany his young friend who accepted.

"Look here," said he to Fifi, after kissing her in turn on the forehead, "here's the sugar for you from the café all the same, and three four-sou pieces for your money-box. Be a good girl until I tell you what to do."

The girl modestly plied her needle with exemplary diligence. A ray of sunlight, falling athwart a neighbouring roof, brightened up the little room, touching with its gold this innocent nook, where not the noise of traffic below might ever come. It roused all Bachelard's latent poetry.

"May God bless you, Monsieur Narcisse!" exclaimed aunt Menu, as she showed him out. "I am easier now. Only listen to what your heart says to you; that will inspire you."

The cabman had again dropped off to sleep, and grumbled when Bachelard gave him Monsieur Desmarquay's address in the Rue Saint-Lazare. No doubt, the horse had gone to sleep too, for it needed a veritable hailstorm of blows to make it move. At length the cab jolted uncomfortably along.

"It's hard lines, all the same," continued Bachelard, after a pause. "You can't imagine how upset I was at finding Gueulin there in his shirt. No, that's a thing one must go through before one can understand it."

So he went on, touching upon details without ever noticing Auguste's increasing uneasiness. At last the latter, who felt his position becoming more and more false, told him why he was in such a hurry to find Duveyrier.

"Berthe with that counter-jumper?" cried Bachelard. "You astonish me, sir!"

His astonishment, seemingly, was mainly on account of his niece's choice. But, after reflecting somewhat, he grew indignant. Eléonore, his sister, might well blame herself for a great deal. He meant to drop the family altogether. Of course, it would not do for him to be mixed up with this duel; but, nevertheless, he deemed it indispensable.

"Like me, just now, when I saw Fifi with a man in his shirt, my first impulse was to murder everybody! If such a thing had happened to you——"

Auguste started painfully, and Bachelard stopped short.

"True, I wasn't thinking. My story can hardly be very amusing to you."

Then there was once more silence, as the cab swayed dismally from side to side. Auguste, whose valour ebbed with each turn of the wheels, submitted resignedly to the jolting, cadaverous of mien and blind of one eye through neuralgia. Whatever had made Bachelard think that the duel was a *sine qua non*? As the guilty woman's uncle, it was not his place to insist upon bloodshed. His brother's phrase yet buzzed in his ear: "It's ridiculous; you'll only get spitted!" A phrase that came back to him importunately, obstinately, until it seemed a very part of his neuralgia. He was sure to be killed; he had a sort of presentiment that he would; such mournful forebodings completely overwhelmed him. He facied himself dead, and bewailed the grievous event.

"I told you Rue Saint-Lazare," cried Bachelard, to the cabman. "It's not at Chaillot. Turn up to the left."

At last the cab stopped. For caution's sake they sent in to ask for Trublot, who came out bare-headed to talk to them in the doorway.

"Do you know Clarisse's address?" asked Bachelard.

"Clarisse's address? Why, in the Rue d' Assas, of course."

They thanked him, and were for getting into the cab again, when Auguste in his turn enquired:

"What's the number?"

"The number? Oh, I don't know what number!"

Hereupon, Auguste declared that he would rather give the whole thing up. Trublot tried his best to remember; he had dined there once—just at the back of the Luxembourg, it was; but he couldn't recollect if it was at the end of the street, or on the right or on the left. But the door he knew perfectly well, and could have recognised it at once. Then Bachelard had another idea and begged Trublot to accompany them, despite Auguste's protestations and assurances that he would trouble no one further in the matter, but would go home. However, with a somewhat constrained air, Trublot refused. No; he wasn't going to that hole again. But he avoided giving the real reason, a most astounding adventure, a tremendous smack in the face that he had got from Clarisse's new cook one evening when he had gone to give her a pinch as she stood over her fire. It was inconceivable! A smack like that in return for a mere civility of that sort, just in order to get to know each other! Such a thing had never happened to him before; it amazed him.

"No, no," said he, trying to find an excuse, "I'll never set foot again in a house where one's bored to death. Clarisse, you know, has become simply impossible; her temper's worse than ever, and she's quite the lady now. And she's got all her family with her, ever since her father died—a whole tribe of pedlars; mother, two sisters, a big blackguard of a brother; even an old invalid aunt, with a head like one of the hags that sell dolls in the street, don't you know! You can't think how dirty and distressed Duveyrier looks among them all!"

Then he told how one rainy day, when the counsellor had found Clarisse standing in a doorway, she had been the first to upbraid him, as, sobbing, she declared that he had never had any regard for her. Yes, she had left the Rue de la Cerisaie, stung to exasperation by a slight upon her personal dignity, though for a long while she had hidden her feelings. Why did he always take off his decoration whenever he came to see her? Did he think that she would sully it? She was ready to make it up with him, but he must first of all swear upon his honour that he would always wear his decoration, for she valued his esteem and was not going to be perpetually mortified in this way. Discomfited by this passage of arms, Duveyrier swore that he would do as she asked. He was completely won over, and deeply touched; she was right; he deemed her a noble-spirited creature.

"Now he never takes his ribbon off," added Trublot. "I fancy she makes him sleep with it on. It flatters the girl, before all her own people, too. Moreover, as that big fellow Payan has already spent her twenty-five thousand francs' worth of furniture, this time she's got him to buy her thirty thousand francs' worth. Oh, it's all up with him! she's got him completely under her thumb. How fond some people are of real jam, to be sure!"

"Well, I must be off, as Monsieur Trublot can't come," said Auguste, whose vexation was only increased by all these tales.

Trublot, however, suddenly consented to accompany them; only he would not go upstairs, but would show them the door. After fetching his hat and making some excuse, he joined them in the cab.

"Rue d'Assas," cried he to the cabman. "Straight along, and I'll tell you when to stop."

The driver swore. Rue d'Assas, of all places! Some blokes liked driving about, damned if they didn't! However, some time or other they'd get there. The big white horse, as it ambled, steaming, along, made hardly any headway, its neck arched at every step in a sort of excruciating nod.

Meanwhile, Bachelard had already begun to tell Trublot about his misfortune. Bad news made him noisy. Yes, that pig of a Gueulin with a dainty little girl like that! He had caught them both in their shirts. But at this part of the story, he suddenly remembered Auguste, who, glum and doleful, had collapsed in a corner of the cab.

"Ah! of course; I beg your pardon," he muttered. "I always keep forgetting." Then, turning to Trublot: "Our friend has just had some trouble in his own home, too; and that is why we are trying to find Duveyrier. Yes, you know, last night he caught his wife with——" With a gesture he completed his sentence, adding, simply: "Octave, don't you know?"

Plain-spoken as he was, Trublot felt inclined to say that this did not surprise him. But he forbore to use this phrase, substituting another, full of angry scorn, for an explanation of which the husband dared not ask:

"What a born idiot that Octave is!"

At this criticism of the adultery there was a pause. Each of the three men became plunged in thought. The cab could go no further. It seemed to be lumbering along for hours on a bridge, when Trublot, the first to awake from his reverie, ventured upon this sapient remark:

"This cab doesn't go very fast."

But nothing could quicken the horse's pace; by the time they got to the Rue d'Assas it was eleven o'clock. When there, they wasted nearly another quarter of an hour, for, despite Trublot's boast, he did not know the door, after all. First he let the cabman drive right along the street without stopping him, and then made him come back again. This he did three times running. Acting on his precise instructions, Auguste called at ten different houses, but the hall-porters replied that they "hadn't got such a person." At last, a fruit-seller told him the right number. He went upstairs with Bachelard, leaving Trublot in the cab.

It was the big blackguard of a brother who opened the door, a cigarette between his lips, and he puffed smoke in their faces as he showed them into the drawing-room. When they asked for Monsieur Duveyrier he first stared mockingly at them, without answering, and then slouched off, presumably to find him. In the middle of the drawing-room, the new blue-satin furniture of which was already stained with grease, one of the sisters, the youngest, was sitting on the carpet, wiping out a kitchen saucepan, while the elder girl thumped with clenched fists on a splendid piano, of which she had just found the key. On seeing the gentlemen enter, they both looked up, but did not stop, as they went on thumping and scrubbing with redoubled energy. Five minutes passed, and nobody came. Deafened by this din, the visitors looked at each other, until shrieks from an adjoining room filled them with terror. It was the invalid aunt being washed.

At last an old woman, Madame Bocquet, Clarisse's mother, peeped round the door, dressed in such filthy a gown that she dared not show herself.

"Whom do the gentleman want?" asked she.

"Why, Monsieur Duveyrier, of course!" cried Bachelard, losing patience. "We've told the servant so already! Say, Monsieur Auguste Vabre and Monsieur Narcisse Bachelard."

Madame Bocquet shut the door again. Meanwhile, the elder of the sisters, standing on a stool, thumped the keyboard with her elbows; while the younger was scraping the bottom of the saucepan with a steel fork. Another five minutes elapsed. Then, in the midst of this din, which seemingly had no effect upon her, Clarisse appeared.

"Oh, it's you!" said she to Bachelard, without even looking at Auguste.

Bachelard was quite taken aback. He would never have recognised her, so stout had she grown. The big, gaunt hoyden, with her fluffy mop of hair like a poodle's, had been transformed into the dumpy matron, with hair neatly plastered and lustrous with pomade. However, she did not give him a chance of uttering a word, but at once told him with brutal frankness that she did not want a mischief-maker like him at her place, who went and told Alphonse all sorts of horrid stories. Yes, yes, just that; he had accused her of sleeping with Alphonse's friends, and of carrying on with scores of men behind his back. It was no use his saying he had not, for Alphonse had told her so himself.

"Look here, old cock," she added, "if you've come here to booze, you may as well clear out. The old days are over and done with. Henceforth I mean to be respectable."

Then she proclaimed her passion for what was proper and gentle—a passion that, growing, had become a monomania. Thus, in her periodical fits of prudery, she had one by one sent all her lover's friends to the right-about, not allowing them to smoke, insisting upon being styled madame, and upon receiving formal calls. Her old superficial, secondhand drollery had vanished; all that remained was her exaggeration in her attempt to play the fine lady, who sometimes broke forth into foul language and fouler gestures. By degrees, solitude again surrounded Duveyrier; no amusing nook for him now, but a grisly middle-class establishment, amid whose dirt and din he encountered all the worries of his own house. As Trublot remarked, 'the Rue de Choiseul was not more boring, while it was certainly far less filthy."

"We've not called to see you," replied Bachelard, recovering himself, being used to the lively greetings of ladies such as she. "We want to speak to Duveyrier."

Then Clarisse glanced at his companion. She thought he was a bailiff, knowing that Alphonse's affairs had latterly become rather involved.

"Well, what do I care, after all?" said she. "Take him and keep him, if you like. It's not much fun for me to have to look after his pimples!"

She no longer even sought to hide her disgust, feeling, moreover, certain that her unkindness only made him more attached to her. Then, opening a door, she exclaimed :

"Here, come along, as the gentlemen insist on seeing you."

Duveyrier, who apparently had been waiting behind the door, came in, shook hands with them, and tried to smile. He no longer had the youthful air of former days, when he used to spend the evening with her in the Rue de la Cerisaie. Languor overcame him; he looked thin and depressed, trembling nervously now and again, as if alarmed by something behind him.

Clarisse stopped to listen. But Bachelard was not going to speak before her, so he invited the counsellor to lunch.

"Say you'll come, because Monsieur Vabre wants to see you. Madame will be good enough to excuse you——"

At that moment madame caught sight of her youngest sister thumping on the piano, whom, slapping violently, she drove out of the room, while she boxed the other child's ears and packed her off with her saucepan, too. There was a most infernal row. The invalid aunt in the next room started screaming again, thinking they were about to beat her.

"Do you hear, my love?" murmured Duveyrier. "These gentlemen have asked me to lunch."

She was not listening, but shyly, tenderly touched the keys. For the last month she had been learning to play the piano. This had been the unuttered longing of her whole life, a remote ambition, which, if attained, could alone stamp her as a woman of fashion. After making sure that nothing was broken, she was about to stop her lover from going, merely in order to be disagreeable to him, when Madame Bocquet once more popped her head round the door.

"Your music-master's come," said she.

Hereupon Clarisse instantly changed her mind, and called out to Duveyrier :

"All right, you can hook it! I'll have lunch with Théodore. We don't want you."

Théodore, her music-master, was a Belgian, with a big rosy face. She at once sat down at the piano, and he placed her fingers on the key-board, rubbing them, to make them less stiff. For an instant Duveyrier hesitated; evidently he was much annoyed. But the gentlemen were waiting for him. He had to go and put on his boots. When he came back she was playing scales in slap-dash style, strumming forth a perfect hailstorm of wrong notes, to the utter disgust of Bachelard and his companion. Yet Duveyrier, driven wild by his wife's Mozart and Beethoven, stood still for a moment behind his mistress, apparently enjoying the sound, despite his nervous facial twitchings. Then, turning to the other two, he whispered :

"Her talent for music is quite amazing."

After kissing her hair, he judiciously withdrew, and left her alone with Théodore. In the ante-room the big blackguard of a brother asked him chaffingly for a franc to buy some tobacco. Then, as they went downstairs and Bachelard expressed surprise at his conversion to the charms of the piano, Duveyrier swore that he had never hated it, and spoke of the ideal, saying how greatly Clarisse's simple scales stirred his soul, thus yielding to his perpetual desire to bestrew with flowers of innocence the rude pathway of his grosser passions.

Trublot, down below, had given the cabman a cigar, and was listening to his talk with the keenest interest. Bachelard insisted on lunching at Foyot's; it was just the right time for it, and they could talk better whilst eating. Then, as the cab at last succeeded in starting, he informed Duveyrier of all that had happened, who thereupon grew very grave. Auguste's indisposition seemed to have increased during the visit to Clarisse, where he had not uttered a single word. Now, completely exhausted by this interminable drive, with throbbing temples, he sank back, prone, in a corner. When Duveyrier asked him what he meant to do, he opened his eyes, paused for a moment as if in anguish, and then repeated his previous phrase :

"Why, fight, of course!" His voice, however, sounded fainter; and, closing his eyes, as if asking to be left in peace, he added: "Unless you can suggest anything else."

Then, as the vehicle lumbered along, these good gentlemen held a grand council. Duveyrier, like Bachelard, deemed a duel indispensable. He seemed much affected because of the shedding of blood, of which in fancy he saw a dark stream staining the staircase of his own house. But honour demanded it, and with honour no compromise was possible. Trublot took a broader view of the case; it was too silly, said he, to stake one's honour upon what, for courtesy's sake, he called a woman's frailty. With a faint movement of his eyelids, Auguste expressed his approval, being exasperated by the warlike fury of the other two, who certainly ought to have been wholly for reconciliation and peace. Despite his fatigue, he was obliged once more to tell the story of that night, of the box on the ear which he had given and which he had received. Soon the question of the adultery was forgotten; the sole topic of discussion was the two boxes on the ear. It was these that were subjected to comment and analysis, to try and discover therein a satisfactory solution.

"Talk about hair-splitting!" cried Trublot at last, in disdain. "If they boxed each other's ears, why, they are quits."

Duveyrier and Bachelard looked at each other aghast. But by this time they had reached the restaurant, and Bachelard declared that, first of all, they had better have lunch. It would give them clearer ideas upon the subject. He invited them to a copious luncheon at his expense ordering dishes and wines extravagant in cost, so that for three hours they sat over their meal in a private room. The duel was not even once mentioned. Immediately after the *hors-d' oeuvres,* the talk irresistibly turned upon women—Fifi and Clarisse were perpetually explained, overhauled and plucked. Bachelard now declared the fault to be on his side, so that to Duveyrier he might not seem to have been grossly jilted, while the latter, to make up for having let uncle Bachelard see him weeping on that night in the lonely apartment at the Rue de la Cerisaie, expatiated upon his present happiness, until he actually began to believe in it, becoming quite sentimental. Prevented by his neuralgia from eating or drinking, Auguste sat there, apparently listening, with one elbow on the table, and a woe-begone look in his eyes. During dessert, Trublot recollected the cabman, who had hitherto been forgotten, down below. Brimful of sympathy, he sent him the remains of the feast and the heeltaps of the bottles, for, from certain remarks that the fellow had made, he had an inkling that he was a quondam priest. It struck three. Duveyrier grumbled at having to be assessor at the next assizes. Bachelard, now very drunk, spat sideways on to Trublot's trousers, who never noticed it, and there amid the liqueurs, the day would have ended, if Auguste had not roused himself with a sudden start.

"Well, what's going to be done?" he enquired.

"Look here, my lad," replied Bachelard, in familiar fashion, "if you like, we'll manage the whole thing nicely for you. It's too stupid; you can't fight a duel about it."

At this conclusion no one seemed surprised. Duveyrier nodded approvingly. Bachelard went on :

"I'll go with Monsieur Duveyrier and see the chap, and make the brute apologise, or my name isn't Bachelard. The mere sight of me will make him knuckle under, just because I am an outsider. I don't care a damn for anybody, I don't!"

Auguste shook him by the hand, but did not seem much relieved, for he had such a splitting headache. At length they left the private room. Beside the kerb, the driver was still having his lunch inside the cab. He was quite drunk; and had to shake all the crumbs out, while giving Trublot a fraternal poke in the stomach. It was only the poor horse that had had nothing, and, with a despairing wag of the head, it refused to budge. By dint of urging, however, it reeled forward, along the Rue de Tournon.

It had struck four before they stopped at the Rue de Choiseul. Auguste had had the cab for seven hours. Trublot, who stopped inside, said that he would hire it himself, and meant to wait for Bachelard, whom he was going to invite to dine with him.

"Well, you *have* been a long while!" said Théophile to his brother, as he ran forward. "I began to think you were dead!"

And, as soon as the others had gone into the shop, he related the day's experiences. Ever since nine o'clock he had been watching the house, but nothing had happened. At two o'clock, Valérie had gone with Camille to the Tuileries. Then, about half-past three, he had seen Octave go out. Nothing else; nothing stirring, not even at the Josserands'; so that Saturnin, who had been looking under all the furniture for his sister, had at last gone up to ask for her, when Madame Josserand, to get rid of him, had slammed the door in his face, saying that Berthe was not there. Since then the madman had gone prowling about, grinding his teeth.

"All right!" said Bachelard, "we'll wait for the gentleman. We shall see him come back from here."

Auguste, his head in a whirl, strove all he could to keep on his feet, until Duveyrier advised him to go to bed. It was the only cure for migraine.

"Just you go upstairs; we shan't want you any more. We'll let you know the result. My dear fellow, it's no good being upset about it—not a bit."

So upstairs to bed went the husband. At five o'clock the two others were still waiting for Octave. He, going out for no particular reason, except to get a little fresh air and forget the disagreeable adventures of the night, had walked past "The Ladies' Paradise." Madame Hédouin, in deep mourning, stood at the door, and he stopped to bid her good-day. On telling her that he had left the Vabres, she quietly asked him why he did not come back to her. Without thinking, the whole thing was settled there and then, in a moment. After bowing to her once more, and promising to come the next day, he went strolling along, full of vague regrets. Chance always seemed to upset his calculations. Absorbed by various schemes he wandered about the neighbourhood for more than an hour, when, looking up, he saw that he was in dark alley leading out of the Passage Saint-Roch. In the darkest corner opposite to him, at the door of a queer sort of lodging-house, Valérie was bidding good-bye to a gentleman with a big beard. She blushed and tried to get away through the padded door of the church. Then, seeing that Octave smilingly followed her, she preferred to wait for him in the porch, where they chatted cordially to each other.

"You avoid me," said he. "Are you angry with me?"

"Angry?" she rejoined. "Why should I be angry with you? They may scratch their eyes out, if they like; it is all the same to me."

She was alluding to her relations. She immediately gave vent to her old spite against Berthe, at first sounding the young man by various allusions. Then, feeling that he was secretly tired of his mistress and furious still at the events of last night, she no longer restrained herself, but blurted out everything. To think that that woman had accused her of selling herself, she who never would take a penny, not even a present! Well, a few flowers sometimes, a bunch or two of violets. Everybody knew now which of the two sold herself. She had prophesied that some day they would find out how much it cost to have her.

"Ah! it cost you more than a bunch of violets, eh?"

"Yes, it did," he basely muttered.

Then, in his turn, he rapped out some rather disagreeable things about Berthe, saying how spiteful she was, even asserting that she was too fat, as if revenging himself thus for all the worry that she had caused him. All day long he had been expecting her husband's seconds, and he was now going home to see if anybody had called. A silly business altogether; she could easily have prevented a duel of this sort. Then he finished up by giving an account of their absurd assignation, of their quarrel, and of Auguste's arrival on the scene before they had so much as kissed each other once.

"By all that I hold most sacred!" said he, "I'd not even touched her yet."

Valérie laughed excitedly. She was being allowed to share his confidences in the most tenderly, intimate way, and she drew closer to Octave as if to some woman friend who knew all. At times, some devout worshipper coming out of church disturbed them; then the door closed again gently and they found themselves alone, safely shrouded in the green baize hangings of the porch as if in some secure and saintly harbour of refuge.

"I can't think why I live with such people," she continued, referring to her relatives. "Oh, I'm not blameless, no doubt! But, frankly, I can't feel a bit sorry, as I care so little for any one of them. And if you only knew how boring all these love affairs are!"

"Come, now, it's not so bad as all that," cried Octave, gaily. "People are not always as silly as we were yesterday. They have a good time now and then!"

Then she made a clean breast of it. It was not merely hatred for her husband, the fever that perpetually shook him to pieces, his impotence, and his eternal whimpering—it was not all this that drove her to misconduct herself six months after marriage. No, she often did this without wanting to do so, simply because things came into her head, for which she could give no sort of explanation. Everything was all to pieces, and she felt so ill that she could have committed suicide. Since there was nothing to check her, she might as lief take that plunge as any other.

"Well, but come, now, did you really never have a good time?" asked Octave again, who apparently was only interested in this particular point.

"Well, not such as they describe," she answered. "I swear I didn't!"

He looked at her full of sympathy and pity. All for nothing, and without getting any pleasure out of it! Surely it was not worth all the trouble she took, in her perpetual fear of being caught. He specially felt that his wounded pride was soothed, for her old scorn of him still rankled. Then, that was why she would not let him have her one evening! He reminded her of the incident.

"Do you remember, after one of your fits of hysterics?"

"Yes, yes; I recollect. I did not dislike you, but I felt so utterly disinclined for that sort of thing! But listen, now; it was far better; for by this time we should both have loathed each other."

She gave him her little gloved hand. Squeezing it, he repeated:

"You are right; it was better so. In fact, one is only fond of the women that one has never had!"

It was quite an affecting interview. Hand in hand they stood there for a moment, full of emotion. Then, without another word, they pushed open the padded church-door, as she had left her son Camille inside in the charge of the charwoman. The child was asleep. She made him kneel down, and herself knelt down for a moment, her head in her hands, as if breathing a most fervent prayer. Just as she was about to rise, the Abbé Mauduit, coming out of a confessional, gretted her with a fatherly smile.

Octave merely walked across the church. When he got home the whole house was in a flutter. Only Trublot, asleep in the cab, did not catch sight of him. Tradespeople at their shop-doors eyed him gravely. The stationer opposite still stared at the house-front, as if to scrutinise the very stones themselves. The charcoal-dealer and the greengrocer, however, had grown calmer, and the neighbourhood had relapsed into its frigidly dignified state. Lisa was gossiping with Adéle in the doorway, and, as Octave passed, she was obliged to be satisfied with staring at him; then they both went on complaining about the dearness of poultry, while Monsieur Gourd eyed them sternly as he bowed to the young man. While he was going upstairs Madame Juzeur, on the watch ever since the morning, gently opened her door, and, catching hold of his hands, drew him into her ante-room, where she kissed him on the forehead, murmuring:

"Poor boy! There, I won't keep you now. But come back for a chat after it's all over."

He had hardly got to his room before Duveyrier and Bachelard called. Astonished at seeing the latter, he at first sought to give the names of two of his friends. But, without replying, these worthies spoke of their age and read him a lecture upon his bad behaviour. Then as, in the course of conversation, he announced his intention of leaving the house as soon as possible, his two visitors both solemnly declared that this proof of his tact would suffice. There had been scandal enough; it was time for him to make a sacrifice of his passions in the interest of respectable folk. Duveyrier accepted Octave's notice to quit then and there, and departed, while Bachelard, behind his back, asked the young man to dine with him that evening.

"Look here, I've been counting upon you. We're out for a lark. Trublot's waiting for us downstairs. I don't care a damn about Eléonore. But I don't want to see her, and I'll go on ahead, so that they mayn't catch us together."

He went downstairs. Five minutes later Octave joined him, in high glee at the way in which the matter had been settled. He stealthily got into the cab, and the melancholy horse, which for seven hours had been dragging the husband about, now limped along with them to a restaurant at the Halles, where some astonishing good tripe was to be got.

Duveyrier went back to Théophile in the shop. Just then Valérie came in, and they were all chatting, when Clotilde herself appeared, on her return from some concert. She had gone there, however, in a perfectly calm frame of mind, for, said she, she was certain that some arrangement satisfactory for everyone would be made. Then came a pause; a moment of embarrassment for both families. Théophile, seized with a fearful fit of coughing, was almost spitting out his teeth. As it was in their mutual interest to make it up, they at last took advantage of the emotion occasioned by these fresh family troubles. The two women embraced each other; Duveyrier declared to Théophile that the Vabre inheritance was ruining him. However, by way of indemnity, he promised to remit his rent for three years.

"I must just go up and pacify poor Auguste," said Duveyrier, at last.

On the staircase he heard hideous cries, like those of an animal about to be slaughtered, which came from the bedroom. Saturnin, armed with his kitchen-knife, had noiselessly crept into the apartment, when, with eyes like gleaming coals, and frothing lips, he had leapt upon Auguste.

"Tell me where you've hid her!" he cried. "Give her back to me, or else I'll bleed you like a pig!"

Startled thus from his painful slumber, Auguste attempted to escape. But the maniac, in the strength of his one fixed idea, had caught hold of him by the tail of his shirt, and, throwing him backwards, placed his neck at the edge of the bed, with a basin immediately undereath it, and held him there just as they hold brutes in a slaughter-house.

"Ah! I've got you this time. I'm going to bleed you; yes, bleed you like a pig!"

Luckily, the others came in time to release the victim. Saturnin had to be shut up, for he was raving mad. Two hours later, the commissary of police having been summoned, they took him once more to the Asile des Moulineau, his family having consented to this. With chattering teeth poor Auguste remarked to Duveyrier, who had informed him of the arrangement made with Octave:

"No, I'd rather have fought a duel. One can't protect oneself from a maniac. What the deuce is he so anxious to bleed me for, the ruffian, after his sister had made a cuckold of me? Ah, I've had enough of it, my good fellow! upon my word, I have!"

XVI

On the Wednesday morning when Marie had brought Berthe to Madame Josserand, the latter, aghast at a scandal which touched her pride, turned very pale, and said not a word. She took her daughter's hand as brutally as if she were a school-mistress clapping some naughty pupil into a dark closet. Leading her to Hortense's bedroom, she pushed her in, and at last exclaimed :

"Hide in here, and don't show yourself. You'll be the death of your father."

Hortense, who was washing, seemed astounded. Crimson with shame, Berthe flung herself on the tumbled bed, sobbing violently. An immediate and stormy explanation was what she had looked for, and she had prepared her defence, having resolved to shout, too, directly her mother's wrath went beyond bounds. But this mute severity, this way of treating her as if she were a naughty little girl who had been eating jam on the sly, entirely upset her, recalling all the terrors of her childhood and the tears shed in corners when she penitently made solemn vows of obedience.

"What's the matter? What have you been doing?" asked her sister, whose amazement increased on seeing that she was wrapped in the old shawl lent by Marie. "Has poor Auguste been taken ill at Lyons?"

But Berthe would not answer. No, later on; there were things that she could not tell, and she begged Hortense to go, and leave her alone to weep there quietly by herself. Thus the day went by. Monsier Josserand had gone to his office, never dreaming that anything had occurred, and when he came home that evening Berthe was still in hiding. Having refused all food, she at last avidly devoured the little dinner which Adèle secretly brought her. The maid stopped to watch her, and, noticing her appetite, said :

"Don't take on so; you must keep up your strength. The house is quiet enough, and as for the killed and wounded, why, there's nobody hurt at all."

"Oh !" said the young woman.

Then she questioned Adèle, who gave her a lengthy acount of the day's proceedings, telling her of the duel which had not come off and what the Duveyriers and the Vabres had done. And Berthe, listening, took fresh heart of grace, devoured everything, and asked for some more bread. It was really too silly to let the thing distress her so much when the others had apparently got over it already.

So when Hortense joined her about ten o'clock, she gaily greeted her, dry-eyed. Smothering their laughter, they had great fun, especially when Berthe tried on one of her sister's dressing-gowns and found it too tight for her. Her bosom, which marriage had developed, almost split the stuff. Never mind, by shifting the buttons she could put it on to-morrow. They both seemed to have gone back in the days of their girlhood, there in the old room where for years they had lived tgether. This touched them, and drew them closer to one another in an affection that for a long while they had not felt. They were obliged to sleep together, for Madame Josserand had got rid of Berthe's old bed. As they lay there side by side, with outstretched limbs, after the candle was out, they talked on and on, their eyes wide open in the dark, for sleep they could not.

"So you won't tell me?" asked Hortense once more.

"But, my dear," replied Berthe, "you are not married. I really can't. It's a dispute that I had with Auguste. He came back, don't you know, and——"

Then, as she hesitated, her sister struck in impatiently :

"Go along, do! What rubbish, to be sure! As if at my age I couldn't know !"

So then Berthe confessed all, choosing her words at first, but finally telling everything about Octave and about Auguste. Lying there on her back in the dark, Hortense listened, uttering a word or two every now and then to question her sister or express an opinion : "Well, what did he say then?" "And how did you feel?" "That was rather odd; I shouldn't have liked that!" "Oh, really! so that's the way, is it?' Midnight struck, then one o'clock, then two o'clock, and still they kept talking the thing over as their limbs grew warmer beneath the bedclothes, though sleep did not come. In this sort of trance Berthe forgot she was with her sister, and began to think aloud, relieving both mind and body of the most delicate confidences.

"As for Verdier and myself," said Hortense, abruptly, "I mean to do just as he likes."

At the mention of Verdier, Berthe gave a start of surprise. She thought the engagement had been broken off, for the woman with whom he had lived for fifteen years had had a child just as he was on the point of getting rid of her.

"Do you mean to say that you think of marrying him, after all?" she asked.

"Well, why shouldn't I? I was a fool to wait so long. The child won't live, though. It's a girl, and one mass of scrofula."

Then, in her disgust, she spat out the word "mistress," revealing all her hatred, as a respectable middle-class spinster, for a creature like that, who had been living all that while with a man. It was just a manoeuvre, nothing else, her having a baby—a pretext which she had invented on discovering that Verdier, after buying chemises for her, to prevent her being dismissed without a rag to her back, was trying to accustom her to a separation by sleeping out more and more frequently. Ah, well! one must just wait and see.

"Poor thing!" exclaimed Berthe.

"Poor thing, indeed!" cried Hortense, bitterly. "It's evident that you've got things to reproach yourself with as well."

But the next moment she was sorry for such a cruel speech, and, putting her arms round her sister, she kissed her and declared that she never meant to say such a thing. Then they both became silent. Yet they did not go to sleep, but continued the story with eyes wide open to the dark.

Next morning Monsieur Josserand felt somewhat unwell. Up till two o'clock he had persisted in working away at his wrappers, although for months past he had complained of depression and gradual loss of strength. However, he got up and dressed, but just as he was starting for his office he felt so exhausted that he sent a commissionaire with a note appraising Bernheim Brothers of his indisposition.

The family were just going to have their coffee. It was a meal, graced by no table-cloth, taken in the dining-room, which still reeked of the greasy residues of last night's repast. The ladies appeared in dressing-gowns, wet from their basins and with hair twisted up anyhow. Seeing that her husband was going to stop at home, Madame Josserand determined not to keep Berthe hidden any longer, for she was already disgusted at all this mystery; besides, she expected every moment that Auguste would come up and make a scene.

"Hullo! you here at breakfast? How's that?" cried the father, in surprise, on seeing his daughter, her eyes puffy with sleep and her bosom squeezed into Hortense's undersized dressing-jacket.

"My husband wrote to say that he was going to stop at Lyons," she replied, "so I thought that I would spend the day with you."

The sisters had arranged to tell this fib. Madame Josserand, who maintained her rigid governess air, forbore to contradict. But Berthe's father eyed her uneasily, as if aware that something was wrong. As the tale seemed to him somewhat unlikely, he was about to ask how the shop would get on without her when Berthe came and kissed him on both cheeks in her old sunny, coaxing way.

"Now, honour bright! you're not hiding anything from me?" he whispered.

"The idea! Why should I hide anything from you?"

Madame Josserand merely shrugged her shoulders. Of what use were all these precautions? To gain an hour, perhaps, not more. It wasn't worth while. Sooner or later the father would have to receive the shock. However, breakfast passed off merrily. Monsieur Josserand was delighted to find himself once more with his two girls; it seemed to him like old times when, scarcely awake, they used to amuse him by narrating their childish dreams.

For him they still had their fresh sweet aroma of adolescence, as, with elbows on table, they dipped their bread in their coffee, laughing aloud with mouths chock-full. All the past came back, too, as facing them he beheld their mother's rigid countenance, her enormous body bursting through an old green silk dress, which she was now using up of a morning without stays.

Breakfast, however, was marred by an unfortunate episode. Madame Josserand suddenly addressed the servant:

"Whatever are you eating?"

For some few moments she had been watching Adèle, who, shod in slippers, plodded heavily round the table.

"Nothing, madam," she replied.

"What do you mean by nothing? You're chewing something; I am not blind. Why, your mouth's quite full. Ah, it's no good your drawing in your cheeks! I can see all the same. You're got something in your pocket, too, haven't you?"

Adèle, in her confusion, sought to withdraw; but Madame Josserand caught hold of her petticoats.

"For the last quarter of an hour I've watched you taking something out of here and stuffing it into your mouth, hiding it in the hollow of your palm. I daresay it's something very nice. Just let's see."

Thrusting her hand into the girl's pocket, she pulled out a handful of stewed prunes, with all the syrup dripping from them.

"Why, what's this?" she furiously exclaimed.

"They're prunes, madam," said Adèle, who, aware that she was found out, grew insolent.

"Oh! so you eat my prunes, do you? That's why they disappear so quickly. Well, I never! Prunes! and in your pocket, too!"

Then she accused her of drinking the vinegar. Everything vanished in the same way; one couldn't even leave a cold potato about without being sure that one would never see it again.

"You're a regular pig, my girl."

"Give me something to eat, then," replied Adèle, rudely; "then I'll leave your cold potatoes alone."

This was the climax. Madame Josserand rose, majestic, terrible.

"Be quiet; don't dare to answer me like that! I know what it is; it's the other servants that have spoilt you. No sooner does one get some stupid noodle of a girl fresh from the country into one's house, than all the other sluts in the place put her up to every sort of disgraceful conduct. You no longer go to church; and now you've begun to steal!"

Spurred on by Lisa and Julie, Adèle was not going to give in.

"If I was such a noodle as you say, you ought not to have taken advantage of it. It's a bit too late now."

"Leave the room; I give you warning!" cried Madame Josserand, as with a tragic gesture she pointed to the door.

Then she sat down, quivering; while the maid, without hurrying herself, dawdled about in her slippers, and munched another prune before going back to her kitchen. She was regularly sent flying in this way once a week; it no longer alarmed her in the least. At the table an awkward silence prevailed. Hortense at last observed that it was not a bit of good sending her to the right-about one day, and keeping her on the next. Of course, she was a thief, and had grown insolent; but they might as well have her as anybody else, for she at least condescended to wait upon them; while any other maid would not tolerate them for as long as a week, even though she were so accomplished as to drink the vinegar and stuff her pockets full of prunes. However, there was a charming intimacy about their breakfast, despite this episode. Monsieur Josserand, in the tenderest of moods, spoke of Saturnin, poor boy, whom they had been obliged to take back there last evening while he was away; and he believed the tale they had told him about an attack of raving madness in the middle of the shop. Then, when he complained of never seeing Léon, Madame Josserand, hitherto mute, curtly remarked that she was expecting him that very day. He was probably coming to lunch. A week ago the young man had broken off his intimacy with Madame Dambreville, who, to keep faith with him, wanted him to wed a stale, swart widow. He, however, was minded to marry a niece of Monsieur Dambreville's, a creole, of great wealth and dazzling beauty, who had only arrived at her uncle's house last September, after the death of her father in the Antilles. So there had been terrible scenes between the two lovers. Consumed by jealousy, Madame Dabreville refused to give her niece to Léon, feeling it impossible to yield in favour of so fascinating a flower of youth.

"How's the match going on?" asked Monsieur Josserand, discreetly.

At first the mother made answers in expurgated phrases, because of Hortense. She now worshipped her son, a fellow who was going to be a success; and at times she flung his triumph in the face of his father, saying that, thank God, he at least took after his mother, and wasn't going to let his wife go naked. By degrees she got up the steam.

"Well, there, he's just about sick of it! However, it's all right; the whole thing has'nt done him any harm."

For decency's sake, Hortense began to drink her coffee, pretending to hide behind her cup; while Berthe, who now might listen to everything, looked somewhat disgusted at her brother's success. They all rose from table, and Monsieur Josserand, feeling much better, talked jauntily of going on to the office after all, when Adèle brought in a card. The lady was waiting in the drawing-room.

"What? Is it she, at this hour?" cried Madame Josserand. "And I without my stays on! Never mind; I shall have to tell her some home truths."

It just happened to be Madame Dambreville. So the father and his two daughters remained chatting in the dining-room, while the mother made for the drawing-room. Before pushing the door open she uneasily surveyed her old silk gown, tried to button it, removed stray threads that had got on to it from the floor, while with a tap she sent her exuberant bosom back to its place.

"You will excuse me, dear lady," said the visitor, smiling, "I was passing and thought I would call to see how you were."

Corseted and coiffed, her toilette was perfect in every detail, and her easy manner suggested the amiable lady of fashion who had just dropped in to wish a friend good morning. Her smile, however, was tremulous, and lurking beneath her worldly suavity, one could note the grievous anguish which shook her whole being. At first, she talked of a thousand trivial matters, avoided mentioning Léon's name, and at last furtively drew from her pocket a letter of his which she had just received.

"Such a letter, such a letter!" she murmured, as her voice, changing, became choked with tears. "Why is he vexed with me, dear madam? He won't even come near us now."

And she feverishly held out the agitating missive. Madame Josserand coolly took it and read it.

It was to break matters off; three lines, most cruelly concise.

"Well," said she, handing back the note. "I dare say it isn't Léon's fault."

Madame Dambreville forthwith began to sound the praises of this widow, a woman scarcely thirty-five yet, a most worthy person, fairly well-off, and of such energy that she would not rest until she had got her husband a place in the ministry. She had kept her promise, she said, after all; she had made a good match for Léon; so why should he be angry with her? Then, without waiting for an answer, in a sudden nervous impulse she mentioned Raymonde, her niece. Could such a thing really be possible? A hoyden of sixteen, a raw minx that as yet knew nothing of the world.

"Why not?" Madame Josserand kept repeating in reply to each question. "Why not, if he's fond of her?"

"No, no! he's not fond of her, he can't be fond of her!" Madame Dambreville cried, losing all command of her feelings. "Listen to me!' she exclaimed; "all I ask from him is a little gratitude. It's I who made him; he has me to thank for his position as auditor, and, as a wedding present, he will have his nomination as *maitre de requetes*. Madam, I implore you, tell him to come back; ask him to do so for my sake. I appeal to his heart, to your heart as a mother, to all that is noblest in you."

She clapsed her hands, and her voice faltered. There was a pause, as they both sat opposite to each other. Then, all at once, she burst into tears, sobbing out, hysterically:

"Not with Raymonde; oh, no, not with Raymonde!"

It was the fury of passion, the cry of a woman who refuses to grow old, who clings convulsively to her last lover at that burning moment before old age arrives. She seized hold of Madame Josserand's hands, bathed them in tears, confessing all to her, the mother, humiliating herself before her, repeatedly saying that she, and she alone, could influence her son, declaring that she would serve her devotedly if only she would restore Léon to her. Doubtless she had not come there to say all this; on the contrary, she had resolved to let nothing be guessed; but her heart was breaking, she could not help it.

"Hush, my dear! you make me feel quite ashamed," replied Madame Josserand, with a vexed look. "My girls there might overhear you. For my own part, I don't know anything, and I don't want to know anything. If you've had any differences with my son, why, you'd better make it up between you. I never undertake to interfere."

However, she overwhelmed her with good advice. At her time of life one ought to be resigned. In God she would find great succour. But she ought to give up her niece, if she wished to offer an expiatory sacrifice to Heaven. Besides, this widow would not suit Léon at all, who required a wife of pleasant mien to preside at his dinner-table. And she spoke admiringly of her son, full of maternal pride, enumerating his good qualities and showing him to be worthy of the most charming of brides.

"Just think, my dear friend, he's not yet thirty. I should be grieved to seem disobliging, but you might be his mother, you know. Oh! he is aware of what he owes to you, and I myself feel full of gratitude. You shall be his guardian angel. But, you know, when a thing's over, it's over. Surely you didn't imagine that you could keep him for ever, did you?"

Then, as the unhappy woman declined to listen to reason, merely desirous to get back her lover at once, the mother lost her temper.

"Look here, madam, you'd better be off! It's too good-natured of me to show any concern in the matter. The boy doesn't want to; and there's an end of it! You look after yourself! It's now my place to remind him of his duty if he again should yield to your importunities; for, I ask you, of what interest can it be to either of you now? He'll be here himself directly; and if you counted on my——"

Of all this speech Madame Dambreville only heard the last phrase. She had been pursuing Léon for a whole week, without ever getting to see him. Her face brightened as she uttered the heartfelt cry:

"If he's coming, I shall stop here!"

Whereupon she stolidly sank down into a chair, gazing vacantly into space and making no further reply, stubborn as some brute that even blows cannot force to budge. Distressed at having said too much, and exasperated at this wet blanket of a woman who had got into her drawing-room and whom she could not very well eject, Madame Josserand at last withdrew, leaving her visitor to herself. Moreover, a noise in the dining-room made her uneasy; she fancied she heard Auguste's voice.

"Upon my word, madam, such behaviour is unheard of!" she exclaimed, as she slammed the door violently. "It shows a most preposterous want of tact!"

As it so happened, Auguste did come upstairs to make some arrangement with his wife's parents upon terms which he had been planning the evening before. Monsieur Josserand, growing ever more chirpy, had given up all idea of the office; he was bent on fun, and just as he was proposing to take his daughters out for a walk, Adèle announced Madame Berthe's husband. There was general astonishment at this; the young wife turned pale.

"What! Your husband here?" said the father. "Why, I thought he was at Lyons. So you told me an untruth? I was sure that there was something wrong. I felt as much these two days past!"

Then, as she rose to go, he stopped her.

"Tell me; you've had another quarrel of some sort? About money eh? Perhaps about the dowry of ten thousand francs that we've never yet paid him."

"Yes, yes, that's what it was!" stammered Berthe, as she shook him aside and escaped.

Hortense got up also, and ran after her sister, whom she rejoined in her bedroom. The rustle of their skirts left behind a sort of shiver of fear for their father, who suddenly found himself seated alone at table in the middle of the silent dining-room. All his old feeling of illness came back, his ghastly pallor, lassitude and want of vitality. The hour he dreaded, awaiting it with shame and anguish, had come; his son-in-law was going to mention the insurance, and he would have to admit the dishonesty of the scheme to which he had consented.

"Come in, come in, my dear Auguste," said he, in a choked voice. "Berthe had just told me all about your quarrel. I'm not very well, so they're coddling me. I am most awfully sorry that I cannot let you have this money. I ought never to have promised, I know."

So he faltered on, like some guilty person who is making a clean breast of it. Auguste listened to him in surprise. He had already been informed about this bogus insurance, but had never dared claim the payment of the ten thousand francs for fear that that terrible Madame Josserand might first of all send to old Vabre's tomb to get his own paternal inheritance of ten thousand francs.

Whenever the subject was mentioned to him, he always urged this as an objection.

"Yes, yes, sir," said he; "I know everything; you've absolutely let me in with all your fine tales and promises. As to not getting the money, that wouldn't matter so much; it's the hypocrisy of the whole thing that enrages me! Why all this complication about an insurance that never existed! Why pretend to be so tender-hearted and sympathetic, offering to advance sums which, as you said, would only come to you three years afterwards, when all the while you hadn't got a brass farthing! There is but one word for such conduct!"

Monsieur Josserand was on the point of retorting, "It was not I, it was they who did it!" But a sense of family shame restrained him, and he hung his head in acknowledgment of the scurvy trick, while Auguste went on:

"Besides, everybody was against me; Duveyrier, with his scoundrel of a notary, behaved shamefully as well, for I requested them to insert a clause in the contract, guaranteeing the payment of the insurance money, but they hushed me down. If I had insisted upon that, you would have been guilty of forgery, sir, yes, forgery!"

White as a sheet, the father at this accusation rose and was about to reply, offering to work hard for the rest of his life, if only he might purchase thereby his daughter's happiness, when Madame Josserand rushed in like a whirlwind, lashed to fury by Madame Dambreville's stubborness. She no longer gave heed to her old green silk dress, the bodice of which was split by her heaving bosom.

"Eh? What's that?" she cried. "Who talks of forgery? You, sir? You'd better go to Père-Lachaise first, sir, and see if your father's cash-box is open yet!"

Auguste was expecting this, but, nevertheless, he was dreadfully annoyed. However, with head erect, she went on with amazing self-possession:

"We've got your ten thousand francs all safe. Yes, they're in that drawer yonder. But we're not going to let you have them until Monsieur Vabre comes back to give you your inheritance. A nice family, indeed! The father a gambler, who swindles us all, and the brother-in-law a thief, who collars the inheritance!"

"Thief? thief?" spluttered Auguste, beside himself with rage. "The thieves are here, madam!"

With burning cheeks, they both stood facing each other, and Monseiur Josserand, utterly prostrated by turbulent scenes of this sort, strove to separate them. He besought them to be calm. His whole frame quivered, and he was obliged to sit down.

"At any rate," said Auguste, after a pause, "I won't have a strumpet in my house. You can keep your money and your daughter, too. That's what I came up to tell you."

"You're changing the subject," coolly remarked Madame Josserand. "Very well, we'll talk about that presently."

But the father, powerless to rise, looked at them aghast. He no longer understood what they meant. What did they say? Strumpet? Who was the strumpet? Then, as listening to them, he learned that it was his daughter, his heart was torn as by a gaping wound through which all that remained to him of existence ebbed away. Good God! So his daughter would be his death! For all his weaknesses she was to serve as punishment, she whom he had never known how to educate! Already the thought that she was living in debt and always quarrelling with her husband, saddened his old age, and revived within him all the petty worries of his own existence. And now she was an adulteress, having sunk to that lowest grade of infamy for a woman. The idea was revolting to his simple, honest soul. He grew cold as ice, listening, mute, while the others wrangled.

"I told you that she would be unfaithful to me!" cried Auguste, in a tone of indignant triumph.

"And I told you that you were doing your best to make her so!" screamed Madame Josserand, exultantly. "No, I don't say Berthe was right; in fact, she's behaved like an idiot, and I mean to let her know what I think, too; but, as she's not here now, I repeat, you, and you alone, are to blame!"

"What do you mean? *I* am to blame?"

"Of course you are, my good fellow! You don't know how to treat women. Now, look here, here's an example. Did you ever condescend to come to one of my Tuesdays? Not you; and if you did, you only stayed half-an-hour at the most, and then you only came three times during the whole season. It's all very well to say you've always got a headache. Manners are manners, that's all. I don't say it's a great crime, no; but there it is, you don't know how to behave!"

She hissed out the words with a venom that had gradually accumulated, for when her daughter married she had above all things counted upon her son-in-law to fill her drawing-room for her with desirable guests. But he had brought no one, and never even came himself; thus another of her dreams vanished as she saw that she could never hope to rival the Duveyrier choruses.

"However," she added, with a touch of irony, "I don't force anybody to seek amusement at my house."

"The fact is, nobody ever *is* amused," he retorted, petulantly.

Her blood was up in a moment.

"That's right, lavish your insults upon me, do! I'd have you know, sir, that, if I chose I could get the best society in Paris to come to my parties, and I certainly never depended upon you for my social position."

It was no longer a question of Berthe's misconduct; in this personal quarrel the adultery had disappeared. As if the victim of some hideous nightmare, Monsieur Josserand sat there listening to them. It was not possible; his daughter could never have caused him such grief as this. At last, rising with difficulty, he went out, without saying a word, to find Berthe. As soon as she came, thought he, she would fling her arms round Auguste's neck; everything would be explained, everything would be forgotten. He found her having a dispute with Hortense, who kept urging her to ask forgiveness of her husband, for she was already tired of her, and feared that she might have to share her room in this way for some time to come. At first Berthe refused, but finally followed her father. As they came back to the dining-room where the dirty breakfast-cups still stood, Madame Josserand was crying out:

"No, upon my word, I don't pity you in the least!"

Then, at the sight of Berthe, she was silent, relapsing into her severely majestic mood, while Auguste, when his wife appeared, made a grand gesture of protest, as if to sweep her from his path.

"Now, see here," said Monsieur Josserand, in his low, tremulous voice, "what's the matter with all of you? You're driving me mad with these bickerings; I don't know where I am. Tell me, my child, your husband's mistaken, isn't he? You explain it to him, do. You ought to have some compassion for your poor old parents. Now, kiss and be friends for my sake."

Berthe, who anyway would have embraced Auguste, stood there half-throttled in her dressing-gown, looking very awkward as she saw him recoil from her with a mien of tragic repugnance.

"What? You won't kiss him, my darling?" continued the father. "It's you who ought to make the first advance. And you, my dear fellow, you should encourage her, and show yourself indulgent."

Then finally Auguste burst out :

"Encourage her, forsooth ! I like that ! Why, I caught her in her nightdress, sir, with that fellow ! Are you making game of me to suppose that I should embrace her? In her night-dress, do you hear, sir?"

Monsieur Josserand was thunderstruck. Then, seizing Berthe's arm, he exclaimed :

"You don't speak. So it's true, is it? Down on your knees, then !"

But Auguste had reached the door; he was going to escape.

"That's no good whatever. Don't come any of your old tricks over me, nor try and saddle me with her again. Once was more than enough. No more of it, do your hear? I'd rather get a divorce. Hand her on to someone else, if you find her a nuisance. And, if it comes to that, you're just as bad as she is."

He waited until he had got into the hall before relieving his feelings of this final taunt :

"Yes, when one has made a whore of one's daughter, one does not force her down an honest man's throat."

The front-door was slammed, and profound silence reigned. Berthe mechanically seated herself at the table with downcast eyes, examining the dregs in her coffee cup, whilst her mother strode up and down, swayed, as it were, by the tempest of her emotions. The father, utterly worn-out, with white, agonised countenance, sat aloof in the far corner of the room, leaning against the wall. The room reeked of rancid butter, of the cheap kind on sale at the Halles.

"As that insolent fellow has gone," said Madame Josserand, "we may come to some understanding. Now, sir, this is all the result of your incapacity. Do you at last see how much at fault you have been? Do you think that quarrels of this kind would ever have occurred in the house of one of the Brothers Bernheim, owners of the Saint-Joseph glass factory? No, I should think not ! If you had listened to me, if you had got the whip-hand of your employers, this insolent person would now be grovelling at our feet, for, obviously, all that he wants is money. Only get money, and people will think you're somebody, sir. Far better be envied than pitied. If I only had twenty sous, I always pretended I had got forty. But you, sir, you don't care a rap whether I go barefoot or not;

you've deceived your wife and daughters in a most disgraceful fashion by letting them drag on their existence in this hand-to-mouth way. Oh, it's no good protesting! all our misfortunes are due to that."

Monsieur Josserand stared blankly, without moving. His wife stopped short in front of him, full of mad desire for a scene. Then, observing that he was motionless, she resumed her march.

"Yes, yes; put on your scornful air, but it doesn't affect me in the slightest, you know that. Just you dare abuse my family after what has happened in your own! Why, uncle Bachelard is a saint, and my sister, too! Now, listen; do you want to know my opinion? Well, if my father had not died, you would have killed him. As for yours——"

Monsieur Josserand's pallor increased as he gasped:

"Eléonore, I beg of you—say what you will about my father, about my whole family; only I beg of you, leave me in peace; I do not feel well!"

Berthe looked up compassionately.

"Mamma, do leave him alone," said she.

Then, turning round upon her daughter, Madame Josserand went on with greater fury:

"As for you, I was waiting to let you have it. Ever since yesterday I've been keeping it in. Now, I give you notice, it's a little bit too much, this is! With that bounder, of all people! You must have lost all pride! I thought that you were only making use of him, showing him just sufficient cordiality to keep him zealous as a salesman at the counter downstairs. And I helped you. I encouraged him——! Now, tell me, what advantage did you hope to gain by such a thing?"

"None, whatever; that's very certain!" stammered Berthe.

"Then, why did you carry on with him? The folly of it seems to me greater than the scandal!"

"How odd you are, mamma! One never reflects in matters of that sort!"

Madame Josserand resumed her march.

"One never reflects! Bah! That's just what one ought to do. Fancy misconducting yourself like that! Why, there's not a grain of common-sense about the whole thing—that's what enrages me! Did I ever tell you to deceive your husband? Did I ever deceive your father? There he sits; ask him. Let him say if ever he caught me with a man."

Now she walked slower; her gait grew majestic and she lustily slapped the green bodice.

"No, never; not a slip, not an indiscretion, nor the thought of one, even! My life has been a chaste life, and yet the Lord knows what I've had to put up with from your father! I had every excuse, and lots of women would have revenged themselves. But I had common-sense; that's what saved me. There, you see, he's not got a word to say! He sits there on a chair, powerless to protest. I've every right to rank as a virtuous woman! Oh, you great ninny you surely see what a fool you've made of yourself!"

Then she delivered a learned discourse upon domestic morality with regard to adultery. Was not Auguste now entitled to lord it over her? She had furnished him with a terrible weapon. Even though they were to make it up, she could never have the least quarrel with him but that would instantly be flung in her teeth. A nice state of affairs, eh? How delightful it would be for her always to eat humblepie! It was all over, and she could never hope to enjoy any of the little privileges obtained from a dutiful husband, little kindnesses, attentions and the like. No! rather live a virtuous life than not be able to have the last word in one's own house!

"Before God, I swear it," cried she; "I would never have yielded, even if the Emperor himself had persecuted me! The loss is too great!"

She strode on, silent for a time, as if lost in thought, and then added:

"Besides, it's the most shameful thing of all."

Monsieur Josserand looked at her, and then at his daughter, moving his lips without speaking, his whole dejected frame protesting against such harrowing explanations. Berthe, however, daunted by violence, felt hurt at her mother's moral lecture. And at last she rebelled, for, true to her old training as a marriageable maiden, she failed to recognise the gravity of her sin.

"Why, bless me!" she cried, planting both elbows on the table, "you shouldn't have made me marry a man I didn't care for. I hate him now, and have taken up with somebody else."

So she went on. The whole story of her marriage was rehearsed in short phrases; rapped out at random—the three winters devoted to man-hunting; the various youths at whose heads she was hurled; the failure of this offer of her body in the public marts of middle-class drawing-rooms. Then she spoke of all that mothers taught their dowerless daughters. A complete series of lessons in polite prostitution—the touch of fingers in the dance, the relinquishing of hands behind a door, the indecency of innocence speculating upon the prurient appetites of the foolish then, one fine evening, the full-blown husband, landed just as some pavement courtesan lands her man; the husband trapped behind a curtain, who, in his hot sexual excitement, falls into a snare.

"Well, there, he bores me, and I bore him!" she exclaimed. "It's not my fault that we don't understand one another. The very next day after our wedding he seemed to fancy that we had swindled him; yes, and he looked as glum and disagreeable as he does now when one of his bargains falls through. As for me, I was never smitten with him. If that's all the fun one gets out of marriage! It all began from that, as I tell you. Never mind, it was bound to happen, and it's not all my fault."

She was silent, and then, with an air of profound conviction, added:

"Ah, mamma, how well I understand you now! Do you remember how you told us you'd had more than enough of it?"

Standing before her, Madame Josserand listened to her, indignant and aghast.

"*I* said that?" she screamed.

But Berthe was worked up, and would not stop.

"Yes, you did, lots of times. And I'd like to see how you'd have behaved in my place. Auguste is not easy-going, like papa. You'd have had a fight about money before the week was out. That's the sort of fellow about whom you would have said that men were no good except to be swindled!"

"*I* said that?" cried the mother, beside herself with rage.

So threateningly did she approach her daughter that the father held out both hands, as if begging for mercy. The ceaseless storming of these two women struck him to the core; each fresh outburst seemed to widen the wound. Tears filled his eyes as he stammered out:

"Do have done; spare me all this!"

"No; but it's monstrous," continued Madame Josserand, raising her voice. "The wretched girl actually taxes me with her lascivious conduct! She'll tell me next that it was I who helped her to be unfaithful to her husband! So it's my fault, is it? For, after all, that's what it comes to. My fault, eh?"

With elbows on table, Berthe sat there, pale, but resolute.

"It's very certain that if you had brought me up differently——"

She never finished the sentence. Her mother gave her such a swinging box on the ear that it laid her head prone on the oil-cloth table-cover. Since last night this smack had lurked in her palm, her fingers itched with it, as in the far-off days when her little girl used to oversleep herself.

"There, take that for your education!" she cried. "Your husband ought to have killed you!"

Without raising her head, Berthe burst into tears, holding her cheek to her arm. She forgot that she was four-and-twenty; this slap reminded her of bygone slaps, and of all the timorous hypocrisy of her girlhood. Her resolution, as a personage emancipated and important, was lost in the sharp pain of a little girl.

Hearing her sob thus violently, her father was well-nigh overmastered by emotion. Tottering forward, he pushed his wife aside, saying:

"Tell me, do you both want to be the death of me? Must I go down on my knees to you?"

Having relieved her feelings, and finding nothing further to say, Madame Josserand withdrew in regal silence. Opening the door suddenly she caught Hortense listening behind it. This caused a fresh outburst.

"So you've been listening to all this scandal, have you? One of you does shocking things, and the other gloats over them! A pretty couple, indeed! Gracious me! whoever could have brought you up?"

Hortense came calmly in, and said:

"There was no need to listen; one can hear you from the far end of the kitchen. The maid is in fits. Besides, I'm old enough to get married now, and so there's no reason why I shouldn't know."

"Verdier, I suppose!" was the mother's biting reply. "That's the sort of satisfaction you afford me. Now you're waiting for the bastard to die; but you'll have to wait, as it's a big, fat baby, so they say. A good job, too!"

A flood of bile dyed the girl's gaunt visage yellow, as she replied, with teeth hard set:

"If it's a big, fat baby, Verdier can get rid of it. And I'll make him get rid of it quicker than you think, just to teach you all. Yes, yes; I can find myself a husband, for the matches that you make are such utter frauds!"

Then, as her mother approached:

"Now then, you won't box *my* ears; so look out!"

They glared at each other, and Madame Josserand was the first to yield, masking her retreat by an air of disdainful superiority. The father, however, thought that hostilities were about to recommence. Watching thus these three women, the mother and her daughters, beings that he had loved and who now were ready to murder one another, he felt as if the whole world were giving way under his feet; and he, too, escaped to his room as if he had got his death-blow and desired to die alone. And he repeatedly sobbed out:

"I cannnot bear it, I cannot bear it!"

Silence reigned once more in the dining-room. Berthe, breathing hysterically, with her cheek on her arm, had grown calmer. Hortense sat at the other end of the table, buttering a piece of toast by way of recovering her equanimity. Then, with various gloomy remarks, she wrought her sister to a pitch of desperation, saying that life at home had become unbearable; if she were in her place she would prefer to have her ears boxed by her husband rather than by her mother, as that was a far more natural thing. Moreover, when she had married Verdier, she would simply send her mother to the right-about, as she was not going to have rows of this sort in her home. Just then Adèle came in to clear away; but Hortense went on, saying that if there was any more of this she should give warning; and the maid was of this opinion also. She had been obliged to shut the kitchen-window because Lisa and Julie had both been peeping out to see what was going on. The whole thing, however, had amused her vastly, and she still chuckled thereat. What a jolly smack Madame Berthe had got! She was the worst off, after all. And as she sidled about, fat-waisted Adèle uttered a phrase full of profound philosophy. After all, said she, what did the people in the house care? The world wagged on, and before the week was out nobody would even remember madame's affair with the two gentlemen. Hortense, who nodded approval, here broke in to complain of the butter; her mouth was tainted by the filth. Gracious goodness! Butter at twenty-two sous! Why, it could only be poison! And, as in the saucepans it left a nauseous deposit, the maid proceeded to explain that it was not even economical to buy such stuff, when a dull sound, as of a thud upon the floor, set them all listening.

Berthe at last looked up in alarm. "What's that?" she asked.

"Perhaps it is madame and the other lady in the drawing-room," suggested Adèle.

On going through the drawing-room, Madame Josserand had started back in surprise. A lady sat there, all by herself.

"What? you here still?" she exclaimed, on recognising Madame Dambreville, whose presence she had entirely forgotten.

The visitor had never moved. Family wranglings, stormy voices, the banging of doors, all this had passed over her, yet she was wholly unconscious of it all. There she remained, motionless, gazing vaguely into space, absorbed in passionate despair.

But something was at work within her; this advice of Léon's mother had upset her, and she had half decided to pay dearly for the last few fragments of happiness.

"Come, now," cried Madame Josserand, with brutal candour, "You can't sleep here, very well. I have heard from my son, and I no longer expect him."

Then with parched dry tongue, as of one awaking from sleep, Madame Dambreville spoke.

"I am going directly; pray excuse me. Tell him from me that I have thought the matter over, and I consent. I will reflect still further, and, perhaps, will arrange for him to marry that girl, as he wants to. But it is I who am giving her to him, and I want him to come and ask me for her; ask me, me only, do you see? Oh, make him come back to me, make him come back!"

Thus in ardent tones did she plead, and then, lowering her voice, like a woman who, after sacrificing all, yet obstinately clings to one last consolation, she added:

"He shall marry her, but he must live with us. Otherwise, nothing can be settled. I'd rather lose him altogether."

Then she departed. Madame Josserand grew quite gushing, making various consolatory speeches in the hall. She promised to send Léon that very evening, in a contrite, affectionate frame of mind, declaring that he would be delighted to live with his new aunt. Then, having shut the door after Madame Dambreville, full of pity and tenderness, she inwardly observed:

"Poor lad! A nice price he'll have to pay her!"

But at that moment she, too heard the dull thud which shook the flooring. What on earth could that be? Had the maid smashed all the crockery?

She rushed back to the dining-room and eagerly questioned her daughters.

"What's the matter? Did the sugar-basin fall down?"

"No, mamma, we don't know what it is."

Turning round to look for Adèle, she caught her listening at the bedroom door.

"What are you about?" she cried. "Everything's being smashed to bits in your kitchen while you stand there spying upon your master. Yes, yes, you start with prunes and you end with something very different. For some time past, my girl, I haven't liked the looks of you : you smell of men——"

Wide-eyed, Adèle looked at her, observing :

"That's not it. I think it's master who's fallen down inside there."

"Good gracious me, I believe she's right!" cried Berthe, turning pale. "It was just as if someone had tumbled down."

Accordingly, they entered the room. On the floor, near the bed, Monsieur Josserand lay in a swoon. His head had struck against a chair, and blood issued in a thin stream from his right ear. Mother, daughters, and maid servant stood round to examine him. Only Berthe burst into tears, sobbing convulsively, as if still smarting from the blow she had received. And as the four of them lifted up the old man and placed him on the bed, they heard him murmur :

"It's all over. They've killed me."

XVII

Months passed, and spring had come. In the house in the Rue de Choiseul everybody was talking of the approaching marriage of Octave and Madame Hédouin. Things, however, had not yet got so far as that. Octave had resumed his old post at "The Ladies' Paradise," and every day the business grew greater. Since her husband's death Madame Hédouin had not been able to undertake the sole management of an ever-growing business. Old Deleuze, her uncle, was a martyr to rheumatism, and could attend to nothing; so that, naturally, Octave, young, active and full of ideas as to trading on a large scale, soon assumed a position of decided importance in the house. Still sore about his ridiculous love-affair with Berthe, he now no longer thought of making use of women: he even fought shy of them. The best thing, as he believed, would be for him quietly to become Madame Hédouin's partner, and then to pile up the dollars, Recollecting, too, the absurd snub which she had given him, he treated her as if she were a man, which was exactly what she wanted.

Henceforth their relations became most intimate. They used to shut themselves up for hours together in the little back room. Here in former days, when he had determined to seduce her, he had followed a complete set of tactics, trying to profit by her excitement about business, breathing on the back of her neck as he mentioned certain figures to her, waiting for a time when takings were heavy to profit by her enthusiasm. Now he was merely good-tempered, with no end except business in view. He no longer felt wishful to enjoy her, although he still remembered her little thrill of excitement as she leaned against his breast when they waltzed together on the evening of Berthe's wedding. Perhaps she had been fond of him, after all? Anyhow, it was best to remain as they were; for, as she rightly observed, perfect order was necessary in a business like that, and it was foolish to want things which would only upset them from morning to night.

Seated, both of them, at the narrow desk, they often forgot themselves after going through the books and settling the orders. Then it was that he reverted to his dreams of aggrandisement. He had sounded the owner of the next house, who was quite ready to sell. The umbrella-maker and the second-hand dealer must have notice given them to quit, and a special silk department must be opened. To this she gravely listened, not daring as yet to make the venture. But her liking for Octave's business capacity grew ever greater, for in his ideas she recognised her own; her aptitude for commerce, and the serious, practical side of her character showed as it were beneath his urbane exterior of a polite shopman. Moreover, such zeal, such boldness were his—qualities lacking in herself, and which filled her with enthusiasm. It was imagination applied to trade, the only sort of imagination that ever troubled her. He was becoming her master.

At length, one evening, as they sat side by side, looking over some invoices, under the hot flame of the gas, she said slowly:

"I have spoken to my uncle, Monsieur Octave. He has consented, so we will buy the house. Only——"

But, merrily interrupting her, he cried:

"Then that'll snuff out the Vabres!"

She smiled, and reproachfully murmured:

"So you hate them, do you? It is not right of you; you're the last person to wish them any ill."

She had never once made any remark about his intrigue with Berthe, so that at this sudden allusion he was greatly disconcerted, without exactly knowing why. He blushed and stammered out some excuse.

"No, no! that does not concern me," she continued, still smiling and very calm. "Forgive me; the remark escaped me involuntarily, for I determined never to open my mouth to you on the subject. You're young. All the worse for such as want it, eh? Husbands ought to look after their wives if they can't look after themselves."

He felt relieved to observe that she was not angry. He often had feared that if she got to know of his old liaison she might grow cold.

"You interrupted me, Monsieur Octave," she went on gravely. "I was about to add, that if I purchase the adjoining house, thus doubling the importance of my present business, I cannot possibly remain a widow. I shall be obliged to marry again."

Octave was astonished. So she had already got a husband in view, and he knew nothing about it. At once his position there seemed to him compromised.

"My uncle," continued she, "told me as much himself. Oh, there's no hurry about it just yet! I've been eight months in mourning, so I shall wait until the autumn. But in trade all matters of the heart must be put aside, and the necessities of the situation ought to be considered. A man is absolutely necessary here."

She calmly discussed all this as if it were a business matter, while he watched her, with her beautiful regular features, clear healthy complexion, and neat wavy black hair. And he felt regretful that since her widowhood he had not again sought to become her lover. "It is always a very serious thing," he faltered. "It needs reflection."

Of course she thought so, too. And she mentioned her age.

"I'm getting on, you know. I'm five years older than you are, Monsieur Octave."

Then, overcome, he interrupted her, thinking he took her meaning. Seizing her hands, he exclaimed :

"Oh, madam! Oh, madam!"

But she, rising, freed herself. Then she turned down the gas.

"Well, that'll do for to-day. Some of your ideas are excellent, and it's only natural that I should have thought of you as the proper person to carry them out. But there will be some bother about it, and we must think the whole thing out. I know that at bottom you're a steady fellow. Just you think the matter over, and so will I. That is why I mentioned it to you. We can discuss it some other time, later on."

Things remained thus for weeks. The business went on as usual. As Madame Hédouin always maintained her calm and smiling demeanour towards him, never once hinting at any tenderer feeling. Octave at first affected similar serenity, and soon, like her, grew healthfully happy, trusting implicitly in the logic of things. It was her favourite remark that reasonable things always happened of their own accord. So she never was in a hurry about anything. None of the tittle-tattle respecting her intimacy with the young man touched her in the slightest. All they had to do was to wait.

Everyone in the house in the Rue de Choiseul declared that the match was made. Octave had given up his room there and had got lodgings in the Rue Neuve-Saint-Augustin, close to "The Ladies' Paradise." He no longer visited anyone, and never went to the Campardons' nor the Duveyriers', who were shocked at his scandalous intrigue. Even Monsieur Gourd, when he met him, pretended not to recognise him, to avoid having to bow. Only Marie and

Madame Juzeur, if they met him of a morning in the neighbourhood, stopped and chatted for a moment or two in some doorway.

Madame Juzeur, who eagerly questioned him as to his reported engagement to Madame Hédouin, wanted him to promise that he would come and see her and have a nice chat about it all. Marie was in despair at being again pregnant, and told him of Jules' amazement and of her parents' dreadful wrath. However, when the rumour of his marriage was confirmed, Octave was surprised to get a very low bow from Monsieur Gourd. Campardon, though he did not yet offer to make it up, nodded cordially to him across the street, while Duveyrier, when looking in one evening to buy some gloves, appeared very friendly. By degrees, the whole household seemed ready to forget and forgive.

Moreover, the inmates had one and all regained the beaten track of middle-class respectability. Behind the mahogany portals fresh founts of virtue played; the third-floor gentleman came to work one night a week as usual; the other Madame Campardon passed by, inflexible in her integrity; the maids sported aprons of dazzling whiteness, while, in the tepid silence of the staircase, all the pianos on all the floors flung out the self-same waltzes, making a music at once mystic and remote.

Yet the taint of adultery still lingered, imperceptible indeed to common folk, but disagreeable to those of fine moral sense. Auguste obstinately refused to take back his wife, and so long as Berthe lived with her parents, the scandal would not be effaced; material trace of it must remain. Yet not one of the tenants openly told the exact story, as it would have been so embarrassing for everybody. By common and, as it were, involuntary consent, they agreed that the quarrel between Berthe and Auguste arose about the ten thousand francs—a mere squabble about money. It was so much more decent to say this; and one could allude to the matter before young ladies. Would the parents pay up, or would they not? The whole farce became so perfectly simple, for not a soul in the neighbourhood was either amazed or indignant at the idea that money matters should provoke blows in a domestic circle. As a matter of fact, this polite arrangement did not affect the actual situation, and, though calm in the presence of mischance, the whole house had suffered a cruel shock to its dignity.

It was Duveyrier in particular who, as landlord, bore the brunt of this misfortune so persistent and so undeserved. For some time past Clarisse had been worrying him so much that he often returned to his wife in tears. The scandal of the adultery, too, stung him to the quick, for, as he said, he saw the passers-by look up at his house, the house that his father had sought to adorn with all the domestic virtues. Such a thing as this could not be allowed to go on. He talked of purifying the whole place, to satisfy his own personal honour. And, for the sake of public decency, he urged Auguste to effect a reconciliation, who unfortunately refused, being backed up in this by Théophile and Valérie, who had regularly usurped the post of cashier at the pay-desk, and revelled in the domestic quarrel. Then, as the Lyons business was in a bad way, and the silk warehouse likely to come to grief for want of capital, Duveyrier had the following practical idea. The Josserands were doubtless most anxious to get rid of their daughter, and Auguste should offer to take her back, but only on condition that they paid the dowry of fifty thousand francs. Possibly, if they entreated him, uncle Bachelard would consent to give the money. At first Auguste vehemently refused to be a party to any such arrangement; though the sum were a hundred thousand francs it was not nearly enough. However, feeling very uneasy about his April disbursements, he at last yielded to Duveyrier's persuasion, whose plea was in favour of morality, his sole aim being, as he said to, perform a righteous act.

When all was settled, Clotilde chose the Abbé Mauduit to negotiate matters. It was rather a delicate thing; only a priest could intervene without compromising himself. As it so happened, the abbé had been much grieved by all the shocking things which had occurred in one of the most interesting households of his parish. Indeed, he had already offered to use all his wisdom, experience, and authority to put an end to a scandal over which enemies of the Church would only gloat. Yet when Clotilde mentioned the dowry, and asked him to inform the Josserands of Auguste's conditions, he bowed his head and maintained a painful silence.

"The money which my brother claims is money due to him, you understand," said Clotilde. "It is not a bargain. He absolutely insists upon it, too."

"It must be, so I will go," said the abbé, at last.

For days past the Josserands had awaited a proposal of some kind. Valérie must have said something, for everyone in the house was talking about the matter. Were they so hard-up that they'd have to keep their daughter? Would they manage to find the fifty thousand francs so as to get rid of her? Ever since the subject was broached Madame Josserand had been in a perfect fury. What!

after all that bother to get Berthe married once, they were now obliged to marry her a second time? Nothing had been settled, the dowry was again asked for, and all the money worries had begun afresh. No mother surely had ever had to go through such a thing twice over. And all through that silly fool whose stupidity was such that she forgot her duty! The house became a sort of hell upon earth; Berthe suffered perpetual torture, for even her sister, Hortense, furious at not having the bedroom to herself, never spoke now without making some cutting remark.

Her very meals were made a matter of reproach. It seemed rather odd, when one had a husband somewhere, to come and sponge upon one's parents for a meal, who had little enough to eat in all conscience! Then, in despair, poor Berthe slunk away, sobbing, calling herself a coward, and afraid to go downstairs and throw herself at Auguste's feet, and say:

"Here I am. Beat me, do; for I can't be more wretched than I am!"

Monsieur Josserand alone treated his daughter with kindness. But her sins and tears were killing him; the cruelty of his family had dealt him his death-blow, and, with unlimited leave of absence, he lay almost always in bed. Doctor Juillerat, who attended him, said it was blood-poisoning; it was actually an entire break up of the whole system, each organ being affected in turn.

"When you've made your father die of grief, you'll be happy, won't you?" cried the mother.

Berthe, indeed, was afraid to go into her father's room now, for when they met they both wept, and only did each other harm. At length Madame Josserand decided to make a grand move. She invited uncle Bachelard to dine, having resolved to humiliate herself yet once again. She would gladly have paid the fifty thousand francs out of her own pocket, had she got them, so as not to be saddled with this hulking married daughter of hers, whose presence brought a slur upon her Tuesday parties. Moreover, she had heard some shocking tales about her brother, and if he did not behave nicely, she meant to give him a piece of her mind, just for once in a way.

Bachelard behaved in a singularly disgusting way at dinner. He had come there half-drunk: since the loss of Fifi, he had sunk to the very deepest depths. Luckily Madame Josserand had not invited anyone else, for fear of disgrace. He fell asleep during dessert, while telling certain rakish and ribald anecdotes, and they were obliged to wake him up before taking him into Monsieur Josserand's room. Here, signs of skilful stage-management were evident; with a view to working upon the old drunkard's feelings, beside the bed two chairs had been placed, one for the mother, the other for the uncle, while Berthe and Hortense were to stand. They would just see if the uncle again dared to deny his promises when face to face with a dying man, in so mournful a room, half-lighted by a smoky lamp.

"Narcisse," said Madame Josserand, "the situation is a grave one."

Then, in low, solemn tones, she explained what the situation was, telling of her daughter's deplorable misfortune, of Auguste's revolting greed, and of their painful obligation of having to pay the fifty thousand francs, so as to put a stop to this scandal which covered their family with shame. Then she said, severely :

"Remember what you promised, Narcisse. The night the contract was signed, you slapped your chest and again swore that Berthe might rely upon her uncle's kindness of heart. Well, where is that kindness of heart? The moment has come for you to give proof of it! Monsieur Josserand, join me in showing him what his duty is, if, in your ailing state, you can do so."

Deeply repugnant though it was to him, the father, from sheer love for his daughter, murmured :

"It is quite true; you did promise, Bachelard. Now, before I'm gone, do act like an honourable man."

Berthe and Hortense, however, hoping to soften their uncle, had filled his glass somewhat too frequently. So maudlin was his state, that they could no longer take advantage of it.

"Eh? what?" he stuttered, without needing to exaggerate his drunken air. "Never promise—don't know—least what you mean! Just tell me that again, Eléonore."

Accordingly Madame Josserand began anew, and made Berthe, sobbing, embrace him, begging him to keep his word for the sake of her sick husband, and proving to him that in giving the fifty thousand francs, he was fulfilling a sacred duty. Then, as he dropped off to sleep again, without apparently being affected in the least by the sight of the sick man or the mournful chamber, she suddenly broke out violently :

"Look here, Narcisse, this has gone on far too long; you're a regular blackguard! I have heard all about your swinish behaviour. You've married your mistress to Gueulin, and given them fifty thousand francs—the very sum that you promised us. Nice, isn't it? And that little beast of a Gueulin cuts a pretty figure, eh? As for you, you're far worse, for you take the very bread out of our mouths, and squander your fortune; aye, squander it, robbing us of money that was our due for the sake of that bitch!"

Never before had she vented her feelings to such an extent as this. To hide her embarrassment, Hortense had to busy herself with her father's medicine, while, wrought to fever-pitch by such a scene, the sick man tossed about restlessly on his pillows, as he tremblingly murmured:

"Eléonore, be quiet, I entreat you! He won't give anything. If you want to say all that to him, take him away, so that I mayn't hear you!

Berthe began to sob with greater vehemence as she joined in her father's entreaties.

"That'll do, mamma; for father's sake, do stop! Gracious me! how wretched I am at being the cause of all these quarrels! I'd much rather go away somewhere and die quietly!"

Then Madame Josserand bluntly put the question to Bachelard:

"Now, will you or will you not give the fifty thousand francs, so that your niece may hold her head up?"

In his bewilderment he sought to explain.

"Listen to me a moment. I caught Gueulin and Fifi together. What could I do? I had to marry them. It wasn't my fault!"

"Will you or will you not give the dowry that you promised to give?" she furiously reiterated.

His speech faltered, being, seemingly, so fuddled now that words failed him.

"Can't do it, 'pon m'honour, can't! Utterly ruined! Else I would, directly! Honour bright, I would!"

She cut him short with a terrible gesture.

"Very well!" she exclaimed, "I shall call a family council, and pronounce you incapable of managing your affairs. When uncles become doddering idiots, it's time to have them shut up in some asylum."

Hereupon Bachelard was at once greatly overcome. The room seemed to him very gloomy, with its one flickering lamp; he looked at the sick man, who, supported by his daughters, was about to swallow a spoonful of some black liquid, and he straightway burst into tears, accusing his sister of never having understood him. Gueulin's treachery had been quite grievous enough for him, he said. They knew how sensitive he was, and it was not right of them to ask him to dinner, and then harrow his feelings directly afterwards. Instead of the fifty-thousand francs, they could have every drop of blood in his veins; there, that was all he could say!

Utterly worn out, Madame Josserand gave up persecuting him when the maid announced Doctor Juillerat and the Abbé Mauduit. They had met on the stairs, and they came in together. The doctor found Monsieur Josserand much worse, for he was still upset by the scene in which he had had to play a part. As the abbé sought to take Madame Josserand into the drawing-room, having, as he said, a communication to make, she instinctively guessed whence he came, and majestically replied that she was in the bosom of her family and could bear to hear everything. The doctor himself would not be in the way, for a physician was a confessor as well.

"Then, madam," said the priest, with somewhat awkward gentleness, "what I am doing is, as you will see, actuated by an ardent wish to reconcile two families."

He spoke of God's pardon, and of his great delight at being able to reassure honest hearts by putting a stop to so intolerable a state of affairs. He alluded to Berthe as a wretched child, which drew from her fresh tears, and there was such fatherly tenderness in all he said, and his expressions were so carefully chosen, that Hortense was not obliged to leave the room. However, he had at last to touch on the subject of the fifty thousand francs. Husband and wife had, seemingly, only to kiss and be friends, when he mentioned the formal condition of the payment of the dowry.

"My dear abbé, excuse my interrupting you," said Madame Josserand, "we are deeply touched by your efforts. But the thing can never be, you understand! We can never traffic in our daughter's honour. Some people, too, have already made it up behind the child's back! Oh! I know all about it; they were first of all at daggers drawn, and now they're inseparable and abuse us from morning to night. No, my dear abbé, such a bargain as this would be disgraceful."

"But, madam," the priest ventured to observe, "it seems to me——"

She cut him short, as she went on, with glorious assurance:

"Listen! here's my brother, ask him what he thinks. Only a moment ago he said to me: 'Here, Eléonore, I've brought you the fifty thousand francs. Do settle this wretched business.' Well, just ask him what my answer was. Get up, Narcisse! Get up, and speak the truth!"

Bachelard had gone to sleep again in an armchair at the end of the room. He merely moved and uttered a few incoherent words. Then, as his sister continued to address him, he placed his hand on his heart, and stammered out:

"When, duty calls we must obey. Family before everything!"

"There, you hear what he says!" cried Madame Josserand, triumphantly. "No money! it's a disgrace! Just tell those people that we are not in the habit of dying to avoid having to pay. The dowry is here, and we should have paid it; only when it is exacted as the price of our daughter, the whole thing really becomes too disgusting. First let Auguste take Berthe back; then we'll see what can be done afterwards."

She had raised her voice to such a pitch that the doctor, examining his patient, had to tell her to be quiet.

"Gently, please, madam," he said. "Your husband is in pain."

Then, growing more embarrassed, the Abbé Mauduit approached the bed, and made a few sympathetic remarks. Hereupon he withdrew, without further allusion to the matter, hiding the confusion of his failure beneath a good-humoured smile, while his lip curled with vexation and disgust. As the doctor also went away he bluntly informed Madame Josserand that there was no hope; they ought to take the greatest possible care, as the least emotion might prove fatal. Appalled at the news, she went into the dining-room, whither Bachelard and the girls had gone, so as to leave Monsieur Josserand in peace, as he seemed inclined to go to sleep.

"Berthe," she murmured, "you've done for your father this time. The doctor has just told me so."

Then the three, sitting at the table, began to cry, while Bachelard, who also wept, mixed himself some grog.

When Auguste was told of the Josserands' reply he grew more furious than ever with his wife, and swore that he would kick her off if ever she came and asked his pardon. But, as a matter of fact, he missed her greatly. There was a void in his life, and with all these new worries in his solitude he seemed lost, for they were quite as serious as those of his married life. Rachel, whom, to vex Berthe, he had kept, robbed him and showed her bad temper now, being as coolly impudent as if she were his wife. He began to miss the many little pleasures of their dual life, the evenings of mutual boredom, following by costly reconciliations beneath warm sheets.

Above all things, he was heartily tired of Théophile and Valérie, who had installed themselves down below, and filled the whole shop with their importance. He even suspected them of casual tampering with the till in the most barefaced way. Valérie was not like Berthe; her delight was to sit enthroned at the cashier's desk, only, as it seemed to him, she had a way of attracting men, openly, under the very eyes of her imbecile husband, whose perpetual catarrh for ever made his eyes dim with tears. Thus he preferred Berthe. At least she never turned the shop into a thoroughfare for oglers. Then another thing worried him. "The Ladies' Paradise" was prospering, and threatened to rival his own business, where the takings grew daily less. True, he did not regret the loss of that wretched Octave; yet he was just, and fully recognised his excellent business capacities.

How smoothly things would have gone if only there had been a better sort of understanding! Moods of tenderness and regret assailed him, and there were moments when, sick of solitude, and finding life a blank, he felt as though he must go upstairs to the Josserands and take Berthe back from them for nothing.

Duveyrier, however, did not despair, but constantly urged Auguste to make matters up, being more and more grieved at the moral blemish which the whole affair had cast upon his property. He even effected to believe what Madame Josserand had told the abbé, that, if Auguste would take back his wife unconditionally, her dowry-money would be paid down the very next day. Then, if Auguste at such a proposal flew in a passion, the counsellor would appeal to his heart. He would walk with him along the quays, on his way to the Palais de Justice, preaching the doctrine of pardon for injuries in a voice half-choked with tears, endeavouring to imbue him with the philosophy, at once dismal and cowardly, which sees the only possible happiness in tolerating the wife since she may not be got rid of.

The whole of the Rue de Choisuel was depressed and uneasy at the sight of Duveyrier's lugubrious gait and pallid face, on which the red blotches grew larger and more inflamed. Some hidden grief seemed to be weighing him down. It was Clarisse who ever grew fatter, more insolent, and more presuming. In proportion as her middle-class plumpness increased, her fine-lady airs and affected good-breeding were to him the more insupportable. She now forbade him to address her familiarly when members of her family were present, though before his face she flirted in most outrageous fashion with her piano-teacher, to his uncontrollable grief. Twice had he caught her with Théodore, when, after storming, he begged her, on his knees, to pardon him, accepting whatever terms she chose to make. Then, with a view to keeping him docile and submissive, she would constantly express her disgust at his blotchy face; and she had even thought of handing him on to one of her cooks, a buxom wench accustomed to rough work of all sorts. However, the cook declined to have anything to do with her master. Thus, each day for Duveyrier life grew more and more bitter at the house of his mistress, which had become a vertitable hell. The tribe of parasites—the mother, the big blackguard of a brother, the two little sisters and the invalid aunt—robbed him right and left, sponging on him mercilessly, and even emptying his pockets at night when he was asleep. Other things helped to aggravate the situation; he was at his wits' end for money, and trembled at the thought of being compromised in his magisterial capacity. True, they could not dismiss him from his post; only young barristers looked at him roguishly, which embarrassed him when administering justice. And when, driven thence by the dirt and the noise, in self-disgust he fled from the Rue d'Assas and took refuge in the Rue de Choiseul, the hateful coldness of his wife served to exasperate him yet more. It was then that he would lose his head, glancing Seine-wards on his way to the court, being resolved to drown himself one night when emboldened thereto by some supreme touch of anguish.

Clotilde had, indeed, remarked her husband's nervous state with some anxiety, and she felt incensed at this mistress of his, who, despite her immoral conduct, still failed to make him happy. She for her part, was much annoyed by a deplorable incident, the consequences of which served to revolutionise the whole house. On going upstairs one morning to get a handkerchief, Clémence had caught Hippolyte and that little wretch Louise, on her own bed; since when she boxed his ears in the kitchen at the least provocation, which had a disastrous effect upon the other domestics. The worst of it was, that madame could no longer shut her eyes to the illicit relations that existed between her parlour-maid and her footman. The other servants laughed thereat; among the tradespeople the scandal was spreading, and if she wished to keep the guilty couple it was absolutely necessary to make them marry. Thus, as she still found Clémence a most satisfactory maid-servant, all her thoughts were set upon this marriage. To negotiate matters, however, seemed a somewhat delicate task, especially with lovers who were always scratching each other's eyes out; so she determined to entrust the

Abbé Mauduit therewith, for, under the circumstances, he seemed to be marked out for the part of moral mediator. For some time past, indeed, her servants had caused her great anxiety. When in the country, she had become aware of the intrigue between her big lout of a son Gustave and Julie. At first she thought of dismissing the latter, regretfully indeed, for she liked her cooking. Then, after much sage reflection, she kept her on, preferring that the young cub should have a mistress in her own house—a decent girl, who would never make herself objectionable. Elsewhere, one never could tell what sort of woman a lad got hold of, especially when, as in this instance, he started all too early. So she kept her eye upon them, without saying anything and now the other two must needs come and plague her with their wretched affair.

One morning it so happened that as Madame Duveyrier was about to go and see the Abbé Mauduit, Clémence informed her that the priest was just on his way to administer the Sacrament to Monsieur Josserand. The maid, being on the staircase, had crossed the pathway of the Holy Ghost, and hastened back to the kitchen, exclaiming :

"I knew that He would come back again this year !"

Then, alluding to the various mischances which had befallen the various inmates of the house, she added :

"That brought us all bad luck !"

This time the Holy Ghost had not come too late—an excellent portent for the future. Madame Duveyrier hastened to Saint-Roch, where she awaited the priest's return. He listened to her, sadly, silently; and then could not refuse to enlighten the footman and the chamber-maid as to the immorality of their actual position. Besides, he would have to get back to the Rue de Choiseul very shortly, as poor Monsieur Josserand could surely never live through the night; and he hinted that in this circumstance, distressing though it was, there lay the possibility of a reconciliation between Auguste and Berthe. He would endeavour to arrange both matters at one and the same time. It was high time that the Almighty gave their efforts His blessing.

"I have prayed, madam," said the priest. "The Lord God will triumph."

That evening, indeed, at seven o'clock, Monsieur Josserand's death-agony began. All the family had assembled except uncle Bachelard (whom they had sought vainly in all the cafés) and Saturnin, who was still in the Asile des Moulineau. Léon, whose marriage, owing to his father's illness, had unfortunately to be postponed, showed a dignified grief, while Madame Josserand and Hortense bore up bravely. Only Berthe it was who sobbed so loud that, out of consideration to the sufferer, she escaped to the kitchen, where Adéle, profiting by the general muddle, was drinking mulled claret. However, Monsieur Josserand died very quietly—a victim to his own honesty of heart. He had lived a useless life, and he went hence, like an honest wight, weary of all life's petty ills, done to death by the heartless conduct of the only human beings that he had ever loved. At eight o'clock he stammered out Saturnin's name; then, turning his face to the wall, he expired.

No one thought that he was dead, for all had feared a long and dreadful death-struggle. They waited awhile, letting him sleep. But, on finding that he was already cold, Madame Josserand, amid the general sobbing, began to scold Hortense, whom she had charged to fetch Auguste, thinking to have given Berthe back to him just as the sufferer was about to expire.

"You never think of anything!" she exclaimed, wiping her eyes.

"But, mamma," said the girl, weeping, "we none of us thought papa was going to die so soon! You told me not to go down and fetch Auguste before nine o'clock, so as to make sure that he was there at the end!"

This wrangle helped to divert the family in their grief. Another thing that had gone wrong! Somehow, they never managed to get anything done! Fortunately, though, there was the funeral, which might serve to reconcile husband and wife.

The funeral was fairly well-appointed, yet not on so grand a scale as Monsieur Vabre's. Nor did it create nearly as much interest either in the house or in the neighbourhood, for Monsieur Josserand was not a landlord, but merely an easy-going old soul whose death had not even troubled the slumber of Madame Juzeur. Marie, who the day before had been hourly expecting her confinement, was the only one who said how sorry she was not to be able to help the ladies in laying the poor old gentleman out. Downstairs Madame Gourd thought it sufficient to stand up and bow from her room as the coffin passed, without coming to the door. Everybody, however, went to the cemetery; Duveyrier, Campardon, the Vabres, and Monsieur Gourd. They talked about the spring and how the crops had been affected by the recent heavy rains. Campardon was surprised to see Duveyrier looking so ill; and noticing his ghastly pallor as the coffin was lowered into the grave, the architect whispered:

"Now he's smelt churchyard mould. God save our house from further bereavements!"

Madame Josserand and her daughters had to be supported as far as their coach. Léon, with uncle Bachelard's help, proved most attentive, while Auguste walked sheepishly in the rear, and got into another carriage with Duveyrier and Théophile. Clotilde went with the Abbé Mauduit, who had not officiated, but put in an appearance at the cemetery so as to give the mourners a proof of his sympathy.

The horses set off homewards more gaily; and Madame Duveyrier at once begged the priest to come back to the house with them, deeming the moment a favourable one. So he consented.

The three mourning coaches silently deposited the sorrowing relatives at the Rue de Choiseul. Théophile at once went back to Valérie, who, as the shop was shut, had stopped at home to superintend a grand cleaning-up.

"You can pack up your things," he furiously exclaimed. "They are all egging him on. I'll bet you what you like that he'll beg her pardon!"

They all, as a matter of fact, felt the urgent necessity of putting an end to this deplorable business. It was an ill wind that blew nobody good. Auguste, in their midst, could easily see what it was they wanted. There he sat alone, strengthless and confused. One by one the mourners slowly passed in under the porch, hung with black. No one spoke. On the staircase the silence was unbroken, a silence fraught with deep cogitation as the crape petticoats sadly and softly went up the stairs. In a last attempt at revolt, Auguste hurried on ahead, intending to shut himself up in his own rooms, but Clotilde and the abbé, who had followed him, detained him just as he was opening the door. Behind them, on the landing, stood Berthe, in deep mourning, accompanied by her mother and her sister. The eyes of all three were red; Madame Josserand's condition was, indeed, quite distressing to behold.

"Come, now, my friend," said the priest, simply, with tears in his eyes.

That was enough. Auguste at once gave in, aware that there was no fitter moment than this in which to make his peace. His wife wept, and he wept also as he stammered:

"Come along!" repeated Auguste, quite unnerved.

Then there was general kissing, while Clotilde congratulated her brother, saying that she had fully relied upon his kindness of heart.

Madame Josserand displayed a sort of disconsolate satisfaction, as that of a widow whom unlooked-for joys may no longer touch. And with their happiness she linked her poor dead husband's name.

"You are doing your duty, my dear son-in-law. He who has gone to heaven thanks you for this."

"Come along!" repeated Auguste, quite unnerved.

Hearing a noise, however, Rachel came out into the hall, and, noticing the maid's mute look of rage, Berthe momentarily hesitated. Then she sternly passed in, and her black mourning dress disappeared in the gloom. Auguste followed her, and the door closed behind them.

All along the staircase there floated a deep sigh of relief; it filled the whole house with joy. The ladies shook their pastor by the hand; God had answered his prayers. Just as Clotilde was taking him along with her to settle the other matter, Duveyrier, who had stopped behind with Léon and Bachelard, came wearily up. They had to explain the good news to him, yet he hardly seemed to understand, though for months past he had been wishing for it. His face wore a strange expression, as if he were haunted and overcome by one idea. As the Josserands went back to their flat, he followed his wife and the abbé. They were still in the hall when the sound of stifled screams made them tremble.

"Don't be alarmed, madam," explained Hippolyte, complacently. "It's the little lady upstairs what is took bad. I saw Doctor Juillerat run up just now." Then, when alone, he philosophically added: "One goes, t'other comes."

Clotilde took the abbé into the drawing-room, and, bidding him be seated, said that she would send Clémence to him first. To while away the time, she gave him a copy of the *Revue des Deux Mondes,* in which there were some really charming verses. She must first of all prepare her maid for what was coming. But in the dressing-room she found her husband seated on a chair.

Ever since the morning Duveyrier had been in a state of agony. For the third time he had caught Clarisse with Théodore, and when he protested all her parasite relatives—mother, brother, and little sisters—had fallen foul of him, driving him downstairs with kicks and blows, while Clarisse grossly abused him, threatening in her fury to send for the police if ever he dared set foot in her place again. It was all over; the hall-porter had told him downstairs that for the past week a rich old fellow had offered to provide a comfortable home for madame. Being thus driven away, with never a snug corner to call his own, Duveyrier, after wandering about the streets, went into an out-of-the-way shop and bought a small revolver. Life for him had become too sad; he had better leave it at the first opportunity. It was the search for some quiet place which preoccupied him thus, as mechanically he went back to the Rue de Choiseul to attend Monsieur Josserand's funeral. On the way to the grave he conceived the notion of suicide in the cemetery; he would withdraw to a secluded spot behind a tombstone. This appealed to his sense for the romantic, to his yearning for a tender ideal—a yearning that made all his stiff matter-of-fact existence dreary and a wreck. But as the coffin was lowered into the grave he began to quake in every limb, shuddering at the chill churchyard mould. This was certainly not the right place; he must find one somewhere else. Then, coming home more distressed than ever, haunted by this one idea, he sat meditating on a chair in the dressing-room, trying to choose the best place in the house—the bedroom, perhaps, near the bed, or here in the dressing-room, just where he was.

"Would you be good enough to leave me alone?" said Clotilde to him.

He had already got the revolver in his pocket.

"Why?" asked he, speaking with difficulty.

"Because I want to be alone."

He thought she wanted to change her dress, and would no longer even let him see her bare arms, so great was her disgust for him. For a moment, blear-eyed, he looked at her, standing there so tall and beautiful, her complexion the hue of marble and her hair bound up in burnished coils. Ah, had she but consented, how all might have been arranged! Tottering forward, he stretched out his arms and sought to embrace her.

"What is it?" she murmured, in surprise. "What can have possessed you? Not here, surely? Have you not got the other person any longer? So that beastliness has to begin again, has it?"

So great seemed her disgust that he recoiled. Without another word, he went out into the hall, where he stopped for a moment. A door faced him—the door of the water-closet. He pushed it open, and leisurely sat down on the seat. This was a quiet place, where nobody would come and disturb him. Putting the barrel of the revolver into his mouth, he pulled the trigger.

Meanwhile Clotilde, who all the morning had felt uneasy at his strange manner, listened to see if he was going to do her the favour of going back to Clarisse. As the creak peculiar to that door told her where he had gone, she gave no further heed to him, but rang for Clémence, when the dull report of a pistol started her. What could it be? It was just like the report of a revolver. She ran out into the hall, not daring at first to ask him what was the matter. Then, as a strange gurgling sound came from within, she called to him, and getting no answer pulled the door open. It was not even bolted. Duveyrier, stunned by fright more than by actual pain, was huddled up on the seat in a woebegone posture, his eyes wide open, and with blood streaming from his face. The bullet had missed its mark, after grazing his jaw, had passed through the left cheek. He had not pluck enough left to fire a second shot.

"So that's what you've been about in there, is it?" cried Clotilde, beside herself with rage. "Why don't you go outside and shoot yourself?"

She was indignant. Instead of unnerving her, the whole scene utterly exasperated her. Catching hold of him, she roughly pushed him out, endeavouring to get him away from such a place before anybody saw him. In the closet! And to miss the mark, too. That really was too much!

Then, as, holding him up, she led him back to the bedroom, Duveyrier, half choked with blood, kept spitting out his teeth, as he gurgled:

"You never loved me!"

And he burst into tears, bewailing his lost ideals and the little blue flower of romance that it had never been his lot to pluck. When Clotilde had got him to bed, she at last broke down also, as her anger gave way to hysterics. The worst of it was that both Clémence and Hippolyte came to answer the bell. At first she told them it was an accident, that their master had fallen down on his chin; but this fabulous account she was soon obliged to abandon, for when the manservant went to wipe up the blood on the seat, he found the revolver, which had fallen behind the little broom. Meanwhile, the wounded man was losing a deal of blood, and the maid suddenly remembered that Doctor Juillerat was upstairs at Madame Pichon's confinement, so she ran out and caught him on the stairs as he was coming down after a most successful delivery. The doctor instantly reassured Clotilde; possibly there might be some disfigurement of the jaw, but there was no danger whatever. He hastily proceeded to dress the wound, amid basins of water and bloodstained rags, when the Abbé Mauduit, alarmed at all the commotion, ventured to enter the room.

"Whatever has happened?" he asked.

This question sufficed to upset Madame Duveyrier. At the first words of explanation she burst into tears. The priest, indeed, had guessed all, knowing as he did all the secret troubles of his flock. Already, in the drawing-room there, despondency had seized him, and he felt half sorry at his success in having once more joined that wretched young woman to her husband, without her showing the least sign of contrition. Awful doubts assailed him; maybe God was not with him, after all. His anguish only increased as he saw Duveyrier's fractured jaw. Approaching him, he was about to denounce suicide in the most fervent manner, when the doctor, busy with his bandaging, pushed him aside.

"Wait a bit, my dear abbé! Don't you see that he has fainted?"

Indeed, no sooner had the doctor touched him, than Duveyrier became unconscious. Then Clotilde, to get rid of the servants, who were no longer of any use, and whose staring eyes disconcerted her greatly, murmured, as she dried her eyes:

"Go into the drawing-room. The Abbé Mauduit has something to say to you."

The priest had to take them thither—another disagreeable task. Hippolyte and Clémence, vastly surprised, followed him. When they were alone, he began by a series of vague exhortations; Heaven rewarded good conduct, while one sin alone was enough to bring one to hell. Besides, it was high time to put a stop to a scandal, and think of saving one's soul. While thus he harangued them, their surprise changed to utter bewilderment. With arms hanging down, she, with her slight figure and screwed-up mouth, and he, with his flat face and hulking limbs, exchanged mutual glances of alarm. Had madame found some of her napkins upstairs in a trunk? Or was it because of the bottle of wine which they took up with them every night?

"My children," quoth the priest, in conclusion, "you are setting a bad example. The greatest sin of all is to corrupt others—to bring one's own household into disrepute. Yes, you are living in a disorderly way, which, alas! is no secret to anyone, for you have been fighting with each other for a whole week."

He blushed; a certain prudish hesitation made him pick his words. The two servants heaved sighs of relief. They smilingly drew themselves up, quite perky and gleeful. So that was all! They needn't have been in such a funk.

"But it's all over, sir," declared Clémence, giving Hippolyte a look as of a woman reconquered. "We have made it up. Yes—he explained how it was."

The priest, in his turn, seemed amazed and grieved.

"You do not understand me, my children. You cannnot go on living together like this; it is an offence to God and man. You must get married."

At once their look of astonishment came back. Get married? What was that for?

"I don't want to," said Clémence. "I've no idea of such a thing."

Then the abbé tried to convince Hippolyte.

"Look here, my good fellow, you're a man; so persuade her to do so; tell her that her reputation is——It won't alter your life in any way. You must get married."

The servant laughed a waggish, awkward laugh. At length, surveying the tips of his boots, he blurted out:

"That's quite right; I daresay we ought; but I am married already."

This reply soon cut the cleric's moralising short. Without another word, he stowed away his arguments, and put God back again, as useless, into his pocket, distressed at having sought to invoke Divine aid to suppress such barefaced debauchery as this. Clotilde, who now joined him, had overheard their talk, and, with one gesture, she let out all. In obedience to her orders, the footman and maid left the room one after the other, chuckling inwardly, though apparently very grave. After a pause, the abbé bitterly complained. Why expose him in this fashion? Why stir up things that were best left alone? Now the situation was absolutely scandalous. But Clotilde repeated her gesture. So much the worse; she had other worries now. However, she certainly could not dismiss the servants, lest the whole neighbourhood should get to know the story of the suicide that very evening. Later on they must see what could be done.

"Now, recollect; he must have absolute rest," enjoined the doctor, as he was leaving the room. "He will soon be all right again, but he must on no account be subjected to the slightest fatigue. Don't lose heart, madam." Then, turning to the priest: "You shall preach him a sermon later on, my dear abbé, I can't give him up to you just yet. If you're returning to Saint-Roch, I'll accompany you, and we'll go back together."

They both went downstairs together.

Gradually the whole house regained its calm. Madame Juzeur had loitered about the cemetery, trying to make Trublot flirt with her as they together deciphered the inscriptions on the gravestones, and, albeit indisposed for fruitless philandering of this sort, he had to drive her back in a cab to the Rue de Choiseul. Louise's sad experience deeply grieved the good lady. At their journey's end she was still talking about the wretched girl, whom yesterday she had sent back to the home for destitute children. It was a bitter experience for her, a final disillusion, which bereft her of all hope that she would ever get a respectable maidservant. Then, at the door, she asked Trublot to come and see her sometimes and have a chat. But his excuse was that he was always so busy.

At this moment the other Madame Campardon went by. They bowed to her. Monsieur Gourd informed them of Madame Pichon's successful accouchement, when they all shared the opinion of Monsieur and Madame Vuillaume—three children for a mere clerk was sheer madness; and the porter hinted, moreover, that, if there were a fourth baby, the landlord would give them notice, as too many children about a house did not look well. At this they were silent, when a lady, wearing a veil and leaving behind her a faint scent of verbena, passed swiftly through the vestibule, without speaking to Monsieur Gourd, who pretended not to see her. That morning he had got everything ready in the distinguished gentleman's apartment on the third floor, preparatory to a night of work.

He had hardly time, however, to call out to the other two:

"Look out! They'll run over us as if we were dogs!"

It was the second-floor people driving past in their carriage. The horses pranced under the vaulted doorway, and, leaning back in the landau, the father and mother smiled at their two pretty fair-haired children, each struggling to possess a large bunch of roses.

"What queer folk, to be sure!" muttered the porter, furiously. "They never even went to the funeral, for fear of seeming to be as polite as anybody else. They splash you from head to foot, and yet, if one liked to talk——"

"What then?" asked Madame Juzeur, greatly interested.

Then Monsieur Gourd told how they had had a visit from the police—yes, the police! The second-floor tenant had written such a filthy novel that they were going to imprison him at Mazas.

"Horrible stuff!" he went on in accents of disgust. "It's full of all the beastliness that gentry do. They do say our landlord is took off in it—yes, Monsieur Duveyrier, his very self. Pretty good nerve, eh? Ah, it's well for them they keeps themselves to themselves, and don't visit any other tenants; We know now the sort of stuff they make, in spite of all their stand-off airs. Yet, you see, they can afford to keep their carriage, as their filth is worth its weight in gold!"

It was this reflection which above everything exasperated Monsieur Gourd. Madame Juzeur only read poetry, while Trublot admitted that he was not well versed in literature. Yet, as both censured the novelist for smirching by his books the very house in which he and his family dwelt, they suddenly heard wild shrieks, which came from the far end of the courtyard.

"Go on, you great cow! You were glad enough to have me when your lovers had to be hidden! You understand me right enough, you cow."

It was Rachel, whom Berthe had sent to the right-about, and who was now giving vent to her feelings on the servant's staircase. All of a sudden this quiet, respectful girl, whom the other servants could never get to gossip, broke out into this rabid fit of fury. It was like the bursting of a sewer. Incensed at madame's return to monsieur, whom since the estrangement she had calmly plundered, Rachel looked very wicked when told to fetch a commissionaire, who was to remove her box. Berthe, aghast, stood listening in the kitchen, while Auguste, with an air of authority, remained at the door, and received all this revolting abuse full in his face.

"Yes, yes!" the infuriated maidservant went on, "you never kicked me out when I used to hide your chemises, so that your cuckold of a husband shouldn't see them! No, nor that night when your lover had to put on his socks in my kitchen, while I prevented your cuckold of a husband from coming in. Ah, you bitch! get out with you!"

Berthe rushed away in disgust. But Auguste was obliged to show a bold front, as, pale and trembling, he heard all these nauseous revelations bawled out at him on the back-stairs. He could only exclaim:

"Wretched woman! wretched woman!"

It was the sole word available to express his pain at learning all these crude details of his wife's adultery, at the very moment that he had condoned it. Meanwhile all the servants had come out of their kitchens, and, leaning over the railings, lost not a single word. Even they were amazed at Rachel's fury. By degrees they withdrew, appalled by the whole scene, which was positively beyond all bounds. Lisa echoed the general sentiment when she remarked:

"Well, well! talking's one thing; but one shouldn't pitch into gentry that way."

Thus everyone slipped away, leaving the girl to vent her wrath by herself, for it became unpleasant to have to listen to all these horrid things, which made everybody uncomfortable, the more so as she now began to abuse the whole house. Monsieur Gourd was the first to withdraw to his room, observing that nothing could be done with a woman when she was in a temper.

Shocked beyond measure at these ruthless disclosures, Madame Juzeur seemed so upset, that Trublot, greatly against his wish, was obliged to see her safely to her own apartment, lest she might faint. Wasn't it unfortunate? Matters had been nicely arranged; there was no longer the least ground for scandal; the house was relapsing into its former dreamy respectability; and now this horrid person must needs go and rake up matters that had been forgotten, and about which nobody cared now!

"I'm only a servant, it's true, but I'm respectable," she screamed with all her might, "and there's not one of you bloody genteel bitches as can say the same in this God-damned house. Don't you worry; I'm going, for you all make me sick, you do!"

The abbé and Doctor Juillerat quietly came down stairs. They had heard all this, too. Then came a great calm; the courtyard was empty, the staircase deserted. The doors seemed hermetically sealed; not a window-blind stirred; each flat seemed shrouded in majestic silence.

In the doorway the priest stopped, as if exhausted.

"What miseries!" murmured he, sadly.

The doctor, nodding, answered:

"Such is life!"

Remarks of this sort they were wont to make as they came away together from the chamber of birth or of death. Despite their opposite beliefs, they occasionally agreed upon the subject of human frailty. Both were sharers of the selfsame secrets; if the priest heard the ladies' confessions, the doctor, for the last thirty years, had attended the mothers in their confinements while prescribing for the daughters.

"God had forsaken them," said the abbé.

"No," replied the doctor; "don't drag God into it. It's a question of bad health or bad training, that's all."

Then, going off at a tangent, he began violently to abuse the Empire; under a republic things would surely be better. And amid all this rambling talk, the flighty speech of a man of mediocre intelligence, there came the just remarks of the experienced physician thoroughly cognisant of all his patients' weak points. He did not spare the women, some of whom were brought up as dolls and made either corrupt or crazy thereby, while others had their sentiments and passions perverted by hereditary neurosis, who, if they sinned, sinned vulgarly, foolishly, without desire as without pleasure. Nor was he less merciful to the men—fellows who merely ruined their constitutions whilst hypocritically pretending to lead sober, virtuous, and godly lives. And in all this Jacobin frenzy one heard, as it were, the inexorable death-knell of a whole class, the collapse and putrefaction of the bourgeoisie, whose rotten props kept cracking of themselves.

Then, getting out of his depth again, he spoke of the barbarous age, and foretold an era of universal bliss.

"I am really far more religious than you are," quoth he, in conclusion.

The priest appeared to be listening silently. But he heard nothing, being completely absorbed in his own mournful meditations. After a pause, he murmured :

"If unconscious of their sin, may Heaven have mercy upon them !"

Then, leaving the house, they walked slowly along the Rue Neuve-Saint-Augustin. Fear that they had said too much kept them silent; it behoved each of them to be discreet. At the end of the street they spied Madame Hédouin, who smiled at them from the door of "The Ladies' Paradise." Octave stood close behind her, and smiled too. That very morning, after serious talk, they had decided to get married. They were going to wait until the autumn. And they were both very glad that the matter had at last been settled.

"Good-day, my dear abbé," said Madame Hédouin, gaily. "Always on the trot, eh, doctor?"

And as he told her how well she was looking, she added :

"Ah, if you'd only got me as a patient, you wouldn't do much business !"

They stood chatting for a moment. When the doctor mentioned Marie's accouchement, Octave seemed glad to know that his quondam neighbour had got over it safely. And when he heard that number three was a girl too, he exclaimed :

"So her husband can't manage to knock a boy out of her, eh? She was in hopes of getting Monsieur and Madame Vuillaume to put up with a boy; but they'll never stand another girl."

"I shouldn't think they would," said the doctor. "They've both gone to bed, so upset are they by the news. And they have sent for a notary so that their daughter may not inherit a stick of their furniture even."

Then there was more joking. Only the priest was silent, and kept his eyes on the pavement. Madame Hédouin asked if he were unwell. Yes, he was very tired; he was going to rest for a little while. Then, after cordial greetings, he walked down the Rue Saint-Roch, still accompanied by the doctor.

At the church-door the latter abruptly said : "Bad sort of patient that, eh?"

"Who?" asked the abbé, in surprise.

"Why, the lady who sells the calico. She don't care a damn for either of us. No religion wanted there, nor physic either. There's not much to be got out of folk like that, who are always well!"

With that he went off, while the abbé entered the church.

A bright light fell through the broad windows with their white panes edged with yellow and pale blue. No sound, no movement in the deserted nave; marble facings, crystal chandeliers, and gilded pulpit, all slumbered in the peaceful light. It might have been, in its drowsy quietude, some middle-class drawing-room, when the furniture covers have been removed for some grand evening party. Only a woman, in front of the chapel of Our Lady of the Seven Dolours, stood watching the tapers as, guttering, they emitted an odour of melted wax.

The abbé thought of going straight up to his room. Yet, so great was his agitation that he felt impelled to enter the church and remain there. It was as if God called to him, vaguely and in a far-off voice, so that he could not rightly hear the summons. He slowly crossed the church, striving to read the thoughts that arose within him and allay his fears, when suddenly, as he passed behind the choir, an unearthly sight set all his frame a-tremble. Behind the lily-white marble of the Lady chapel and the chapel of the Adoration, agleam with its seven golden lamps, golden candelabra, and golden altar glittering in the aureate light from gold-stained windows, there in this mystic gloom, beyond this tabernacle, he saw a tragic apparition, the enactment of a drama, harrowing yet simple. It was Christ nailed to the cross between the Virgin and Mary Magdalene, who wept at His feet. The white statues lighted from above, and so set in bold relief against the bare wall, moved forward, seemingly, grew greater, making this human tragedy in its blood and tears the divine symbol of eternal sorrow.

Utterly overcome, the priest fell upon his knees. It was he who had whitened that plaster, contrived that method of lighting, and prepared so appalling a scene. Now that the hoarding was removed and architect and workmen gone, he it was who first was to be thunderstruck at the sight. From that Calvary, austere and terrible, there came a breath that smote him to earth. It seemed as if God swept past his face, and he bowed beneath the breath of His nostrils, tortured by doubts, by the hideous thought that possibly he was a wicked priest.

Oh, Lord! had the hour come when no longer all the sores of this festering world might be hidden by the mantle of religion? Should he no longer help the hypocrisy of his flock, nor always be there, like some master of the ceremonies, to regulate its vices and its follies? Should he let all collapse, even at the risk of burying the church itself in the ruins? Yes, such was his behest, no doubt, for the strength to probe human misery yet deeper was forsaking him, and he yielded in utter impotence and disgust. All the nauseous evils with which that morning he had come in contact seemed to choke him, and with outstretched hands he craved pardon—pardon for his lies, forgiveness for his base complacency and infamous time-serving. Dread of God's wrath seized hold of his vitals; he seemed to see God disowning him, forbidding him to take His name in vain, a jealous God bent upon the utter destruction of the guilty. All his worldly airs of toleration vanished before such reckless stabs of conscience. All that remained to him was the faith of the believer—a faith, shaken, terror-struck, struggling in its uncertainty of salvation. Oh, Lord God! what road should he take? What should he do amid this festering society, which brought infection even to its priests?

Then the Abbé Mauduit, as he gazed up at the Calvary, burst into tears. He wept, just as the Virgin and Mary Magdalene wept; he wept for truth which was dead, for heaven which was void. Beyond the marble walls and gleaming jewelled altars, the huge plaster Christ had not in its veins one single drop of blood.

XVIII

It was in December, after she had been in mourning for eight months, that Madame Josserand for the first time consented to dine out. The Duveyriers had invited her, so it was almost a family dinner, to celebrate the recommencement of Clotilde's Saturday "At Homes." On the previous day, Adèle had been told that she would have to go down and help Julie with the washing-up. When giving parties, these good ladies were wont to lend each other their servants in this way.

"Now, above all things, try and put some go into you," was Madame Josserand's advice to her maid. "I can't imagine what has come to you lately. You're as limp as a rag. Yet you're round and plump enough."

The fact was, Adèle was nine months gone with child. For a long while she thought she was getting stouter, and this astonished her somewhat. Famished as she always was, it enraged her when madame triumphantly pointed to her before all her guests, remarking that if anyone accused her of doling out food to her servant they might come and see what a great glutton she was, whose belly had never got as round as that by licking the walls, eh? When the dull-witted girl was, at last, aware of her misfortune, she was often within an ace of telling her mistress the whole truth, who thus took advantage of her condition to make all the neighbours believe that she was feeding her up, after all.

From that moment, however, she became besotted by fear. Within her dullard brain surged up all the crude fancies of her native village. She believed herself lost, that the gendarmes would come and carry her off, if she confessed that she were pregnant. Then all her low cunning was employed to hide her condition. Her intolerable headaches, nausea, and terrible constipation she was careful to conceal, though more than once, when mixing sauces at the fire, she thought she was going to drop down dead. Fortunately, it was her flanks that grew big, and her belly, though widening, did not stick out too much, so that madame never suspected anything when exultant at her astounding plumpness. Moreover, the wretched wench squeezed in her waist till she could scarcely breathe. Her belly seemed to her fairly well-proportioned, though, all the same it was awfully heavy when she was scrubbing her kitchen. The last two months had been months of dreadful pain, borne in stubborn and heroic silence.

That night Adèle went up to bed about eleven o'clock. The thought of to-morrow's dinner-party terrified her. More slavery and more bullying from Julie! And she could hardly stand; her limbs were all to pieces! Yet her confinement seemed to her vague and remote, as yet; she preferred not to think about it. She'd rather carry that for a good while longer, hoping that, somehow, she might get all right again. Nor had she made the slightest preparation, being ignorant of any symptoms, incapable of recollecting or of calculating a date, devoid of any idea, any plan. She was only comfortable when she was in bed, lying on her back. As it had been freezing since the previous day, she kept her stockings on, blew out her candle, and waited until she could get warm. At length she fell asleep. All at once slight pains caused her to open her eyes—faint twinges, as if a bee were stinging her close to her navel. Then the pricking pains ceased; and they caused her little discomfort, used as she was to all the strange, unaccountable things which went on inside her. Yet suddenly, after half-an-hour's uneasy sleep, a dull throb woke her up again. This time she grew quite angry. Was she going to have the stomach-ache? How fit she'd feel next day, if all night long she would have to be running to the po! All that evening she had been thinking that what she wanted was a good clear-out; her stomach was so tense and heavy. Yet she would stave if off, and, rubbing her belly, believed that she had soothed the pains. But in a quarter of an hour they returned with greater violence.

"Blast it all!" she muttered, under her breath, as she determined to get up this time.

Groping about in darkness for the pot, she squatted down, and exhausted herself by fruitless efforts. The room was icy cold; her teeth chattered. In ten minutes' time the pains ceased, and she got back into bed. But soon they returned. Again she rose, and again she tried, without success, going back to bed chilled through, where she enjoyed a moment's rest. Then so violent was the pain that she stifled a first cry. What humbug it was! Did she want to do something or did she not? Now the pains became persistent, almost perpetual, and more excruciating—as if some hand had ruthlessly gripped her belly from within. Then she understood; and shivering beneath the coverlet, she muttered :

"Good God! good God! That's what it is!"

Birth-pangs tortured her; she felt obliged to get up and walk about in her agony. She could no longer stop in bed; so she lighted her candle and began to pace up and down the room. Her tongue grew parched, burning thirst overcame her, while her cheeks grew red as fire. When some sudden spasm bent her double she leant against the wall and caught hold of the back of a chair. Thus, in this pitiless tramping up and down, the hours passed; while she never dared put on her boots for fear of making a noise. Her only protection from the cold was an old shawl, which she wrapped round her shoulders. Two o'clock struck; then three o'clock.

"There's no such thing as God!" she muttered, as if impelled to talk to herself—to hear the sound of her own voice. "It's too long; it'll never be over!"

The first stage of parturition had, however, been reached; the weight lay now in her hips and her thighs. And, when her belly gave her a moment's respite, she felt there a perpetual gnawing pain. In order to get relief she grasped her hips with both hands, and supported them thus while she swayed about barelegged, with only coarse stockings on up to her knees. No, there was no such thing as God! Religion disgusted her; her patience, her brute submission, which hitherto had made her bear her pregnancy as merely one more misery, forsook her. So it wasn't enough to be starved to death, and the dirty drudge which everybody bullied; but her masters must needs get her with child as well! Filthy brutes! She couldn't say if it was the young one or the old one that had done it. However, neither of them cared a damn; they had got their pleasure, while she had to smart for it! If she went and had her baby on their doormat, wouldn't they just stare! Then her old fears came back; she would be put in prison; it was best to say nothing. And between two spasms she kept repeating in a choked voice :

"Dirty beasts! How dared they let me in for all this! Oh, my God! I'm going to die!"

And, with hands clenched, she pressed her hips with greater vigour, her poor aching hips, stifling her cries of pain as she rocked from side to side. Next door no one stirred; everybody was snoring; she could hear Julie's sonorous trumpeting, while Lisa's breathing sounded shrill and sibilant as a fife.

Four o'clock struck, when suddenly she thought that her belly had burst. During one of the spasms there had been a rupture of some kind, followed by a flow of liquid, which trickling down, soaked her stockings. For a moment she remained motionless, terror-struck, stupefied, thinking that perhaps in this way she would get rid of her burden. Perhaps she had never been pregnant, after all. Then, fearing she had some other malady, she looked at herself to see if all the blood in her body were not running away. Feeling somewhat relieved, she sat down for a few moments on her trunk. The mess on the floor worried her; and the flickering candle was on the point of going out. Then unable to walk about, and aware that the crisis was near, she had just sufficient strength left to spread out on the bed an old piece of oil cloth that Madame Josserand had given her as a toilet-cover. Hardly had she lain down than the process of expulsion began.

For nearly an hour and a half the pains assailed her continually and with increasing violence. The internal spasms had ceased; she it was who now with all the muscular force of her loins and belly kept straining to free her frame from this intolerable weight. Each fresh effort was accompanied by shivering her face grew burning hot, perspiration broke out on her neck, whilst she bit the bed-clothes to stifle her groaning, that sounded like the grim, involuntary grasp of a woodcutter who fells an oak. After each effort to expel she murmured as if addressing someone :

"It is'nt possible! It'll never come out. It's too big."

With tumbled breasts and legs wide apart, she clutched hold of the iron bedstead, which, with her struggling, shook again. Happily it was a splendid accouchement, a cranial presentation of the normal sort. The head as it emerged kept slipping back again, sucked in by the elasticity of the surrounding tissues that were dilated to cracking point, while as the travail proceeded, excruciating cramps begirt her as with a girdle of iron. At last her bones cracked; everything seemed going to pieces. An awful feeling came over her that her bottom and belly had burst, forming one hole through which her life was ebbing away; and then between her thighs the child rolled out on to the bed in a pool of viscous bloody evacuations.

Loud was the cry she uttered, the wild triumphant cry of a mother. At once folk in the adjoining rooms began to move, while drowsy voices asked, "Hullo?—What's up?—Some one being murdered or outraged?—Don't shout out in your sleep like that!"

Alarmed, she thrust the blanket between her teeth, squeezed her thighs together, and pulled up the coverlet over the baby, which cried plaintively like a little kitten. Soon she could hear Julie snoring again after turning over in bed; Lisa was asleep once more; her shrill breathing had ceased. Then for about a quarter of an hour she felt indescribable relief, a sense of infinite calm and repose. She lay there as one dead, as one glad to give up life.

All at once colic seized her again. She woke in a fright. Was she going to have another? On opening her eyes she found herself in pitch darkness. Not even a tiny bit of candle! There she lay, all by herself, in a pool, with something slimy between her thighs that she did not know what to do with. There were doctors for dogs, but not for such as she. She and her brat might kick, for all anyone cared. She remembered having lent a hand when Madame Pichon, the lady opposite, was confined. Ought she to be careful not to kill the youngster? It was not crying now. She stretched out her hand and caught hold of a cord that hung out of her belly. Dimly she seemed to recollect having seen this cut and tied in a knot. Her eyes had got used to the gloom; the garret was now dimly lighted by the rising moon. Then, groping about blindly, impelled thereto by instinct, without rising, she performed a tedious and painful operation. Pulling down an apron from a hook behind her, she tore off one of its strings, tied the cord in a knot, and cut it with a pair of scissors which she got out of the pocket of her skirt. The effort threw her in a perspiration and she lay down again. Poor little thing! she didn't want to kill it, not she!

The griping pains continued. Something uncomfortable was still there which, with straining, might be expelled. She tugged at the cord, first gently, then with all her might. Something was coming away; it fell out in a great lump, and she got rid of it by throwing it into the po. Thank goodness, this time it was over and she would not suffer any more! Tepid blood trickled down her legs.

She must have dozed thus for nearly an hour. It struck six, when, conscious of her condition, she awoke. There was no time to lose.

Rising with difficulty in the cold moonlight, she began to do whatever came into her head first, inconsequently, at random. After dressing herself, she wrapped the child in some old linen and rolled it up in two sheets of newspaper. It was quiet now, but yet its little heart was beating. As she had forgotten to look if it were a boy or a girl, she undid the parcel. It was a girl! One more unfortunate! A tit-bit for some brawny groom or footman, like that Louise, whom they had found behind a door! The servants were still asleep, and after getting somnolent Monsieur Gourd to pull back the front-door latch, she managed to go out and deposit her bundle in the Passage Choiseul just as the gates were being opened. Then she crept upstairs again, without meeting a soul. For once in her life, luck was on her side!

She at once began to put the room to rights. She rolled up the oilcloth under the bed, emptied the po, and sponged the floor. Then, strengthless, white as wax, and with blood still streaming down her thighs, she lay down again after wiping herself with a towel. Here Madame Josserand found her when, about nine o'clock, she determined to go upstairs, being amazed that Adèle wasn't down. The maid complained of a violent attack of diarrhoea which had kept her awake all night, when her mistress exclaimed:

"Ah, I expect you've over-eaten yourself again! You only think about stuffing!"

Alarmed at the girl's pallor, however, she talked of sending for a doctor, but was glad enough to save the three francs when Adèle declared that all she wanted was rest. Since her husband's death Madame Josserand lived with Hortense, on a pension allowed her by the Brothers Bernheim. This did not prevent her from vilifying them as cheats, and she now lived in more stingy style than ever, rather than lose caste by leaving her apartments and giving up her Tuesdays.

"Yes, that's what you want, sleep," she said. "There's some cold beef left, which will do for lunch, and to-night we're dining out. If you can't come down and help Julie, she must get on without you."

That evening the Duveyriers' dinner passed off very pleasantly. The whole family was there—the two Vabres and their wives, Madame Josserand, Hortense, Léon, and even uncle Bachelard, who was on his best behaviour. They had also invited Trublot as a stop-gap, and Madame Dambreville, so as not to separate her from Léon, who, after wedding the niece, had fallen back into the aunt's arms again, as she was most useful to him. They went about everywhere together as before, making excuses for the young bride. She had a cold, or was tired, and could not come, so they declared. Everyone at table expressed regret at not seeing her more often, for they were all so fond of her; she was so charming! They talked of the chorus which Clotilde was going to have at the end of the evening. It was the *Benediction of the Poniards* again, but with five tenors this time—something first-rate. For the last two months

Duveyrier, who had become quite agreeable, went about buttonholing all his friends, addressing to each the same stereotyped phrase, "You're quite a stranger; do come and see us; my wife's going to begin her choruses again." Thus, by the time the sweets were on the table, they talked of nothing but music. Perfect good fellowship and lighthearted gaiety prevailed from start to finish.

Then, after coffee was served, while the ladies sat round the drawing-room fire, the gentlemen, grouped in the dining-room, began to engage in grave debate. Meanwhile, other guests arrived. Soon there were Campardon, the Abbé Mauduit, Doctor Juillerat, besides those who had dined, with the exception of Trublot, who, as they rose from table, had straightway disappeared. They at once began to talk politics, for these gentry were deeply interested in the parliamentary debates, and still eagerly discussed the success of the Opposition candidates, who had all been returned for Paris at the May elections. This triumph of the Fronde democracy vaguely alarmed them, despite their apparent satisfaction.

"Well," said Léon, "Monsieur Thiers has great talent, certainly. But his speeches about the Mexican Expedition were so biting that they lost all their weight."

Léon had just got his appointment as *maitre de requêtes,* owing to Madame Dambreville's influence, and he had at once joined the Government party. There was nothing of the starveling demagogue about him, save an utter and absolute intolerance of all doctrine.

"You used to say it was all the Government's fault," remarked the doctor, smiling. "I hope that you, at least, have voted for Monsieur Thiers."

The young man avoided making any reply. Théophile, a martyr to indigestion and to fresh doubts as to his wife's fidelity, struck in :

"Yes, I voted for him. Directly men refuse to live together as brothers, why, so much the worse for them."

"Exactly, and so much the worse for you, eh?" quoth Duveyrier, who, though he said little, uttered words of deep wisdom.

Théophile stared at him, aghast. Auguste no longer dared admit that he also had voted for Monsieur Thiers. Then, to their surprise, Bachelard professed to be a Legitimist; there was something uncommon about that, he opined. Campardon warmly seconded him; he himself had refrained from voting, as the official candidate, Monsieur Dewinck, did not offer sufficient guarantees as regarded religion. Then he broke out into wild abuse of the "Life of Jesus," which had just appeared.

"It's not the book that ought to be burnt, it's the author," he repeated.

"Perhaps you are too much of a Radical, my friend," interposed the abbé, in a conciliatory voice. "Yet certainly the signs of the times are dreadful. They talk of deposing the Pope; Parliament is in revolt. Truly we are on the brink of a precipice."

"All the better," said Doctor Juillerat, drily.

At this they were all scandalised. Once more he abused the middle-classes, declaring that if once the masses got the upper hand the classes would soon be swept away; but the others, interrupting, loudly protested that in the bourgeoisie lay the virtue, energy, and thrift of the nation. Duveyrier at last made himself heard above the general babel. He roundly confessed that he had voted for Monseiur Dewinck, not because that senator exactly represented his own opinions, but because he was enrolled beneath the banner of order. Aye, it might be that they would have a repetition of the saturnalia of the Reign of Terror. Monsieur Rouher, that very remarkable statesman, who had just replaced Monsieur Billault, had formally prophesied as much from the Tribune. Then, with this graphic metaphor, he ended:

"The triumph of the Opposition is but the first shock to the whole edifice. Beware lest in falling it crush you to death!"

His hearers were silent, vaguely afraid that they had let themselves be carried away so far that now their own personal safety was in jeopardy. Visions floated before them of workmen, begrimed with dust and soaked in blood, who broke into their houses, raped their maidservants, and drank up their wine. Doubtless, the Emperor deserved a lesson; yet they began to be sorry for having given him so severe a one.

"Never fear," added the doctor, mockingly, "you shall yet be rescued at the point of the bayonet."

However, he always exaggerated, and they set him down as an original. It was just this same originality of his which kept him from losing his practice. Then he proceeded to pick his eternal quarrel with the Abbé Mauduit about the speedy disappearance of the Church. Léon now was on the side of the priest; he talked of Divine Providence, and on Sundays went with Madame Dambreville to nine o'clock Mass.

Meanwhile, guests kept arriving, and the large drawing-room was filled with ladies. Valérie and Berthe, just like old friends, were exchanging confidences. The architect had brought the other Madame

Campardon with him, doubtless in place of poor Rose, who, a-bed upstairs, lay reading Dickens. She was giving Madame Josserand an economical recipe for bleaching linen without soap, while Hortense, sitting apart, waited for Verdier, and kept her eyes fixed on the door. Suddenly Clotilde, while chatting to Madame Dambreville, rose and held out both her hands. Her friend, Madame Octave Mouret, had just arrived. She had been married early in November, directly her term of mourning was at an end.

"And where's your husband?" asked the hostess. "I hope he won't disappoint me."

"No, no," replied Caroline, smiling. "He's coming on directly; something detained him at the last moment."

Everybody, whispering, surveyed her curiously, so calm, so comely was she, in manner just the same, with the bland assurance of a woman who succeeds in everything. Madame Josserand shook hands with her as if delighted to see her again. Berthe and Valérie stopped talking to examine the details of her dress, which was straw-coloured and covered with lace. But just as all the past seemed thus calmly forgotten, Auguste, whom politics had left frigid, began to shows signs of wrathful amazement as he stood at the dining-room door. What! His sister was going to receive the wife of Berthe's former paramour? And to his marital rancour there was added the bitter jealousy of the tradesman ruined by a successful rival; for "The Ladies' Paradise," now that it was enlarged and had opened a special department for silks, had so crippled his resources, that he had been obliged to find a partner. While everyone was congratulating Madame Mouret, he approached Clotilde and whispered:

"I say, I'm not going to stand that!"

"Stand what?" asked she, in surprise.

"I don't mind the wife; she's done nothing to me. But if the husband comes, I shall catch hold of Berthe's arm and leave the room before everybody."

Clotilde stared at him, and then shrugged her shoulders. Caroline was her oldest friend, and she certainly wasn't going to give up seeing her merely to satisfy one of his fads. As if anybody ever recollected the matter now! Far better not to rake up things that everyone but him had forgotten. Then, as he excitedly turned to Berthe to back him up, expecting her to rise and leave with him there and then, she tried to pacify him with a frown. Was he crazy? Did he want to look a bigger fool than ever?

"But it's just because I don't want to look a fool!" he exclaimed, in despair.

Then Madame Josserand, leaning forward, said severely:

"This is positively indecent; people are looking at you. Do, for goodness' sake, behave yourself, just for once in a way!"

Though silent, he did not submit. At once a certain uneasiness was perceptible among the ladies. Madame Mouret alone, as she sat opposite Berthe and next Clotilde, preserved her tranquil, smiling mien. They watched Auguste, who had disappeared in the bay window, where once his marriage had been brought about. Anger had started his neuralgia, and every now and then he pressed his forehead against the icy window-panes.

However, Octave did not arrive until very late. He met Madame Juzeur on the landing. She was coming downstairs, muffled in a shawl. She complained of a cold on her chest, but she had got up on purpose so as not to disappoint the Duveyriers. Her feeble state did not prevent her from flinging herself into the young fellow's arms as she congratulated him on his marriage.

"How pleased I am, my friend! I had really begun to despair about you; I never thought that you would succeed. Tell me, you naughty boy, how did you manage to get round her, eh?"

Octave smiled, and kissed her finger-tips. Just then someone running upstairs, lightly and swiftly as a doe, disturbed them. To Octave's astonishment it was Saturnin. He had left the Asile des Moulineaux a week ago, as Doctor Chassagne again declined to keep him there any longer, as his mania was not sufficiently marked. No doubt he was going to spend the evening with Marie Pichon, just as he used to do when his parents had a party. On a sudden all those bygone days came back. Octave seemed to catch the sound of Marie's voice upstairs, as she faintly crooned some old song in her solitude. And he saw her once more sitting by Lilette's cot waiting for Jules' return, complacent, feckless, gentle as ever.

"I wish you every happiness in your married life," said Madame Juzeur, as she tenderly squeezed Octave's hand.

In order not to enter the room with her, he loitered behind and took off his overcoat, when Trublot, in evening clothes and bareheaded, emerged from the kitchen passage.

"She's not at all well, do you know!" he whispered, while Hippolyte was announcing Madame Juzeur.

"Who's that?" asked Octave.

"Why, Adèle, the maid, upstairs."

On hearing of her indisposition, he had gone up in fatherly fashion to see her as soon as dinner was over. Probably it was a violent attack of colic. What she wanted was a good stiff glass of mulled wine; but she had not even got such a thing as a lump of sugar. Then, observing Octave's smile of indifference, he added:

"Oh, I forgot! you're married now, you humbug! It's poor sort of fun, that is, to you now, I suppose? I never thought of that when I caught you just now in the corner with Madame Anything-you-like-except-that."

They both went into the drawing-room together. The ladies were just talking about servants, and, in their excitement, never noticed them at first. One and all affably accepted Madame Duveyrier's faltering explanation as to why she still kept Clémence and Hippolyte. He was a brute, it was true; but she was such an excellent lady's-maid that she willingly forgot her other failings. Valérie and Berthe both declared that they could not find a decent girl. They had given it up as a bad job after all the registry offices had sent them no end of disreputable sluts. Madame Josserand abused Adèle like a pick-pocket, recounting fresh and amazing instances of her filthiness and stupidity. However, she had not discharged her, she said. The other Madame Campardon praised Lisa to the skies. She was a pearl; there was no fault whatever to be found with her; she was one of those rare servants that are worth their weight in gold.

"She's quite like one of us now," quoth Gasparine. "Our little Angèle attends lectures now at the Hôtel de Ville, and Lisa always goes with her. Oh! they might be out together for days, but we should never feel the least anxious."

Just then they caught sight of Octave. He came forward to shake hands with Clotilde. Berthe looked at him and coolly went on talking to Valérie, who exchanged with him a friendly glance. The others, Madame Josserand and Madame Dambreville, without being too gushing, surveyed him with kindly interest.

"Well, you've come at last!" said Clotilde, in her most gracious voice. "I had begun to tremble for our chorus."

And when Madame Mouret gently chid her husband for being so late he proffered his excuses.

"But, my love, I could not get away. Madame, I am sorry. I am entirely at your disposal now."

Meanwhile, the ladies glanced uneasily at the bay-window, whither Auguste had fled. For a moment they were frightened when they saw him turn round on hearing Octave's voice. Evidently his neuralgia was worse; his eyes were all dim after gazing out into the gloomy streets. Yet, making up his mind, he came up close to his sister, and said :

"Get rid of them, or else we shall go."

Clotilde again shrugged her shoulders. Then Auguste, apparently was going to give her time to consider the matter. He would wait a few minutes longer, particulary as Trublot had taken Octave into the other room. Among the ladies, uneasiness still prevailed, for they heard the husband whisper to his wife :

"If he comes back here, you must at once get up and follow me. If you don't, you can just go back to your mother's."

Octave's reception by the gentlemen in the parlour was equally cordial. If Léon's manner was somewhat cool, uncle Bachelard, and even Théophile, seemed desirous to show, as they shook hands, that the family was ready to forget everything. Octave congratulated Campardon, who for the last two days had been wearing his new decoration, a broad red ribbon. The architect, beaming, scolded him for never coming to see them and spend an hour or two with his wife, now and then. It was all very fine to say he had got married; all the same, it wasn't nice of him to forget his old friends. But at the sight of Duveyrier, Octave was positively startled. He had not seen him since his recovery, and it was painful to him to notice his distorted jaw, which gave a lopsided look to his whole face. His voice, too, begot fresh surprise; deeper by a couple of tones, it sounded quite sepulchral.

"Don't you think he looks much better now?" said Trublot, as he led Octave back to the drawing-room door. "It makes him positively majestic. I heard him the day before yesterday at the Assizes. Hark ! they're talking about it."

The gentlemen had, indeed, passed from politics to morals. They were listening to Duveyrier, who was giving details concerning a case in which his attitude had called for much remark. It was even proposed to appoint him President and an officer of the Legion of Honour. The case was one of infanticide which had happened more than a year ago. The unnatural mother, a regular savage as he styled her, was none other than the boot-stitcher, his former tenant, the tall, pale, sad-looking girl whose enormous belly had excited Monsieur Gourd's ire. What a stupid fool, besides ! For, not even reflecting that a belly like that would betray her, she actually cut the child in two, and then hid it in a band-box ! Of course, she told the jury a ridiculous tale; how her seducer had deserted her, and how, hungry and wretched, mad despair overcame her at the sight of the baby that she could not nourish. In a word, the usual story. But an example must be made of such people. Duveyrier flattered himself that he had summed up with such striking clearness that the verdict was a foregone conclusion.

"What did you give her?" asked the doctor.

"Five years," replied the counsellor, in his new voice, which sounded cavernous and hoarse. "It is high time to put a check upon the debauchery which threatens to engulf all Paris."

Trublot nudged Octave, for they both knew about the unsuccessful attempt at suicide.

"There, you hear what he says?" whispered he. "Chaffing apart, it really does improve his voice. It stirs one more, eh? It goes straight to the heart now. And if you'd only seen him standing there in his long red robes, with his chops all awry! My word! he quite frightened me, he looked so odd; so solemn, too! He fairly gave me the shivers."

Here he stopped to listen to what the ladies were saying in the drawing-room. They had begun about servants again. That very day Madame Duveyrier had given Julie a week's notice. Certainly she had nothing to say against the girl's cooking; in her eyes, however, good conduct was the first thing. The real fact was that, acting on the advice of Doctor Juillerat, and uneasy about her son's health, whose goings-on at home she tolerated so as to control them better, she had cross-questioned Julie, who for some time past had been ailing. Julie, as behoved a first-class cook, of the sort that never quarrel with their employers, had taken her warning without even condescending to retort that maybe she had misbehaved herself, but, all the same, she would not have got anything the matter with her if it had not been for the unclean state of Master Gustave, her son. At once Madame Josserand joined in Clotilde's wrath. Yes, in matters of morality it behoved one to be absolutely inflexible. For instance, she kept on that slut of an Adèle, with all her filthy, stupid ways, merely because the dolt was so thoroughly virtuous. Oh! on that score she had nothing whatever to say.

"Poor Adéle! When one only thinks of it," muttered Trublot, touched at the thought of the poor wretch lying half-frozen upstairs under her thin counterpane.

Then in Octave's ear he whispered, sniggeringly:

"I say, Duveyrier might at least send her up a bottle of claret."

"Yes, gentlemen," continued the counsellor, "statistics show that infanticide is assuming alarming proportions. Sentimental reasons now-a-days carry far too much weight; people trust too much to science, to your so-called physiology, which before long will prevent us from distinguishing good from evil. For debauchery there is no cure; we must destroy it at its very root."

This retort was mainly directed at Doctor Juillerat, who had sought to give a medical explanation of the boot-stitcher's case.

All the other gentlemen, however, displayed great severity and disgust. Campardon failed to understand vice; uncle Bachelard spoke in defence of children; Théophile asked for an enquiry to be made; Léon discussed prostitution in its relation to the State, and Trublot, in reply to Octave, told him all about Duveyrier's new mistress, who this time was quite a presentable person, somewhat elderly, but of romantic disposition, able to understand that ideal which her keeper declared was so necessary to the perfect purification of love—in short, a worthy woman, who would make his establishment tranquil and orderly; imposing upon him and sleeping with his friends, but never kicking up a row. The abbé alone was silent, as, with downcast eyes, he listened, sorely troubled at heart.

They were now going to sing the *Benediction of the Poniards.* The drawing-room soon became full; there was a crush of gay dresses under the bright light from chandeliers and lamps, and laughter rippled along the rows of chairs. Amid the general murmur, Clotilde roughly remonstrated with Auguste as he caught hold of Berthe's arm and tried to make her leave the room when he saw Octave and the other chorus-singers enter. But his resolution wavered as neuralgia now completely overcame him, while the mute disapproval of the ladies served to increase his confusion. Madame Dambreville's austere gaze utterly disconcerted him; even the other Madame Campardon sided against him. Madame Josserand it was who achieved his defeat. She abruptly interfered, threatening to take back her daughter and never to pay him the dowry of fifty thousand francs, for this she was always promising in the most unblushing manner. Then, turning to Bachelard, seated behind her and next to Madame Juzeur, she made him renew his promises. Hand on heart, the uncle declared that he would do his duty; family before everything. Auguste, baffled, was obliged to beat a retreat; he fled to the bay-window, where he pressed his burning brow against the ice-cold panes. Then Octave had a strange feeling as if all were beginning anew. The two years of life in the Rue de Choiseul were as a blank. There sat his wife, smiling at him, yet no change had come into his life; to-day was yesterday, with neither pause nor stop. Trublot pointed out the new partner to him, a fair, dapper little fellow, sitting next to Berthe. He was said to give her heaps of presents. Uncle Bachelard, grown poetical, was disclosing the sentimental side of him to Madame Juzeur, who was quite touched at certain confidential details respecting Fifi and Gueulin. Théophile, a prey to doubts and doubled-up by violent fits of coughing, took Doctor Juillerat aside and begged him to give his wife something to soothe her nerves. Campardon, watching cousin Gasparine, talked about the Evreux diocese, and then of the big alterations in the new Rue du Dix-Décembre. God and art; the rest might go hang, quoth he, for all he cared; he was an artist! Behind a flower-stand even, one caught sight of a gentleman's back, which all the young ladies contemplated with the utmost curiosity. It was that of Verdier, who was talking to Hortense. They were having a somewhat acrimonious discussion about the wedding, which they again postponed until the spring, so as not to turn the woman and her brat into the street in mid-winter.

All at once the chorus burst forth. With mouth wide open, the architect declaimed the opening phrase, Clotilde struck a chord, and uttered her usual cry. Then the voices broke forth into ever-increasing uproar; so great was the din that the candles flickered and the ladies all grew pale. Trublot, found wanting as a bass, was once more on his trial as a baritone. The five tenors, however, made the most effect, especially Octave; Clotilde was sorry that she had not entrusted him with a solo. As the voices fell and, with the aid of the soft pedal, she imitated the footfall of a patrol departing in the distance, there was loud applause, and both she and the gentlemen were covered with compliments. Meanwhile, in the room beyond, behind a triple row of black coats, one could see Duveyrier clenching his teeth to keep from shouting out in anguish, while his jaw was all awry and his blotches inflamed and bleeding.

Then, when tea was served, the same set filed past, with the same teacups, the same sandwiches. For a moment the Abbé Mauduit stood alone in the middle of the empty drawing room. Through the wide-opened door he watched the throng of guests, and, feeling as if vanquished, he smiled as once more he flung the mantle of religion over this corrupt middle-class folk, as if he were some master of the ceremonies, veiling the fester in an endeavour to delay the final moment of decomposition. Then, as usual on all Saturdays, when it struck twelve the guests one by one departed. Campardon was one of the first to leave, accompanied by the other Madame Campardon; Léon and Madame Dambreville were not long in following, quite like husband and wife. Verdier's back had long since vanished, when Madame Josserand took Hortense off with her, scolding her for what she called her sentimental obstinacy. Uncle Bachelard, who had got very drunk on punch, kept Madame Juzeur talking at the door for a moment. Her advice, based on wide experience, he found quite refreshing. Trublot, who had pocketed some sugar to take to Adèle, was going to make a bolt by the back-stairs but, seeing Berthe and Auguste in the hall, he was embarrassed, and pretended to be looking for his hat.

Just at this moment Octave and his wife, accompanied by Clotilde, also came and asked for their wraps. There was an awkward pause. The hall was not large; Berthe and Madame Mouret were squeezed against each other, while Hippolyte was turning all the things topsy-turvy. They smiled at each other. Then, as the door was opened, the two men, Octave and Auguste, brought face to face, stepped aside and bowed civilly. At last Berthe consented to pass first, while slight bows were exchanged. Then Valérie, who, with Théophile, was also leaving, gave Octave another glance, the glance of an affectionate, disinterested friend, as much as to say that they two alone were able to tell each other all.

"*Au revoir!*" said Clotilde, blandly, to the two couples before going back to the drawing-room.

Octave suddenly stopped short. Downstairs he caught sight of Auguste's new partner going away, the dapper little fair man. Saturnin, who had come down from Marie's, was squeezing his hands in a wild outburst of affection, as he stammered, "Friend, friend, friend!" At first he felt a strange twinge of jealousy; then he smiled. The past came back, with visions of his bygone amours and reminiscences of his whole Parisian campaign—the complacence of that good little thing, Madame Pichon; Valérie's rebuff, of which he had an agreeable recollection; his stupid intrigue with Berthe, which he only regretted as so much lost time. Now he had done what he had come to do. Paris was conquered; and he gallantly followed her whom, in his heart of hearts, he still styled

Madame Hédouin, stooping at times to prevent her train from catching in the stair-rods.

Yet once again the house wore its grand, dignified, middle-class air. He seemed to hear a faint echo of Marie's wailing tune. In the porch he met Jules coming home; Madame Vuillaume was dangerously ill, and refused to see her daughter. Everybody had gone; the doctor and the abbé were the last to leave, arguing as they went. Trublot slily crept up to see after Adèle; and the deserted staircase slumbered in its warm atmosphere, with its chase portals shut close upon so many righteous hearths. One o'clock struck, when Monsieur Gourd, whose buxom spouse awaited him in bed, turned out the gas. Then all the building was plunged into solemn darkness, lulled by chaste and holy dreams. Not a trace of evil now; life there fell back to its old level of apathy and boredom.

Next morning, when Trublot had gone, after watching over her like a tender parent, Adèle languidly tottered down to her kitchen, to allay suspicion. During the night it had thawed, and she opened the window, feeling stifled, when Hippolyte shouted up, furiously from the bottom of the narrow courtyard :

"Now then, you pack of sluts! who's been emptying the slops out again? Madame's dress is done for!"

He had hung one of Madame Duveyrier's gowns out to dry after getting the mud off it, and now found it splashed with greasy slops. Then all the maids from the top of the house to the bottom looked out of window and violently denied the charge. The floodgates were opened, and filthy language surged up out of this pestilent sewer. When it thawed the walls dripped with damp, and a stench arose from the little dark quadrangle. All the secret rottenness of each floor seemed fused in this stinking drain.

"I did not do it," said Adèle, leaning over. "I've only just come down."

Lisa looked up sharply.

"Hullo! you on your pins again? Well, what was it? Did you nearly croak?"

"Yes, I had stomach-ache beastly bad, I can tell you."

This interruption put a stop to the quarrel. The new maidservants of Berthe and Valérie, christened "The Big Camel" and "The Little Donkey" respectively, stared hard at Adèle pale face. Victoire and Julie both wanted to have a look at her, and they craned their necks in the attempt. They both suspected something, for it wasn't usual for anyone to wriggle about and groan in that way.

The others burst out laughing, and there was another flood of beastly talk, while the unfortunate girl stammered out in her fright:

"Do be quiet with your filthy jokes; I'm bad enough as it is. Do you want to finish me off?"

No, not they. They didn't want to do that much. She was the biggest fool going, and dirty enough to make the whole parish sick, but they were too clannish to want to do her any harm. So, naturally, they vented their spite upon their employers, and discussed last night's party with an air of profound disgust.

"So it seems they've all made it up again, eh?" asked Victoire, as she sipped her syrup and brandy.

Hippolyte, sponging madame's gown, made answer:

"They've none of 'em any more feelings than my old boot! When they spit in each other's faces they wash themselves with the spittle, to make believe that they're clean."

"It's better they should be on friendly terms," said Lisa, "or else it would soon be our turn."

Suddenly there was a panic. A door opened and the maids rushed back to their kitchens. Then Lisa said it was only little Angèle. No fear of the child; she was all right. And from the black hole all the spite of these menials once more arose amid the stale, poisonous smell of the thaw. All the dirty linen of two years' standing was now being washed. How glad they were not to belong to the middle-class when they saw their masters living in this filthy state, and liking it too, for they were always beginning it all over again.

Brutal giggles re-echoed through the stinking cesspool. Hippolyte actually tore madame's dress; but he didn't care a damn; it was far too good for her as it was. "The Big Camel" and "The Little Donkey" split their sides with laughing as they looked out over their window-sill. Meanwhile, Adèle, terrified and dizzy with weakness, reeled backwards. Above the coarse shouting came her answer:

"Get out, you heartless things! When you're dying I'll come and dance round your beds, I will!"

"Ah, mademoiselle," continued Lisa, leaning over to address Julie, "how glad you must be to leave this rotten house in another week! My word! one becomes bad in spite of oneself. I hope you'll find something better."

Julie, with bare arms, all bloody with cleaning a turbot for dinner, leant out again, by the side of the footman. She shrugged her shoulders, and, in conclusion, delivered herself of the following philosophic speech :

"Dear me, mademoiselle, if it's this hole or that hole it don't matter. All are pretty much alike. If you've been in one of 'em you've been in all. They're all pig-sties."

THE END